What people are saying about

Marx R

An outstanding work of fiction   f
Marx's revolutionary thinking.
Slavoj Žižek, Birkbeck Institute for the Humanities

This book is fabulous. The descriptions of steam are stunning!
Andreas Malm, author of *Fossil Capital*

An imaginative, uplifting, and sometimes disturbing alternative
history.
Nina Power, *Los Angeles Review of Books*

This is a stimulating book, which manages to wear the immensity of its learning lightly.
Peter Beilharz, *The Australian*

Set in a putrid prerevolutionary London marinating in the miasma of oppression and exploitation, *Marx Returns* is an uncanny alt-fiction that blows the past out of the continuum of history to revivify Marx the man, his life and his thought for our own age. Mixing tragedy with farce, mathematics with alcohol, *Marx Returns* gives us a great new take on a grand old tale.
Justin Clemens, author of *The Mundiad*

Curious, funny, perplexing, and irreverent – an inspired divagation that casts unexpected light on Marx's thought.
Ray Brassier, author of *Nihil Unbound: Enlightenment and Extinction*

For years we've been led to believe that "Marx was right". On the evidence of Jason Barker's debut novel, however, it seems we may have grossly underestimated him. Joyful, artful and playfully anachronistic, *Marx Returns* is a book you're unlikely to want to end.

Yong Soon Seo, Professor of Philosophy, Sungkyunkwan University

MARX
RETURNS

Marx
Returns

Jason Barker

Winchester, UK
Washington, USA

JOHN HUNT PUBLISHING

First published by Zero Books, 2018
Zero Books is an imprint of John Hunt Publishing Ltd., Laurel House, Station Approach,
Alresford, Hants, SO24 9JH, UK
office1@jhpbooks.net
www.johnhuntpublishing.com
www.zero-books.net

For distributor details and how to order please visit the 'Ordering' section on our website.

ISBN: 978 1 78535 660 5
978 1 78535 661 2 (ebook)
Library of Congress Control Number: 2017945654

A CIP catalogue record for this book is available from the British Library.

Cover and title page by Jason Barker and Eugen Slavik
Illustrations to Parts I, II and III by Kerstin Hille
All illustrations copyright: Jason Barker 2017

UK: Printed and bound by CPI Group (UK) Ltd, Croydon, CR0 4YY
Printed in North America by CPI GPS partners

We operate a distinctive and ethical publishing philosophy in
all areas of our business, from our global network of authors to
production and worldwide distribution.

A Note on the Text

This is a work of historical fiction. Although it portrays true incidents in Karl Marx's life and includes original correspondence, the story often departs from the facts. Furthermore, in Part III especially, the timeline has been greatly abbreviated.

Some of the made-up incidents are more plausible than others. For example, the meeting between Marx and Mikhail Bakunin in Part I, Chapter 3 could not have taken place, since in November 1849 the latter was in prison in Königstein. However, this is not to say that the two men would not have met had Bakunin managed to escape to London: they almost certainly would have done. As for the implausible incidents, readers are free to judge them in the context of the story. It was never my intention to write a Marx biography and I make no apologies for not having written one.

The novel draws on Marx's unpublished and published writings of the period. All translations from the *Marx Engels Werke* are my own unless otherwise stated. I am grateful to G. M. Goshgarian for his German translations.

Minor references to Marx and Engels's works are to English editions. Mindful of the fact that too many notes can be distracting, especially in a work of fiction, I have tried to keep them to a bare minimum. Mostly they contain contextual and historical information, references to real persons and primary and secondary literature. For quotations from Shakespeare's plays I have chosen not to cite publishers or editions. There are several unacknowledged quotations from other works, notably Dante's *Divine Comedy* (all such works are in the public domain). There are also anachronisms, particularly in relation to chess.

Marx's interest in differential calculus dates from the final years of his life, whereas in the novel I have him grappling with mathematical formulas from the beginning. I am grateful to

Anindya Bhattacharyya for his help and corrections of my use of mathematics. I am also grateful to Igor Koršič for his many comments and suggestions on the manuscript, and for the engaging conversations on Marx, Marxism and revolution.

Jason Barker, Seoul, 12 June 2017

PART I
CREATURES OF THE BOG

Chapter 1

News from Paris[1]

Neue Rheinische Zeitung, No. 27
June 27, 1848

Cologne, 26 June. The latest news from Paris takes up so much space that we have no choice but to omit all analytical articles.

We accordingly offer our readers only a few briefs. *Ledru-Rollin, Lamartine* and their Ministers *Resign; Cavaignac's Military Dictatorship* Transplanted from Algiers to Paris; *Marrast, A Dictator in Civilian Clothing; Paris Awash in Blood; Uprising* Developing into the *Greatest Revolution of All Time,* the *Proletariat's Revolution against the Bourgeoisie.* There is the latest news we have received from Paris. The three days that sufficed for both the *July Revolution* and the *February Revolution* will not be enough for this gigantic *June Revolution,* but *the victory of the people is ever more certain. The French bourgeoisie has dared to do what the French Kings never did:* it has itself cast the die. With this, *the French Revolution's second act,* the *European tragedy* is just beginning.

Chapter 2

On the Upper Lambeth Marsh the air was threatening to induce dizziness in any wayward soul. Not that any soul would ever be so possessed as to visit what Dietz had described as Hell's waiting room. From sulphurous clouds the smouldering armour of the Whig parliament emerged in homage to the Great Fossil Lizard that once roamed the Thames Basin. On the South Bank, chimney stacks blasted out their molten debris in a barrage of volcanic eruptions. In Lambeth, the munitions factories sent projectiles skywards with such ferocity that the clouds seemed to ignite before returning the glowing debris back to earth.

In a democratic understanding of sorts, perhaps the signal achievement of the times, the fiery rain fell on top hats and flat caps in equal measure. For anyone crossing the damp element by Westminster Bridge, the threat of tumbling masonry compounded that of falling debris; which, on occasion, would seal the thanks-offering fate of drunks, college-goers[2] and lunatics. On the narrow stretch offshore, in easy range of the cannonade, steamboats and Thames barges jostled for control of the quays and wharfs. Lighters ferried cargo from the bulkier craft and, as if to complete the aquatic food chain, workers in rowboats hawked beer to the lightermen.

Whether or not the seismic activity of bourgeois industry would one day come to rival the Triassic extinction event in its environmental impact was unclear. For the moment, however, what struck the spectator—the one inclined to doubt the evidence of their own eyes—was not remotely how things had evolved thus, or where they might in future, but whether or not any of "it" could really be described at all. What exactly was one looking at?

'Sir! Pay me a penny for my cat, say.'

Marx glanced up from his notebook. A gang of street urchins approached, rehearsed in their own variety of extinction event. The ringleader, genderless and caked in mud, dangled an animal from a cord, more rodent than feline, though not long for this world. He thrust the petrified creature at Marx in plain ignorance of the fact that both animal and tormentor shared a common ancestor.

'I-I-I...' Marx faltered and the creature responded in kind.

'You-you-you,' replied the tormentor and the apprentice demons cackled.

'*Raus mit euch, Ihr Tierquäler!*'[3] Marx would have declared next, had his English been up to the mark.

The creature was almost human. Its bloodshot eyes and pulsating nostrils might have been those of Marx's landlord on rent day. Indeed, but for the unfortunate mystery of the animal's capture, the break in the organic chain might have been minutely deferred. Of such unpredictable encounters was history woven. (The class struggle could surely be traced back to the dark wood of savagery—if not before—when man was a mere tree-dweller among beasts.)

The animal was more attuned to survival than its tormentor and in a gymnastic effort, it wriggled from the latter's hand and catapulted itself forward in a spasm. Landing in a heap, it righted itself then zigzagged through the melee of baying urchins, finding time to bite the ringleader on the ankle before hurtling through the wrought-iron gates of the factory opposite.

Could this be the place? Marx squinted through his tar-stained handkerchief at the smudged outline of a building—an impression, Engels had called it, 'But you'll recognize the thing once you're there.' *Genau*. "There" was precisely where Marx was trying to be. But the sketch bore little resemblance to the thing itself, to any discernible landmark, moreover. A map would have served his purposes; though, again, the difficulty lay in locating where he was in the first place.

Marx paced along the mud track that separated the factory wall from the wood panel frontage of Field's Candle Works. At the entrance he paused and peered inside the container of darkness. He tried to imagine the synchronized horrors that lay in store for the proletarians as the day shift filed in and the night shift shuffled out, dazed and dishevelled like a community displaced by war.

He brushed a fresh deposit of volcanic debris from the page on which he had jotted down, at some ungodly hour, his latest attempt to master the differential calculus. On reflection, Engels's sketch had its merits. Was that the solution? The whole difficulty in understanding the differential operation—which repeats the negation of the negation—lays precisely in seeing its results.[4] *Charles Bloodworth, 11 Vauxhall Walk, Maudslay's Ironworks.* At which point the address collapsed into the derived function and careered off the page. If we divide both $a(x_1 - x)$ and the left side of the corresponding equation by the factor $x_1 - x$, we then obtain:

$$\frac{y1 - y}{x1 - x} = a$$

Since y is the dependent variable, it cannot carry through any independent motion at all; y_1 therefore cannot equal y and $y_1 - y = 0$ without x_1 first having become equal to x. Shouldn't one be able to infer the economic crisis from the incremental changes expressed by the derived function in a manner wholly in keeping with the qualitative law of the dialectic?

Mathematics was no mere measure of matter in motion any more than wages were a measure of factory labour. Equally, the patch of inflamed skin threatening to expand into a pus-filled furuncle at the entrance to Marx's anal passage was no mere indicator of pain: it actually hurt. Mathematics *was* something and as adept in accounting for it as philosophy was. That was the general gist of it, but he would need to go back and derive the theorems later that day in the pub.

Suddenly a proletarian convoy exited a slow-moving mist, their faces shrouded in shawls like a Bedouin tribe and heading toward the river. Or so it seemed. Marx stumbled, almost falling head first down an escarpment that jutted out of nowhere. Wasn't this supposed to be reclaimed marshland? That's what Dietz had said: *eben*. Dietz! The man could no more give directions than prepare soothing balms for the treatment of haemorrhoids. The reform of consciousness depends on rudely awakening men from their bedridden slumbers. But how would that be possible if men were not in fact asleep, or even capable of sleep, or even bedridden, owing to their incapacity to lie down?

No sooner had they appeared than the proletarians disappeared back into the mist. As the molten dust reignited the coal-black heavens, Marx understood everything in an instant. *Come with your gods into a country where other gods are worshipped and you will be shown to suffer from fantasies and abstractions. And justly so.*[5]

Marx tiptoed along the escarpment and by the grace of forces unknown descended it in one continuous motion. The ground was sodden underfoot; despite the poisonous stench weeds sprouted obstinately in the bog terrain, their wire-drawn growth a cry to escape the earth. No doubt a botanist from the Royal Society would soon announce the discovery of a new local species.

Across the street a mound of fish garbage had been left to fester, neatly at first, then scattered in piles, as if their owner had suddenly lost interest and decided that preserving the tidiness of the neighbourhood was a lost cause. Nearby, a pig's carcass retained the aspect of wonder at the spectacle of its own demise. What other accursed creatures were lurking in this primeval soup, threatening to rise up and take revenge on the living?

Marx began to retch convulsively. Aware that a minor miscalculation would be enough to land him in a rival state of wonder, he inhaled sharply. Such exertion, however, was too much for his lungs to take in and this provoked a fall the major indignity of which even his gods, unencumbered by the majesty of Reason, did not see fit to avert. The problem, dear fellow, is not that Spirit is a bone, but that your bones are bones.

It was approaching eight on the Upper Lambeth Marsh and Marx's carbuncle lay submerged in a carbuncular-shaped crater in the carbuncular outcrop of this godforsaken carbuncle of a city. *Every portion of matter can be thought of as a garden full of plants, or as a pond full of fish. But every branch of the plant, every part of the animal, and every drop of its vital fluids, is another such garden, or another such pool.*[6] But such recursion was useless if it only led back to God. Marx rose trembling and braced himself for the pain. Nothing. Had he severed a vital nerve? He shuffled forward shin deep in mud, then paused. Still nothing. Might this be the cure? The New Cut reinvented as a spa town. Pottery had been produced in the region since Roman times and there was a plentiful supply of clay. With its low-lying aspect and mild climate, wasn't this the prime location for the ablutionary treatment of chronic ailments?

It was then Marx realized that it wasn't an escarpment he had just descended, but a dung heap piled six-feet high with human excrement, entrails and coagulating industrial fluids. Some malefactor had disguised the cesspool by raking it over with coal ash.

A clump of green-red ivy clinging to a farmer's cottage beckoned his eye. From the door frame its trail extended along the length of the building, then dropped at a right angle into the gutter. He followed the glistening trail to the source of the strange foliage. It wasn't exactly ornate. But on the other hand, neither was its meandering progress entirely at odds with its surroundings. He reached out to touch the plant, which seemed to recoil from his hand. Odd. Sensing a faint noise, Marx edged closer to the rubbery petals; it was as if they were conversing in a thousand tiny voices. Like the evanescent proletarians, Lambeth was producing species all unto itself that confounded the most up-to-date thinking of the life scientists.

The path began to taper into a dark alleyway between two private dwellings. One of them was so badly subsided that its windows were in danger of being swallowed by the black earth. Through the open window of the adjacent cottage Marx could see a man and his daughter limewashing the walls. The man started and bellowed, either in salutation or rebuke, it was impossible to tell. Marx hurriedly squeezed his way through the alleyway and out into a vacant courtyard, where there, before him, lay the source of the alien plant life.

It was high tide. The green-red ivy fanned out in one continuous expanse from the waterfront all the way to the archway of Millbank Prison on the North Bank. But this wasn't ivy; it was a thick crustaceous blanket of algae, thriving on human waste and factory chemicals. Once enriched by this diabolical concoction, the algae would migrate ashore with the malicious intent of Frankenstein's monster, infecting everything in its path.

As if to confirm Marx's thesis, the daughter emerged moments later from the alleyway carrying a bucket of limewash. The slime on this section of river being at least six-inches thick, she made her way along the shoreline to where the Lambeth ferry was disembarking its passengers and began washing out her bucket there; a mere stone's throw upstream from a woman filling hers.

Earlier that morning the stench of effluvium from the bone-crushing factories had stymied Marx's senses. Looking south from Westminster Bridge had convinced him that Lambeth Marsh, instead of buttressing an eastward bend in the river, was in fact a peninsular jutting out into the Thames and that the carpet of algae was pastureland. In fact, it was the opposite:

no outcrop of molten industry, Lambeth was a vast floating sewer at constant risk of being swept away by the tide. Indeed, wasn't the close proximity—nay, osmosis—of land to water the aggravating cause of the recent cholera epidemic, from which hundreds of local residents had perished? Feeling the urge to vomit, he reached for his handkerchief and pulled out the sodden remains of his notebook. *Scheisse.* A month's worth of research reduced to mush. Perhaps he could dry out the pages once back at the hotel; assuming Jenny hadn't squandered the coal.

A chimney stack started to move. He felt the ground shake and the rumbling steam engine hissed and clattered past. And then it came to him: *All that is solid melts into air.*

Marx presently came to his senses, conscious that the sulphur was starting to play tricks on his mind. He buttoned his overcoat against the stiffening breeze. Time to disembark the shores of happenstance for firmer ground.

Chapter 3

From the steaming engines of the Waterloo Bridge, to the coffee houses of Covent Garden, to the monstrous facades rising from the Piccadilly slime pools, Marx's theory was everywhere. But as he made his way to the pub his only positive thought was Wang's vapour bath. For a shilling the Chinaman could probably be cajoled into washing his clothes and lending him something suitable in the meantime, given the unlikelihood of there being anything clean to wear back at the hotel. Once refreshed he could finally put his treatise to bed and have the manuscript in the post on the morrow, midweek at the latest. Who knows? Perhaps Duncker would even see fit to advance the 1500 talers before the end of the month, thus enabling him to settle up and relocate the family into more suitable lodgings. A study and separate bedroom for Helene and the children would be ideal, thus affording him and his wife some privacy at long last.

The Red Lion stood at the north end of Great Windmill Street opposite some of the most notorious landlords in London. Diagonally it faced a knacker's yard. A construction boom had been threatening the neighbourhood with demolition for donkey's years, but the unwillingness of landlords to sell up, coupled with the latest economic shock, had conspired in its social neglect. It wasn't the most salubrious part of town, which suited the pub's outsider reputation. Its elevated street view appealed to men on the run. In its 70-odd-year history just about every revolutionary worthy of the name—or pretender riding on the coat-tails of someone else's—had passed through its doors and in many cases been thrown back out again. Marx belonged to the first category and in all likelihood the second.

Once inside an arm seized his and veered him through the fug of the saloon bar.

'You'll never guess what Bonaparte's gone and done now,'

said the voice in his ear. 'Only gone and locked up his own judges!'

Marx took a moment to acclimatize and put a face to his old comrade. One could never be too careful in the Red Lion; it was a breeding ground for spies. The news from Paris was predictably dire. Louis-Napoléon Bonaparte,[7] France's first elected president, was cracking down on his allies this time, most of whom appeared to have fled to this pub.

'How was your field trip?' said Engels, looking his comrade up and down.

'Are you taking the piss?' said Marx. He raised his voice: 'You never told me the city was sinking!'

'What?' screeched Engels, straining to hear above the drunken din of *the Marseillaise*.

'That district you sent me to. It's a swamp! It's like a proletarian Venice!'

'Menace?'

'Not menace! Venice! A proletarian Venice!'

'Pah!' Engels waved his hand in the manner of someone mildly inebriated. 'It'll burn before it drowns!'

'Are you growing a moustache?' enquired Marx, noticing something altered in the other's regard.

'I'm a moustache, you're a moustache, we are *all* moustaches!' retorted Engels, spinning round and swinging his arms gaily.

'What?'

'Hang on.' Engels broke off to light his cigar. *The Marseillaise* sounded as if it were being sung in a dozen languages and the singers all competing against rival renditions. 'What did you say?' he resumed, struggling to stay afloat on the riptide of bodies.

'All that is solid melts into air!' screamed Marx. 'That book on the Macellum of Pozzuoli by the Scotsman, Lyell. Remember it?' Engels was flagging. Marx persevered: 'Darwin cites him. In fact, it's the bedrock of the evolutionary theory. It forces the geologists to give up theology. It's indispensable for anyone seeking to revive the natural philosophy. You need Lyell. He's a dialectician. He envisages incremental changes that encompass the more convulsive tectonic activity—volcanoes, earthquakes and the like—along with large meteor strikes and other gravitational phenomena. I thought I might include something about it in the appendix. *C'est une piste*! What do you say?'

Engels was far worse for wear than he had first appeared. 'Not later, *now*,' he mouthed, jumping up and down dementedly in his own world.

Marx could make out a feminine profile through the smoke. Engels was chatting up the barmaid.

Marx's compatriot was exceptionally handsome for a revolutionary. His blond mane defied gravity, his blue-eyed stare melted hearts and his tall, athletic build owned its own wardrobe. Both he and Marx shared a great deal of history, but when it came to natural charm they were separated by an era. Engels could stand out in a crowd. Marx, on the other hand, blended in perfectly well, with a physique somewhat adapted to serving the revolutionary cause on his rear end. It was all just as well. Better off taking the five pounds Engels had promised him and wrapping the manuscript alone, with minimal fuss, then seeking his friend's sober criticisms once he was in a fit state to offer them.

'I say, Marx! Come and join us in a bacon sandwich,' said Liebknecht, who had managed the impossible feat of ordering food in a Soho pub at lunchtime. 'They're awfully good, you know.'

Perhaps he would splash out and treat himself. Then again, no need. He would eat at Wang's. On his previous visit there he had eaten a plate of dumplings in his bath. Barring some minor anomaly in the Asiatic mode of production (which he would need to address in a sequel to his book), Chinese dumplings, which Wang always served with a steaming hot bowl of vegetable and ginger soup, bore out Marx's theory of history.

Engels went on swaying from side to side, rambling and bemoaning the German donkeys and the French parvenus and the appalling state of European democracy in general. The bulletins from Paris fell into two categories. The first: disasters. The second: harbingers of disasters.

'Moor,' said Engels, 'it's bad news, I'm afraid. I couldn't get the cash I promised you.'

Marx felt a sharp pain in his nether regions as if penetrated by a red-hot poker.

'You're not desperate, are you?'

'Well! I am rather,' Marx meant to say; although what actually came out of his mouth was more like the noise a Devonian tetrapod would have made.

'It's not a problem,' continued Engels, mistaking the noise for affirmation, 'I'll sweet-talk my old man. I'll have him eating out of my hand before the month's out. See if I don't.'

A commotion swept through the pub. The anarchist contingent was hailing the arrival of the Russian revolutionary Mikhail Bakunin.[8] *The Marseillaise* struck up again, this time with a superhuman gusto that made the walls tremble.

'Oh, shit,' said Engels.

'What?' Marx sensed catastrophe on a different scale.

'Bakunin. He and I have had a falling-out.' Engels rifled through his pockets as if divesting himself of incriminating evidence. He puffed out his cheeks and set off. 'Most humbly do I take my leave, sir.'

'Wait,' said Marx.

'N-O-W,' mimed Engels, waving his arms at the barmaid. 'Listen, Moor, before I go…'

'Yes?'

Engels leaned into Marx like a falling spruce, almost toppling both of them. He steadied himself on the smaller man's shoulders.

'You look like shit. Ask Liebknecht to give you some second-hand clothes. He's been taken in by the Methodists.'

Then, stuffing his copy of *The London Illustrated News* into Marx's pocket, he shepherded the barmaid out into the dank November afternoon.

'*Frère* Marx,' announced Bakunin, pacing forward in long strikes and parting the crowd like the Red Sea.

The Russian was dressed in the cassock of a Lutheran priest. He appeared taller than Marx remembered him. Perhaps his Saxon gaolers had stretched him on the rack. He made the sign of the cross and began reading from a volume of poetry. At the end of each line he paused. Failing to rouse the other's interest he eventually gave up.

'Charles Baudelaire,' said the giant, peering down his beard. 'Ever heard of him?'

'No,' said Marx.

'No? Oh. Well... poets! Who needs them? Bunch of filthy layabouts.' He threw off his wide-brimmed hat. 'Deus did weep; I'm as dry as a Spanish goat herder's cock. Landlord!' He signalled to the bar and tipped out coins of various currencies from a leather pouch. 'You look... *well*,' he offered, registering Marx's mud-caked appearance. Then, grabbing him in a bear hug, 'Come! We shall drink till we vomit.'

Chapter 4

Cd4.

'You took my castle,' squealed Jenny in a passable imitation of her adolescent self.

'And?' said Helene.

Jenny was hyperventilating. 'And… and… and…'

Jenny Marx, née Johanna Bertha Julie Jenny von Westphalen, the daughter of Baron von Westphalen of Trier, County Sheriff of the Landrat and Regional Advisor to the Prussian government, had long since parted company with her adolescent self. On such occasions, however, her impetuousness got the better of her, and she would channel the energies of bygone days when she and Sophie would fight over boys and ball gowns, and perform tricks on her incontinent cocker spaniel Voltaire. They had been born within days of each other and when he died she regretted having teased him so. Like the time she put him inside one of her stockings and hung him from the bedroom window.

'What's wrong with you?' exclaimed Helene, ducking the shoe that narrowly missed her head and slammed into the window.

Jenny removed the clay pipe from Helene's mouth and took a puff. 'You're winning,' she said.

'And *you're* losing,' replied Helene, snatching back the pipe and jutting out her chin.

Helene Demuth, née Helene Demuth, the daughter of south German peasants, was rarely impetuous; although her temper was a force to be reckoned with. In her teenage years she never attended balls and felt equally at home among livestock as she did people. Dogs, which in the Rhineland were simply part of the landscape, never stood still long enough in her home town of Sankt Wendel to be placed inside stockings and hung from bedroom windows.

Since joining the von Westphalens as a maid 15 years ago, she and Jenny had become close friends and confidantes. And, ever since the Baron had introduced her to chess, rarely did a day pass when she and Jenny wouldn't play. Perhaps this was the reason why Jenny's hissy fits were wasted on Helene; although, of course, the hissy fits were, as both players knew, an integral part of Jenny's strategy.

'Now I'm a queen without a castle,' said Jenny, reclining on the bed. 'Could there be anything worse? What do you think is worse: a queen without a castle or a queen without a king?' She considered her next move.

'Citizen,' announced Jennychen, the eldest daughter, 'I arrest you in the name of the Revolution.'

'On what charge?' demanded Laura, the younger one, waving defiantly the tricolour she and her sister had made by sewing together their father's handkerchiefs and nailing them to his cane.

'Sedition.'

Helene tapped the hourglass. 'Time.'

'Wait!'

'Time!' Helene repeated.

'Edgar!' Jenny snapped at her hyperactive two-year-old. 'Mummy's trying to concentrate!'

On reaching the mound of clothes at the foot of the bed, Edgar reversed his toy locomotive, then charged into them at full pelt, catapulting himself into his father's writing desk. The paperwork, which resembled a papier-mâché pyramid—a fascinating accomplishment that a colony of ants would have been proud of—scattered everywhere. The child thought about this for a moment, then burst into tears.

'Come here,' said Helene, hauling him up onto her knee. 'That was a silly thing to do, wasn't it?' She swept the matte of black curls from his face. 'Is that why we call you Musch?' she whispered. 'Is it? Because you're always flying around? You know what happens to flies, don't you? They better mind they're not careless. Otherwise...' She slapped her thigh and Edgar sat bolt upright, newly primed for mischief, one misdemeanour having merely paved the way for another.

'Edg-arrr,' said Jenny solemnly, her eyes fixed on the chessboard, 'do you want me to tell the landlord's dog you've been naughty?'

The boy buried his face in Helene's apron and wriggled, blowing hard through his nose in a concerted effort not to cry.

Re7.

Helene set down the child instinctively and reached for the hourglass, already anticipating her next move.

'Citizen,' declared Jennychen, 'either you come of your own accord or we shall be forced to take extreme measures.'

Jenny got up from the bed and leaned against the window. Dusk was falling and the orange debris was drifting in on a southerly breeze. On the corner of Leicester Square, off-duty Redcoats were being goaded by Soho tearaways. The Redcoats congregated there in the evenings, since the beer was cheap and the view was free. Standing in a line they joked with their tunics unbuttoned, wagering on who could steal a glance from the passing ladies, whose husbands took umbrage at the objectification of their wives; although, of course, they were powerless to do anything about it.

Leicester Square was located at the fringes of social respectability. The square itself was an overgrown thicket and dumping ground for drunks and unidentified creatures. Anyone passing that way after dark was sure to encounter mischief.

'That dog was growling again last night,' said Helene, picking up her king and suddenly unsure what to do with it. 'It must have been three. I swear this place is haunted.'

'Do you think?' mused Jenny, gazing distractedly at the Redcoats in their devilishly handsome uniforms.

'Course!' said Helene, spotting an opening. 'How else do you explain all that moaning?'

'Somebody getting laid, I imagine,' muttered Jenny to herself. 'Don't blame them.'

Kb6.

Helene turned over the hourglass. 'Your move.'

'You're right,' replied her opponent, resuming the formalities of the game, 'a queen without a castle would be quite undignified.' She stood over the board and raised her nightgown up above her waist, exposing her pregnant belly and gyrating the fleshy bulge from side to side.

'Do you mind!' said Helene, dodging a second projectile.

'I always had a thing for soldiers. So... sacrificial.' Jenny toyed with her queen. She always played White. Helene said it was her prerogative.

Qd4.

'You lucky...'

'You were saying? That'll teach you for taking my castle. Who's the mummy now, eh?' Jenny clapped her hands in a flutter of excitement.

'It isn't over, my lady, until the fat tenor sings,' replied Helene, who always played Black. Jenny said it was her colour.

Helene spied a weakness on her opponent's left flank. Jenny had played a King's Pawn Opening, to which Helene responded with a Caro-Kann Defence; although it hadn't prevented Jenny from developing the diagonals. Helene's reading of her opponent's strategy confirmed what she always suspected: namely, that Jenny's moves were simply facsimiles of countless other moves, unconsciously absorbed over time and redeployed more or less at random. Then again, perhaps Jenny was bluffing. Perhaps she did have a strategy after all; a hidden variation nesting inside this one. As things stood, Black looked invincible. But White always had the opening move.

'I thought we might go to a concert,' said Jenny, perching herself on the windowsill.

'Really?'

'Yes, really.'

Jenny pulled down her chemisette and inspected her bosom in the pane. Despite being naturally dark, her skin glowed pink at the temples owing to her *condition très intéressante*. The evening luminescence painted her in a fiery light that seemed to transport her entire being and she imagined for a moment hovering above the street outside, floating among the orange debris, not as herself but in a different form, like an angel or a snowflake. *Nihil movetur nisi corpus, ut probatur.*[9]

'And what do you suggest we do for money?'

'I have my ways,' said Jenny, tracing the outline of her reflection with her index finger.

There was a long pause, then Helene said, 'You can count me out, anyway.'

'What do you mean?'

'What do *I* mean? Huh. After the rubbish you made me sit through last time? Do me a favour. Even his lordship fell asleep; and he started snoring; and you disappeared to God knows where.'

Jenny stifled a giggle, still seething at the capture of her castle and loathe to concede any moral advantage to her opponent.

'All them hysterical madams carping on about this, that and what have you; how they've been wronged by some selfish brute and just want to throw themselves in front of a locomotive. "I burn, I burn! I rage, I rage!"'

Jenny, unable to contain herself, burst out laughing. 'I'm not sure Handel had locomotives in mind when he wrote that.'

Outside the early evening preludes had segued into a boisterous symphony of night hawkers, theatregoers and the Soho tearaways, whose hellraising antics were amplified by the maze of alleyways that led off Leicester Square. It all sounded quite deranged, as if one were trapped inside a huge concrete wind instrument.

'Your justice is a sham! Unhand me at once!' demanded

Laura, whose playful reprimand was threatening to turn violent.

Ka5.

'You were saying?' said Helene, raising the hourglass above her head as if claiming a trophy.

'A knight for a king,' said Jenny. '*Wunderbar*. And for a baroness?'

Between the bustle of the streets and the focal point of the game there wasn't much in it; not much, that is, if one read the minute chasm separating Black from White as a meeting between strangers. Would it help if the board were bigger? Might it then offer spaces to hide in the monstrous proportions of a city under siege, provide multiple lines of retreat and counterattack, safe houses and cracks to crawl into without ever being found? Or was she, she wondered, a pawn in someone else's game? Feeling tired, irritated and inclined to kick the board up in the air, Jenny picked up Helene's king and stuck it between her breasts.

'Hey! What do you think you're doing?' demanded Helene.

Jenny poked out her tongue. 'Changing the rules.'

Chapter 5

In the space of 50 minutes Bakunin's disquisition had managed to establish the following, no less: operas in German were superior to those in Italian; the word "art" could be applied to things that had nothing to do with art, such as mass uprisings; life was not a book; all literature should be banned; all laws should be banned; Saxon women were whores; cabbage was an aphrodisiac; philosophy was a form of buggery; the German philosopher Fichte had been a Russian spy in the pay of the Romanovs; for all Bakunin knew, so was Marx; and for all Marx knew, so was Bakunin.

The differential formula that Marx had scribbled in the margin of *The Illustrated London News* was more diverting than anything printed in that portentous bourgeois gossip sheet. A valid addendum; an improvement. Albeit a deeply troublesome creature:

$$\frac{dy}{dx}$$

Even a glance at the thing was to experience being flung off a cliff while still refuting the laws of gravity, convinced that the Almighty would reach out His hand just in time. The formula that confirmed that Hell had no bottom. Although x and $x1$ were meant to account for quantitatively different states of a moving body in time, wasn't change thus conceived a complete illusion? Wasn't it a contradiction in terms?

'Marx.'

After all, a variable could "vary" as much as it liked, passing from one state to the next by infinitely small degrees. But if that were the case then there was no sense in saying that x could approximate to zero, since in so doing one would—

'Marx!'

'Mmm?'

'When did you arrive?' Bakunin was reclined imperiously on a dilapidated chaise longue and resembled a giant sloth. 'From Paris?'

'Last month. Six weeks ago,' Marx corrected himself. 'My head's crammed so full of ideas I don't know where the time goes.'

'I know the feeling,' said the sloth, dangling a leg the size of an anchor. 'What are you working on?'

'Nothing.' Marx stuffed the paper inside his coat. 'It's finished.'

'Finished? Why, congratulations! This calls for a toast. Landlord!' Bakunin raised his arm as if hailing a cab. 'Who's your publisher?'

'Duncker of Berlin.'

Bakunin rolled his eyes in dismay. 'Duncker? Should I tell you the man's a swindler? Mind you, all publishers are. I never sign their sordid contracts. What's the book about, anyway?'

'Capital.'

'Capital?' Bakunin eyed Marx suspiciously. 'How... interesting. I must admit, I don't profess to know much about these... *theories* of yours. Your book's about capital, you say?'

'Yes—'

'Good!' Bakunin lurched forward and set down his tankard on the table. 'So. Explain to me your thesis.'

'My thesis?' Marx sounded baffled.

'Yes. The general gist; the kernel of it.'

'Well,' said Marx, retrieving the newspaper from inside his coat, 'things don't simply vanish.'

Bakunin banged the table. 'Damned right! That reminds me: add conjurers to the list of undesirables.'

'Quite,' said Marx, 'but listen: take the accumulation of capital.'

'The accumulation of capital...' Bakunin shifted uncomfortably in his seat, reluctant to do any such thing.

'It's just an example, mind.' Marx pointed at his scribble. 'One can't accumulate surplus value indefinitely.'

'One can't?' said Bakunin, sounding dismayed.

'No,' affirmed the theorist. 'There must be a limit to it.'

Bakunin scratched his beard. 'A limit, you say...'

Marx shook his head. 'But.'

'But?'

'The concept of limit in Leibniz and Newton[10] is incompatible with that of qualitative change!' Marx nervously gulped down his ale.

Bakunin looked perplexed and somewhat disturbed. 'Well, it's... fascinating. Truly it is. But in all honesty, Marx, I can't get as worked up as you about it. I mean: political economy. Well. It's hardly a page-turner. There was a time when I felt sure you and I might collaborate on a great work together. But in the end you chose a different partner and I set out on a different path. Capital? I mean I can see the overriding point. But when it comes to all these formulas... Granted, the capitalists are degenerates and its bourgeois class pimps. But the way you break things down makes it all seem so...' Bakunin plucked an imaginary apple hanging from a branch and bit into it. 'Abstract.' He spat out the imaginary core.

Bakunin was an inspired performer. One could never simply converse with the man. To be in his company was to join in a secret cabal of rites and rituals and constant allusions to all things past, present and future. Imaginary worlds. His assertions would often cloud serious analysis. Where most people would reason one step at a time, Bakunin would do so all at once, ascending and descending the logic staircase in unpredictable leaps and bounds. It was a wonder the capricious critic didn't fall and break his neck.

'I'm losing my faith in books,' he went on, undeterred by Marx's failure to conceal a look of utter depression. 'All these philosophical bibles are just another form of idolatry. Trifles and tricks. Free the shelf space of the mind, that's what I say. We are all walking books. Our library should be out on the streets, in the alleys of the faubourgs and up and down canals. That's where you'll find real volumes of poetry; poetry of the living, breathing kind.' Bakunin gestured toward the drunken brawl that had broken out in front of the pub, probably over the price of a bacon sandwich or a woman. 'As for your eminent theory of capital,' he said, rummaging in his pouch for British currency, 'man produces, man consumes. What more is there to understand?' He leered diabolically at the barmaid, newly returned from her afternoon adventure with Engels, as she set down two tankards on the table.

'Спасибо, дорога́я,' said the Russian in his native tongue.

'Пожалуйста,' replied the girl.[11]

'To death on the barricades!' declared Bakunin, wielding his tankard like a hand grenade, then crashing it into Marx's and spilling most of the latter's ale on the floor.

'And you, Mikhail,' enquired Marx, wiping his trousers, 'what are you working on?'

Bakunin placed an envelope on the table and his hand on Marx's shoulder. 'In this envelope you will find top-secret plans for the seizure of the British Parliament. I have placed you in charge of procuring weapons. I count on you absolutely in this affair.'

Marx opened the envelope. 'This is a blank sheet of paper.'

'Oh!' exclaimed Bakunin, collapsing on the chaise longue as if struck by a stray shell. 'You'd prefer if I took out a front-page advertisement in *The Times*? It's written in invisible ink.'

'How… ingenious.'

'Look,' said Bakunin, whispering in the sceptic's ear, 'this is the last thing those bastard Whigs will expect, see. By seizing their parliament we shall resurrect the Parisian dynamic here in London. Who on Bog's Earth would ever think of storming

Westminster Palace? Eh? Exactly! No one. But how to pull it off? Let the doubters and the cynics wonder. I'll say no more for now, but prepare yourself for a dastardly hostage-taking. It's November. Read up on your English history, and you'll manage to put two and two together. I've seen you're well versed in arithmetic. I've said too much already. Mind!'

Marx was intrigued, albeit with the detached fascination of a witness to a train crash. 'Tell me, who else have you recruited for this mission?'

'A vow of secrecy prevents me from divulging names and addresses,' muttered the Russian.

'*Genau*. But roughly how many persons?'

'Roughly? Six.'

'Six.'

'*A peu près.*'

'More or less.' Marx nodded. The strategy would need to be more sophisticated than the numbers. 'Yes. So, to be clear, you intend to seize the British Parliament with all of *six* men?'

Bakunin smiled. 'The brilliance of it, no?'

Marx took a sip of his beer and pondered. The man seated next to him was either a raving lunatic or a deluded fantasist. But then a brief survey of the bar told exactly the same story. Every table was a microcosm of world revolution; a fisherman's tale of the one that got away; a cabal of gunpowder plotters who'd lost the plot, hatching plans in a world entirely of their own making. All the world was a stage. But one without wings. It was a tragicomic end to the Parisian debacle. But what crowned the achievement was Bakunin himself, whose arrogance went beyond mere provocation and who had the temerity to compare his own saloon bar "philosophy" to Marx's path-breaking research on capital.

'Mikhail?' said Marx, turning to face the giant.

'Yes, Marx,' said Bakunin, inclining to meet him.

'You are out of your mind.' And with that he got up to leave.

He hadn't got very far before the giant made his riposte.

'I say! *Frère* Marx? The revolution will make a relic of you!'

Marx turned on his heels and brought his fist down hard on the table, feeling the thud in his nether regions. 'Listen here! I should be *scandalized* by your arrogance and insensitivity, but I'll put that down to the fact that you're clearly sleep-deprived — not that I should excuse it. I don't need you or any other crazed fanatic to tell me what revolution entails! I am perfectly acquainted with its triumphs' — Marx paused to register the banks of startled faces — 'and its failures.'

Bakunin didn't flinch, his blank face confirming that Marx probably hadn't been the first to spurn his suicidal mission. No doubt he wouldn't be the last.

'You're living in a dream world, Marx,' offered the Russian.

Marx leaned over the table and let drop the blank sheet of paper. 'Am I?' he said, then cut a slow and deliberate path to the door.

A French youth burst in reciting from a book of poetry. He slammed into Marx, knocking him sideways. The German barked his disapproval and the youth fled onto the stage of the outside world.

Chapter 6

In the street outside the minor scuffle had become a pitched battle. Self-styled Jacobins in frilly shirts (in reality Parisian students on a pub crawl) were taking on Hungarian anarchists and German social democrats, at least one of whom Marx recognized from the German Workers Educational Society on Drury Lane. Jacobin, anarchist, democrat: x_1, x_2, x_3. Variables to be plotted in Cartesian space. But then on second thoughts, no. There was nothing to postulate here, since it was nothing more than a territorial dispute between rival clans of primates. If only the monkeys had been lions then at least their sense of *shame* might have been a revolutionary force.

The anarchists had pinned down a Jacobin while another laid into him with a lump of wood. The Germans, to their credit, were trying to diffuse the situation with language, but a Jacobin, who spoke no English and mistaking them for anarchists, responded by taking up a length of rope and beating at them wildly. It was all too much for one of the youngsters—whose parents, no doubt, had already raised the alarm back in Saint-Germain or Versailles—in whose desperation to escape dived head first into a coal chute. *A different sin downweighs them to the bottom; if thou so far descendest, thou canst see them.*

Locals stood outside their cottages and formed the contours of a boxing ring. Some of them were wagering on the outcome. An old-timer wearing a long white beard sat in a rocking chair appraising the scene with the sobriety of an aboriginal chief.

Marx covered his throat with one hand and his head with the other and dodged the projectiles as far as Coventry Street. He caught his reflection in the window of an upmarket boutique selling French revolutionary *habits*, "celebrating the 60th anniversary of the French Revolution in tricolours; velvets, silks and shawls; the choicest selection from sashes to furs".

From there he crisscrossed the Piccadilly slime pools on wooden planks, fantasizing as he bounced over the open drains at how much filthier falling into the shit would make him, and lamenting his botched plans for the vapour bath and Chinese dumplings (that'd teach him for counting his chickens), before continuing along Haymarket and left on Panton Street, thus avoiding the baker's on Covent Street, whom he owed two pounds and a shilling plus interest (that'd teach him for counting his).

At the entrance to the alleyway next to Lyle's the greengrocers, which doubled as a public urinal, Marx saw something move under a sack; most likely a rat or—gods forbid—a hybrid creature of the bog returned to wreak vengeance on its human tormentors. Marx bent down—the smarting had lessened now—and flipped over the corner of the hessian, revealing a shoeless foot, chapped and frost-bitten, then a bare leg covered in ulcers, followed by the rest of the rag-clad torso of a young boy, no more than six years of age: emaciated, flea-ridden, barely breathing. The eyes of the miserable wretch registered the daylight before shutting tight, as if unable to be reconciled to whatever images flashed in front of them. As for his body it remained quite calm, as if sunk in a dreadful despair, dead to the world.

Marx held out a hand but the boy shrank away, no doubt in reminiscence of some phantom blight. But something more than fear was mirrored in the boy's regard, something far more disquieting: a look of pure anxiety or shame turned on the world. Not the anxiety of being seen, the spectacle of his own wretched existence, which was enough to frighten the life out of anyone. But that awful state of being ignored and of the social energy invested in pretending the child wasn't there, that he didn't exist, of making him invisible. Dead to the world.

Even Satan had his entourage to pester him with compliments. But this poor devil bore Hell within, the deep-rooted Hell of the dark wood of solitude. Where did this unhappy consciousness fit in to the revolutionary scheme of things? Did he so much as enter the minds of the pissed-up tribes scoring points against each other on Great Windmill Street? Or the purveyors of this season's French revolutionary chic?

'Where are you from, son?' said Marx, wondering where his family were and whether or not the child even knew.

The boy rested mute. Then the tears welled and he started to cry.

'I am hungry,' he sobbed. 'I am hungry, mister.'

Instinctively Marx pulled out a penny from his pocket, the only money he had, placed it in the boy's lap and walked away.

On Leicester Square he hesitated. He thought about returning to the boy and offering more in the way of solidarity. The penny was charity and the gesture misguided. Perhaps money would complicate things for the child. Nothing at all was better than next to nothing. Then again, what counted as nothing? In London who could really say? In any case the deed was done.

Nearby a jester banging a gong danced round a man dressed as a fir tree. At this point Marx felt one of his migraines coming on. The performance had gathered quite a crowd, mostly of American tourists strayed off the beaten track on their way to Covent Garden. They dispersed when the Soho tearaways began their Beast of Leicester Square impressions. At the north end a tightrope walker balanced, a juggler stood praying for a miracle and a war veteran wearing a sandwich board with "laugh more, worry less" written across it rocked on his heels. The émigrés were still queuing to get into the German Hotel as far back as the Gun and Pistol Repository at Savile House.

Marx considered his strategy *du jour*: either he could aim to sneak in with one of the new arrivals or else try his luck at the tradesman's entrance (since it was already evening it was bound to be locked). However, once it became clear that the queue wasn't moving and that shinning up the drainpipe wasn't a viable option (the less said about last night's attempt the better), he settled on the counter-intuitive approach and bowled up to the front door like he owned the place. He pressed his way in and made a beeline straight for the stairs, forgoing his usual good evenings and tips of the hat, which since Friday was in the pawn shop, anyway.

To his surprise, the hotel lobby was brightly lit but completely empty, save for a man in overalls hanging a pendulum clock on the wall. However, no sooner had he reached the foot of stairs than his bête noire, the hotel hound, sounded the alarm. At that moment nothing would have given Marx greater pleasure than to have placed an iconoclastic hand over the snout of its sphinx-like expression and wrung its neck.

'Good boy, good dog,' he pleaded, placing a finger to his lips. The dozy-looking mutt clicked its jaws together and huffed. 'Gooo-oood boy.' The animal was probably hungry, that's all. Marx could relate to that.

With the nimbleness of the tightrope walker, he began the perilous climb to the landing.

'Shhh! Gooo-oood boy,' he breathed, carefully observing the minute geography of the 18 stairs, every creak and crack and knot in the wood. Nine, eight, seven... 'Shhh!' Nearly there. Six, five, four... 'Gooo-oood boy.'

He was home and dry. The mutt contemplated Marx's gymnastics with the sobriety of a judge, quite content to respect the rules of the game and permit the tightrope walker his passage, so long as he managed to complete the course in silence. However, on the last stair Marx miscalculated, and the creaky floorboard set the animal off again in a volley of woofs and howls that could have sprung a stiff to life.

'Monsieur Ramboz!' said the landlord.

'Mmm?' said Marx, feigning surprise.

'Your bill is two weeks overdue.'

'Is it?'

'It is,' the man affirmed.

'Well, I was not aware of that.' Although he was, as was the landlord, as Marx knew well.

'I spoke to you about it yesterday,' said the landlord.

'Did you?' said Marx, feigning surprise.

'I did,' the man affirmed.

'Well, I do not recall that.' Although he did, as did the landlord, as Marx knew well.

'And the day before that. At a quarter past six in the evening.'

'Ah! so you did,' conceded Marx, trying to appeal to the man's innate sense of fair play and good sportsmanship. It was rather a tall order given that the eminent doctor, smeared in mud and raw sewage, looked more like something one should promptly flush away than enter into serious negotiation with. 'Look,' Marx began candidly, 'my good sir, I've been so overwhelmed with my writing lately—'

'Monsieur Ramboz,' the landlord cut in, 'I must have payment forthwith or else—'

'Or else?'

'Or *else*,' the man affirmed, 'I shall have you and your family removed from the premises.'

The landlord's ultimatum sounded more decisive than usual; less rhetorical.

'I see,' said the debtor. 'Well, in that case I shall settle the outstanding sum no sooner than I receive your account. Good day.'

Marx knew perfectly well how much the landlord's "account" amounted to and how little his own contained: nothing. As he traipsed dispiritedly to his room he decided that Plato was wrong about the poets. Their Dionysian frolics were harmless; let them dance their socks off. It was those deranged creatures the mathematicians who posed the true threat to law and order. The Pythagoreans should have been banished from the community for their discovery of irrational numbers. As for the mercantilists, they could all go to Hell in a handcart: zero minus a debt was still zero. Blood couldn't be got out of a stone.

Chapter 7

'Give me that!' demanded Jennychen, snatching away the tricolour from her sister and almost ripping it in half.

'Give it back to me!' squealed Laura, this time succeeding in the feat.

Jennychen recoiled from the debris. 'I don't want it now. You can keep it.'

'*Nonnn!*' Laura howled. 'I don't want it either,' she said and promptly flung it back at her.

Jennychen picked up the cane and thrashed it against the dressing table. The metal tip came off and ricocheted into the wall.

'Look!' she exclaimed, quite startled. 'You've broken it now.'

Marx entered the room to a curtain of silence. 'What is the meaning of this insufferable din? Well, now! That's a fine way for young ladies to behave! Isn't it?'

The girls fled to their mother.

Marx took a moment to survey the scene. It was difficult to know where to start.

'What's this?' he said, holding up the remains of the flag. 'Jenny? What have the children been up to?'

'Playing—haven't you, girls?' The mother beamed at her offspring.

'That was a present from your grandfather,' said Marx in a grave voice. 'Do you hear me, young ladies?' He pointed the cane witheringly at each of his daughters in turn. 'You didn't know your grandfather. But I can assure you he would have been horrified by this... this... decadence. As am I; and don't think I'm not!'

'Are we still playing the game now?' said Laura through her baby teeth.

'No!' squawked Marx, his voice shooting up an octave. 'This

is definitely *not* a game! And just look what you've gone and done to my handkerchiefs!'

Jenny suppressed a giggle.

'Oh! Well, frankly, I'm glad their mother is amused,' he said.

'Girls,' said Jenny, looking up from the chessboard, 'go and kiss Papa and tell him you're sorry.' The girls froze. 'Go on,' she chimed, suddenly re-energized by her change in fortunes. Somewhat miraculously White was in a winning position.

The girls took turns in pecking Marx on the cheek, each making a little chirping noise as she did.

'Good. Now, how's my little class warrior getting on? Musch! Come, Colonel. Come to Papa.'

Marx held out his arms and Edgar obligingly rode his locomotive over the father's foot. Marx took off his mud-caked boots and left them at the door, followed by most of his other soiled things. He placed them inside the laundry sack in the corner, which bulged and exhaled a caustic smell.

'How long is your game going to last?' said Marx as he hobbled over to his desk. 'A week? A month? A year?'

Kb4.

'It shall last,' said Helene, inverting the hour glass, 'as long as it takes.'

He reached down and plucked a daguerreotype in a silver frame from the rubble beneath his desk. It was the picture of his father whose frightened expression paled in comparison to how the man himself would have looked on witnessing the scene.

'Jenny?' said Marx, holding up the frame in bemusement, 'I thought we pawned this already.'

c3.

'Check,' she said, inverting the hourglass.

Kc3.

Qa1.

'Check,' repeated Jenny, inverting the hourglass again.

Marx turned to the mountain of gravity-defying notes

masquerading as a manuscript. That wasn't how he had left it this morning. There had been an avalanche on the western face. Someone had been interfering again. Jenny, perhaps, or more likely the children, who knew on pain of savage chastisement to stay clear of his desk.

Somewhere in the environs a drunk was singing. One would need to intervene should that persist. He sat down and looked up in awe at the monster, bracing himself for the climb. Slowly he began unpeeling the jigsaw, lightly removing the layer at the summit first. He could barely make sense of all that was written down.

'Two pork sausages?' he wondered out loud. Category mistake. He peeled off another layer. 'Bed linen 2d?' The entire edifice comprised bills, bills and nothing but unpaid bills. There was no manuscript here. Marx dived into the pile and started tunnelling for his vanished masterpiece. 'Jenny?' he implored, rapidly approaching wits' end.

Qb2.

Jenny turned over the hourglass. 'Check.' The game was reaching its climax.

'Jenny!'

'Yes! What on earth's the matter, Karl?'

'Where's my manuscript?'

'Manuscript? What do you mean *manuscript?*' Jenny pronounced it awkwardly, as if the word were quite foreign to her lips.

'What do you mean what do I mean manuscript?'

Jenny stifled a giggle. 'We could go on forever like this, Karl.' Kd1.

'I know what you mean now when you said you wished the board could be bigger,' said Helene, lighting her pipe.

'Ah. Now *that* was only because I was losing.'

Bf1.

'At least you're honest.'

Rd2.

'I *am* honest. When needs must.'

Marx wondered whether by "bigger" Helene meant a board of infinite dimensions. On such a scale checkmate might be achievable in a finite number of moves. It seemed plausible on condition that the parameters of the game provided for the possibility of checkmate in n-moves which, despite being a very, very large number was still *not* infinite.

Rd7.

'My manuscript, Jenny,' said Marx. 'You know very well what I'm talking about.'

'I haven't seen it,' she said, taking a drag from Helene's pipe.

Marx looked on in horror. 'Are you mad? You'll poison the child.'

'It's just one puff,' she insisted, handing the pipe back to Helene and reclining on the bed.

The singing was becoming unbearable; he would have to intervene.

He contemplated the pile of bills. Some of them were from Paris and predated the family's arrival in London. One could safely discount those. But a cursory inspection of the remainder revealed at least 70 pounds' worth of what were effectively loans, all of them rapidly accruing interest.

'Did you get round to writing that letter to Weydemeyer?' enquired Marx.

'Karl, do I look like I'm in any fit state to write letters? I told you already: you write it and I'll sign it.'

'What!' he scoffed. 'What good will that do if it's written in my handwriting?'

'So? Just tell him I dictated it to you.'

'And *why* would you do that, Jenny?'

'Because I'm *pregnant*, of course,' said she, tutting at the husband's silliness.

'Jenny, why would *you* dictate a confidential letter to *me* that *you* wished to send Weydemeyer?'

Bc4.

'This is going round in circles,' Jenny sighed, inverting the hourglass.

bc4.

'I need that shilling you promised me,' said Helene.

The singing stopped.

'A penny's all I have,' replied Marx distractedly.

'That'll do.'

He checked himself. 'No. I... gave it away.'

'What?'

'To a beggar.'

'You—did—*what?*' Helene rose from the bed.

'I gave the money to a homeless child collapsed in the street. Clear enough? He was dying in a pool of his own filth. What else was I supposed to do?'

Helene leaned over Marx's desk and jutted out her chin. 'Do you *know* how much we owe the butcher? Our credit's spent with Fairbrass and we're two weeks in arrears with Grayson. And what about the baker?'

'All right, all right, I heard you the first time. How am I supposed to work with you carping on?'

'But that's just it!' exclaimed Helene. 'You don't *work*, do you? If you *worked* for a living then we wouldn't be in this mess in the first place!'

'I should mind your tone with me if I were you, woman,' said Marx, whose red jowls and bulging veins bespoke seismic activity.

But the woman wasn't finished yet.

'For a man who spends so much time crapping on about capital, what about making some for a change!'

Marx leapt up and almost instantly collapsed as Edgar rode over his father's foot again.

'This is impossible!' he yelped through clenched teeth, and

on retrieving his soiled clothes from the laundry sack, he fled from the room in a fit of despair.

Chapter 8

On exiting the hotel and crossing Leicester Square Marx felt a crumbling conviction that seemed to weaken his heart and made his bowels bubble like a cauldron of acid, so that by the time he reached St Martin's Lane his constitution was shot to pieces. Nothing stood still. The church bells clanged a frenzy. The traffic was a blur, the people buzzed like flies and everything went off spontaneously without the slightest pause or compunction. To say nothing of the smell—a mind-altering stench of burnt coffee, coal ash, horse manure, sulphur, factory effluvium or whatever all mixed together in a concoction worthy of the Inferno itself (probably the Sixth Circle, since the miasma assaulting his nostrils must have been payback for his Epicureanism).

In Trafalgar Square he watched a pigeon describe the arc of a parabola and land on Nelson's statue. The bird turned in circles three times before emptying its bowels on the Admiral's nose. There must have been a formula for that, Marx surmised. There wasn't the remotest chance of him having the manuscript ready by next week. Nor by the end of the month at this rate, owing to whatever catastrophe had befallen the thing in its previous state. Meaning he could give up any realistic hope of receiving the 1500 talers from Duncker; which, *caeteris paribus*, also meant he could give up any realistic hope of completing the manuscript at all. The domestic straightjacket of the hotel simply didn't allow for it. And with his application for a reader's pass to the British Museum still undecided, there was no indication of how long this intolerable situation might last. Unless, by some fortuitous circumstance, funds could be acquired in the meantime.

Engels had gone down considerably in his estimations since this afternoon and could no longer be relied upon. Who, then? Schramm? The lad had mere pennies to his name; although he would readily give them up at Marx's behest. Wolff had money.

Marx already owed him 300 talers, 30 silver groschen and the five pounds in paper money he had practically swindled from him on his previous visit to London.

Who, then? Liebknecht? Dietz? Now he really was scraping the bottom of the barrel. Even if Dietz had a small fortune to his name, which he most certainly did not, Marx couldn't bear the moral indignation of accepting money from the acting chairman of the Communist League. Marx would have jumped at the chance of a three-bedroom Chelsea apartment. But not with the enforced guilt of being constantly reminded that Dietz had put up the deposit. The very idea was intolerable.

There was but one thing for it. Petition Weydemeyer.[12] By all reports the man was doing very nicely in Frankfurt as editor of the *Neue Deutsche Zeitung*, having walked away from the collapse of the *Neue Rheinische Zeitung* a little too subtly and painlessly for Marx's liking, in stark contrast to his own fortunes (the cursed venture had swallowed up 3000 talers of his own cash). Aside from whatever strictly moral case could be made for remuneration, Weydemeyer had taken more out than he had put in, and far more than Marx.

A friendly dispatch was in order, conciliatory yet firm. A word or two inquiring as to the health of his good wife—Marx had forgotten her name—who Jenny and he had visited six months ago and who was also expecting a child. Followed by something sober yet sanguine yet Dickensian about the Marx children. How the fourth was due any day now. The shocking state of the hotel and its dysfunctional central heating, its fleas, the cutthroats who lined up outside come nightfall and what have you. Rounded off with a paragraph spelling out the "negative" state of Marx's account, the fixed capital costs paid out to the *NRZ*, how much was outstanding on Weydemeyer's side and, finally, the sum that Marx felt was needed to get their relationship back on an even keel and draw a line under the whole affair.

The pigeon's arc was most likely given by the Cartesian

equation $y^2 = 4ax$. As for its turning in circles and defecating on the Admiral's nose, that was anyone's guess.

Marx turned off Charing Cross and continued down to the end of Craven Street, then south over the wharfs toward Whitehall Stairs. On the dark grey mudflats, seafarers sat huddled round a fire watching the sun go down. One of them plugged away on a squeezebox. He listened to their sea shanty, which worked wonders for his migraine, and stayed there long enough for the words to sink in. And the men went on singing in spite of him, since looking the way he did he could have easily passed for one of their number. There was only one verse:

> Is this land still mine
> When the sea washes it away
> Or as a point in space
> When the seas evaporate
> And the earth explodes
> And space is replaced
> By a new notion

Stumbling on an empty can of sardines, he continued along the shoreline below the India Board to the Swan Hotel where a lone lighterman was riding the ebb tide. On the horizon another of the mobile chimneys was crossing the Vauxhall Viaduct, while on the South Bank the mass extinction was gathering pace. A rhapsody in orange. *Through me the way to the infernal city.* Across the water the rag-and-bone men hatched from their coffins. Pink-faced and dressed in sackcloth and gossamer shirts they traipsed back to their nests in vulture steps.

Marx hastened to the pier, experiencing as he had done earlier that day the nausea and fractured vision. Spots came before his eyes so big and bright that he began to doubt the veracity of their descriptions. A light tremor sounded beneath his feet, radiated out into the deep channel of the river then returned, causing the sand to tear and tumble, opening a crater here, a fissure there, and shaking the shoreline like a sink full of crockery.

He steadied himself, unable to look away from the water and the source of the next implausibility. The pier was deserted as he climbed the last flight of steps up to the Swan, spluttering through clouds of sulphur. The tremors grew and rattled the wooden pier in staccato signals: a message from the other side or a tribal beacon buried in the deep time of the river.

A crowd had gathered on Westminster Bridge. On the central turret the watchman gazed out like a ship's captain. He was pointing at something. A sunken vessel or falling star, perhaps. The river swelled then gushed violently to the sound of splitting timbers. Slowly, in a kind of whirlpool of being and appearance, the dark outline of a figure rose up from the waters.

At first the thing seemed to lack form; then the apparition grew and took on the outlandish proportions of a 50-foot giant. Wearing a top hat and cloak, the monster found its feet on the riverbed and turned to face the shore. His deadpan orbits, each the size of a cave, peered over the upturned collar of his cloak, which swished in the breeze, making the sound of a spinnaker flapping downwind. A note of wonder went up from the crowd. Wielding a cane the size of a poplar tree, he prodded the sky as if turning the dying embers of a fire, which kindled the heavens.

'Uncanny,' Marx mouthed in astonishment.

Then it registered that the crowd's attention was in fact being drawn elsewhere. On the South Bank a flurry of activity was afoot and only when the lightning tore through the sky again, briefly turning night to day, was its true nature revealed. A colossal proletarian army was gathered on the shoreline. Extending all the way to Lambeth upstream, the manifestation started funnelling across Westminster Bridge, spreading faster than the poison algae or hybrid creatures of the bog could ever have done.

'Off with you now!' shouted the watchman.

The crowd of early evening *flâneurs* gathered their petticoats, held on to their top hats and took to their heels as the leviathan lurched forward as one. Marx stood rooted to the spot, his face animated by an utterly incongruous smile. The produce of the workshops of the Upper Lambeth Marsh had matured and taken form. It was no longer private property and certainly wasn't adapted to the market's needs. What had been building in those waterside receptacles was something as miraculous as the atmospheric conditions for life on earth. It was the wild and dysfunctional breed of living-dead labour that refused to stop working, the rebel power with nothing else in mind other than the fabrication of the tools for the takeover of society.

As the cursed gathering drew near, Marx caught a glimpse of his future rulers: a many-headed hydra of foul-mouthed apoplexy; a riotous mass of contorted faces, every one of which was the double of his own.

On freeing himself of the nightmarish vision something else hit home. The proletarians had downed their tools. They came unarmed. Unencumbered by the capitalist instruments they no longer were, they themselves had become the new machines, or the steam power that the atmospheric engines could no longer contain.

It was ironic that the factory line had brought this about. The universal army had assembled itself from component parts that were never meant to be combined and now the amalgam was headed straight to the nerve centre of power. They looked and sounded a savage bunch whose impropriety preceded them. Unlike the march of those feudal petitioners of old charged with doffing their caps as they filed past the town hall, the universal army had no formalities to dispense with.

No sooner had they reached the Westminster Palace than its doors were flung open and they swarmed inside, filling its enlightened corridors and reception halls, toppling statues and smashing stained glass, not through revenge but through sheer weight of numbers, the natural side-effect of direct democracy. Marx reclined on the balcony of the Swan and felt roundly disappointed. Was he giving due service to the revolution from a seated position? Was he now a theatre director? Instinctively he reached for his notebook before remembering the unfortunate business that same morning. It made no difference. On the contrary, the revolution was being written over there.

On crossing Parliament Square he ran into a crowd of Celtic festivalgoers. A man in a cotton sack coat stood holding a lantern, while next to him his wife wondered whether or not lighting their bonfire was the "done thing" in the circumstances.

'I say we light it, Richard,' said the woman, as if pondering the fate of a cat stuck up a tree.

'I s-s-s-say, Mildred,' exclaimed the man, 'they're b-b-burning the place.'

The windows of Westminster Hall shattered in a trickle of ecstasy and the gothic facade of the Palace burst into flames. Marx looked on with the same sense of pride he had felt at Jennychen's first words ("treason" and something garbled from *Hamlet*). He squeezed the bridge of his nose and slapped his hollow cheeks the better to have his wits about him should things go awry. In the revolution's opening hours there were bound to be excesses, gratuitous acts.

He hastened away and walked up Whitehall, marvelling at the serene calm of the moment of truth. On reaching the Banqueting House and the spot where 200 years ago Charles I had been beheaded, another festive crowd appeared, laughing boisterously and holding children aloft. Behind them, or somewhere in front or to the side, a fire raged.

As he approached Trafalgar Square he entered a thermal corridor encased in an icy mist. A street vendor was handing out hot snacks on wooden skewers, and people were singing and dancing. Either they had come to celebrate the fall of Parliament or hasten its demise; or perhaps both at once.

A nefarious detachment surged onto the square causing panic and confusion. Projectiles flew and the flames began to spread, rapidly engulfing the shops and private dwellings. Marx considered his next move as if it were a chessboard. What piece was he? And which Circle of Hell was he in? Perhaps the Seventh: Violence (Ring 3, probably), whose entrance was guarded by the Minotaur. Marx thought of possible candidates for the role, at last settling on the stuttering nincompoop from Parliament Square. *Pàrtiti, bestia! ché questi non vene ammaestrato da la tua sorella...*

The heat grew more intense. Marx stood his ground, fascinated by this novel danger to his person. He could think now; fire was his element. This incendiary revolution appeared to be bearing out his fledgling theory and rendering the missing manuscript superfluous. Perhaps it even solved the extinction problem of the Great Fossil Lizard. Might the factories and locomotives be replaced by real volcanoes? Would the West End consumers notice the difference? That was where humanity was headed, Marx thought, at last being forced back from the inferno. That was the nearest the machines came to an identity and a goal: the return of man to the dawn of time.

On Trafalgar Square the scaffolding on Nelson's Column served a daemonic purpose. There were more uses for a scythe than reaping corn. Three silhouettes came swinging down from the platform on ropes and the few remaining people below began to scatter. The statue lunged forward, a few degrees at first, slackening the ropes wrapped around the head of the condemned man. A few degrees more and the ropes went taught again, and the Admiral bowed down in submission. Nelson's torso snapped off leaving his legs where they stood on the plinth. Meanwhile the rest of him hit the ground in a cascade. Then a huge explosion erupted that sent masonry sky high and a tremor down below, covering everything in between in white powder. No confirmation were needed that the column was down.

Marx parried the falling debris and took shelter in an alleyway. As he edged along the wall blindly he recited the opening lines of the *Communist Manifesto*. 'A spectre is haunting Europe, the spectre of communism,' he intoned in the style of Hamlet's soliloquy. He exited the alleyway on Scotland Yard and collapsed on a bench, realizing he was being followed but too exhausted to do anything.

•

Chapter 9

No wonder Hell was on the banks of a river. The capitalist mode of production was the synthesis of fire and water. Steam was the creature's medium. Land colonization by the atmospheric engines was humanity's Late Devonian moment. A primitive form of capitalism had emerged in the Po Valley in the 13th century,[13] its mad inventors having thrown up improbable hydropowered contraptions hacked from wood. Whether or not this primitive race of the possessed really believed in the wisdom of its inventions, and that Promethean offspring, in the absence of fire, could be cast from the desolate crags and high precipices of the western Alps, we may never know. In the event the experiment had failed.

Then, four centuries later, steam power was harnessed. The industrialists hit upon the novel idea of turning the boilers on their sides and wheeling them round on casters. The random walks of the early machines made revolutionary strides. They put the fear of God into clergymen and animals, and laughed the Luddites out of history.

Marx had first set eyes on one as a child. 'These things are the future, Heinrich,' Baron von Westphalen told his father, 'the future of invention and democracy.' But it was equally possible that Marx's recollection of the blades and wheels and the whole unruly contrivance coming over the hill was unsound, and that the sight of it perched there next to the cherry orchard was a product of his imagination, a phantasmagoria of all the machines he had ever seen. In any case, something had gone horribly wrong with those machines. The roads were abandoned in favour of the railways, which began to spring up everywhere.

The Baron had been right about the future, albeit not quite in the way he meant. From the confluence of democracy and invention the tracks would soon radiate out of every metropolis;

from its gravitational centre to the X of every satellite district and back of beyond, paving the way and constructing the track for the revolutionary breakdown and its diaspora, the mass expulsions and deportations; preparing to enshrine victory in the grand public works and their joint stock ventures, in awe-inspiring bridges spanning ravines, rivers, high mountain passes and plunging through subterranean tunnels; all unprecedented in scale. All for the sake of ensuring that necessity remained the master of invention.

Marx couldn't decide between the roast veal and the Wiener schnitzel. There was also something to be said for the steak and fried potatoes, a hearty simplicity that appealed to his ravenous hunger. The bill of fare didn't extend to the sweets. For some reason the sheet of paper had been torn off just below "cucumber 2d", which struck him as expensive. The abridgment had no meaning in relation to his actual scholarship, which would be doomed if ever it abandoned the scientific method and started writing recipes for the cookshops of the future.

The surplus value of agricultural products corresponded to the unpaid work of agricultural labourers. The scientific method exposed the conceit. Ideally every menu should be a statement of the real value of commodities. However, it was doubtful that the principle could be extended to the domestic sphere. Love, sharing and mutual need were incalculable. How could Marx ever hope to calculate Helene's wages? Food for thought. But best set aside for the time being, seeing as he couldn't afford the price of a glass of water. File under "sweets". Perhaps that had been his point in writing the differential formula in the right margin. In any case, there was so little light here that he would need to take a proper look at it back at the hotel.

'Get your snowdrops 'ere! A penny a bunch!'

They wouldn't be fresh for long, thought Marx, as the sulphurous clouds descended on Whitehall. *Schneefall*: the winter flowers that Jenny used to decorate their Brussels apartment with and that always reminded him of her porcelain skin. They grew plentifully along the tree-lined avenue of the Théâtre Royal du Parc, where he and his wife would walk His Majesty Qui Qui and Hottentot as infants.

'But is there any *law* against it, Karl?' Jenny would ask rhetorically as she scooped up bundles of the flowers from the verges in front of the Palais de Justice, transferring them to the children's perambulator as Marx grappled a baby under each arm.

Philosophically speaking, no "law" as such, no. But one could still wind up in prison for it.

'The King's hardly going to expel you for picking a few flowers, is he?'

What did she mean "you"? In the event of their arrest Marx pitied the poor prosecutor with the task of facing off his wife in the dock. Only the most heartless of monsters or one of Greek mythology's most malicious gods could deport Jenny for picking flowers. And woe betide any who did.

Nelson's Column was still standing on Trafalgar Square and on the corner of St Martin's the congregation filed in to church for the evening service. A top hat in a fur coat stepped down from a Hansom cab and offered his hand to his female companion, who wasn't his wife despite wishing she were. From his wallet he selected a paper bill and handed it to the cab driver. The client made a great show of this simple act of exchange. The tradesman tipped his hat before picking up the horse's reins and taking off in a deft manoeuvre that exposed the nincompoop's stupidity for having forgotten to attend his change. The top hat thought about this momentarily—his face markedly altered for the purpose—before waving the fault away and turning to the important task of finding a pocket large enough to house the wallet.

The couple, heavily inebriated, bumped into each other before swaying arm in arm up the steps to the church. The man tried to light a cigar as he went. Marx considered doing the decent thing and pointing out that Covent Garden was a mile further on, but in the end he decided to let nature take its course.

For all its manifold diversity—the circus-like freakishness and philistinism of its "individuals"—one had to admire the bourgeoisie *as a class*. Granted they drank too much, lived too long, were rapacious philanderers and the lousiest of hypocrites. However, one was inclined to be less cynical, even reassured by their progressive contribution to society as a whole in having placed the dynamite for their own destruction.

Marx set off along St Martin's Lane laughing hysterically. He couldn't rightly say why. The mood had taken him by complete surprise and for the following minute, which he counted down in English, he failed to shake off the regard of that universal class—his own—and the darts of resentment directed at him for what he knew and could prove by resorting to the scientific method.

'53, 52, 51...' The countdown to detonation had begun.

He picked up his pace in order to avoid the indignity of being crushed by the church steeple.

'37, 36, 35...' he continued, loud enough to be heard across the street.

He registered the presence of the mysterious figure from the alleyway. He decided to run across St Martin's Lane to Castle Street—a bad decision, since the pain in his nether regions confirmed something had burst.

'16, 15, 14...'

He beat a path through the throng on Bear Street and once arrived back in Leicester Square, began to remark at how quiet it all was and where the tearaways were when the first of the explosions went off.

'5, 4, 3...'

He doubled up on the rubble-strewn ground. This time it was real, the countdown proved it—the existence of real numbers was irrefutable—and for several moments the shock of having managed to predict—miracle of miracles—a revolutionary event rendered him a useless writhing mess.

'Marx! It's star-ted!'

A second explosion, to the south this time, confirmed that the uprising was on a different scale entirely and certainly nothing to do with the Great Windmill Street ruffians. The opening salvos confirmed it would take time, patience, persistence, intelligence. Then his heart sank at the thought of Bakunin and his "invisible" plans for the seizure of Parliament. Could this be his doing? Surely not. It couldn't be allowed.

Explosions dotted the sky in a series of constellations, each one pulsing then fading. Red, blue, white and gold. The colours no doubt a coded signal. He considered raiding the Gun and Pistol Repository at Savile House but the premises were deserted.

'Marx! It's star-ted!'

He bit his lip so hard to quell the pain from his backside that his canine came loose. He ran toward the voice. It was Helene declaiming from the hotel window, her words striking an unprecedented note of solidarity. It all depended on him. *Los.*

As he started through the thicket of Leicester Square he was buoyed by the first faint echo of a new rapport between men and women. This was how the new society could be, it struck him, as he overtook the crowds marching down Whitehall, past Horse Guards—the erstwhile defenders of the state apparatus a novel tourist attraction now—and on to Parliament Square, where a huge crowd was congregating. The atmosphere was robust yet relaxed with workers, artisans and bourgeois all in fraternal liaison. A huge bonfire was ablaze.

Negotiating the maze of bodies, Marx fell upon Harney[14] and the Chartists. He might have known the people's friend would be first on the scene. He saluted the General Secretary of the Provisional Government of the British Republic, who peered out from a large circle of supporters and aides-de-camp, his collar pulled up over his side whiskers, a self-styled Oliver Cromwell with a self-righteous morality to match.

Harney recognized Marx immediately and came over to greet him. As he held out his hand a pair of navvies cut a path between them, conveying the lifeless body of a child toward the fire.

'Stop!' shouted Marx, but the men took no notice, intent on inflicting the revolution's first arbitrary act of justice, something he couldn't be associated with and wouldn't allow to happen.

Bracing himself for the pain yet determined to set an example he launched himself at the navvies. He managed to grasp one of them round the waist but the brute was so muscle-bound he didn't flinch. Marx held on and caught the other's knee in his face, who then buckled, promptly splitting in half the Guy Fawkes effigy he was carrying. It was the annual bonfire festival for marking the Gunpowder Plot of 1605, when Robert Catesby, Fawkes and their fellow conspirators had packed explosives into the cellars of the Houses of Parliament with the aim of assassinating the King. Every 5 November a public festival was held to celebrate the failed revolution.

Marx hobbled back to the hotel, determined to get there while he had the use of his legs. People were still converging on Parliament Square as he made his way home against the grain. On the stroke of midnight and with Jenny in the final throes of labour, he entered the nativity scene. She heaved and cried and heaved again, and in a peal of agony the child was free.

'It's a boy,' said Helene, cradling him in a sheet as he separated from the mother.

She wiped his face and massaged his back then held up the son for the father's inspection. The child opened his mouth and raised a tiny fist, filling his lungs and abhorring his first intake of London air. Good things come to those who wait. As to this evening's errand to nothing, at least it had supplied the child with a name.

'Welcome, Guido,' said Marx, embracing him with a frenzied grin.

Chapter 10

London, 20 May 1850[15]

Dear Herr Weydemeyer,

It will soon have been a year since the days when you and your dear wife showed me such friendly, affectionate hospitality, the days I felt so happy and so much at home in your house. I haven't shown the least sign of life the whole time. I kept silent when your wife wrote me a very friendly letter; I even remained mute when we received the announcement of the birth of your child. This silence of mine often weighed heavy on my own heart but, most of the time, I was incapable of writing. It's hard, very hard, for me to write even today.

Circumstances, however, have thrust the pen into my hand. I ask you to send us, *as soon as possible, the money collected or being collected by the* Review. We need it *very, very badly.* Certainly no one can accuse us of ever creating much of a fuss about all the sacrifices we've made and everything we've borne up under for years: the public hasn't been troubled much, or at all, by our personal affairs. My husband is very sensitive when it comes to such matters and would rather sacrifice his last penny than resort to the democratic begging that the great official men do. But surely he had a right to expect active, energetic participation in his *Review* from his friends, especially in Cologne. He had a right to expect it above all in the place where the sacrifices he'd made for the *Neue Rheinische Zeitung* were well known. Instead, the enterprise has been completely ruined by negligent, sloppy mismanagement. It's hard to say what was worse, the bookseller's shilly-shallying or that of the business manager and our acquaintances in Cologne; or whether the worst thing of all wasn't the behaviour of the Democratic movement as a whole.

My husband has been very nearly crushed by the pettiest

53

worries of bourgeois life, in so outrageous a fashion that it took all the force, all the calm, clear, quiet self-possession of his character to sustain him amid these daily, these hourly struggles. You know, dear Herr Weydemeyer, what sacrifices my husband made at the time: he invested thousands in cash and took over ownership of the newspaper, talked into it by the petty-bourgeois democrats who, if he hadn't, would have had to assume the debts themselves, at a time when the prospects for making a go of it were already dim. To save the paper's political honour and the public reputation of our Cologne acquaintances, he took on all the liabilities, gave up his machine, gave up all revenues, and even borrowed three hundred *Reichsthaler* to pay the rent for the newly rented premises, the arrears on the editors' salaries and so on—and then he was forcibly thrown out.

You know that we've kept nothing at all for ourselves. I came to Frankfurt to pawn our silverware, the last thing we owned; I arranged to have my furniture sold in Cologne, because of the risk that a lien would be put on everything, even our linen. When the unhappy period of the counter-revolution began, my husband went to Paris and I followed him with my three children. Hardly had he settled down in Paris than he was expelled, and my children and I were denied an extended residency permit. I followed him again, over the sea this time. A month later, our fourth child was born. You would have to know London and conditions here to understand what three children and the birth of a fourth means. We had to spend forty-two *Taler* a month on rent alone. We were able to meet all these costs using our own assets. But our meagre resources ran out when the *Review* was published. Despite what had been agreed on, the funds didn't arrive, or arrived only in such small amounts that we continually found ourselves in the most terrible predicaments.

Let me describe *One Day* of this life for you the way it was, and you'll see that few refugees, perhaps, have gone through anything of the sort. Because nursemaids are unaffordable here,

I made up my mind to breastfeed my child myself, despite constant, terrible pains in my chest and back. But the poor little angel drank so many worries and silent cares in with my milk that he was constantly sickly, and in severe pain night and day. He hasn't slept a single night since he came into the world; he sleeps, at most, two or three hours at a time. In the last little while, he's been beset by violent convulsions as well, so that the child has been permanently suspended between death and a miserable life. He sucked so hard because of his pain that my breast was rubbed raw and started to bleed; the blood would often pour into his little quivering mouth. I was sitting there this way one day when the house manager—to whom we'd paid more than 250 *Reichstaler* over the winter, and with whom we'd come to a contractual agreement to pay money in future not to her, but to her landlord, who had earlier had her property put under distraint—burst in, denied that we'd made such a contract, and demanded the five pounds we still owed her. When we were unable to produce the sum right away (Naut's letter arrived too late), two bailiffs walked into the house, put a lien on everything I owned—beds, linen, clothing, everything, even my poor child's cradle and the better quality toys belonging to the girls, who stood there crying their eyes out. They threatened to take everything in two hours—I was lying on the bare floor with my shivering children and sore breast. Our friend Schramm rushed off to find help in town. He climbed into a cab, the horses bolted, he sprang out of the coach and was carried bleeding into the house where I was wailing with my poor trembling children.

We had to vacate the house the next day. It was cold, rainy and grey outside. My husband went looking for lodgings for us, but no one was willing to take us when he mentioned our four children. Finally, a friend came to our aid: we paid up and I sold all my beds in short order so that we could pay off the pharmacists, bakers, butchers and the milkman, who'd been alarmed by the scandal of the lien and had suddenly taken me by storm with their bills.

The beds I'd sold were carried out of the house and loaded onto a cart—and what happened then? It was already gone sunset and that's against English law. The landlord charged our way, accompanied by constables, affirming that some of his own things might well be mixed in with the rest and that we were bolting for a foreign country. In fewer than five minutes' time, better than two hundred to three hundred people were standing outside our front door rubbernecking—the whole Chelsea mob. The beds came back; they could only be turned over to the buyer the next morning after sunrise. After we'd been put in a position to pay off every last penny that way, by selling all our possessions, my little darlings and I moved into the two tiny rooms we now occupy in the German Hotel, 1 Leicester Street, Leicester Square, where we found a humane reception for £5/10 a week.

Forgive me, my dear friend, for describing so lengthily and in such great detail just One Day of our life here; it's improper, I know, but my heart gushed into my trembling hands this evening, and I had to pour my heart out in front of one of our oldest, best and most faithful friends. Don't imagine that these petty trials and tribulations have broken my spirit; I know only too well that our struggle isn't an isolated one and, especially, that I'm still one of the happy, favoured few, since my beloved husband, my mainstay in life, is still by my side. But what really shatters me to my very depths and makes my heart bleed is that my husband has to endure so much pettiness, that it would have taken so little to help him and that he had so little help here; although he himself has been ready and willing to help so many others. But as I said, dear Herr Weydemeyer, don't imagine we're making claims on anyone. If we *receive an advance from anyone*, my husband *is still capable of paying it back out of his personal assets*. The one thing my husband could rightfully expect from those indebted to him for many an idea, many an uplifting insight, and a great deal of support was that they muster up more commercial zeal and greater personal commitment in connection with his *Review*. I'm proud and bold enough to contend that people owed him that much. And I also can't say that the ten farthings my husband earned for his work were more than his due. *I don't believe anyone was ever cheated on that score.* That pains me. But my husband sees things differently. He has never lost faith in the future, not even in the most terrible moments, or lost his most jovial good humour; and he was always very happy whenever he saw that I was light-hearted, with our beloved children cuddling up to their beloved mother. He doesn't know, dear Herr Weydemeyer, that I've written to you at such great length about our situation, so don't make any use of these lines. He knows only that I've asked you, on his behalf, to speed up collection and transfer of the funds in any way possible. I know you'll only put these lines to a use inspired by your *tactful, discreet* friendship for us.

Farewell, dear friend. Extend my most affectionate greetings to your wife and kiss your little angels on the part of a mother who has let many a tear fall on the baby at her breast. If your wife too is breastfeeding, tell her nothing about this letter. I know that agitation of any kind causes strain and is harmful for the little ones. Our three eldest children are flourishing, despite everything. The girls are pretty, blooming, jovial and in good spirits, and our chubby boy is a model of humour and brimming over with the funniest ideas. The little rascal sings funny songs all day long with tremendous emotion and in a booming voice, and when, in a fearsome voice, he lets the words from Freiligrath's *Marseillaise*:

> 'Come, O June, and bring us deeds,
> Our hearts are longing for fresh deeds,'

ring out, the whole house resounds. Perhaps it's the world-historical vocation of this month, like that of its two unfortunate predecessors, to usher in the gigantomachy in which we shall all stretch our hands out to each other again.

Farewell.

Chapter 11

The revolution entered a period of hibernation. It suited Marx to remain hotel-bound in the first few days following Guido's birth and in any case, the winter weather prohibited all but essential excursions. Marx was no longer a producer; he was a hunter-gather. The revolution would return — as surely as spring followed winter — but for the time being there were more important fish to fry. He was determined for his health to improve in the new decade — he planned to swim and go on long country walks — and the fallow phase provided a novel opportunity for praxis in the domestic sphere. He read to the children, reasoned with his daughters that revolutionary violence was no end in itself and tried to stop Musch from wheeling round on that wretched toy of his by hiding it in the laundry sack or under the bed.

Guido became his joy and salvation. The child was a dreadful worry to begin with. Feeding time irritated him, and he cried day and night. Bauer, the family doctor, would call round more often, sometimes twice a day, armed with potions and prescriptions for medicines Marx couldn't afford. Within a few weeks things quietened down and with Jenny fully recovered, and on a diet of red meat, fruit and vegetables, the child began to settle into regular patterns. Guido soon became fascinated by everything around him and began to explore his new world. He had his father's eyes, coal-black and furtive, only far more handsome according to Helene.

'I think he'll be a ballet dancer,' mused Jenny. 'Look, Karl,' she said as she swung the baby round the room by his tiny hands, 'don't you think he's got the knack? That's what you'll be, little man,' she cooed. 'We're going to enrol you in the Ecole de Danse. Yes we are! What do think about it, my darling *petit bonhomme*?'

'Jenny,' said the husband, 'if you think I'm sending that boy to ballet school in Paris then I've some disappointing news for you. In any case, by the time he reaches maturity there's not likely to be a ballet school any more.'

'Don't be ridiculous, Karl. Why ever not? One needs ballet. It's… necessary. It's part of life.'

'Because by mid-decade, '57 at the latest, I expect a major economic crisis to have set the ball rolling on a thoroughgoing political upheaval in England, France and Germany. That's what the data's telling me,' said Marx, waving a clump of paperwork that resembled a fish-and-chip wrapping.

'Oh, you're such a scaremonger,' said Jenny, whirling Guido round again. 'Isn't Papa a scaremonger? Yes he is. Yes he is.'

The child looked positively worn out by it all.

Some weeks later and with more career suggestions for the father to mull over—pianist, opera singer, actor, theatre director—the hibernation period came to an abrupt end when the great power of the clan knocked off Marx's horns and sent him out into the ranks of the warriors with nothing besides a cup of tea and a mouthful of porridge to keep him going. Had Marx been at home when Bauer arrived it would have implied that he wished to settle the account. In the event, Helene's intuition worked like a charm. Not only did the doctor not even mention the money he was owed, but the pre-Raphaelite apparition of Jenny sitting up in bed with her hair down must have melted his heart. The upshot being that instead of asking for money, the doctor actually handed over the price of a week's rent *in cash*, along with a free batch of Marx's anal concoction. (When it almost blew the patient's brains out the philanthropic gesture seemed less philanthropic, prompting Marx to label the benevolent doctor a semi-erudite plebeian quack and an anti-communist).

Marx set off toward Whitehall but had barely reached St Martin's when he was so overcome by exhaustion that he very nearly curled up on the pavement. However, the north wind concentrated his mind sufficiently for him to make it down to Westminster Bridge, where he sat on a bench watching the workers construct the clock tower at Parliament.

At first he couldn't really understand what was going on. Most of the labouring was hidden inside what must have been the base of the tower, a rectangular red brick wall resembling a secret garden. From time to time a stonemason's head would poke up above the wall. The men worked only from within the structure. There was little to suggest to passers-by that any work was going on. Why had scaffolding not been erected? A whistle sounded and almost immediately the artisans clambered out on ladders, far more of them than he expected, like a colony of ants in response to some communal emergency.

In human terms, however, one could see the problem perfectly well: the division of labour. Could such alienated working practices ever satisfy democratic imperatives? Certainly not. One wasn't dealing with polyvalent workers here, but with workers divided by the unequal possession of acquired skills. Only the factory system could proletarianize—and so modernize—such gothic construction projects in such a way as to meet the wider needs of society. Then again, if such work were proletarianized then sooner or later the proletarians would come bursting over the bridge to knock the blasted structure down again.

'Young man! I have heard the rumour.'

'What rumour?' answered Marx mechanically, without knowing where he was. His eyes were almost frozen shut and the rest of him had shut itself down in an unconscious act of self-preservation.

Engels heaved him up from the grass verge in front of the Swan Hotel where, like a giant hedgehog rolled into a furry ball, he had come to rest. It took a minute or two for the poor creature to be revived and unkinked.

'Even hedgehogs manage to find proper shelter in winter,' said Engels, helping his friend to his feet.

'I'm fine, really,' said Marx, attempting to make light of his near-death experience. 'I slipped.'

'Did you hit your head?'

'I don't think so.'

Engels embraced Marx with a great sigh. 'Congratulations, Moor!' It seemed gratuitous to congratulate someone for being alive, but then Marx realized he was talking about Guido.

'Let's drink something. Come. In there.'

Engels ordered them whiskies in the Swan. The place didn't cut it as a watering hole but the elixir worked as well as any of Bauer's medicines. After downing a second glass and washing his face in a bowl of warm water he was ready for the trek to the Red Lion, where the Communist League was presently due to meet. On the march up Whitehall Marx fantasized over a bacon sandwich as big as a table and a Chinese bath filled to the brim with steaming soup, which he would slurp up like a hound on all fours. Seeing as the upstairs of the pub had been reserved for the meeting there would be no difficulty this time in finding a comfortable seat. Since there was nothing of any consequence on the agenda he could profit from the occasion and work through some formulas while his comrades took care of business.

'Mary's been having some problems,' Engels related as they turned on to Haymarket.

Marx felt an agitation building in his bowels. There was no reason why they couldn't have caught an omnibus or taken a cab the rest of the way.

'What's she done now, then?'

Engels glowered. 'Done? Why, I'm talking about Mary—you remember her?' He looked offended, which made Marx question how much he should have known about his friend's romances and how much he actually did. Mary: the Irish girl Engels had taken a shine to on his first stint working as a junior clerk in Manchester. She and Jenny had got on rather well. 'I don't know what to do. She wants me to get her a job in Manchester but doesn't seem to understand how much I loathe the place. This could easily drive a wedge between us.'

Marx suddenly became alert to everything Engels was saying. 'What do you mean "us"?'

'I want to settle in London eventually,' Engels went on, who might have been talking to himself. 'Manchester's just a stopgap. Of course I daren't tell her that straight out, since her family's there and I don't want to upset her. But living up there is going to be like a death sentence for me. Most of all, I worry about the toll it's likely to take on my constitution. I love the girl but—'

'Well, you're right to be worried,' cut in Marx, aiming for the appropriate balance between empathy and all-out selfishness. 'One has to think logically, especially in affairs of the—'

'Weerth[16] lived in Bradford for years,' Engels reasoned, 'so it's not completely out of the question that I'd be able to put up with the Manchester life. The man's proved life north of London is liveable.'

Reaching the top of Haymarket and crossing the Piccadilly slime works on planks—a no-man's-land resembling a pirate's graveyard—Marx's carbuncular pain returned with a vengeance. It felt as if his right buttock were being sliced off with a cutlass. The pain might have lessened had he been at liberty to relieve himself. Then again, he had taken to doubting the evidence of his physical constitution, which was well and good given what a lamentable state it was in.

Walking up Great Windmill Street he thought how convenient it would be if he could just dispense with his body altogether and have his brain carried around in a vat. But he preferred old Spinoza's doctrine that the mind's consciousness of itself is no more adequate than its consciousness of its own body.

At the entrance to the pub Engels blocked his path. 'Moor, I want to tell you something,' he declared solemnly. 'Mary and I have an open relationship.' He paused and loosened his cravat. 'It's nothing you weren't aware of. I'm telling you because I'm immensely fond of the girl and don't wish to be judged for it.'

Marx nodded, awkward at the prospect of where this might be leading.

'I want to tell you something,' Engels repeated. 'Mary spoke to your wife.'

Marx steadied himself against the door frame. 'About what?' he gulped.

'Love,' said Engels, sweeping back his golden mane with both hands and almost swooning, 'the perennial *joy* of it, Moor. She wants a child—Mary, that is, not your wife.'

The husband felt oddly reassured.

'Please say you don't mind me telling you this.' He seized Marx by the wrist. 'It's the Vaud air; I can still smell it, you know. Its wistful perfume... It embarrasses me. Switzerland? I know, I know. But the girls are so ravishing there. Their... *musk* works like a drug. I used to believe in channelling my carnal energies, but I'm no longer ashamed of the art of seduction. Think about what Plato says in the *Symposium*. Eros guides the soul. But one mustn't confuse Eros with desire. Eros is superior; he stands like a towering erection above *epithymia* and *thymos*. The soul is courted by Eros to create things of universal beauty. One can serve the revolution each according to one's own... talents.'

Engels's eyes sparkled and his lashes fluttered.

'There was this one beauty in particular I took a shine to. God, the creature almost made me lose my marbles. But the strange thing is, Moor, the liaison—which I threw myself into wholly—made me, well... ever more... *faithful*. Is that the word? Yes, truly it is. Faithful, I'd say; committed in my commitment to Mary. Does that sound odd? Why, it's more than just *odd*. It's unprecedented! And yet perfectly rational. Ever since I arrived I've been convinced... you know? On the way back from Genoa we stopped off in Gibraltar and the captain of the schooner I was on took me to this brothel. All the girls were Jewesses. Most of the clients were priests. Priests and soldiers! But Gibraltar, I ask you! It's all paid for by the Brits. It's the only way they can prevent the soldiers from deserting.'

Marx shifted his weight onto his other foot as Engels breathed in the still morning air.

'You know, Moor,' he said, breathing out again, 'if only love were a real... *advance.* A genuine leap. Do you know what I mean?'

Marx nodded, trying to reconcile his bemusement with the coming pain.

'Quite unlike Elberfeld. Scythes and pickaxes. That's all most of them had, the ones who wanted the fight. Anyone with a flintlock... why, those bourgeois needed rifles to keep the scythe and pickaxe-wielders in check. They had no intention of pointing them at the Prussians. We need a revolution more like love. What was it you wrote to Ruge?[17] Shame is already a kind of revolution such that, if an entire people felt it, it would be like a lion ready to spring. I've had enough of running away... But I want you to promise me that you'll keep this strictly between us. Mary's the woman I love. I won't marry her, but I love her unconditionally.'

'Of course, of course,' said Marx, quite unsure what he was agreeing to but dying to sit down.

It was all horribly confusing and more than slightly overwhelming, and in his present state of nervous exhaustion made him feel desperately small, insignificant and alone.

They climbed the stairs to the meeting in the garret above the pub. There was adequate light and a decent view of the street from up here. And it was warm. It certainly made a change from Brussels and the damp cellars in which they used to convene. On the face of it the Communist League had gone up in the world and despite not being a remotely "respectable" political organization, there was no longer any reason to operate as a secret society.

'Gentlemen comrades, I make that four and twenty minutes past the hour,' said Dietz as the latecomers arrived.

'We started half an hour ago,' put in Heinzen, whose hairy face was buried deep in a copy of *Le Proscrit*.

The others stood up to greet them. There was Oswald Dietz,[18] the League's acting chairman and archivist; Wilhelm Liebknecht,[19] an ex-schoolteacher recently arrived from Switzerland; Konrad Schramm,[20] young and loyal enthusiast; Gottfried Kinkel,[21] revolutionary poet now making a name for himself in London literary circles; and Karl Heinzen,[22] professional mischief-maker.

Next to the stairwell a large red flag had been unfurled with "Workingmen of All Countries Unite!" embroidered on it in gold lettering.

'That's nice,' said Engels admiringly, running his hand across the fabric. 'These dyes they use nowadays... I wonder if it's one of my old man's.'

'Damned unnecessary expense if you ask me,' said Marx, warming his hands over the stove in the corner. 'Who gave that the go-ahead?'

'Is there any coffee?' asked Engels.

'Apparently not,' replied Marx, shaking the empty pot.

'Gentlemen comrades,' interrupted Dietz, 'time is against us this afternoon, as we only have the room until two o'clock. So if you would very kindly take your places, please.'

'Two?' said Marx. 'But it's usually booked for the entire afternoon.'

'We're broke,' came Heinzen's voice from behind the news-sheet. 'Imagine that.'

Marx sat down on a rickety stool thoroughly ill-suited to the rigours of scientific reflection. Heinzen had commandeered the only decent chair in the place. Judging by his simmering impatience it was unlikely Marx would have been able to claim the prize for himself, even if he and Engels had arrived on the hour. This fact devalued the entire proceedings in Marx's eyes. In any case, that was that. There was no chance of him turning his mind to the manuscript here, for his mind felt less like his own with each passing minute and his body had long since rebelled in its own fashion.

'Would all those in favour of the motion please raise their hands?' said Dietz.

'Motion, motion, motion...' Marx hummed under his breath.

'All those against? Anyone? No one? Anyone? Good. Any abstentions? Anyone? No one? Anyone? Good. Which means that... the motion to *amend* clause 3, paragraph ii, sub-paragraph iv, of the statutes is passed... unanimously? Can we say unanimously, gentlemen?' Dietz wore the concentrated expression of a dentist pulling teeth, while the others looked like his patients.

'You just said it,' whispered Schramm.

'I know I did. But for the vote.'

'Unanimously,' confirmed Engels, raising his hand. 'A bit of solidarity, perhaps?' The comrades did likewise. 'That's the spirit.'

'Are we all sure?' Dietz glanced round the table again.

Heinzen peered over his news-sheet in the manner of a devil looking down on reason. His presence at the meeting was unusual. The same went for Kinkel, the beautiful soul in a raggedy brown overcoat. Marx had lapsed from the chessboard of late. Mapping the current state of play required a separate organization.

'In which case the motion is passed unanimously, gentlemen.' Dietz tapped the table with his finger. 'Now. Moving on to point 34 of the agenda. No. Oh, dear. Wait. Now I'm confused: 35. Silly me. Point 35... of the agenda... it... is. Following on from the previous point—point 34. Point 35—'

'Comrade Acting Chairman,' cut in Engels, 'I think we all know how to count.'

'Comrade Engels?'

'Perhaps we could...' Engels motioned for things to speed up.

'I'm afraid I don't follow you, comrade,' said Dietz. 'You wish to make a point of order?'

'No,' said Marx, 'he wishes you to put a move on.'

Dietz sighed. 'Comrade Marx, I am going just as fast as is practicable in light of an *extremely* weighty—'

'But let's make it faster. I don't want to be carried out of here in a coffin.'

'Well, quite,' the chairman confessed, wringing his hands. 'Perhaps we might... Does anyone else... *concur* with Marx's point?'

'Acting Chairman,' ventured Liebknecht after a time, 'I do feel Comrade Marx might have a point. Perhaps in future we might try to make things—'

'Faster,' said Marx.

'I second that,' said Engels.

'Hang on,' said Liebknecht, backtracking, 'I hadn't proposed it yet.'

Dietz politely intervened. 'Comrade Liebknecht, if you wish to propose an item then can I suggest you do so at the end of the meeting? We do have rather a weighty agenda to get through and—'

'Enough!' cried Heinzen, leaping from his chair. 'The clock is ticking, gentlemen. The countdown has already begun. In the real world, that is. I know not for the life of me what *you* all make of this *horseplay*,' he declared, his eyes fixed on Marx. 'But by the look on your faces your hearts aren't in it. What good is this talking shop? Tyrants and oppressors are set against us on all sides and meanwhile we split hairs over—what? Agendas? In France I need hardly remind you that there's a Bonaparte in power riding roughshod over the constitution and anyone who dares stand in his way. So, enough of idle banter! We must act! We must embark on our sacred mission, the one etched on the heart of every revolutionary fighter. The future is calling, gentlemen. I propose we raise a revolutionary workers' army and march on Paris this night! That's what is needed and that's what must be done. *Ici et maintenant*. So! Are you with me, brothers?'

Somewhere outside a bottle smashed and a woman screamed.

'Should I add this to the any other business, Comrade Chairman?' whispered Schramm.

Dietz shook his head.

'I have news for you, friend,' said Marx, finally breaking the spell. 'The revolution in France and everywhere else is finished. Anyone with half a brain can see it.'

Heinzen feigned surprise. 'Brain, you say, comrade? Brain? Or brawn? "The philosophers have only interpreted the world; but the point is to change it."[23] That's what you *wrote*, isn't it? Then, why not change it? Oh, I forgot: do as I say and not as I do. That's more your creed, isn't it? Dr Marx?'

'What are you getting at?' Marx demanded.

'Getting at?' said Heinzen. 'You don't see? So permit me to clarify things, seeing as your memory is so vague on the matter. I dare say our comrades might like to know. Last 5 November, just here, outside the pub, I was rallying the workers for a march on Whitehall. The men were gathered as far as the main road. Comrade Kinkel was with me and will back me up. Things were just getting moving and the men were in fine spirits. Then, who should make an appearance? Why, Comrade Marx. And yet not walking but *running away* from the march! In the opposite direction! I called to him, thinking I'd mistaken him for another. "Will you not join us, brother?" I shouted, but he slipped away faster than the words from my mouth. I was quite surprised— stunned, indeed—to see one of our own turn his back on us.'

'What!' Marx was incensed. 'How dare you! I refuse to tolerate such an outrageous slander.' He rose in a theatrical show of indignation. 'What "workers' march" are you referring to? There was no march on that day. Unless you count the antics of the drunken rabble who nearly landed a bottle on my head as I was walking home. That's what I was "running away" from, if sheltering from a hail of glass counts as running away. Is that what you're referring to? Surely not. In any case, I resent your insinuation and advise you to withdraw. I was exiled from Paris at gunpoint for my political convictions, as everyone here will know. My political credentials are not in question here.'

'Nor indeed mine,' said Heinzen, yielding the point with a bow. 'Forgive me, Marx, but a man of your calibre—the joint author of this party's manifesto no less—who appears, to me at least, so... indecisive. I must admit to being confused.'

'You're welcome to it,' said Marx, regaining his seat.

'You trouble me, brother.'

'Likewise.'

Heinzen began a tour of the room. 'Why, it's almost as if you're embarrassed of revolutionary activity and of getting involved. Why *is* that? Why are you so unwilling to join in a workers' march?'

'Where there are marches to join, I'll join them.'

'But not mine.'

'There was no march,' Marx scoffed. 'It was a drunken brawl.'

'All revolutions are brawls in the beginning,' put in Kinkel, the poet.

'That,' Heinzen affirmed, running his hand across the red flag, 'is so very true. Well said. Of course, I don't wish to suggest that you harbour any... workingman phobia; any grudge. That would be just plain wrong. What intrigues me, however, is what *practical* alternative you have and, indeed, what this party's politics are going to be from now on. What is *your* alternative, Marx? I must say, I hardly know. What *exactly* do you want?'

All eyes turned on the chief theoretician.

'I shall present my "alternative", as you put it, in the form of a treatise on capital at our next meeting,' he announced.

Chapter 12

'The world is richer by a citizen,' said Engels, holding aloft tankards of ale. It was gone lunchtime in the Red Lion but the place was thronged alive. 'Long live Guido!'

'Indeed,' said Marx, 'and I am poorer by a crown.'

'May he live to see the Workers' Republic. How is the young fellow doing? He must be getting strong.'

'The child is well and blissfully ignorant of his father's virtual destitution. What am I to do now with seven heads to feed?'

Engels nodded feebly. The pub's revolutionary songbook put paid to such weighty talk. Besides, the Red Lion was no place for it, where the talk was mostly bigger than reality itself.

'How's Jenny?' he asked.

Marx sighed, 'When the child came along I'd forgotten she was even pregnant.'

'Good!' said Engels, mishearing. 'She's a fine communist woman, your wife.' He made a vulgar face.

Marx realized the look was aimed over his head at the barmaid.

'Moor,' Engels resumed, 'I really owe you an apology for running out on you the last time. Bakunin and I are no longer on speaking terms.' He pursed his lips and took a sip of ale. 'Mind you, you really went for Heinzen. Bravo. I thought you were going to challenge him to a duel.' Engels laughed and shook his head at the prospect.

'Ha!' said Marx, puffing out his chest. 'And I.'

'Just as well you didn't, though,' Engels cautioned. 'He probably would have killed you. He's a crack shot.'

Across the bar, Heinzen was leaping about in animated conversation with a cabal of workingmen. He was working up the passions and drawing quite a crowd.

'That man's up to something,' estimated Engels. 'I wonder

what. Some hare-brained scheme, no doubt.' He downed his ale in one and handed Marx a five-pound note. 'Here, take this. It's all the spare money I have.'

'What? You're going already?' Marx panicked. 'But wait! You promised me 10. That's not even enough to pay the rent.'

'I have to. Business calls,' said Engels, landing his hands on his comrade's shoulders. 'Moor, listen to me. You need to forget your domestic worries and finish your book on capital. I know things are far from ideal *chez vous*. But please do your best.'

'But I can't—'

'Show Heinzen what he's up against.'

'But I can't—'

'*Show* him. Give us more than just hope for a change,' and with that Engels turned on his heels and in military quickstep shot out of the door in hot pursuit of the barmaid.

In his hotel room Marx did his best to make some headway. Or at least make a start. Again. There was something inordinately frustrating about that damned formula. It was rather difficult to put into words. It was mathematics, after all—a subject he hadn't studied seriously beyond high school.

'Jenny?' he said, distracted for the umpteenth time. 'What's with the singing? I say!'

The room, which might have been a microcosm for any of the worlds outside, contained ample distractions of its own. Jennychen and Laura had enlisted Edgar in their class war game, and Guido was asleep on the bed. The child was restless and every few seconds let out a perturbed yawn. As for the women, as usual they did battle on the chessboard.

'It's such a relief to have my figure back,' said Jenny, pouting in the mirror. 'I'd forgotten what it's like to be thin.'

Rc8.

'Your move,' said Helene, inverting the hourglass.

'I could do with your boobs, though.' Jenny resumed her

place at the board. 'Then I'd really turn heads.'

'You could do with a new dress,' said Helene, raising her voice, 'that I'll grant you. What with all your unpaid *labour*.'

Jenny laughed. 'Right. I can see that happening.'

'Jenny?'

'Karl,' she said, exposing her left breast. 'Do you think my boobs have sagged?' The miraculous object might have been modelled on one of Michelangelo's Virgins.

'Jenny,' said the husband, gawping in spite of himself, 'I've been attempting to ask you something. The singing. Do you hear it?'

She slipped the breast back inside its drapery. 'Singing? I can't hear any, no.'

'Are you playing this game or not?' demanded Helene.

'Am I the only one to hear it, damn!' exclaimed Marx.

'Shhh!' said Helene, pointing at Guido on the bed.

'Ah! Look at the little man.' Jenny jumped up to inspect the thick nest of blankets that contained her child. '*Mon petit bonhomme*. I still think he'll be a ballet dancer, you know. I had thought opera singer, but if he takes after his father his lungs will be too weak. I suppose he might be a lawyer…'

Rae1.

'Are you letting me win, Helene?' enquired Jenny as she doubled her rooks on the e-file.

She was experiencing a run of form of late that made Helene out to be a novice. The strategy of Black's opponent, insofar as strategy there were, was gallingly simplistic. There was nothing admirable, as far as Helene was concerned, about the manner in which Jenny played. Of course, this was not to say that the moves themselves in combination weren't intelligently conceived and weren't to be admired in a more "thoughtful" player. But Helene refused to concede to Jenny the credit that her last few implausible victories might have merited. And no, Helene wasn't losing on purpose.

Marx rifled through his notes, counting the number of parchment sheets as he went. There must have been a good 60 of them. If a book's merits could be weighed in pounds and ounces, then it was getting on for a decent work. In any case, what he had was a quarter of a book once typeset and bound. A third, say. Whether the formulas added up was less important for now than getting the damned thing *looking* like a manuscript and posting it off to Duncker before the end of the month.

Suddenly a thought struck him. 'What happened to that silver picture frame?'

'This court finds the defendant *guilty* on all charges,' announced Jennychen.

'No!' cried Edgar.

'Shhh!' said Helene.

'Jenny?'

'You pawned it, Karl. Along with my best linen. Shame. I could have done with a change of sheets.' The wife flashed the husband a lascivious smile. 'Couldn't you?'

Qd7.

'Your move,' said Helene, inverting the hourglass.

'I am *referring* to my theoretical treatise here,' replied Marx, wielding what resembled the leftovers of a fish supper.

'Helene, you *do* insist on making it easy for me,' Jenny chided her opponent.

Bf6.

'The moment you stop concentrating is the moment you lose the game,' Helene replied.

'What makes you think I'm not concentrating?'

Qg4.

'This try-boon-er-all isn't fair!' cried Edgar, stamping his foot in protest.

'Shhh!' Helene covered the boy's mouth.

The singing was reaching a crescendo. Marx looked out the window and counted at least 50 refugees queuing round the block in what was likely to have been their first encounter with orange hail. He placed his hands over his ears in order to muffle the singing, forgetting that he needed both of them for turning the parchment pages. Perhaps he could make do with assessing the thing differently.

A caricature of the French president Louis-Napoléon that Engels had scrawled in the margin came to life. It surveyed the unruly landscape of jottings and crossings-out before offering its own verdict: 'Why, my dear fellow,' the President squeaked, 'this is no manuscript. It's nothing but a bunch of meaningless squiggles.' Marx leaned back from his desk. It was true. What he had was utter nonsense.

'Aaa-oooh!' he shrieked as the wheels of Edgar's toy ran over his foot. 'You damned stupid child!' he cried, leaping up and accidentally flattening the boy.

Edgar wavered in that uncanny zone of confusion before the tears flowed: in sobs at first, then a delirious heart-wrenching cry. The noise woke Guido, who wasted no time in showing solidarity with his elder brother.

'Happy now?' said Helene as she carted off Edgar to safety.

'It's impossible!' said Marx, storming out of the room. 'It's nigh impossible!'

Chapter 13

At night, when the clouds opened to the sublunary world, the moon would appear, throwing light in strange ways, revealing those hidden dimensions of the city that ordinarily escaped the eye. It wasn't a matter of magnifying life, but of seeing it through a different lens. Under moonlit refraction the dust became green, purple, ochre—not so much colours as thick slabs of hanging sediment that made up the atmosphere. The London air aggravated Marx's ears, eyes, nose and throat, and the visual delight was little consolation to him, any more than it was to the unfortunate college-goers forced to ingest the stuff in the toxic delivery rooms of the Upper Lambeth Marsh.

When Marx called on him, Engels was lounging in his Chelsea digs reading the latest dispatches from Paris. Mary Burns[24] was there, much to Marx's surprise, since only that afternoon had he seen Engels leave the pub with the barmaid. The three of them wasted no time in jumping in a cab and heading across the river to the open countryside of Rotherhithe. Marx did his best to ignore the fact that Mary had her hand down Engels's trousers for most of the way.

They turned off Jamaica Row and on the outskirts of Seven Islands south along the Deptford Lower Road, then east toward Limehouse Reach, where the bend in the river briefly makes south Londoners more northern than their northern cousins. Eventually they pulled up in a place called the Plough Public House, which was situated on the Kent county border.

'These are the busiest ports in the world,' said Engels, stepping out of the cab into the pitch-black. 'You wouldn't credit it, would you? That canal we just crossed goes all the way up to the Grand Surrey Dock, but the river's less than 200 yards away over there.' Engels put his arms round Mary's waist. 'Can you find your footing, my love? Watch yourself. There's no lantern and it's quite marshy here.'

'Where is this place?' said Marx as the door of the cab swung out into the glowing virus of space, the addendum to the sublunary world and its refracted particles.

The change of air heightened his senses as much as the sulphur clouds of the Upper Lambeth Marsh stymied them. There was clarity here; not that endured, but that flashed with the perfection of his wife's breast. A light breeze ruffled his collar, hinting at something partly understood. It was part of the all and nothing, the all without limit. Even the college-goer on his way home from the alehouse was perfectly attuned to the raging inferno, or the offshoots thereof, which stood no more "out there" than the factory furnaces on the banks of the Thames. In fact, what real difference was there between the sublunary gas clouds that obscured this "higher truth" and the starry constellations themselves, which in any case were only visual records of time, of congealed time? The time that could be retraced to the first fiery inferno.

'There are more docks here than in the city,' said Engels, leading the party down a muddy path dotted with cowpats, 'and this is only the beginning. In five years all the big container vessels will be unloading here. And five years after that they're sure to be building more docks further east.'

Inside the Plough, Marx sat opposite Mary while Engels went to fetch the drinks. So here was the object of Engels's erotic confession. The girl had a strong and healthy complexion, and her hair was blacker than Jenny's. Her hands were badly stained and when she touched his—which she often did—they felt as rough as sandpaper, attesting to the factory labour that defined her and her class. Nothing in her speech revealed much else about her and this suited Marx, since the barn they were in—which must have housed livestock at some point—was a cavernous echo chamber.

Mary gushed with political convictions, the history of her

people, her aspirations to learn German and travel with Engels to Italy; all this and more came forth in a torrent of words. Marx had to infer most of the detail, owing to the girl's dialect, the intelligibility of which deteriorated in proportion to the amount of alcohol they both consumed. If he had stayed sober for long enough he could have plotted the problem using the Cartesian coordinates.

The entrance to the pub faced out onto East Country Dock, a deep and narrow finger of water just below the Commercial Docks, and must have been set that way in order to entice foreign sailors. Marx could make out the masts and rigging of at least four freight ships and judging by the look of the drinkers, most of their crews were inside.

'I think they must have arrived this afternoon,' said Engels, meaning the sailors of Malay extraction stumbling round to the rhythm of an Irish folk ensemble. 'And I bet they won't stop downing ale until they've spent every last penny they have. Cheers!'

Mary brandished her tankard of ale with ease. Marx remarked at her muscular forearms. She quaffed a good third of the measure at once, as did Engels, who mirrored his lover's every move. She whispered something in his ear and they rolled back their heads in synchronized cackles of laughter.

'Mary wants to know why you're such a genius,' said Engels.

'What did you tell her?'

'That it's all German ideology.'

Marx watched the Malays prancing and pirouetting, and wondered at the distances they must have travelled to be here. The ocean charts might have been pinned to the sky according to nature's whims, but it required those men to read them and steer the ship.

He felt inebriated and needed to relieve himself; an urge that made him queasy at the prospect of what might be unleashed when he undid his trousers. In the end the operation passed off without incident—the volcano being dormant for the time being—and Marx returned from the outhouse, which was a muddy slope emptying directly into the dock, through the heaving crowd and back to the table, where Engels and Mary were locked in a passionate embrace.

'Come,' said Engels, coming up for air and grabbing Marx by the wrist.

'Where?'

'I told Mary you were an excellent dancer of the Irish jig.'

'What?'

'Don't worry. She didn't believe me.'

Engels and Mary hauled the reluctant dancer into the centre of the room. He couldn't prance or pirouette like the Malays, or manage anything that wasn't a waltz. But then no one in the glorified cowshed was wearing a tuxedo or a bow tie. Some of them were wearing very little indeed, and most were as drunk as skunks.

Gradually he began to throw caution to the wind, at first by tapping his right foot. It was a significant concession. Then one foot led to two and the knee joined in, and before long his entire body was gyrating to the Celtic music and flailing to the rhythm with all the grace of an epileptic walking a tightrope.

On downing his third tankard and with his inhibitions gone, Marx rolled up his trousers in a Lederhosen style and commanded the floor, slapping his thighs and jumping around like a Kosak with his pants on fire. Such was the vitality if not dexterity of his interpretation that the revellers stood back, and began to clap and cheer and goad him into ever more outlandish gymnastics. But in the abstract individuality of his solipsistic gyrations reality dawned on Marx, reminding him that repulsion was the first form of self-consciousness and that in any event he needed to urinate again. He flew off the floor, seemingly in a straight line; although the manner of his deviation raised the possibility of there being no such thing. After all, how is the idea of a straight line compatible with the principle of matter in motion? The thought rekindled as he tripped on the stairs on his way to the outhouse, landing flat on his back and knocking himself unconscious.

The mysterious figure stood over him, looking down into the staring eyes which, despite registering the other's presence, saw nothing.

On the cab journey home, Mary and Engels treated Marx to a mobile peepshow which—mercifully—none of them would remember the next day. Hands and tongues combined with whispered pleadings and moans. On managing to extricate himself from the paralytic assemblage on the corner of St Martin's Lane, Engels handed Marx 10 shillings and told him to 'keep the change'—obviously mistaking him for the cabdriver—before instructing the phantom coachman to 'drive on, Horatio!' Or at least that's what Marx heard. As for the 10 shillings, at some point they must have dropped out through the hole in his trouser pocket, the one Helene was supposed to have mended for him.

The church clock struck three. Why the final chime sounded different from the others, so forlorn as it resounded all unto itself, he could not fathom, not at this ungodly hour. What was it about the final number in a series? 1, 2, 3... Was the "final" number intrinsically different?

He broke wind loudly in the freedom of knowing that his solitude served some purpose and then swung the lantern he had pilfered from the dock, which threw bewitching shadows backward and forward, assisting neither his sense of direction nor locomotion. Where he was on this falling gas cloud was itself a work in progress, he thought, as he urinated against a wall upon which the solution to the differential paradox might have been inscribed. He began to sing *the Marseillaise*. It sounded like a chorus from *The Magic Flute*. '*Entendez-vous dans les campagnes!*'

he screeched at the top of his voice, nearly bringing up bile, and strangely minded to commit a random act of violence. Seeing as no one was around he started throwing stones at street lights. One smashed.

'Ho! You there!' a French wine merchant berated him from a first floor window. 'You are disturbing the quarter!'

'*Monsieur! Veuillez accepter mes plus sincères excuses pour le désagrément,*' Marx replied sarcastically, before ripping down the tricolour from the merchant's shop front. '*Je me mettrais volontiers à plat ventre devant vous, mais je crains que, ce faisant, je resterais par terre indéfiniment,*' he added, launching another stone. '*Dans le mille!*'[25]

It missed the street lamp by a mile but smashed glass somewhere else. Aside from the objections of the wine merchant, the noise alerted a constable.

'You there! Stop!'

'Fuck off, peeler!' Marx heard himself cry.

He retreated in haste and hit the rubble of Leicester Square on a second wind. By a stroke of luck the front door of the hotel had been left unlocked. On gaining the lobby he was so desperately parched that he gulped down the water from a vase of carnations. There was only one more hurdle to negotiate: the hotel hound.

The Sphinx was plonked in his usual spot at the top of the stairs and Marx gravitated upward in the routine he knew by heart. Things passed off in textbook fashion until the seventh stair when, for no apparent reason, he abandoned the challenge and stumbled the rest of the way to his room in the nonchalant spirit of a shameless drunk, and without provoking so much as a peep from the hound.

Presently his entrance was worthy of his new-found animal magnetism. He crept into the room holding the lantern aloft with the tricolour draped over his head.

'Behold,' he whispered, 'I am the Ghost of Revolution Future and I bring you... the Light of Truth. Hooo-oooer! You have nothing to lose but your chains. Brothers and sisters, the Future is already arrived and it goes by the name of... Karl Heinzen. Hooo-ooo—'

Helene, who had been lying in ambush, leapt from the bed and onto the ghost's back.

'While you were pissing away our money on booze,' she snarled, 'your children went starving tonight!'

The ghost began to laugh; she grabbed him by the jowls.

'Find that funny, do you?'

'I am dealing with higher truths,' rasped the ghost, accidentally smashing the lantern.

'Oh, really?' she replied, her hands tightening by degrees. 'And what have your *truths* achieved lately, then? Answer me that! All your fine-sounding phrases never earned us a farthing.'

'Go on,' said Marx, struggling to speak through the deformed hole where his mouth should have been, 'out-philosophize me: I dare you.'

Helene let go his face and he dropped to the floor. She hauled him up again, this time by the lapels.

'You think you're so fucking clever. You and your bullshit philosophy. You're nothing but a selfish, arrogant, insensitive, egotistical bastard! D'you hear?'

'You don't understand,' he mumbled, 'you poor peasant girl. You poor lumpen proletarian girl. History has no use for you. History will laugh at you.' He flopped to the floor.

It took another half an hour for him to find his way to bed, but he was asleep before his head hit the mattress and too drunk to dream.

Chapter 14

In 1810 Peter Durand had invented the tin can. It would be another 60 years before it occurred to anyone else to invent the tin opener. Capitalism could hardly be described as a *system*. There was no joined-up thinking. It certainly wasn't a leviathan. It was Frankenstein, *res singulares*, an amalgam species of the living dead, a lunatic fringe cult. A non-system.

Ever since the mad inventors of the Po Valley had let loose the reins on their perversions, the history of private manufacture had been littered with useless inventions. Stillborn ideas, half-baked and petrified, washed up on the banks of rivers, left to rot in attics, cellars, barns and factories, which would then be abandoned themselves.

Sometimes the ideas would be recycled, as in the case of the steam locomotive. The machines couldn't have gone on idly chugging up and down country lanes indefinitely. The social revolution represented by the steam train had to be harnessed, coordinated and regulated by the private corporations. On the threshold of every social revolution stood a bank manager spoiling things, judging them on their utility. If a revolution were deemed profitable, capital would be advanced by the bank, then shares in the enterprise issued. In a parallel universe the steam locomotive was one of the useless inventions, along with portable windows and beard umbrellas.

The lords of the imagination railed against the miserable details of commerce. Invention was a law unto itself at one with life's melancholy reflections. For every Newton there were a dozen Cornelius Agrippas;[26] countless others, no doubt. In his mind every experimentalist was a seer tasked with abstracting rules from the human condition and perfecting a machine for its description. Mankind might have vanished without trace, dropped off in the dark wood of savagery, had it not been for the arrival of some evil genius harbouring a vision.

And yet the seers underestimated the extent to which every botched invention, every stillborn idea, bestowed an animation of its own. They created monsters, conjured negative apparitions, bloodcurdling infusions, formless mummies, accursed demons, disfigured shapes, ghoulish projections from the dark rooms of their souls, all the accidents of history unfit for human eyes. The singular delirium possessed entire communities and the laboratories emptied of their half-baked specimens in turn.

In the hovels of Long Millgate and Ducie Bridge,[27] teetering on high parapets of necrotized debris, a new breed arose, a malign stain, an indecent caricature of civilization: the proletariat. The random impulses of the machines became a monstrous reproductive cycle driven by commercial rationale, a massive accumulation exercise facilitated by blind transactions.

Where previously wealth had been a matter of pandering to the sovereign's every whim, in the capitalist age everything changed. Now, wealth hinged upon the organic composition of capital or the capitalist's ability to marshal entire populations, aided and abetted by the latest technological contrivances.

But the new breed resisted and would go on resisting integration. They wouldn't be caged. They wouldn't be *defined*. Indeed, their alleged excrescence, plague, mass, indiscriminate expansion and multiplication—even their rebellions—were a function of the social alienation that "the system" engendered as a condition of its reproduction. There was no such thing as the human condition. One could no more unearth this unruly thing than predict volcanic eruptions. There was no law of capitalism; it was contingent by necessity.

Perhaps one day people would wake up to discover that the proletariat had never actually existed. Erstwhile creatures of a parallel universe.

Chapter 15

Jenny adored the trappings of the West End. There was nothing like it in her native Germany. Cologne was a cattle market by comparison; whereas in London the cattle were far more cultivated. Paris came a close second, but the recent social upheavals had ruined it.

During her formative years the idea of the city had always seemed so remote. Then her father took out a subscription to the *Revue de Paris*. Suddenly, the world arrived on the back of a speeding locomotive. She remembered taking the first issue to Sophie's house and the two of them being too breathless to read as they sat in the orchard overlooking Trier. They kept the subscription secret from Jenny's mother, who wouldn't have approved; although the Baroness was liberal enough not to be scandalized. The *Revue* was delivered every Friday morning to the Baron's chambers and on the weekend the girls would indulge in the same ritual, even in winter when the snows came, only giving in to the elements when Jenny almost lost her thumb to frostbite.

Her father reasoned in his usual phlegmatic manner. 'Is it sensible,' wondered the Baron, 'to want to read one's *Revue* outside when the mercury is showing minus ten?'

'No, Father,' replied Jenny as she sat by the fire wrapped in five blankets, 'but it was Balzac.'

The Baron didn't understand the new writers. They were a means of transport. They drove one to delirious heights of joy and depths of despair, to new pastures where wild and intoxicating plants grew. He was right, of course. The *Revue* wasn't worth losing a thumb for. But it was worth catching a train for. Reading Balzac delivered Paris to Trier. The problem was that in doing so it only exaggerated the distance between her and the real thing.

London brought it all back. The excitement she felt when

exploring the West End was exactly the same as when she immersed herself in her *Revue*. It was different now, in the sense that whereas in Trier the stories had opened the door to a fantasy world, in London she became part of the story. In Trier she could only take a peek inside the pages of the book, skipping in and out. Whereas in London she mixed with the central characters. It was always so invigorating to be inside the book; and more than slightly disturbing. She didn't much like Balzac's *Vendetta*. But she couldn't help thinking of Ginevra and how romantic the idea was of being married to the "wrong" man. The parallel was perfectly valid, she thought—as long as she didn't end up dying in poverty.

The West End was like that. It could alter one's mind. But it offered the kind of intellectual stimulus that she rarely found in books these days; or at least in the stories she wasn't in. Jenny enjoyed being seen in public. It provided her with the opportunity to twist things, especially a gentleman's prerogative for flattery and condescension. She rather detested what passed for such quaint English "manners", which she put down to the English humour. Her aversion was peculiar and certainly didn't stem from the vindication of women's rights. It was more personal and had everything to do with her upbringing.

Her father was to blame. She could never make the Baron love her enough however much she craved his affections, even by surpassing herself in her role as the dutiful daughter. The incident with Voltaire was a prime example. If she couldn't attain *all* the love she longed for and rightly merited from her father simply by being herself then there was nothing else for it but to exceed his expectations. Why, she could go beyond good: she could be bad, instead. But it never worked. Her transgressions would always be met with the same sufficient reason, rather than genuine chastisement.

'Do you think Voltaire should be placed inside your stocking and hung from your bedroom window?' the Baron rhetoricized.

'He's an animal, Father.'

'That's quite correct; so he is. But does that mean he should be deprived of his dignity? Rights aren't limited to human beings.'

'What do you mean "rights"? If animals have rights it's only because humans say they have.'

'Is that really so? Is it true in our case? Do we have rights merely because other humans say we have? I should say humans have rights because they are human. Likewise, our animal friends have rights because they are our friends.'

Jenny could never keep pace with the Baron's gymnastic mind. He was too practised in the liberal arts of diplomacy. Law was his profession. Her ever more outlandish attempts to shock and confound him always ended up falling flat. Such as the time she took her pony, Rousseau, into his study as an April fool's prank, where he defecated on the floor and ate one of his books. However far she went in her unconventional attempts to make him love her more, the Baron would always go that one step further, always using the knight's move of reason to temper her enthusiasm. Perhaps she should have been more grateful and less self-obsessed. After all, he had intervened during her relationship with Karl, her one true love, when she felt sure she was losing her mind. The Baron had steered her through the pain and heartbreak. Then again, what sense was there in "true love" without the pain and heartbreak?

'Where shall we go first?' Jenny gushed as the female party plus Guido ambled along Bond Street.

It was all the same, thought Helene, seeing as they wouldn't be spending any money. But that wasn't Jenny's concern at all, since what was on display in the boutiques was only on sale as a kind of afterthought. The sale was always "second-hand" in her eyes. In any case, such was the principle she was determined to live by. Despite living in poverty she was still the Baron's daughter. Her husband's attempts to differentiate between all varieties of "value" confused her no end, since each and every individual was cut according to the cloth. Helene was made for service and it was Marx's responsibility to pay her for it. The fact that he couldn't was a scandal. But it couldn't make her resent the fact that she and Helene were different by nature. Then again, perhaps this attitude of hers was her affliction or a mark of her perversity, which was hardly her fault. The Baron had always preached *amour-propre* or a communal form of self-respect. It was the very thing that seemed designed to frustrate Jenny's quest for inner happiness.

'Look at all the beautiful cakes, girls!' announced the mother to her daughters.

'Can I have a cake, Mummy?' asked Laura.

'Let them eat cake!' replied Jennychen, whose younger sister had been chosen to play Marie Antoinette in today's class war game. 'You can't have cake,' said the big sister, 'it's counter-revolutionary.'

Laura's bottom lip curled and she began to cry.

'Now listen here, you two!' Jenny snapped. 'I don't want any of your tantrums today. Is that clear? No play-acting!' She took out her handkerchief and wiped away Laura's tears. *'Pas d'histoires et gentil. C'est vu?'*[28]

Jennychen, who always had an answer for everything, simply folded her arms.

Burlington Arcade was a covered shopping market designed in a mixture of the high Regency and Ionic Renaissance styles. It had been commissioned by Lord Cavendish in 1817 in order to shelter his garden from flying oyster shells. The building marked a giant leap in leisurely perambulation. The idea of strolling beneath a domed firmament bathed in natural light greatly appealed to shoppers. It made for an unusual vista one couldn't experience anywhere else.

The central aisle was flanked on either side by 60 shopping bays, each decorated in a style most suited to its wares. It resembled a cathedral; albeit one open to through traffic and without a central altar. Jenny thought it a very progressive idea. It was perfect for browsing. And with God out of the equation one could shop more or less at one's convenience. In addition to the patisserie (where the Marx family's credit had already been exhausted), there were: milliners, hosiers, glovers, five linen shops, shoemakers, perfumeries, hairdressers, jewellers, watchmakers, lacemen, hatters, umbrella and stick sellers, case-makers, tobacconists, florists, a shawl seller, ivory turner, goldsmith, glass manufacturer, optician, wine merchant, bookseller, stationer, music seller and engraver. It was a feast for the eyes. It also provided Jenny with the opportunity to converse with the lady shopkeepers, practise her English and see how far the visiting cards her husband had printed could lead her into the realm of commercial speculation.

The women began their grand tour in Monet's Perfumery.

'Smell this,' said Jenny, handing Helene a pink bottle.

Helene read the label. '"Fraternity. A new fragrance of betrayal and hope by Conrad Kleine." Pooh, that's just awful,' she spluttered.

'I know. It smells like stale knickers. What about this?' Jenny handed her another bottle, green this time.

Helene dabbed her wrist with the glass stopper. '"Eden. For a man and for a woman." Oh, yes,' she said, savouring the aroma, 'that's more like it. I'd wear that one.'

'So would I,' said Jenny, liberally dousing her handkerchief with the stuff.

'Jenny!' Helene hissed.

'What?' she replied and returned the half-empty bottle to its display case. 'All property is theft.'

The women did some further sampling in Merlin's Tobacco Shop and Callaghan & Co. Stationers before rounding things off with a visit to Bury Bros & Rudd. Jenny outdid herself in managing to convince the wine merchant to let her and her lady-in-waiting sample three clarets, a port, currant and two gins for a reception at Buckingham Palace.

'I'll send my footman to place the order tomorrow,' Jenny announced, wisely refraining from handing over her visiting card.

'Very good, ma'am,' said the merchant, opening the door for the Royal Party and bowing all the way to his knees.

'What do you think that man's doing, Helene?' said the Baroness who, before her inebriated lady-in-waiting could respond, was already wandering off to investigate.

The man in the red military tunic had been lingering in the alcove all morning and averted his gaze when Jenny approached. The alcove was situated between a tailor's and a hairdresser's. His immaculate grooming clearly demanded neither. From his reflection in the window Jenny glimpsed his face. She stood as if browsing until such time as her conceit, like his, had run its natural course.

'I say,' she ventured.

The man started.

'I was…' Momentarily she lost her English. 'I… Forgive me, but your… flowers.' Jenny pointed to the bunch of red carnations he was holding behind his back.

'These?' he replied as if they had been thrust upon him in error.

'Why, yes,' said Jenny. 'Carnations, if I'm not mistaken.'

'Why, yes,' repeated the man, whose face began to turn the same colour as the flowers.

Jenny was eager to keep up the exchange, but anything more she felt would have exceeded the bounds of the English manners.

'How rare it is to find nice flowers here,' she offered, unsure whether she was making sense.

'I purchased them at Covent Garden,' he stated curtly, regaining his composure.

'Oh?'

'But I have no knowledge of where they come from,' he

conceded. 'Flowers are just flowers.'

It was an amusing formula. 'Covent Garden,' said Jenny, realizing her stupidity. 'Of course. It is near to my hotel.'

Silence reigned. But the strangers lingered at close quarters and in spite of the English manners.

'I take it you are a visitor here, madam,' the man enquired.

Jenny hesitated. 'My family and I are passing through.'

'I see,' said he, intrigued. 'Do I detect a German accent? I'm sure I recognized one just now.'

'Indeed you do,' she affirmed.

The man became animated all of a sudden. 'Ah! And may I ask from where? Forgive me, but had it not been for the flowers—'

'You may,' Jenny interrupted, inclined to answer as many questions as she could. 'From Westphalia, in the western part of Germany. In Westphalia, too, flowers are just flowers.'

The man smiled and his handsome moustache bristled.

'I completed part of my officer training in Westphalia,' said he. 'The people are most pleasant there. In Hanover.'

Hanover wasn't in Westphalia.

'How ironic,' said Jenny. 'Is that the word I'm looking for? Pardon me, I have so few occasions to speak English.'

'Oh, but you speak it perfectly well!' gushed the man, whose flowers and his business with them were ancient history. '*Ich kann nur ein bisschen Deutsch,*' he said.

'What a beautiful mouth you have,' Jenny very nearly exclaimed, but instead settled for: 'I see you know German, too.'

'*Ja, aber nicht viel.*'

'*Es ist immer schön, beim Reisen Leute kennenzulernen, die deine Sprache sprechen,*'[29] she replied, warming to the theme, but the man had already exhausted his German vocabulary.

'*Ja,*' he nodded enthusiastically, without understanding a word.

'How endearing you are,' Jenny thought to herself.

'Are you an English teacher?' he asked.

Jenny looked at him through clenched teeth. 'No! I am a baroness.'

The man's eyes widened and his face reverted to the floral shade.

'Forgive me, Baroness,' he said gravely. 'I… Really, you must think me quite impertinent. I did not mean to pry.' He clasped the flowers behind his back and bowed.

'My good sir,' said Jenny, stifling a giggle, 'I see no need to apologize. Please, think nothing of it. Why, I myself am often mistaken for persons I am not. It's… part of life.'

'I see,' said the man, suddenly distracted by Helene and the others; the girls were reengaging in the class war games under Jennychen's dictatorial leadership. 'Well, Baroness,' he went on, clawing to get away, 'I hope you and the Baron enjoy the rest of your stay in England. There are so many interesting sights to see in this great country of ours.'

'I beg your pardon?' said Jenny, quite confused. 'The Baron?'

'Yes. I assume he must have accompanied you here on your journey from Westphalia.'

'Oh!' said Jenny, at last realizing. 'I see what you mean. No, no, no. The Baron is dead.'

Chapter 16

Marx woke up the next morning but couldn't be sure which day it was. For the first few moments he lay in bed trying to think up a formula that might help. Proving what day it was was like trying to prove that $1 + 1 = 2$. The obviousness of the task only confirmed how misguided one was to believe that such obviousness could properly account for anything real.

Mercifully, he was alone. The room resembled the way he felt. It was carnage. At least the clothes that carpeted the floor saved on shelf space. He searched for a pair of clean trousers. By "clean" he meant a pair whose smell wouldn't attract unwanted creatures, waifs and stray dogs, &c. He retrieved some appropriate garments but a foul lingering smell of rotten meat, sulphur and burnt coffee permeated everything in the room, including the bed. It was even in the walls.

His headache soon passed but the worn-off anaesthetic of the grog exposed the carbuncular pain anew. It felt different this morning, a series of pulses and stabs. The pulses came with clockwork precision. Perhaps there was no *pain* as such. But the stabs were impossible to ignore. They only happened when he moved. He could rest prone indefinitely, or at least until Helene arrived. There came a time in every man's life when he had to climb a mountain. In his case, however, the task would need to be delegated to porters, who would transport him to the summit in his bath chair. It was all about gaining a foothold on the southern face and upwind of the problem volcano.

He reached for his soothing balm and thought about drinking it. "Gone window-shopping," read the note attached to the bottle. "Please fix Edgar's train." The child was in the corner sobbing over his locomotive.

The problem wasn't difficult to solve; it was simply a screw holding a bracket in place that needed tightening. Marx gave the toy back to his son, whose face beamed then dropped.

'What is it?' asked Marx. He surveyed the bomb site. 'Ah. Quite. Debris on the track.'

After a couple of swigs of Jenny's private gin stash—the last dregs of which were impossible to dilute any further—Marx felt well enough to walk his son round the block. Walking was what the body needed, even if it meant running the gauntlet of whatever nasty surprises were out there. He lingered in the upstairs corridor, then ventured out onto the landing. The hound wasn't visible; the landlord must have been out exercising the beast. Seizing the moment and his son by the hand, Marx descended the stairs, only to be swooped on at the entrance.

'Monsieur Ramboz!'

'Mmm?'

'Good morning to you!' The salutation seemed friendlier than usual. 'Monsieur Ramboz,' repeated the landlord, 'you have until tomorrow at midday. This is unacceptable. I'm trying to run a respectable hotel, not a poorhouse.'

There was something strangely affable about the ultimatum. Maybe Marx had heard it all wrong. Maybe what the landlord had really said was: 'Monsieur Ramboz, I fear I've grossly misjudged you. In consideration of my insensitivity and my heinous dog, I hereby write off your bill. Do stay on as long as you can stand us, deplorable petit bourgeois philistines that we are.'

He needed oxygen and in spite of there being so little in the street he went out anyway. The man from the cigar shop on the corner was sweeping up the broken glass from Marx's drunken escapade.

'They woke me up with the din last night,' said the merchant, who must have mistaken Marx for someone who cared less.

'Pardon me?' replied the unrepentant vandal.

'Drunks!' said the man, raising his voice with the broom. 'And they have the *nerve* to call themselves a *working* class? Ha! The idle good-for-nothings wouldn't know work if it landed on a plate in front of them. Lumpen! That's what they are. Lumpen to the core.'

Marx cleared his throat and bid the good citizen good day. He decided on a more meandering excursion. Conceivably, an idea might come to him of how he was going to come up with the 30-odd pounds for the rent by tomorrow lunchtime. He might also be hit by a falling piano or crushed by Nelson's Column. That would solve it—for him, at least.

'Edgar! Slow down, lad!' he shouted, but the boy had already taken off toward Regent Street.

It was the last place on earth Marx wanted to be. The bustle made him sick. He hated crowds, especially when they were spending money. He caught up with his son and steered him across the Piccadilly drainworks, where there was no sign of progress let alone completion. He covered his nose and put the locomotive under his arm, since if the toy fell in there would be no chance of retrieving it. He thought up a mantra: "The wealth of those societies in which the capitalist mode of production prevails presents itself as an immense accumulation of commodities, its unit being a single commodity. One must therefore begin the investigation with the analysis of a commodity."[30] It sounded rather good and once safely across the sewer he paused to jot it down.

His critical reflections never usually took him this far west. The West End wasn't his writing scene. But it was a cleaner and less hazardous laboratory than the Upper Lambeth Marsh. It was the other end of the food chain. Nothing was actually being produced in this bourgeois retail park; the goods were all on sale. But the commodity was the core of the capitalist logic. He took a stab at the next line: "A commodity is, in the first place, an object outside us, a thing that by its properties satisfies human wants of some sort or another. The nature of such wants, whether, for instance, they spring from the stomach or from fancy, makes no difference."[31]

That seemed the decisive point. The capitalist society wasn't a struggle for existence and it wasn't to do with natural evolution. How could it be "natural" that some of the weakest physical specimens came to monopolise entire swathes of the commonwealth? Houses, medicine, transport... The struggle was over something far and away more "human", more prestigious. It was a struggle over the management and control of human desires, and the cultivation of one such variety—bourgeois desire—at the expense of another: proletarian desire. The former desire was a commodity. As for the latter, Marx didn't rightly know what to call that.

Halfway along Regent Street, on the curve of the Quadrant, a garrulous gathering blocked the pavement. Marx craned his head, but not being the tallest of men he couldn't make out a thing.

'What do you think, son? Shall we take a closer look?'

He and Edgar squeezed through the crowd until they reached the shop front. The boy gasped at the man in the vitrine. The promotional event for "The Birmingham Dribbler Model Steam Locomotive Kit" was about to start. "Be the proud owner of a real-life working model steam locomotive" and "marvel at the wonders of the steam age from the comfort of your own home", along with other big top exhortations were painted on placards. Mobile cutouts danced from the ceiling on wires.

Edgar was enchanted. The steam engine was stout and top-heavy; it wasn't a scale replica. However, its carriages were more true to life and had passengers inside. "Respectable" ones, it went without saying, and families too, except for a man seated alone in the final compartment of the rear carriage. He must have been the rebel on board, the villainous proletarian come to wreak havoc and recruit the other passengers in a takeover of the train. The man in the vitrine—who betrayed no proletarian sympathies whatever in his spotless striped apron—tinkered with the pressure gauge and the other brass knobs, and in a puff of smoke the Dribbler was off, true to its name, dribbling a trail of water as it circled the track. *Tröpfeln.*

Edgar beamed and his father found himself quickly entering into the spirit of the thing, willing on the train, which moved like a mouse, and cheering every time it made a circuit of the track.

'One!' Marx began to count.

He and his son really should spend more time together, he thought.

'Two!'

The train brought the Idea home. Granted, the locomotives were all owned by the rail networks.

'Three!'

But once the networks expanded to the point where men were no longer the mere vehicles and instruments of labour, the division of labour would break down; and so too the division between men and machines. At that point the private monopoly of the railways would finally be broken.

'Four!'

The dread conveyor was an intermediary stage on the evolutionary ladder, a mere paraphyletic offshoot of the revolutionary tree that was destined to end up in the British Museum. File under "extinct species".

'Five!'

The Dribbler accelerated. The cylinders turned so fast that they seemed to be going backward and the wheels immobile while travelling forward at the speed of light.

'Look, Edgar!' said Marx in childlike wonder, but the child had gone and when he gazed into the vitrine the train wasn't there either.

It took some moments for it to dawn on him, and more bizarrely still when it did, that *he* was travelling on the Dribbler now, inside one of the compartments. And that Edgar, in the company of his own good self, was standing in the crowd of cheering spectators. An alienating spectacle, there was no other word for it. Desperately he waved at himself as the train came round for what must have been the eighth or ninth time.

'Hey!' he yelled, 'get me off this thing!' but his own good self didn't hear his petrified squeaks, even if the other half of him were making them. Then, on rounding the bend once more, the scenery altered—which relieved him, since he didn't wish to be reminded how gormless he looked—and assumed the appearance of a generic landscape. Some vaguely reminiscent features of the Rhineland popped up; its pastureland and smooth-shouldered hills, deep lakes and rivers. The vista lacked focus; although the speed of the train might have accounted for that. He was travelling ever so fast.

He sat there for an indefinite time, minded not to budge from his compartment, instead mulling over the dark shape drawing near on the horizon. The train rounded the bend and this time he glimpsed momentarily the black wrought-iron bridge crouching over a gorge, as if in anticipation of its prey. Its middle span was missing and the end of the track dangled like a loose cotton thread.

The bridge was a mile away now and in a gathering panic Marx fumbled for an emergency brake. He found a pulley and read aghast the label attached to the handle. "There is no emergency brake on the revolutionary train." Clearly it was a design fault. No doubt they were working on it. Once the network expanded such technical problems would be ironed out. He made his way to the rear compartment, where he expected to find the proletarian busily working up a plan.

'I say!' said Marx, bursting in on the lone flat cap, 'we're reaching the end of the line! Quick!'

To his astonishment the man simply shrugged his shoulders, offering nothing more in return than, 'I'm on my lunch break, boss.'

Marx stared blankly, first at the idle creature, then out of the window at the prospect of doom. There was no time for a backup plan. As the train rattled onto the iron bridge, a familiar tune could be heard. Measuredly he took in his last breath, which at least smelt clean for a change. Progress comes in stages, he thought, settling back and holding on for dear life, a strange witness to fate as the train plunged head first into the void. It kept on falling for some time.

Chapter 17

'Karl? Can you hear me? Karl?'

The eyes opened. 'What happened?'

Jenny placed her palm on his forehead. 'The doctor says it's an infection. You've been running a temperature. You really were quite delirious.'

'Edgar!'

'Edgar's fine—'

'No! I left him at the toyshop! I must go back!'

Jenny leaned across to restrain her husband, pressing down on him with the full weight of her ribcage. She felt unusually strong. Either that or he was weak. He twitched frantically but barely moved.

'Calm down, calm down. Edgar's fine. He's next door with Helene and the girls.'

'I don't remember anything,' croaked the bedraggled patient. 'I must be losing my mind. What happened?'

'Here,' said Jenny, pouring a liquid onto a spoon, 'drink this. It's from Bauer.' She helped him incline his head.

Marx made a face as he gulped down the mixture. 'I feel terrible,' he said, collapsing back on the pillow.

Jenny touched his forehead again, this time to inspect something.

'I don't think you're losing your mind, Karl. But your body is...'

'What?'

She went to grasp the thing between thumb and forefinger, which was the size of a farthing, but quickly thought better of it.

'It's another of the furuncles. Bauer recommends leeches.'

'Oh, no,' he rasped.

'Yes, I'm afraid so.' She went to the stove to pour a cup of tea. 'You've really been in the wars this time. Mind you, we never seem to be out of them, do we?'

Marx could detect perfume; she was wearing a new fragrance.

'They found you on the stairs,' she said, handing him the cup. 'Two days ago.'

'Two days? But I owe rent! They threatened me with eviction—'

Jenny pressed down on him again but the patient didn't struggle this time, the gesture being enough to render him docile.

'Calm down, calm down. Don't worry. It's all been settled... I managed to get us a stay of execution.'

'A stay of execution?' Marx regarded his wife suspiciously. 'How so?'

'I have my ways,' she said, managing to reassure and disconcert in the same breath. 'Don't worry,' she repeated, scratching his beard. 'Just rest. We don't want any more accidents.'

The patient gathered his thoughts. 'I can't rest until I finish the book,' he sighed. 'You know that perfectly well.'

'Yes. The book... I was reading your *Communist Manifesto*. Interesting...' Jenny turned to the bookmarked page of the moth-eared pamphlet. 'Blah blah blah: "Our bourgeois, not content with having wives and daughters of their proletarians at their disposal, not to speak of common prostitutes, take the greatest pleasure in seducing each other's wives—"'[32]

'That's Engels,' Marx cut in.

She went on reading, not remotely finished. 'And... where was I? Here we are: "Bourgeois marriage is, in reality, a system of wives in common and thus, at the most, what the Communists might possibly be reproached with is that they desire to introduce, in substitution for a hypocritically concealed, an openly legalised community of women. For the rest, it is self-evident that the abolition of the present system of production must bring with it the abolition of the community of women springing from that system, *i.e.*, of prostitution both public and private."'[33] Jenny raised a quizzical eyebrow.

'Engels again,' said Marx.

Jenny fidgeted. She leafed through the pages. '"Modern bourgeois society, with its relations of production, of exchange and of property, a society that has conjured up such gigantic means of production and of exchange, is like the sorcerer who is no longer able to control the powers of the nether world whom he has called up by his spells."[34] Engels again?'

'No, no,' said Marx, 'that one's mine.'

'Really, Karl!' exclaimed his wife, shaking her head. The pamphlet was difficult to put down. 'What about this? "What the bourgeoisie therefore produces, above all, are its own grave-diggers. Its fall and the victory of the proletariat are equally inevitable."'[35]

'Me again,' confirmed the author.

Jenny trembled with laughter. 'Where on earth did you get such a warped imagination?' she asked, quickly composing herself.

'How long have you been living in London?'

'Nine months, 12 days, five and a half hours and counting.'

'So, open your eyes once in a while,' said Marx, somewhat confused by the instantaneity of his wife's calculation. 'You might notice some of things I'm writing about.'

'Well!' she declared ironically, 'I won't expect to see *that* many sorcerers on Bond Street.'

'Not literally, no,' said Marx. 'It's rhetorical; stylistic. It's designed to grab people's attention.'

Jenny replaced the book gently on her husband's desk, taking care not to disturb the papier-mâché creature that lived there.

'Oh, I don't know, Karl,' she said, sounding wistful and subdued. 'You and your ghost stories. Sometimes I wonder whether your father—'

'Don't mention that man's name!' he snapped.

She fell silent and averted her gaze, then stood up slowly to inspect the man beneath the white shroud.

'It's all a bit... sad. Is this how you see the world? Is this how you see us?' she asked.

'Don't be ridiculous. Of course not. Why d'you think I'm trying to change it? Why d'you think I'm writing this damned book?'

'But *where* is it all leading?' Jenny insisted, suddenly roused to hysterics.

'Free association. The society without classes. That's where. It's all in the pamphlet. Granted it's submerged and lacking in theoretical detail, but—'

'Did you ever stop to consider that your writing might be making you ill, Karl?'

'Nonsense. It's a physical ailment. A few hours of sleep and I'll be fit and working again. As long as my mind holds out.'

'Correct me if I'm wrong, Karl,' said Jenny, adjusting her hemline, 'but you can't publish a book in your *mind*—wherever that is. That really would be an achievement.'

Barely had he reflected on the idea when there came a knock at the door.

'Get some rest,' she added, rubbing the back of her neck with her handkerchief, 'and no more ghostwriting.' She pointed an accusatory finger. 'I trust we understand each other.'

'Wait a moment!' protested the man beneath the shroud. 'Come back! Where are you going at this hour?'

'Don't wait up,' she whispered, blowing him a kiss and darting out of the door.

Chapter 18

There were 28 sartorial combinations in Jenny's wardrobe. A year ago there had been considerably more than 500. Her debutante's wardrobe had contained at least five times that number counting accessories. It was an appalling regression. Then again, with maturity came the power of discrimination, and nowhere more so than in relation to what a woman wore. She might have had less now than in the past, but Jenny drew consolation from the fact that she had outgrown most of her previous clothes.

Jenny wore her emerald green long-sleeved, floor-length bow ball gown. It was her theatre dress and her *pièce de résistance*. The fabric was Florentine hand-embroidered broadcloth, very finely twilled, with inverted silk pleats at the front. It was made from such fine fabric that the entire dress might have been silk. The dark green embroidery was uniformly finished in ornate damask brocade (handwoven, not jacquard; and notwithstanding her husband's point that the jacquard looms could match the master weavers for fine embroidery). The emerald green crystal choker that Sophie once said made her look like a Spanish harlot she no longer possessed (pawned in Paris). Ditto the green rhinestone earrings (robbed in Brussels by a confidence trickster on the steps of La Monnaie) and most of her costume jewellery (including the hideous tourmaline broaches) that disappeared during a house party gatecrashed by anarchists on the Rue de Lille. Nor, indeed, any of the Persian gold necklaces belonging to the Baron's first wife Elisabeth von Veltheim, which supposedly dated back to the Zand dynasty, or even further back to the reign of Shah Mahmud Hotaki (probably stolen on Jenny's chaotic train ride from Paris to Calais). Instead, she wore the pair of white topaz stud earrings (a twenty-first birthday present from Marx's Uncle Lion), and the pearl and silver necklace she had hidden some weeks ago about her person (in an intimate place that she felt all the more exhilarated for having discovered). As for shawls, gloves and overcoats, most of them had been pawned. However, the navy velvet ruffled cape from the Rue de Rivoli she retained, and although it lacked the sophistication of her Venetian cashmere and taffeta shawl (pawned), her black lace mantilla (bartered for a kettle) and even her dyed black mink capelet (stolen), nevertheless when worn slightly off the shoulder it set off her complexion magnificently. The only overcoat befitting of social functions was her plain single-breasted paletot (the large bow was an addition) and she wore it this evening. However, the cleaners had broken off one of the buttons. As for shoes, Jenny had done the unthinkable and resorted to a pair of black suede ankle boots *à lacet* (an equestrian design inspired by a portrait of Spanish conquistadors and made to measure in Rome). Sophie had assured her they were all the rage in Italy (six years ago), but they attracted disapproving stares every time she went out in them.

All things considered, given the extent to which her wardrobe depended on what was missing from it, and inasmuch as clothes maketh the woman, Jenny's public appearance on that extraordinary evening might best be described as a non-appearance of sorts, and thus nothing to be ashamed of, since her ordinary life was safely confined to the realm of appearances.

The cab made its way along Piccadilly and turned right opposite Hatchetts White Horse Cellar as the evening mail coach was starting out for the West Country. Berkeley Street was eerily deserted.

'The pawnbroker wants my dress back by nine o'clock sharp,' said Helene.

Instantly Jenny grasped the door handle.

'I need time to clean it in case it gets soiled!' Helene protested. 'My, we are in a tetchy mood tonight, aren't we? What did you think I meant?'

Jenny frowned. 'I wasn't planning on staying out all night.'

Then, swiftly changing the subject, 'Once we arrive you'll need to call me "your ladyship" when you address me directly and "her ladyship" when you're referring to me in the third person.'

'You what?'

'For the sake of appearances,' said Jenny, powdering her nose. 'Tonight you're going to be my lady-in-waiting. I shouldn't worry. It's just a posh word for "governess".'

'Your lady-in-waiting. My, my… And who does that make *you* when you're at home? Cinderella?'

'No, I don't quite see it somehow… you as my fairy godmother.' Jenny laughed to her heart's content. 'Anyway,' she added, applying a pencil to her lashes, 'you know who I am. I am the Baroness. There's no need to pretend.'

The Royal Party alighted in Berkeley Square and entered the apartment through the lobby. The concierge greeted them as they came in.

'We have an appointment to see Lieutenant White,' announced the Baroness.

'Allow me to escort you, madam,' said the man and he led the way up the wide spiral staircase to the second floor.

As they climbed the stairs Helene picked up the hem of Jenny's gown.

'Helene,' Jenny hissed, 'behave yourself. What are you doing?'

'I'm carrying your train, Your Majesty,' she replied humbly.

'Lieutenant White's residence is the second door on the left,' said the concierge. 'Number 213.' He departed and the women stood in front of the door.

'How should I knock?' Jenny asked.

'I don't know. However you do normally, I suppose.'

'Yes, but…'

'What?'

'What I mean is, how should the *Baroness* knock?'

Helene became exasperated. 'Look,' she said, 'just let your lady-in-waiting take care of the knocking,' and she rapped her knuckles several times on the door.

Jenny blanched. 'Not like that, Helene! Good grief! It makes us sound like... *bailiffs.*'

'Well, that's all just fine and as it should be,' declared Helene. 'Let them hear how the other half lives.'

Footsteps sounded the approach from some distance away and a small age went by until their owner arrived.

'Good evening,' said the man in a dignified and worn-out voice.

'Good evening,' said Jenny. 'I am the Baroness von Westphalen and this is my lady-in-waiting, Fräulein Helene Demuth. We have an appointment to see Lieutenant White. I imagine you must be his... governator.'

The man looked horrified. 'I am his *butler,* ma'am.'

'I see,' said Jenny, also horrified by the look on his face.

The reception was as large as a tennis court. Jenny removed her paletot and handed it to the butler with the proper degree of decorum.

'This way, please, ladies,' said he and retraced his steps through an antechamber lined to the ceiling with bookshelves, then a sitting room, and finally through white-and-gold Rococo doors into a palatial ballroom.

Jenny could sense that a lavish reception had taken place there recently; one could detect the remnants of garrulous exchanges. Needless to say it was hardly a new experience for her to socialize in an upmarket setting. She had attended her fair share of society balls as a debutante in Trier, and thereafter in Paris and Brussels. The invitations had dried up of late. 'Balls aren't what they were,' her husband would lament. Tonight's reception departed significantly from the routine and on entering the room, she felt herself crossing the threshold of some alien world.

Lieutenant White stood with his back to the guests as they came in, with one hand on the marble mantelpiece, staring intensely into the fire. Jenny thought he must have been practising the pose all day, but from the look of him hadn't quite mastered it. The posing also made him seem exceptionally young and Jenny exceptionally old, she thought, by comparison.

'The Baroness von Westphalen and Miss Helene Demuth, sir,' announced the butler.

'Welcome, Baroness,' said White, spinning round and greeting the Royal Party with a smile, 'and Fräulein Demuth. How do you do? May I introduce Lieutenant Reed? He and I serve in the same regiment together. Lieutenant Reed also completed his officer training in Hanover.'

The second lieutenant seized Jenny's hand and bowed. Both men wore black morning coats and bow ties. She was disappointed not to see her soldiers in red (she had fantasized about the lieutenant wearing a red mess kit jacket and navy lapels with gold mounted buttons, and a ribbed piqué cotton shirt with starched cuffs and a silk bow tie). White was gracious and attentive to a fault and danced round the room like a solicitor's clerk. How seductive this gentle hallucination appeared, whose movements were so deft and refined they were almost feminine.

'It's a great honour to meet you, Baroness,' said Reed who, unlike her dancing flame, was a different prospect altogether.

His name defined him well and his face, though perfectly pleasant to behold, seemed tormented somehow, as if in profound disagreement with its head. He spoke with a slight lisp. On reflection there really was no comparison between the two men. Reed was instantly forgettable. His English irony and euphemisms confounded his every word. It almost made Jenny suspect that her gallant host's intention had been to invite the other along for the sole purpose of enhancing his own admirable qualities.

'And I am most delighted to meet you, Lieutenant,' said Jenny, retrieving her hand. 'I see you play chess, gentlemen,' she added, distracted by the board as big as a double bed.

'Do you play, Baroness?' asked White.

'On occasions, yes. The Baron was a very good player. He taught me all the moves.'

'He sounds a most remarkable man.'

'He was, indeed,' said Jenny, most amused by the English conversational style.

The butler came in with a tray of drinks and on serving Helene tripped, spilling the glass of port down the front of her dress.

'Oh, really! Hoskins,' exclaimed White. 'You are a clumsy clot.'

The butler reacted awkwardly at first by hovering over Helene's bosom. Then, on realizing his indiscretion, he withdrew by walking backward and bowing. On reaching the threshold, he tripped and smashed into a glass-topped display case containing medals.

'I am so desperately sorry, Fräulein Demuth,' said the lieutenant, who couldn't apologize enough and began cursing the butler, labelling him an "awful butterfingers", which made everyone, including Helene, laugh. 'I would ask Violet to help clean your gown, but I'm afraid she's gone home early this evening.' White handed Helene a serviette.

'Early?' said Reed. 'Why, it's barely eight o'clock.'

Hoskins had been the family's butler for "donkey's years" and could be forgiven for such misdemeanours, since he was "over the hill" and "long in the tooth", and mercifully he rarely made "hideous gaffes". But White agreed that house servants weren't what they were "in the old days", which sounded ridiculous, since White was but a mere child himself.

'A house needs servants,' insisted Reed. 'Not this bloody work-shy lot one has to draw from nowadays. Hoskins is all right; he'll be out to pasture in a few years. But who's going to replace him? Why, these new servants one gets don't simply ask for a decent job, they expect all manner of perks and privileges thrown in.'

'What sort of privileges might you be referring to, Lieutenant?' enquired Jenny from the other end of the ballroom. She had to raise her voice in order to attract his attention.

'Privileges?' Reed called back as if his interlocutor had taken leave of her senses. 'Why, money, of course!'

His opinions were compelling in the sense that they saved Jenny the trouble of having to pretend to take him seriously.

'How are the staff in your parts, Baroness?' he persisted. 'Are the servants there as troublesome as the English ones?'

Jenny didn't understand the question, which sounded positively vulgar.

'Do you have many staff in your household, Baroness?' Unlike the other, Lieutenant White was perfectly intelligible.

'We have... some,' decided Jenny. 'But ours really isn't a very large household. Helene's been with us for... why, it must be six years. She does everything for us. She's one of the family.'

The latter sentiment jarred with Reed, who couldn't disguise the fact that in his view servants were becoming too "uppity"; although he admitted he was generalizing and that Fräulein Demuth was no doubt an exception to the rule.

The butler returned with trays of drinks and canapés.

'Thank you, Hoskins,' said White, receiving his offerings. 'May I ask how long you intend to stay in our country?' he enquired.

Jenny declined a second glass of port. 'I am not sure. It depends on... circumstances. You must be aware of the problems presently afflicting my homeland.'

'Indeed!' said Reed. 'These damned revolutionaries! Paris, Berlin, Vienna, Rome... Where's it going to end? They should be rounded up and hanged; all of them, in one fell swoop. No mercy, no trial, just hanged! Bonaparte? He's got the right idea. Strike now when the iron's hot! If you don't crack down on the anarchists right away then you're only storing up trouble. Any government that ignores the revolutionary threat places the public in mortal danger.'

'One can only hope that things are less dangerous in this country,' Jenny opined.

'I am afraid not, Baroness,' said Reed, gravely shaking his head. 'In fact, I would wager that there are men in this very town, located no more than a mile from this room, who are plotting revolution as we speak.'

'Yes,' said Jenny distractedly, 'that is a worry.'

'I'm not sure I wholly agree with Lieutenant Reed,' said White in a diplomatic effort. 'Napoleon's nephew has attracted a great deal of criticism from all quarters. It's said that he acts far too rashly. Moreover, he's a Bonaparte.'

'Who says he acts rashly?' demanded an incredulous Reed.

'I do, of course,' said White with a wry smile.

Jenny was intrigued. 'But tell me, gentlemen: could the danger from the revolutionists not be addressed by different means?'

'Such as?' shot back Reed.

'Apart from suppressing them, I mean? Forgive me; I fear I may be expressing my opinions too freely. They may be unfashionable among the English. They may sound... improper.'

'Please, go on, Baroness,' insisted White, 'this is not France. We English have the freedom to express ourselves as we wish in our own country.'

'Very well,' said Jenny, now unsure whether she should feel more entitled to express herself freely or less. 'What I meant to say, gentlemen, was that surely the danger from revolutionists wielding rifles and grenades poses a threat to everyone, including themselves, and quite irrespective of whether one supports them or not.'

White's expression completely changed, his name now defining him as precisely as Reed's. 'I'm afraid I don't follow you,' he said in a low voice.

'What I mean, Lieutenant, is that the revolutionists are dedicated to changing the world for the better—'

'Well! Damn them for it!' interrupted Reed.

'—and, inasmuch as they are able to achieve it—without interfering with the rights of the other classes, naturally—why not let them try?' Jenny felt giddy and inclined to be sick.

'Because, Baroness,' replied Reed, raising her from her mild delirium, 'one cannot trust a conspirator.'

White laughed. 'I'm afraid you're not going to convert our friend here to the German way of thinking, Baroness. Lieutenant Reed is a British officer through and through, with the accent on "British".'

'I'm sure you're right, Lieutenant. Our cultures must be quite different. In my native Germany, for instance, the revolutionary Communists fight with the bourgeoisie whenever it acts in a revolutionary way, against the absolute monarchy, the feudal squirearchy and the petty bourgeoisie. But they never cease, for a single instant, to instil into the working class the clearest possible recognition of the hostile antagonism between bourgeoisie and proletariat, in order that the German workers may straightway use, as so many weapons against the bourgeoisie, the social and political conditions that the bourgeoisie must necessarily introduce along with its supremacy, and in order that, after the fall of the reactionary classes in Germany, the fight against the bourgeoisie itself may immediately begin. Germany is only beginning to experience a bourgeois revolution that is but the prelude to a great proletarian revolution of world historic proportions.'[36]

One could have heard a pin drop in the room. The tranquillity that overcame the men, this odd and unlikely couple, was total and presumably unprecedented in their short lifetimes. Moreover, the ballroom itself had never heard the like of Jenny's speech and if it had been a person, one rather suspected it would have gathered up its petticoats and run to the hills. Jenny was no more certain of her words now than when they were tumbling from her mouth; neither in their immediate meaning, nor implications, let alone whether or not she agreed with a single one. But they felt necessary, as if it all needed saying somehow, and not least since the English have the freedom to express themselves as they wish in their own country.

The conversation petered out. White took the Baroness's outstretched hand in both of his, thus departing from the royal protocol. Reed bowed from a distance. Perhaps he was a gentleman, after all (if he were then she knew not what to make of White).

'What time did you tell your driver to collect you?' enquired the host.

'9.30,' said Jenny, inventing a number.

'It's only 9.15,' he replied, to the quarter chimes of the clock on the mantelpiece. 'Hoskins will wait with you downstairs. Make sure you take a lantern with you, Hoskins. That lamp has gone again across the street. I noticed it yesterday evening.'

Once downstairs Jenny informed Hoskins that her driver had been given the wrong address and that the Royal Party would need to intercept him on the corner of New Bond Street. Hoskins dangled his lantern in front of Jenny's face as if inspecting the occupant of a coffin.

'Thank you for your attendance, Hoskins,' said Jenny, 'but one simply cannot find the staff these days.'

They were the right words uttered in the wrong context, she thought, and on exiting the apartment she made a note to herself to try to get out more in future. Helene was livid. On reaching the corner where their phantom carriage was pulled up she went on ahead in the direction of Regent Street, cursing and complaining bitterly that she would never be able to clean the dress by nine o'clock the next morning. Jenny took her word for it, reflecting on what it must be like to live in a world free of servants.

Chapter 19

When the human flow drained away, Leicester Square would revert to the denuded tidal zone of the Thames Basin. What then were exposed were the root systems of the city, the prehistoric inclusions that like the Macellum of Pozzuoli provided the clues to a past that can never escape the present.

Marx woke up on the stroke of three. What had the quiet restlessness of his imagination washed up? Nothing. The foreshore of his ideas was a bone-dry desert. It was pitch-black. The street lamp on Leicester Street had gone out, which meant he would need fuel if he wished to work. He fumbled for the lamp. One liked to think that certain objects defied exchange value. Light-giving objects; or light itself. Perhaps human beings were destined to end up in the dark. They already were. *Well grubbed, old mole.* His eyesight was no worse than a mole's, but probably not considerably better in this light.

The objects he managed to dig up from under his desk were an education in themselves and fascinating in combination: the remains of a fish supper wrapped in an old newspaper that probably could have been marketed as hair dye (note to self); a broken fishing rod; a mouse trap (primed minus the cheese); the Book of Common Prayer; a packet of tarot cards; a botched attempt (his?) to forge a 10-pound note; a botched attempt (his?) to forge a 20-pound note; a botched attempt (his?) to forge a 50-pound note; plans for a home-made printing press; the visiting card of a "Madame Jo-Jo, Masseuse, &c."; several copies of a generic begging letter; a patent application "for the commercial manufacture of a clockwork apparatus for the promenading of dogs" —

Marx stopped grubbing. Something sounded behind the silence. It was the singing. Not inside the hotel this time, but on the street. Someone was singing out there in the dark. To themselves? To him? To anyone at all?

He opened the window—it was difficult to see clearly—but there by the street lamp stood the mysterious figure from the alleyway. A shaft of light slanted across his face, which he kept concealed beneath a wide-brimmed hat. The rest of his frame was draped in a long dark overcoat with the collar turned up.

Marx opened the window and shouted down, 'I say! Can I help?'

But calmly the figure walked off and disappeared into the night.

Chapter 20

'This is not a product of my imagination!' yelled Marx.

The pub traffic froze, as the ball would have done in mid-air had the laws of physics been otherwise, before felling the skittles in the corner.

'This is not a product of my imagination,' Marx repeated, toning down the volume. 'Someone is spying on me; he was outside the hotel.'

Engels recalled the time during an absinthe-fuelled brainstorming in a Marais tavern when Marx had accused the landlord of being a hobgoblin. 'You saw him, did you?'

'Yes!' Marx insisted, loosening his collar. 'Not clearly. From a distance.'

'But he was there?'

'Of course he was *there*. Where else would he be?' Marx quenched his thirst before realizing it was Engels's tankard he was drinking from.

'How far away was he? Approximately?'

'You think I'm mad,' said Marx, wiping his neck with a pink floral handkerchief.

'No,' replied Engels. 'I think you're exhausted; you've been burning the midnight oil. Is that perfume you're wearing?'

'It must be Jenny's,' he surmised, inserting the handkerchief down the front of his inexpressibles. 'And?'

'No reason.'

Although he was the junior partner and still in his twenties by the skin of his teeth, as far as revolutionary intrigues were concerned, Engels had seen and heard it all. There wasn't much one could surprise him with. But his equanimity didn't extend to believing everything he heard. On the contrary. Like Marx, he was a stickler for proof.

'How far away was he?'

'Opposite the hotel,' said Marx, distracted by the party at the next table.

'50 metres?'

'Mmm?'

'How far?'

Marx sighed. 'Should I draw you a diagram? What difference does how far make?'

'In London, it's said one is never more than 10 metres away from a rat. It's London. Spies are like rats. They're everywhere. Who knows? They're probably following me. Who cares?' Engels had the sharp and unflustered reasoning of a legal counsel.

'I care!' Marx adjusted the volume again. 'I care,' he hissed, leaning in to his brief. 'I detest rats.'

Engels signalled to the barmaid for more beers.

'Have you spoken to Jenny about it?'

'No,' Marx exclaimed, faintly amused by the idea. 'She'd probably accuse me of being paranoid. That's what she usually does.'

Promptly the beers arrived.

'Did you see them pour that?' Marx fussed. 'No, really, I'm being serious.'

'Surely not,' said Engels, his poker face deserting him.

'No, no. I mean it. That last one tasted… funny.'

'Well, if that was the intention then it's succeeded,' said a deadpan Engels. 'How's the writing coming on?'

Marx shook his head. 'I haven't been able to concentrate.'

'You don't say?'

'There's too much going on. Not just this' —Marx brought the tankard up to his nose and studied the aroma, then took a sip— 'crap. I keep having these dreams.'

Engels lit a cigar and filled his lungs with smoke. 'About what?'

'The past,' Marx reflected.

'Sounds reasonable. Nightmares?'

'Not really. I can't get rid of the moving sensation. I'm on this locomotive. But it travels so fast I can never make out what's going on outside. I'm sure it's perfectly lucid when I'm asleep. But once I'm awake all the images are gone and all that's left are… clouds of mental dust. I can't very well say what it's about. Damned infuriating.'

Marx waved the thought away and gulped down some ale, then removed a wad of parchment from his pocket. He looked confused at first and scratched his beard, before realizing he was holding the thing upside down.

'I can't work any of this out,' he admitted, indicating a sheet of mathematical graffiti.

'The differential calculus,' nodded Engels, albeit merely on account of the fact that Marx never stopped talking about it. Engels had excelled at history and literature at the Elberfeld Gymnasium. But when it came to mathematics he was a complete novice.

'Partial derivatives, derived functions… Look!' Marx began anew on a blank sheet, drawing a diagonal line. Then he sketched a picture of a train with smoke coming out the funnel. The train was climbing the hill. 'Now,' he said, clicking his fingers, 'imagine you're on the slope here at point P.' He drew a dot P on the high point of the slope and another on the low end Q. 'So! What's the formula for the gradient PQ?'

Engels recalled the formula from memory. 'Delta y divided by delta x.'

'Simple.' Marx wrote down the formula: $\Delta y / \Delta x$. 'And what about when the slope's a curve?' He duly added the curve to the diagram so that it just grazed the diagonal.

Engels quickly gave up. 'Algebra's not my forte, Moor—'

'Here,' said Marx, becoming impatient, 'let's abbreviate the thing,' and he added some vertical and horizontal bisections before reverting to his customary scrawl:

$$\frac{f(x + \Delta x) - f(x)}{(x + \Delta x) - x}$$

'Now!' he exclaimed, waving his fingers over the page like a magician. 'What happens when the distance between the two points is infinitely small?' He replotted P and Q to within a hair's breadth of each other, on the tangent of the curve, so close that the points might have been identical.

Engels looked confused. 'Nothing, presumably. I don't understand the question.'

'The slope is still there,' revealed Marx. 'It's simply invisible to the naked eye.'

'Clearly,' replied the other, who could easily follow that.

'If P is equal to Q then the function is zero divided by zero—which is nonsensical.' Marx began writing again. 'The thing is that the gradient formula ceases to have a meaning when P coincides with Q. But when P does *not* coincide with Q, the formula is perfectly legible. Which means we must be able to calculate the gradient of the curve. And yet...' Marx banged his fist loudly on the table and startled the occupants at the next, 'this differential formula makes that calculation impossible.'

'I see,' said Engels, despite being unsure that he did so with perfect precision. Nonetheless, Marx seized Engels's cigar and reclined, blowing a ring of smoke in awe of his negative findings.

'You can see what I mean now,' concluded the rebel mathematician, nodding his head at the floating cipher, which hung there before melting into the fug of the saloon bar. 'It's as if the quantity the formula attempts to describe had vanished and the formula had about as much grasp on reality as... a game of chess. What use are infinitely small quantities if one cannot actually calculate with them? I can hardly visit the butcher and order no mutton chopped into infinitely many portions, can I now?' Marx gave Engels back his cigar, the irony of his statement hardly lost on either man. 'I'm grateful for the money, by the way,' he said, sinking back in his seat.

Engels handed him a bottle of the soothing balm. 'Here. I ran into Dietz. Apparently, it's better than the last batch.'

Marx pulled out the cork stopper and sniffed the contents. 'It couldn't be any worse.'

'Just don't drink it this time.'

Liebknecht ambled over holding a plate up to his chin. 'Comrades,' he said, followed by something unintelligible rendered so by the bacon sandwich he was eating.

'Can't understand a word you're saying,' said Marx.

Liebknecht swallowed hard then tried again. 'You've heard the news, then?'

'What news?'

'Heinzen's called a meeting of the German workers. He says the League's indecisive and the workers don't trust it; they need proper leaders.'

Engels's poker face flushed. 'A putsch! He wants to set up a rival organization.'

'Oh, shit,' murmured Marx, his sentence finally handed down.

'I was wondering why I hadn't seen him recently,' remarked Engels.

'He's changed his drinking habits,' said Liebknecht. 'He goes to the White Bear these days. Schramm saw him in there with a bunch of workingmen last week.'

'I knew it,' Engels enthused. 'I told you he was up to something. Didn't I tell you he was up to something?' He patted Marx on the back. 'Well, well. The hour of truth is at hand. I think it's high time you showed Brother Heinzen who's running the show — don't you?'

Back at the hotel Marx was distracted and couldn't work. Edgar was the younger sibling in a community of women, which made him fair game for devilish plans. His locomotive made an unholy racket, but at least it was *relatively* predictable. Unlike the class war game, which now involved three children running in and out of the room and hurling abuse at each other in three different languages.

Edgar only spoke English, which put him even more at a disadvantage when it came to keeping up with the pan-European dimensions of the game. Most English workingmen were in the same boat. Marx shuffled uncomfortably in his seat and broke wind, loudly and at some length.

'I was thinking of taking the girls to the coast at the weekend,' said Jenny, contemplating her next move. 'You don't mind looking after Guido, do you? You know how sickly they get at this time of year.'

'Is there anything to eat?' Marx demanded. 'I say!'

'Citizen,' announced Jennychen to Edgar, who stood manacled with Marx's cravat. 'You are charged with betraying the revolution. How do you plead?'

'Guilty!' said Laura.

'Silence!' retorted Jennychen. 'Let the citizen speak.'

Bg1.

Helene inverted the hourglass and fetched a bowl of organic matter from the stove. She set it down in front of Marx. The fish head, or that of some other poor creature as yet unclassified, stared at him through the dirty water.

'Is this a joke? I say!'

'A joke?' Helene responded. 'Isn't it just! A man who can't provide for his own family. An almighty fucking joke.'

'What happened to the rest of Engels's money? Jenny?'

e5.

'Money?' replied Jenny, advancing her pawn. 'We spent it.'

Marx rose from his seat, incredulous. 'All of it! On what?'

'Things,' said Jenny.

'Things? What do you mean "things"? Such as?'

'Oh, I don't know, Karl,' she said, exasperated. 'Just things. It doesn't grow on trees, you know.'

'Oh! Does it not?' said Marx, leaning over the board. 'So! *Spend less.*'

He returned to his desk and sat down. He had no intention of eating the head in the bowl, despite being strangely drawn to it.

Qa1.

'Pathetic,' said Helene, turning over the hourglass.

'Excuse me?' said Marx, rising to his feet again. 'Did you speak?'

'You heard,' Helene replied.

'Pathetic? Is that what you called me? Pathetic, am I?'

'Yes,' said Helene, rising defiantly to hers, 'and so you are! Look at yourself! You haven't a penny to your name. All you do is moan and groan: "My manuscript! My ink! My arse!" You carp on at your wife constantly. You treat me like your slave—"do this, Helene! Do that, Helene!" You put the fear of God into your children. You avoid all work, you drink too much, you smell, you scrounge off your friends and you waste your time writing this... economics... *shit* that even you can't understand.'

Marx had already stopped listening, but every word hit its mark.

'Pathetic, am I? I'll show you the meaning of pathetic,' he said, snatching hold of Edgar's locomotive and sending the child into a spasm.

He stormed out of the hotel with what must have been a look of murder on his face, since the landlord backed away from him as he came tearing down the stairs, and out into the street in his dressing gown and slippers. On Whitehall, people cheered as two life-size automata resembling Queen Victoria and the French president Louis-Napoléon Bonaparte rode past in an open carriage. It could have been the real Garibaldi riding a unicycle for all Marx cared, who charged through the crowds in the direction of the pawnbroker's on Pall Mall. Unlike Marx's usual property broker on Drury Lane, whose premises one entered at serious risk to one's reputation, the Pall Mall shop didn't advertise itself as such. Unfortunately, Marx's desire to join the ranks of more upmarket clientele was undermined by the state of his person, which by itself dispelled any illusions as to the quality of his merchandise.

'Take a look in my window, sir,' said the shopkeeper, his eye pressed firmly to his magnifying loupe. 'Most of the items are solid silver, not plated. Fifty per cent of what I'm offered I turn away on account of blemishes. Why should I purchase a block of wood from you?'

'But it's a really rather splendid toy,' protested Marx. 'The wood is... is... Brandenburg oak,' he spluttered, naming the first tree that came into his head.

'It has no resale value, sir.'

'In which case make me a loan.'

'Sir, in order to make you a loan the item must have a minimum wholesale value.'

But this assertion was simply an ideological justification for the classical liberal theory of supply and demand. The idea that the wholesale value of a commodity could be reduced to zero assumed that its "value" was determined in isolation from the average quantity of labour required to produce it.

The shopkeeper removed his panoptic and sighed. 'I can offer you five shillings for the toy,' he said in an almost ceremonial voice, replacing a jewel-encrusted timepiece in its display case.

But Marx couldn't bring himself to part with Edgar's toy and on the way to Drury Lane contented himself with the poetic justice of a proletarian alliance. The toy would be displayed alongside the workingmen's boots and the pickaxe handle in the vitrine on Drury Lane, and the Pall Mall pawnbroker posing as a silversmith could go to Hell. The toy had a history that couldn't be reduced to zero. The four shillings and a thrupenny bit he managed to haggle from the Drury Lane broker was therefore a reasonable price for the loan of Edgar's dream.

'Snowdrops tuppence a bunch!' cried the wandering flower seller on Long Acre.

Notwithstanding, of course, the problem of using differential calculus to explain how the constant tendency of capital (conceived as a variable magnitude) could ever force down the cost of labour to zero.

Marx walked through a mound of festering horse manure on St Martin's Lane. *Scheisse*. Could the differential calculus explain that? Perhaps in some highly abstract form. His slippers were badly soiled and since he hadn't taken a proper bath for weeks, and with money in his pocket, he took a welcome detour via Wang's.

'马克思博士！很高兴再次见到您！' exclaimed the Chinaman with a bow.

'您好, 王先生,' replied Marx, repeating the gesture and wondering why. No matter. One said "comrade" often enough and so might just as well bow.

'最近怎么都没空呢, 再不见我了吗？'

'忙的休息时间都没有啊.'

'马克思博士, 太劳累了. 我也一样啊, 没方法呀 伦敦是劳动者的都市嘛.'[37]

Marx's knowledge of Chinese was so rudimentary that it didn't take long for the conversation to exhaust itself. But Wang kept on regardless. There was a green statue of a dragon in the corner and Marx visualized the words cascading from its tongue. The sound seemed to wash over him. Once in his bath he could have kept on listening to Wang until the sun exploded.

A Chinese girl wearing a red shawl and lotus shoes came in and filled up Marx's tub with hot water. He concealed his orchestra as best as he could. She lit some incense and closed the door behind her, and the steam began to build, misting his eyes and smarting his nostrils with an exhilarating sting that sent a pulse along his spine before entering the catacombs of his anal passage and bursting forth from his chest. From there it simply kept going, pulsating first round the room, then out into the street and radiating in every direction in common cause with Aristotle's five elements.

Chapter 21

Jenny felt quite sure that what she was doing was right. Where this conviction stemmed from, however, was beyond her. Her chess had been more decisive of late, more direct. And she had been winning. Better to trust in the wisdom of whatever strategy she was playing than try to interpret the motives. Having packed her trunk she pondered briefly whether or not she should write her husband a note, concluding it was probably a bad idea, since once she started writing she might get carried away, to the point where au revoir toppled over into adieu. The dividing line wasn't altogether clear. She didn't trust herself to write letters. And why attempt to justify one's pursuit of happiness? The cost in so doing was far too high. Arriving here had taken too much out of her. Was she meant to feel guilty for her self-abnegation? For being victim to a string of public humiliations that read like a poison recipe? Three riots, a soupçon of thefts, a handful of extortions and half a dozen burglaries? She wasn't seeking compensation for lost luggage. She wanted her life back. But how? How to retrieve a history? By changing nothing; by continuing with the game.

'That's where they cut King Charles's head off,' said Jenny cheerily as she and the girls passed the Whitehall Banqueting House.

'Why did they do that, *Maman*?' asked Laura.

'Because there was a war, darling. And the king lost.'

'That's not true!' cried Jennychen. 'The king was a traitor and he had to die.'

'Jenny!' replied the mother, admonishing her eldest daughter's republican blood lust. 'It's easy to call someone a traitor when everyone hates you. If only the king had had some nice friends.'

'Then he might have won the English war!' Laura realized, in awe of her own reasoning.

'Exactly. And if he had won the war who might they have executed instead? Oliver…' Jenny tried to coax out the name.

'O-li-vert…' Laura imitated her mother in a French accent.

The Marx daughters had been raised in the republican tradition. Which meant that History (with a capital letter) prior to 1789 didn't exist for them. Or if it did it always had to pass the test of the French Revolution and the Revolutionary Wars. There was no middle ground and no possible compromise, especially for Jennychen, who saw herself as the custodian of revolutionary virtues, both real and imaginary. What might she make of her mother's decision to spend the weekend with a British army lieutenant? Would she judge her for it? Was a child capable of judging her mother?

On reflection, the girl was probably more like her mother than Jenny imagined, meaning the seeds of independence were already sown. She had suffered fear and deprivation on an unprecedented scale. Future generations would surely marvel at how children ever managed to survive in the past. In Brussels, on one particularly traumatic occasion, the bailiffs had arrived in the middle of Jennychen's pianoforte lesson and carted off the instrument as she was playing. 'Let me finish!' she exhorted, determined to reach the end of Bach's Adagio from BWV 564. After that Jenny would lie awake at night filtering every sound on the Rue d'Orléans. Street altercations didn't trouble her and riots she found strangely comforting. The bailiffs always came minus the banter, the heavy footfall on the stairs raising the tension one floor at a time, followed by the fist announcing their business on the door. Marx said that living in an attic had its advantages; it offered more time. For what? Suicide? Jenny had heard of a philosopher in Berlin leaping to his death cradling his books when the police arrived. If that were true then it was a tad obsessive; although Jenny would happily perish with her children before anyone dared take them from her. No, in other words, she wouldn't be judged by her children, whose welfare and future happiness were conditioned entirely by her own.

They could have done with a timepiece at Waterloo Bridge. Every clock told a different time. Nothing had changed since the family's arrival a year ago. The armies of refugees, arriving from all points south on the compass, still fought their way off the trains and the commuters still fought their way on.

'The train to Brighton departs from platform 3 at around twelve past the hour,' said the man in the ticket office.

'Would you tell me when that is? I don't have a timepiece,' said Jenny.

'It's around twenty to 10 now,' said the man, who didn't have one either.

The magic word was "around". Everything that occurred in the station was always "around". It was a contrary idea that her husband would have delighted in. She didn't care for such approximations. One day she would inhabit a world of pure certainties; certainties that extended right down to the contents of her own mind.

Time wasn't the only problem at Waterloo. The same went for space. The platform layout was a rebus. It could have been designed by Pascal. Perhaps the solution was being serialized on the back page of *The Times*. Not even the porters could agree where platform 3 was. She wondered why the platform indicators often pointed in two directions at once. Perhaps it meant that if one travelled far enough in one direction one would eventually reach the platform from the other. Surely it was impossible to travel in both directions at once. The confusion was typically English.

'Would you direct me to platform 3, please?' Jenny asked the monocled top hat reading his newspaper next to a sign that read:

Platform 1a ↕

'Platform 3, is it?' He thought about the problem for a moment, then offered the following advice: 'Don't go there.'

'I beg your pardon?' said Jenny.

'I'd say you're much better off going to platform 7. Look,' he said, waving his cane at some invisible destination, 'leave the station over there, then come back in through the main entrance, then head for platform 7. It's around there.' There was the magic word again. 'No!' he then corrected himself. '7a.'

It was ridiculous. She wasn't going to leave the station simply in order to come back in and after a period of agonizing she felt ready to wet herself. She commandeered a porter's trolley and sped off with her family baggage through the crowd in search of a water closet.

Some moments later she returned, having failed in her mission, only to be confronted by soldiers marching to the sound of a military band. It served no purpose to be doing that here. Jenny didn't exactly detest military parades, but they did alarm her, and this one instantly set her mind racing, as if to confirm that what she was presently involved in were some awful choreographed mistake. But then no sooner was she back on the main steps above Waterloo Road hailing a cab, one she barely had the money to pay for, than the lieutenant arrived.

'Baroness, my profound apologies,' said he. 'Have you been waiting long?' White was perspiring slightly yet otherwise elegant and inconspicuous in a grey tailored suit and black cravat.

'Lieutenant!' Jenny burst out, very nearly leaping into his arms. 'How frightfully busy it is here. We came the wrong way. Our driver took us over Westminster Bridge—I can't think why—and then it was all so horribly confusing, since none of the staff could tell me the time, or where the platform was, or—'

'No, no. Waterloo Bridge charges a toll, that's why your driver took you further along the river. But tell me, where is your governess?'

'Who?' said Jenny, mesmerized by the lieutenant's pale blue

eyes.

Lieutenant White could have been modelled on Ares, she thought; although none of the Greek statues of him wore moustaches. His was a devilishly handsome one, fine and perfectly manicured, like an English lawn. Whenever he spoke the little furry animal seemed to bob up and down, almost with a mind of its own.

'Fräulein Demuth?'

'Oh, her,' recalled Jenny. 'She... she was called away on urgent business.'

'Oh, I see,' he replied, seeming discouraged.

Lieutenant White wore a fresh carnation in his buttonhole, which Jenny found touching. Then, without seeking her advice on the matter—a youthful impulse that might have been reckless in a different person—the lieutenant bent down and presented the girls with toffee apples. Either he was being extremely brave or naïve. Incredibly, however, they accepted the gifts with the good grace one hardly expected of them. He added something, a remark or observation, to which they nodded vigorously without so much as seeking their mother's approval. Who on earth was this conjurer? She barely recognized the man stood before her.

The lieutenant had made a profound impression on her that evening at his apartment. But the effect was completely disorienting, as if a stick of dynamite had gone off in the room. One struggled to register his perfection. Presumably he had the same effect on the generals he served under. He must have positively frustrated the advance of their armies. In any case, why bother fighting with White on your side? It was said that the Slavs were always being conquered because their women were so beautiful. Soldiering was the last thing on their minds. Likewise, one felt that with two Whites, one on either side, love could replace all war.

'Come! Let's not forget there's a train to catch,' said he, taking control of the trolley, and leading her and the girls through the circus.

But what if he wasn't who he claimed to be? She couldn't for the life of her recall Reed's face. She remembered how tiresome the other lieutenant had been and had come away with the impression that their evening together had been dreamt up by the men as a kind of dare. The thought made her doubt whether or not she would have been able to distinguish White from Reed had the latter turned up instead, passing himself off as the former. Had she been set up as the prize in a *ménage à trois*?

'How exciting!' exclaimed Jenny.

'And so it is!' echoed the lieutenant.

'We're going to Brighton, girls! I haven't been to the coast for ages. I'm so looking forward to breathing some good clean air for a change.'

'Oh, I think any air's preferable to London air,' said the lieutenant, grasping Jenny's enormous trunk with one hand.

As he swung the monstrous container aboard his shirt came undone, revealing a glistening torso. It reminded Jenny of a sirloin steak. She hadn't eaten one of those in a while. The party boarded the first-class carriage.

'Why don't you sit with the girls on that side?' said the lieutenant, indicating the direction of travel.

The coach was luxurious. There were velvet curtains, mahogany inlays, polished brass, plush carpets and handsome waiters serving drinks. A man and his wife at the next table ordered a bottle of wine.

'Fetch a pouffe for my wife, would you?' instructed the man.

'Yes, sir,' replied the waiter obediently, popping open the wine.

It wasn't a train they were on; it was a mobile hotel. Considering this was only the transport, what the real hotel must have been like Jenny was dying to discover. Her curiosity to see a world free of servants vanished at that very moment.

'Can I offer you any food or beverages, madam?' said a voice.

'A gin and tonic,' said Jenny impulsively, 'and lemonades for the children,' as if vocalizing a private wish.

But to her astonishment, the voice returned, 'Very good, madam.'

Finally, she was living in the moment, when time would no longer have any bearing on what happened next. At least for some indefinite time.

As the train pulled away and trundled over the viaducts of the Upper Lambeth Marsh, she saw the new clock tower they were building at Westminster Palace. Enchanted, she recalled Hamlet's speech, 'The time is out of joint, O cursed spite, That ever I was born to set it right.'[38]

Chapter 22

It couldn't have been Mercury—Morning Star, Evening Star—since it was one o'clock in the afternoon. Not that anything above 100 feet was ever visible in the West End. It was on that basis, Marx concluded, that the pinprick of light on the lead screen of the western horizon was a rogue planet on a direct collision course with Earth. Keplerian orbits could account for the straight-line trajectories of celestial bodies, where angular momentum equalled zero. However, instead of estimating the time to impact, all Marx could think about was leaving a note for Jenny. It might have been pointless. But only to those for whom $r = (4.5\mu t^2)^{1/3}$ was pointless. A declaration of love was no less true than a transcendental number. She would never read his note or know of its existence—since gravity would soon be ripping the earth to shreds—but nonetheless it needed saying:

I can read it in the stars up yonder,
From the Zephyr it comes back to me,
From the being of the wild waves' thunder.
Truly, I would write it down as a refrain,
For the coming centuries to see—
LOVE IS JENNY, JENNY IS LOVE'S NAME.[39]

"Aaaahuuiiooo!" or the noise must have sounded something like that. On reflection it was possible that the rogue planet threatening Earth with destruction might in fact be one of the eyespots that appeared on Marx's retina whenever the carbuncular pain reached a critical threshold.

'What have we got up here, then?' said Helene, who was carrying out her task with uninhibited gusto. 'Eh? Maybe this is where you've been hiding your money.'

'Can you see any swelling?' he enquired in a high-pitched

voice.

'I don't know! You really think I want to see up there?' said Helene, whose hand, despite being dexterous, might have been stuffing a turkey. 'You asked me to rub in the lotion. Well! I'm rubbing. You'll have to call Bauer if you want an inspection. And *don't* tell me you owe the man money. If you owe the man then pay the man. If you won't fork out for your health then don't expect any sympathy from me.'

'I don't expect sympathy, just sensitivity. Mind how you go. If you irritate the lesion then I'll be on my back for the rest of the day… Ahhh! What are you doing?'

'Keep still, won't you? My hand slipped. Raise your backside higher. I can't reach with you all slipshod and about-face. You're neither here nor there.'

'I'm not a gymnast, woman,' said Marx, raising his buttocks so they almost sat level with Helene's chin.

'I can't help it,' Helene explained, 'if there's no light in this room. Turn yourself toward the window.'

'Let me stand on my chair,' said Marx.

'What chair?'

'Eh?'

'I already told you,' said Helene, exasperated, 'it's been pawned. How else do you think we've been eating?' She ducked beneath the victim's outstretched leg. 'Hold still! Put your leg up onto my shoulder.'

Despite being smaller than average, and seeming petite to some, she possessed a phenomenal strength—or it possessed her—and when she needed to she could channel this reserve. Most often her robust physicality came into its own at the market, where she was guaranteed to be first in line for discounted fish on a Friday morning. She raised his entire leg with one arm and held it there, like an Athenian wrestler, leaving her other arm inside the burrow.

'That's enough now,' said Marx, eager to extricate himself

from the assemblage as quickly as possible. 'You can go out.'

'What d'you think I've been trying to do for the past five minutes?' said Helene.

'Eh? You mean you're stuck up there?'

An image came to his mind of him addressing the congregation in his present state, "arse first", so to speak. Was there any historical precedent for it? Some of the Greek philosophers were unconventional. Diogenes inhabited a barrel. But none of them had ever, literally speaking, spoken out of the arse. He might have to make his intervention from behind a curtain or inside a commode.

'I'm out!' said Helene, sounding as relieved as the arse in so doing. 'And *don't* ask me to go up there again,' she warned.

'I only asked you to rub in some lotion,' said Marx meekly, collapsing onto the bed, 'not split me in two.'

'I had to clean you first,' she said, reaching for the towel and wiping her hands on his shirt by mistake.

'I'm making a speech,' said he. 'No one is going to inspect my anus.'

'No, but they'll smell you coming. Mind you,' she conceded, 'at least they don't have to sleep in the same bed as you.'

He shifted onto his side and from there onto the edge of the bed. Helene helped him sit up, but to get into his trousers he had to roll backward and raise his legs up onto her shoulders. He probably could have strangled her in that position; though surely not before she had landed a fatal blow to his genitals.

His mood had been more manageable of late, a trend that was bound to continue for as long as the carbuncular pain could be kept at bay. And yet that was the least of his worries for the time being. The immediate challenge, wholly unwarranted in his view, was more onerous simply by virtue of being unknown. In a word: Heinzen.

Marx hadn't asked for this childish confrontation. On the contrary, the showdown had been dropped on his head from a great height. Not only that, but dropped in such a way as to make *him* out to be the challenger. Granted, a renegade must be treated rapidly in order to prevent the infection from spreading. But why confront the enemy on its own terms? Perhaps Engels could be persuaded to take up the reins. He was a first-rate speaker and since Marx's intervention would be a surprise, the surprise might just as well be double. Whether Engels would see it that way and address the gathering in his place was another matter.

As he hobbled along Great Windmill Street massaging his left buttock he questioned the wisdom of prolonging the agony. It was one thing to defend the interests of German refugees, of whom he himself was one. He had done everything in his power since arriving in England to support the workers financially and hadn't taken a penny from the refugee fund. But it was quite another to stand up for the integrity of a political organization— viz. the Communist League—that could barely agree on the content of a weekly agenda, let alone orient the workers politically.

A revolution had nothing to do with the so-called leadership of Heinzen or Bakunin or anyone else, despite the misguided convictions of such "revolutionaries" that they were leading a party. Such fantasies were borne out by the fact that there were now more political organizations in London than supporters capable of joining them. Be a leader, form a party. Those jackasses were putting the cart before the horse. The task of a communist party was to *respond* to the revolutionary movement and *adapt* itself to its dynamic, not mould it from mud and straw. The revolution didn't need alchemists like Heinzen; it needed scientists like Marx. And with the ebb of the revolutionary tide he could just as well retreat into his research all the better to anticipate the real revolution, the radical parabolic trajectory, the one destined to make all previous risings look like a game of swings and roundabouts.

He was no different from Heinzen and the others. He hadn't chosen England; it had chosen him. In an ideal world he would have returned to Cologne. But Louis-Napoléon's expulsion order had forced his hand: leave Paris or fester in the Morbihan marshes. The gendarmes had given him a day to pick up his manuscript, fire off a dozen begging letters, appeal to the good natures of pawnbrokers and pull in favours in a city where charity was in short supply. The dread conveyor had carted him off in a carriage pressed full of workers and a barrel of wine; workers from the faubourgs, not Jacobin fugitives, whose gnarled skin and cross eyes told their own story. They were being driven the wrong way. The Bonapartes knew how to put down a rising: export it across the Channel. The nation of shopkeepers would stock anything. Perfidious Albion was the revolution's last port of call, the discount bazaar where coachloads of refugees were still being delivered to the social factories of London, Birmingham and Manchester. London had never appeared as a light at the end of the tunnel. As far as Marx was concerned they were all still in it, with the prospect of ever emerging receding by the day.

But the unbowed creatures of sorry countenance would rise again.

Halfway up Great Windmill Street the orange stuff dashed in his face and smarted. A black cat crossed his path, swished its tail and skipped through the hole in the fence of the knackery. A profound moan was issuing from in there. He felt an affinity with the condemned creature and the urge to comfort it. On the narrow bend a length of guttering fell off a dilapidated cottage, narrowly missing him. He hobbled the remaining 50 yards to the Red Lion, where Engels and the others were waiting outside. It was hardly a show of strength. Liebknecht could barely make eye contact. As for Schramm, his face had turned the colour of a chameleon.

'What happened?' said Engels.

'My arse,' said Marx. 'How many of them are up there?'

'A hundred,' guessed Engels. 'That's about right, isn't it?'

The look on Engels's face and his trembling hand as he lit his cigar rendered Marx's next question obsolete.

'Fine, fine,' Marx muttered to himself, resigned to whatever fate awaited them all. 'Let's get it over with.'

At the foot of the stairs stood an ape-like creature six-feet high and some.

'Sorry, gents,' said he, barring the way. 'Members only.'

Marx balked. 'Members? *We* are the executive committee.'

'Tickets are a penny each,' replied the unblinking creature.

'Was soll das denn heißen!'[40]

'In which case a ticket for my friend and I,' said Engels, handing over the money.

'And your name is?'

'Louis-Napoléon Bonaparte.'

The great ape stared unblinkingly. He produced a roll of parchment from inside his coat. Since Bonaparte's name didn't appear on the blacklist, the committee members were free to proceed.

The meeting was rammed to the rafters and as they climbed the stairs they could have done with parasols to beat the condensation dripping from the ceiling. Marx attuned his senses to the layout of the place.

'Brothers!' intoned Heinzen like the high priest of the religious sect he was. 'Focus your minds on the coming of the Revolution.'

The windows had been blackened and candles stood at either end of a trestle table. A glass cylinder rested on this altar. As his eyesight returned his ears detected the subtle rendering of a harp. It might have been a dress rehearsal for a West End play. It was difficult to imagine anyone giving Marx a proper hearing in this place, any more than the public at Covent Garden would take kindly to a stage diver interrupting *Rigoletto*.

Kinkel approached the altar and ignited the contents of the

cylinder—phosphorous, probably, with a few Indian herbs and spices from the local market thrown in for good measure. The mixture flashed a variety of colours. Faces gawped at the visual torture unfolding in the dark room. The Marx party carved out a space against the wall. No one batted an eyelid at the latecomers.

'Behold!' declared Heinzen, waving the cylinder in circles in his white gloves, 'the miraculous exploding silver. Brothers, what you see before you is a mere trace of the secret compound that will soon consign the princes of Europe to dust.'

It might have been a production of *Macbeth*. Was he intending to add a fillet of fenny snake, perchance? And the eye of newt and toe of frog? There were gasps and a ripple of applause; though it was difficult to say how seriously anyone was really taking it. Marx had always managed to see through Heinzen's politics, but on this evidence he had considerably underestimated the depths of his rival's desperation. Clearly he had no political programme to speak of. Beyond that Marx could only marvel at the seductive power of the showman in his midst. It was a power worthy of a lion tamer.

'What is this madness?' he grumbled, wiping the sweat from his brow.

'I don't know,' said Engels, 'but I've already seen enough.'

Engels crossed to the window to pull down the curtains and restore the room to light. The audience let go a collective sigh as if shaken from a dream. Heinzen stood expressionless holding the still-burning cylinder. For a moment no one said anything, then Marx introduced himself with a slow handclap. His presence took the room quite by surprise.

'Comrade Heinzen,' said he. 'Love the show. Permit me to make one observation, however. In the event that you decide to take it on tour, your Royal Command Performance may not go down well.'

Heinzen put down the cylinder, which instantly lost its sparkle.

'Dr Marx! Most amusing. Tell me, did you come to pour scorn on the proceedings? Or is there something more pressing you wish to share with us?' He removed his gloves theatrically, one finger at a time. 'You see, gentlemen, Marx is ever so good at critique. But when it comes to offering workingmen such as yourselves *political* alternatives—'

Marx erupted, his voice shooting up an octave. 'The first thing I should offer them is honesty and truth! Not this spurious magic show!'

'Dr Marx studied philosophy at the University of Berlin, you know,' said Heinzen, addressing the room in a Shakespearean aside. 'Although for the life of me I haven't the slightest idea what his philosophy amounts to. Maybe you can enlighten us, Doctor.' He strode out from behind the altar. Despite standing several yards apart, Heinzen towered over his nemesis. Done up in top hat and cape he resembled a villain from Grimm's *Fairy Tales*.

'Well?' said he. 'We're waiting.'

The workingmen growled in a note of menace. Or perhaps it was their own peculiar way of breathing. One hundred pairs of eyes stared and Marx looked fit to burst. It was overwhelming. Sabre-rattling might have been his forte but beyond that he had nothing prepared. The room fell silent.

Hesitating, he began, 'My philosophy, in a nutshell—'

'A very *large* nutshell, it seems,' cut in Heinzen to universal laughter.

He took a deep breath and resumed. 'The *core* of my philosophy… is concerned with investigating the economic causes of social exploitation.' He turned to address the room. 'You see, the class struggle is a mere historical phase in the development of the economic forces and relations of production—'

'What fine-sounding words!' Heinzen interrupted again. 'If only we knew what they meant.'

'Capitalism!' Marx shot daggers at his foe. 'Or bourgeois

society, in plain and simple language, which robs you of your energy and profits from your work while barely paying you enough to live on... Life? Well, now! That's a different matter entirely, since the misery that makes up the workingman's lot is hardly a living, given how the social lords and masters luxuriate in palatial homes and dispose of the free time that only *your* *labour* affords them.

'And then what? The capitalists have the nerve to pretend you're not human, while the economists argue that a workingman doesn't exist unless he's labouring. For them, you're nothing more than a necessary cost, like the oil that greases their machines. Well, now! Do you not exist? Do you feel like a machine? Does your life count for a mere commodity and nothing else besides? There in a nutshell, gentlemen, is what my "philosophy" amounts to. And this is what we must all struggle against.'

Heinzen clapped his hands impatiently. 'Well! I think we've all heard quite enough—'

'Struggle!' cut in Marx this time. 'It won't be easy. Creating a just society is the greatest challenge of our times. The revolution won't materialize in an instant. Neither will it come courtesy of some magic potion.' Marx tapped his fingers against the glass cylinder. 'It'll take time. I can't promise you a better life tomorrow; or the next day, week, month or year after that. I can only promise struggle. Sometimes it might seem pointless, as if nothing is really changing. But it will. Never forget that struggle is part of who you are, not merely what you do; and that unless you're prepared to struggle, so that you workingmen, and you alone, can at last become the owners of your own labour, then there is no future for any of us.'

The proclamation wafted round the room as the audience sat quite still. Marx made his way to the stairwell.

'By the way,' he added, somewhat in awe of his own voice, 'for those of you who may be interested, I'm writing a book on capital. I shall be giving a series of public lectures on the subject in the coming weeks. Admission will be free of charge. Good day.'

Marx descended the stairs in the company of Engels, Liebknecht and Schramm. His intervention had been decisive, surely—but in which direction? The showdown had guaranteed one thing at least, in spite of its success; namely, that no one could accuse him of being a maverick or be left in any doubt as to where he stood politically. Naturally they could still insist on misrepresenting his views if they chose to. And, in truth, there was but one solution to political misrepresentation at the hands of his rivals; namely, complete the manuscript. That was the only public declaration that counted. To achieve it he would gladly see the Communist League frozen beneath the ice of the Cocytus in the Ninth Circle of Hell; which, technically speaking, was meant for traitors, but whose inclusion could probably be justified on the grounds that the organization was plagued by skulduggery.

'Did I overdo it?' said Marx, mopping his brow.

'I don't know,' Engels replied, 'but I think you're about to find out.'

The sound of boots on the stairs confirmed that some common resolution had been reached. The pace of the action was swift and hypnotic. Perhaps Heinzen's "exploding silver" had won out over Marx's calm and sober reasoning after all. On reaching the foot of the stairs the workingmen homed in with the devout purpose of a winged messenger.

'Comrade Marx...' one of them began, a wizened chap in a regimental voice.

Although he spoke at some length those first words were the only ones that registered, since "comrade", not "doctor", said it all. Marx felt a wave of euphoria as the men reached out to him, shaking his hands with their brittle claws, grabbing his arms, ruffling his hair, cheering, laughing and applauding. Drinks were ordered and scores of people arrived, more curious than anything else at the unlikely air of unanimity that held sway in the Red Lion, whose modest dimensions ordinarily housed more diversity of revolutionary conviction than just about any other place on the planet—to say nothing of the layers of intrigue that went far beneath the Cocytus.

Marx was swept away by the tide. It was the feeling of transport that happened, pulsing through his body like a vapour bath, and in the next moment had him running to board an already moving train, just managing to throw on his suitcase and clamber up as the engine put on a burst of speed. Somewhere in the distance he heard the workers chanting his name, hailing his arrival or departure, which confirmed he was on the right track. He pressed his way through the human cargo, reaching the working-class carriage, where passengers were tightly packed inside narrow compartments resembling sheep pens. He opened the window and let out the dead air. Behind him lay the city whence he came; ahead of him nothing, or at least nothing he could make out: a slice of horizon or wad of mountain obscuring it. Nothing of great substance. It was all a blur unprecedented in scale. Not physical scale, since there was no "space" out there. But the true nature of the reality that was.

Travelling at speed fixed the idea of matter in motion with the sublime perfection of Michelangelo's *Battle of the Centaurs* or *Rebellious Slave*. The subject was incidental. What was pressing in those still lives, those complex movements frozen in time, was the idea of time and space as a continuum, as something that could be grasped together in unity.

He ventured further along the corridor, conscious of something that he couldn't quite grasp, but fearing any attempt to do so would distance it still further. Everything fell into darkness as the train passed through a tunnel. On exiting he was back at the pub, only it was dark now, and Engels, Liebknecht, Schramm and the German workers had long since departed.

He set off home convinced he was being watched. But he didn't turn to see who it was, just kept going.

Chapter 23

The Royal Albion was unusual for a seaside resort hotel. Despite being located on the seafront it faced the opposite way. Jenny had revelled in the idea of waking up and staring out at a view from her bed unbroken by obstacles for a change. A view of sea and air. The hotel's inward-facing aspect suited the personalities of its clients, who were mostly dour and over-the-hill.

'My daughters and I would like a different room, please,' she told the concierge.

'Madam—'

'Baroness,' Jenny instantly corrected him.

'Baroness. My apologies. The hotel is deliberately "inward-facing" in order to provide views of the Royal Pavilion. Generally speaking our guests do tend to prefer it.'

She might have insisted, explaining that she had no wish to ogle royalty and that since she resided in a hotel she knew very well what she preferred. The concierge stood before her with a most perplexed look on his face.

'Is there anything else I can assist you with, Baroness?' he asked, bowing in an obsequious manner.

Not wishing to humiliate the little man, Jenny shook her head and the servant scurried off to attend to some other impossible demand before breakfast.

'Free the serfs!' cried Jennychen as she galloped into the dining room to universal consternation.

The hotel was the Palace of Versailles, which provided her and Laura's class war games with the lavish authenticity that the cramped confines of the German Hotel lacked. The girls had been profiting from their sojourn no end and Jenny felt she had been rightly solicitous in shielding them from the overeager attentions of the lieutenant. She would attend to him herself when she was good and ready. Needless to say there was great potential for scandal in this dyspeptic bourgeois reservation. Such was the reason for Queen Victoria's recent falling out of love with Brighton and its "very indiscreet and troublesome" public.

Jenny remarked that the English were inclined to travel to the coast for the express purpose of restocking their metropolitan parlours with meaty gossip. Brighton was the place where the terrifying beasts would come in order to catch unsuspecting prey off guard and savage their reputations. *A hollow gut, full of fear and hope that God will have mercy!* The dowagers in the dining room had excelled on the first morning by complaining to the waiters about everything they could possibly set their minds to—the temperature of the tea, the length of the bay windows, the "sea light", the dining room upholstery, the too many potted plants, the slovenliness of the service—before turning their disparaging tongues on Jenny and her party when the lieutenant joined them for breakfast. Asphyxiated throat-clearing noises greeted Jenny's arrival at dinner and then again at breakfast the following morning, prompting the Baroness to slip a purgative into the crones' teapot. Ultimately she managed to execute her plan with expert subtlety, intercepting their breakfast tray at the kitchen service hatch, which was shielded from the dining room by a large areca palm. The crones weren't seen again after that and Jenny wondered when she overheard the receptionist talking to the waiter about "the lady's seizure" whether or not she might have miscalculated the dosage.

For the rest of the holiday Jenny bounded down to breakfast each morning with the vitality of a proselytizing Presbyterian. The change in her mood since arriving in Brighton had been dizzying to behold. She took on what might best be described as a new lease of life. She would rise in the near pitch-black, rush outside and pace along the seafront with only the seagulls for company, hugging herself madly as the wind blew so hard that she felt ready to take off. Her energy was unprecedented, its source unfathomable, a power so ferocious that it frightened her almost to tears. She would enter into long and loud conversations with herself.

On the third morning she dashed to Seaford Head and arrived in a matter of minutes, then raced back down to the Martello Tower, the raised concrete disc that seemed to defy all purpose, rising from the pebbly beach like the unformed idea of an alien consciousness. She waited for the sun to creep over the South Downs and when it did it bounced off the Tower with the precision of an intergalactic beacon.

She fretted and cursed herself, running back to the hotel in unstockinged feet, convinced that her daughters had been spirited away as punishment for her transgression. She tiptoed into the still-dark room and kindled the lamp, disbelieving the presence of her little ones in spite of their perplexed sighs, until she had harnessed that alien light from the outside and confined it to the small space where her children were still fast asleep, unmoved and untroubled by the epic catalogue of her imagination.

Then, taking deep breaths and pressing her fingers flat to her neck, she realized the true nature of her delirium. It was the lieutenant who was at the centre of it all. He was the new source of gravity in her solar system; the sun to her moon. Her pulse raced as fast as the pistons of the locomotive that had brought them here. The apparatus had installed a new rhythm in her. She went to the bathroom and slowly undressed herself in the mirror, transfixed by the sight of the new being discarding the flesh of its host. She was burning, a wave of heat building from the soles of her feet all the way to her ears, nose, eyes and forehead. She bathed herself, making sure to scrub away every last trace of her old self.

'Baroness? Are you quite well?' The lieutenant's voice wavered in mid-sentence.

It must have been afternoon already, but might have been

the same day or the next. Daylight crept around the edges of the bathroom door. She eased herself out of her cast-iron cocoon, dried herself and dressed, choosing an ensemble that was attractive, practical, yet frivolous at the same time: a black silk dress with ruffled collar and pagoda sleeves, several petticoats (she wouldn't be caged), with her red-and-black fan (a keepsake from Weydemeyer's wife) and, for accessories, her cubic zirconia drop earrings.

She felt her pulse again, which had eased, thus enabling the grace and comportment of the Baroness, to whom, despite feeling indebted, she nonetheless feared. It was a disconcerting prospect to be at cross purposes with someone who answered to the same name, wore the same clothes and occupied the same space as she did. It was unknown territory. It was a new time.

'I know you must think me silly,' said the lieutenant, 'but I was convinced you and the children had left.'

The dining room had emptied in preparation for a gala ball later that evening. Jennychen and Laura were up to their usual games, and hurtled in an out of the conservatory, hiding among the palm trees and scaring the living daylights out of the staff.

'Yes, it is rather. Why ever did you think it?'

'Because I hadn't seen you for a day and a half,' said the lieutenant, trying not to sound aggrieved.

'Was it really that long?' wondered Jenny, reflecting on the correct way to eat a boiled egg. 'Oh, well. We're all here now,' she said to the sound of collapsing foliage followed by a crash.

'What was that?' The lieutenant twisted round in his seat.

He was wearing another of the waistcoats, which in moments of brisk exertion revealed his muscular torso. There was no doubting the physicality of this model specimen sprung from the race of Spartans. But what was lurking beneath?

'Nothing. Tell me about yourself, Lieutenant. I have spent three days in your company so far and—'

'A mere one and a half in your presence, Baroness,' the

lieutenant corrected her, this time with a look of self-mockery.

'But time is such a wearisome notion in our modern world, is it not?' said Jenny, savouring the yellow portion of her egg. 'The idea of spending a day and a half, or two or three in the company of friends... I think it would be so much nicer if we did away with time altogether and just did as we pleased for as long as we liked. Don't you?'

The lieutenant's moustache twitched in a minor act of rebellion.

'Time dominates us. We must always be here or there at a certain time,' added Jenny. 'I'm sure it's the source of untold maladies and bad tempers. Ever since my family arrived in London I've barely had time to think. Some might put that down to the pace of life here, the "industry" or what have you. But on reflection I'm sure it's a widespread affliction. It's a social problem that stems from the unnatural separation between our public and private lives. I do find it unnatural the more I think of it. Instead of our small-minded obligations we should be free to do this today and that tomorrow, to hunt in the morning, go fishing in the afternoon, do cattle breeding in the evening, criticize after dinner, and play chess at all times of the day and night. Indulging in pleasure is the perfect ideal for humankind, I'm sure you'll agree, Lieutenant.'

White shook his head as if attempting to remove a wasp from his ear. 'Why, it does have its attractions,' he politely observed, 'I readily grant you that. And, if you'll forgive me for saying so, I should like nothing better, dear Baroness, than to prolong our acquaintance in your ideal world.' He took a sip of his tea and gently placed the cup on its saucer. 'But... consider for a moment what would become of the world if your ideal became reality. How would it all work, practically speaking? As a military man I have first-hand experience of the situation of peoples deprived of their livelihoods, grown idle and hungry through lack of industry. Would your'—the lieutenant halted abruptly, as if the word refused to come out—'*utopia* make sense in a kingdom like ours?'

What a strange choice of words, Jenny thought, as she scanned the dining room for telltale signs of her children: a broken window, a collapsed ceiling. Did she inhabit a "kingdom"? It occurred to her that she did. How old-fashioned it sounded when phrased that way. How odd the world looked when spied through the prism of the lieutenant's inveterate mind.

'Perhaps it is so,' Jenny conceded, the better to set about contradicting him. 'But tell me: do you regard human suffering brought about by war as the natural state? If so, then we must surely grant to kings their divine right to rule kingdoms and emperors to rule empires. If not, then surely freedom will prevail and people will be at liberty to express themselves as much through their industry as through their leisure.'

This reasoning struck Jenny as rather opaque. It was all hypothetical anyway, since the state of the kingdom made little difference to how she felt and to how she was feeling at this very moment.

Chapter 24

'Monsieur Ramboz!' came the voice from behind the door. 'I shall count to three: one, two, three—'

Marx's life was dominated by numbers. But numbers of the nominal variety, since no one he knew, from mathematicians to bailiffs, bondsmen, shopkeepers and the cursed landlord, could grasp what a number actually was. Anyone could "count", if by counting one meant advancing words in some prescribed order. Marx was constantly being reminded "how much" money he owed and "how much" time he had to settle his account. But to what possible *end?* If the debt could be prolonged indefinitely — as in the case of the national debt — then in what sense was it real?

Marx had already vacated the German Hotel when the bailiffs burst in to number 12. Jenny's departure to the coast had provided the perfect opportunity to write down the family debt to a more manageable sum: namely, zero. The few possessions she had left behind, along with the bulk of Marx and Helene's belongings, had been stuffed inside sacks and thrown down from the second floor to Liebknecht and Schramm at two the previous morning. Helene had left some hours later, having loaded up Guido's perambulator with clothes, linen, broken crockery, bits and pieces of cutlery, and miscellaneous bric-a-brac, and Marx a short time later with nothing more than his precious manuscript tied up in a bundle and stuffed down his trousers. Even before the countdown to jubilee had commenced another one had already started in respect of the family's new abode just round the corner in Soho, which would come no nearer to attaining the desired quantity had Marx been given the rest of his life to pay off the interest, let alone the rent itself, of which he could no more hope to write down than reverse the march of time. An ideal home for Marx's future happiness, in other words, aptly described 64 Dean Street.

'Italians, Poles, Irish, Slavs... People from all over the world live in Dean Street, Dr Mark,' said Mrs O'Sullivan, the landlady, as she wrestled open the door of the second-floor flat.

Marx had rather pinned his hopes on the third, since his mind worked better higher up: better air and less through traffic. The front room was clean and sparsely furnished. The fireplace was a large gaping hole in the wall minus a hearth big enough to swallow a child. The big oak table would do its job at mealtimes. Helene's heart sank when she saw it, since it provided a readymade platform for Marx's intrusive brainwork. She would need to be vigilant and prevent the thing from being taken over by books and parchment. A mattress was propped against the wall of the back room along with two chairs, one of whose seats was missing and the fourth leg on the other. Water was tapped from a lead butt, a welcome feature for a private dwelling; although its operation was unsettled.

'It works best first thing,' ventured Mrs O'Sullivan, doubting the wisdom of her own words. The tap made a gurgling noise that echoed round the building before spitting out some grey matter into the sink. 'There's a standpipe just on the corner,' she added by way of consolation.

Mrs O'Sullivan would intonate every sentence, which made everything she said sound like a question, so that when it came to the rent Marx couldn't be sure whether he owed her for one month or two. This ambiguity reassured him.

'Now, what about your laundry arrangements, Mr Mark? You've a wife and four children besides yourself, and that makes for a great quantity of garments come washday. And,' a thought roused the lady, 'a gentleman doctor like your good self wants his clothes pressed! Demands it in the interests of his clients. Pressed jacket, trousers, shirt, collar and tie,' she went on, nodding vigorously at her own wisdom, undaunted by the diabolical appearance of the shabby specimen whose appearance flew in the face of everything she was saying.

A moment later the penny dropped: Mrs O'Sullivan was as poor as a church mouse and as fretful in her search for additional business as the mouse was for cheese.

'Why didn't you strike a bargain with her?' demanded Helene as soon as the landlady had gone. 'You're not going to pay the rent, so why not *not* pay for the laundry, either?' She was beginning to sound more like Marx every day.

'Engels is my guarantor and if I don't pay he could end up in prison. It was the only way we could get this place.'

'But you won't be able to pay and he'll end up sending you the money anyway. So what's the difference?'

It occurred to him that there were times when Helene's powers of deduction, despite being sound, didn't actually advance the cause of proving him right. He turned to the window. The scene outside resembled a dry riverbed. A lamp post struck through the pavement like a monstrous weed. The curb was broken away, litter and faeces were smeared everywhere, and shoeless urchins were beating a dead cat with sticks. It wasn't the cosmopolitan idyll the landlady had described. But it was relatively quiet and isolated from the main drag (American tourists wouldn't dare get lost here), with the promise of few nocturnal distractions. Marx could operate here and no sooner had Helene gone to bed than he began arranging his notes on the big oak table like a doctor preparing for major surgery. It was touch and go, but by the next morning he felt satisfied: the patient was still alive. Then news arrived that threatened to jeopardize the entire operation.

'Your intervention has made waves,' Engels announced the next day in the pub. 'The venerable Charles Dickens and John Forster wish to attend your lectures on capital.'

'Lectures?'

'The ones you announced last week.'

'Did I?' Marx recalled the startled look on Heinzen's face when the big oaf had left the pub with his tail between his legs.

Engels clicked his fingers. 'I say! Is there anyone at home? "I shall be giving a series of public lectures in the coming weeks..." That's what you said.'

'Oh, I... see,' said Marx after some further prompting.

His announcement had been more an expression of goodwill than a definite plan; a rhetorical flourish whose true meaning was, "and don't bother me again if you can help it"; or, "and don't think anything I've said today entitles you to a running commentary on my work"; or, "and since I specialize in contradictions, this is one of them". As it turned out, however, the announcement had been taken as a genuine invitation, which now threatened to complicate matters considerably.

'This is a capital opportunity,' said Engels, sounding oddly enthused by the idea.

'Do you want me to finish this damned book or not? Yes? So then kindly tell me how presenting introductory lectures on capital is going to assist me in that aim. Really, I'm all ears.'

'But don't you see?' said Engels. 'This could land you a job on *The Examiner*. Forster's a contributing editor. How does International Correspondent grab you? And once Duncker gets wind of it... well, he might advance you the 1500 talers. More, I'd say.'

Marx looked flatly unconvinced. 'Have you read *The Examiner*? It's a liberal rag. It savaged the Chartists and now it's venerating the prime minister.[41] What shall I write about that blasted Lilliputian? Ha! Maybe I could review his arse of a play for the arts pages.'

'They don't want you to write about the prime minister. They want you to talk about overseas news. What Forster wants—'

'Wait a moment! You've spoken to him?'

'Of course.'

Marx jumped in his seat. This was more than just talk. Forster was Dickens's editor and the latter commanded 600 pounds per monthly instalment for his serials. Marx could happily settle for a pound or two less.

'Fine, I'll do the lecture,' he agreed.

'More than one,' said Engels.

'Fine, two lectures.'

'Commit to at least three. That way you're bound to get a pamphlet out of it and I'll talk to Forster about a publication.'

From the few details he was being offered Marx suspected that his friend had already done the deal with Forster. It went without saying, however, that he had Marx's best interests at heart.

'Agreed—on condition that you promise to leave me alone once it's over with.'

'You have my word,' Engels promised, crossing his heart.

'And!' Marx insisted, 'on the understanding that you take on the articles yourself. Pseudonymously or otherwise, I don't care. I don't have time for squalid journalism. Agreed?'

'Moor,' said Engels, holding up his palms, 'as you know, I work in an accounts department. I have all the time in the world to devote to squalid journalism.'

Suddenly the penny dropped. Ever since Engels had arrived in London he had been scurrying hither and thither doing everything in his power to take the pressure off Marx in order that the revolution's chief theoretician could concentrate on his manuscript. Marx had interpreted these antics as those of a careening poseur, when in fact all the seemingly reckless activity—the turmoil in Engels's love life and his constant shuttling between London and Manchester—were owing to the pressures Marx had heaped on his friend. In his blind determination to finish the book, Marx had been too insensitive to see it.

Rather than revolt or complain, Engels had merely stepped aside and sacrificed his literary ambitions for Marx's own, and was doing double the graft in order to provide Marx and his family a roof over their heads. And now he had even gone to the trouble of organizing public lectures that Marx could deliver standing on his head, with the aim of providing him with a supplementary income from newspaper articles that Engels was even offering to write himself. It wasn't just gracious and touching and fraternal and self-deprecating. It was deeply moving and it made Marx want to commission a statue to the man, or at least buy him a box of cigars or a bunch of flowers.

'I'm leaving tomorrow morning for Manchester,' said Engels. 'I'm moving up there for good this time.' An awkward silence ensued. 'I can't put it off any longer. The old man's given me an ultimatum. Either I work in his business or he cuts me off... It'll only be for a short time; just to pay off some of my heftier gambling debts.'

'I don't blame the old man,' said Marx for some reason.

'I thought I could come to your new flat before I go. I've too much to do tonight, but I could spare an hour at least. I'd like to bid au revoir to Jenny and the children.'

'She'd like that, too,' said Marx, disguising his true feelings. 'Wait. She's still in Brighton with the girls. They won't be back until tomorrow night.'

'Ah. But I could see Guido. How's he shuffling along? He must be a grown man by now.'

'*Justement*. You'll see how much. He looks more like me, they say. Like a Chinese dumpling.'

'Reminds me of Goethe: "There are two things children should get from their parents: roots and wings".'

'Well! The child's rooted all right. At any rate, there's more thread on his spool than there is on mine.'

'Ha! Jolly good. And Edgar?'

'The same. That reminds me,' said Marx, downing his ale. 'Give me a couple of hours. There's something I must do first.'

On setting out to Drury Lane Hamlet's soliloquy lodged in Marx's mind and refused to budge. *Conscience doth make cowards of us all*. But the end was surely in sight. He had done his best: as

husband, father, professional revolutionary, critic, philosopher…
In that order of priority. Let them say otherwise—let them dare!
He imagined Dickens and Forster seated in the front row of his
lecture as he derived functions on the chalkboard in a caterpillar-
like sentence. At the end of it Dickens would observe: 'Dr Marx,
much as I'm fascinated by your exposition, I regret that I'm all
the while confused, since you and I and several of the good
gentleman here present in this room belong to the bourgeois
class of which you speak. Are you quite prepared to see your
class "vanish", as you put it, for the sake of the new society you
aim to bring about?'

To which Marx would respond: 'Perhaps, good sir, a time will
come when history finds a different use for men of our class.
Until that day arrives we are free either to assist or get in the
way of progress toward the new type of society. I have made
my choice. As for you, Mr Forster, I don't wish to write for your
Examiner; although you can examine my arse, if you like.'

'Snowdrops tuppence a bunch 'ere!'

The wandering flower seller stood on the corner of Long
Acre. Instead of a clockwork dog perambulator he should
have patented a clockwork one of those. It was probably ahead
of its time. In the new society there would be no demand for
such useless inventions, but he could do with the money in the
meantime.

He turned onto James Street and crossed Covent Garden
holding his handkerchief over his mouth. On Bow Street a
plume of white smoke was venting from a sewer. The odour
was nauseating and so toxic that it had diverted traffic. But it
was a sign, an irrefutable sign, and no less than Vesuvius's first
tendrils of steam had been for the ill-fated residents of Pompeii.

Chapter 25

He arrived back at the flat via Soho Square. It was safer that way than risk bumping into a creditor, most of whom plied their trade farther south. He had coal, some porridge and milk, oranges and a joint of meat for dinner. More importantly, he had retrieved Edgar's toy locomotive from the pawnshop. A stranger opened the door of his flat.

'What are you doing here?' demanded Marx, suspecting foul play or an ill-timed adventure. 'Helene!' History moved in mysterious ways, granted. But this was ridiculous.

'No, no. More high, please,' said the man, an Italian probably, motioning Marx up the stairs to the third floor.

Helene was washing herself by the front window when he walked in. The door was ajar. She was naked from the waist down and looked surprised, before her face reverted to its usual expression. She made no attempt to cover herself. It was nothing Marx hadn't seen before. She held herself there, somewhat defiantly and for several moments, before slowly letting down her petticoats.

'My locomo-iff!' Edgar squealed, seizing the toy from his father and setting off on a tour of the flat.

'There's a leak,' said Helene.

'Why are we here?'

'The landlady says it's cheaper than downstairs and you're bound to like it just as well. If you ask me, the Italian complained about the leak and she caved in.'

'It's bound to be cheaper with a leak. How much?'

Helene grumbled, 'What do you care how much? Found some money down the back of your trousers, did you?'

She began preparing a meal for Guido and Edgar. With a few sparse ingredients the woman could work miracles (unlike Jenny, who couldn't tell one end of a saucepan from the other).

On the corner of Old Compton Street a prostitute stood in a doorway, hand on hip and her elbow propped against the frame. It wasn't clear if she did her business inside or had selected the door at random. Perhaps all doors served the same burrow.

'Nice view,' said Marx.

Helene forced a smile. 'You know what gets me?' she began. 'That with all your highfalutin ideas and university learning, you manage to earn less money than that woman across the street. Why is that?' She sidled up to him, as the prostitute might have done, and placed a hand gently on his shoulder. 'Could it be because her work is more appreciated than yours? What a strange turnabout if true — *if* it were true, mind. But far be it from me to pour scorn on her work — or yours...'

Marx let out a sigh. 'Her "work", as you put it, has a market value. Just like that of any other commodity. But far be it from me to pour scorn on your ignorance — you're welcome to it.'

'So! I am right,' cackled Helene. 'Her market value *is* higher than yours. People appreciate her more than you.'

Marx became irritated. 'No! Now you're confusing things. Her clients aren't purchasing *her*, in spite of her popularity. They're purchasing her labour time. One must separate the individual from the work being produced, as well as from the time taken to produce it.'

'Why?'

'Because labour time is an average measure of the time taken to produce any commodity.'

Helene went on laughing and turned her back on the chief theoretician. 'More of your gibberish.'

He grabbed her by the arm. 'It is not gibberish!' he yelled in her ear. 'Listen to what I am saying! Labour time is a social relation that regulates the exchange value of commodities!'

'Let go of me!'

Helene wrestled herself away, but he clasped her round the waist. She threw out her arms in all directions, but he ducked the blows and pulled her agitated body flat to his, leaving her nowhere to flee but between his legs. She slipped through the hole then rose up behind his back, grabbed him round the neck and yanked down on his beard with the might of a bell-ringer. He caught her hands in mid-flight and managed to turn her entire body so that she faced away from him, and he from her, back to back like ornamental bookends, while maintaining his grip.

For all the sad passion of his bodily state, Marx couldn't help but feel invigorated by the encounter. It felt mutual and his partner less inclined to resist than carry on in pursuit of some shared goal. His behind was their main point of contact: their meeting point, so to speak. He let go of her hands and she stayed put, pushing her buttocks against his, which he took as his signal, the one warning of the momentum already built to the point of no return. Seconds later the entire bodily contraption set off like the Birmingham Dribbler. The thing didn't locomote very far and what counted for the motion consisted of a single piston hitting its stroke. The pressure mounted rapidly towards cut-off. Marx felt a low rumbling, which sounded like a real train and alerted him to mortal danger.

'Mind out!' he yelled, but the locomotive rumbled on regardless and maximum torque was rounded off by his son riding over his foot. He stayed there for a time with his trousers round his ankles, listening to the raindrops landing in the bucket, and finally heard himself announce, to no one and for no particular reason, 'It's fine. Everything's fine.'

After the intercourse had finished Marx went to lie down. Helene came in a few minutes later but didn't say anything. She covered herself with a blanket. When Marx tried to pull it across his legs, Helene wrestled it away and turned onto her side. He felt an overwhelming impulse to console her, but thought it better to wait.

It was a long time before either of them uttered a word. He wondered who would speak first and if they would ever speak again. Some more time passed, during which he tried to gauge precisely the transitioning of day into night.

Helene put on her stockings and shoes, and left the flat, which Marx read as his instruction to prepare what had to be said and done. But it was impossible. He could barely move for one thing—the carbuncular pain radiated out from its source and filled the entire room with bad energy—and as far as saying anything was concerned, anything beyond... well, what was there to say? I'm sorry, Helene? That was sure to be met with her usual contempt for mealy-mouthed excuses, and rightly so; although, he could have made it sound sincere. In any case she deserved an apology, if not for this one appalling incident then for the series of more minor ones stretching back some considerable time, and which *culminated* in this one. If rightly contextualized then the apology could carry the proper weight. Although that hardly solved the problem of critical mass, the transformation of quantity into quality. If he could solve *that* conundrum then not only would he be able to offer Helene a genuine apology, but he could also finish the damned book.

Deranged laughter echoed along the street. Was he being mocked? Was it all a game? All those facetious moves chipping away at his integrity. There was a great clamour, a scuffle, followed by what could have been a skull being cracked on cobblestones. The random violence of a pure decision? Or that of a mortal necessity? Marx pinned his hopes on the former, lest the creature out there rivalled Helene, possessed of a diabolical will. Better he face it now than wait 20 years for the arrival of her offspring, the estranged son come to wreak vengeance on the father. When he heard Helene's footsteps on the stairs he knew it was time.

'Lenchen?' he said.

She froze on the threshold.

'Frankly… I am ashamed. Lenchen… I have acted abominably. It must have been a moment of pure madness. I shall spare us both the indignity of my trying to explain it. That would be quite wrong. Expect no weasel words from me. I detest hypocrisy and you know how much of a dreadful hypocrite I can be.'

There was a knock at the door. It couldn't have been Jenny. Marx held his breath, hoping whoever it was would go away. He thought he detected sobs, but couldn't bring himself to look Helene in the eye.

'I admit things haven't been easy since we left France.' He corrected himself: 'Since we left Belgium.' He corrected himself again: 'Since we left Germany, I mean.'

Helene made a noise like stifled laughter. Marx tensed. He was making it worse.

'If I could change things then I would… in certain respects. You may think me wrong for having made certain decisions. I know you do. But as wrong as they may have been — in certain respects — they have brought us to this place and we have lived by them. I never had a crystal ball. I always made decisions in circumstances that were not of my own choosing. They may have turned out wrong, but they were not all bad. After all, we had the children…' That sounded wrong. 'What I mean to say, Helene, is the children have been blessed with three parents. Three… sources of love and affection. My parents…' He had no idea where this was going. He changed tack. 'I mean, when parents love their children, they… often they…' Marx stopped abruptly. He was confusing himself now.

'Moor,' said Helene.

Marx braced himself.

'Would you like me to wash your anus?'

Chapter 26

'You must be freezing!'

'Yes. I might lose a limb to frostbite.'

'Oh, no! Don't say that.'

'I'm joking. Stop wasting time and jump.'

'No, I'm fine. It's all right. I've changed my mind. Shall I see you back at the hotel?'

'Don't you dare!'

'I think I'll go for a bath instead.'

'Cease with your games and jump. *Springen!*'

'I love it when you talk German!'

'Jump!'

Swimming off the West Pier was prohibited in summer, whereas in November it was simply unheard of. There was little precedent for prohibiting things that no one would ever think to do. The idea had come to Jenny quite by chance. She had packed a huge trunk at the behest of her husband on the understanding that she wouldn't be returning to the German Hotel. Wrapped in a ball and quite forgotten about was the bathing dress she had worn five years ago on a weekend trip to Ostend. Laura had not long arrived in the world and Jenny was determined to reclaim her figure from motherhood. The bathing dress was a gay outfit: a red polka-dot petticoat on the top half and matching knee-length bloomers.

'Is it me?' Jenny had asked her husband in the hosier's.

'Ha! You look like a doily. Take it off.'

'I was hoping you'd say that. In which case I'll have to bathe *nudo come mamma ti ha fatto*.'[42]

'In which case you'll get us arrested,' said Marx, lowering his voice.

'You'd enjoy that, wouldn't you?' said Jenny, raising hers.

The lieutenant had responded meekly, as he often did when

Jenny spoke; although on this occasion the word "bathing" seemed to impact on his pretty little moustache and petrify the poor creature even more than its owner, so that it no longer danced in time to the rhythm of his words and acted as if it might take leave of its perch altogether.

'I... think... it would be...'

'Too cold?'

'No, no... I don't mean that.'

'What, then? Too warm?'

That morning a silver-haired gentlemen had seized the lieutenant by the sleeve at the foot of the stairs.

'Look here, sir,' said the man through his teeth. 'That woman of yours is causing a frightful stink — frightful. Singing and dancing and bawling and screeching like some... lunatic. I don't know. Foreign? Huh. And,' the man tightened his grip, 'yesterday evening my wife informs me that this... *female* of yours was cavorting *naked* — by God! — in the upstairs corridor at some *wretched* hour. No woman of mine... well — I just wouldn't tolerate it. Huh. Eh? Not for a damned second.'

The lieutenant had been appraised of the "cavorting" in real time, which had resulted from his forfeit for losing a game of chess. However, the "female" dimension wasn't strictly part of the forfeit.

'Why should men have all the fun?' Jenny had declared, then streaked the length of the corridor singing *God Save the Queen*.

It was just as well the man's wife hadn't seen the lieutenant, too.

'First of all, sir, for your wife's information — and yours — the "woman" in question is not "mine". And, second of all, neither is she a woman. She's the Baroness. And,' the lieutenant seized the man's other hand, 'kindly note that I'm in love with her.'

The lieutenant's unruly moustache overcame its wearer's modesty and finally gathered itself into a harmonious smile.

'Baroness, I think bathing with you in November would be a

delightful opportunity too good to miss.'

The water beneath the Brighton pier moved in an unpredictable pattern. It was difficult to decide which part of the unruly monster to aim at.

'What are you waiting for?' said the lieutenant, undulating wildly.

'It's too high,' said Jenny.

'You're too scared!'

'Nonsense!'

'So jump. Do it for queen and country.'

'It's not my queen! Or my country!'

'So jump.'

Jenny began to count up in the faint hope of divine intervention. 'One, two, two and a half... God save the queen and the fascist regime!'

She hurled herself into the air and the waves came hurtling toward her. The pier was higher than she expected—15 feet, 18, perhaps—and panic overtook her at the point where the water should have been, and she gasped for breath. The waves churned in a savage rhythm and just before they rose up to break her fall, disappointing her leap to the horizon, her mind contemplated a little prayer, something worthy of the event; a catechism. *Dost thou not think that thou art bound to believe, and to do, as your Godfathers and Godmothers have promised for thee?* — Well, probably. And if I don't live to regret this act of madness, then I pray to continue living the life I want to live forever and ever, so help me God; though don't help me now unless I ask you to—and beyond that, sometime in the future when I've lost the will to live and need some faint glimmer of hope to cling to.

The water wasn't a shock to the system at first and was barely palpable, a light foam floating on air and caressing her feet, before the whirlpool engulfed her whole body and sealed it in a most uncanny place, a kind of echo chamber for crazed ideas.

Gravity took over and she briefly felt the weight of the sky on her back as the tide surged through her, pushing and pulling and turning her upside down and inside out, and she couldn't see or hear a thing for a small age.

'Swim!' urged the lieutenant as she beat at the waves uselessly.

'I'm trying!' she spluttered.

The beach remained where it was, a matter of fact unrelated to the sea, which was once the element of her ancestors. A V-shaped formation of moorhens entered her field of vision. It made her long for home, wherever that was. The horizon dipped sharply. A wave washed over her, then another, and on the third she touched the flint of a steep trough, which seemed to descend vertically into a dark bottomless well. Only then did her body encounter the source of the folly: the water was absolutely freezing.

She gasped for air, but the reflex action of her lungs had already stopped. She surrendered herself to fate before briefly regaining her senses. The tide went heaving out, but she managed to steady herself just in time for the earth to crash into her again, landing her back in her preferred element.

'Did you see the fish?' cried the lieutenant, who was already wrapped in his robe.

'Fish! I didn't see a thing!'

'They were jumping. I think they were trying to communicate with us in their animal language.'

'No doubt. "Dear people! You are safer on dry land! Go there and don't come back!"'

'Yes! Well said, you mighty intelligent animals.'

He offered Jenny his hand, and she came forth on tiptoe tottering and flinching from the pebbles.

'Here,' he said, holding out her robe, 'you look as white as a ghost.'

'Oh, good,' said Jenny through chattering teeth. 'That's what I'll tell Karl—' She checked herself, but from the look on the lieutenant's face he hadn't heard; either that or couldn't have cared.

He took a moment to take her in, from the matching statuettes of her porcelain feet, to the radiant contours of her figure, to the dark veil of hair hanging down by her side like a length of rope. She nestled into him, sheltering in a blind spot and fixing her gaze at some abstract point on the horizon, where everything had slowed down and was barely moving. She waited until the little creature brushed her cheek before turning and raising her hands, grasping its wearer by the jowls. They embraced, merely grazing one another, then turned to face the sea. They repeated the action and separated again, as if the motion of their bodies, despite seeming to be part of everything else around them, were uniquely related.

Jenny and the lieutenant spent the rest of the afternoon in his room. It was more luxurious than hers and twice the size. The reality of their relationship could be inferred from this discrepancy. It was a story of male privilege. This made her doubt the persuasiveness of her deception. She felt a pang of guilt, which made no sense, since she hadn't set out to impress her partner. She certainly didn't owe him a debt of gratitude. He couldn't possibly have known she was married. But even if he did he wasn't so churlish as to punish her for a deception that he was party to.

Ultimately she decided that White didn't need a room quite so large. Perhaps the room told a different story. Perhaps he had planned to sleep with the Baroness all along. Had he booked the room following the reception at his apartment? Even before then? Their carnation encounter was a story unto itself. The hidden stairwell in the Burlington Arcade left little to the imagination. It had been spreading rumours all over the West End like a bout of cholera.

Perhaps she was the consolation prize for a botched affair. An affair with a Burlington lady was botched by definition.

Their contribution to romance was a polished mirror. Burlington ladies were paid to carry mirrors around. They never appeared from behind them, never appeared in their own right. They were shields against Eros, blocking men's desires from reaching their "true" targets. Of course, there were some men for whom the "lady" in the mirror was all they truly desired, fully conscious, even reassured, by the absence of the female gaze. Jenny hoped the lieutenant didn't belong to this last category. After all, romance was one thing, whereas masturbation was quite another.

'I didn't know my mother,' he confided as Jenny contemplated the minarets of the Royal Pavilion. 'She was from Saxony. Did I tell you? She met my father during one of his excursions. He was trying to set up a textile business overseas. He couldn't get on with the government there. "Damned crooks!" he used to say. Europe was impossible for foreigners in the olden days.'

'The revolution,' said Jenny distractedly, remarking how odd the royal palace looked when viewed upside down.

'You might call it that. I prefer to call it "riots". My father had to flee for his life from Dresden.' The lieutenant jumped up from the bed as if riven by the memory. 'The stories he told me were frightening. Things calmed down eventually. But by that stage he had already fled the city with my mother.'

'He was her prize,' said Jenny.

'Prize?' said the lieutenant, somewhat mystified by the thought. 'Why, he loved her. Isn't that enough?'

'I didn't mean to sound callous...'

'Love,' declared he, staring wistfully out of the window. 'We must seize it with both hands. If we lose love then civilization is doomed.'

'Is that what you're fighting for when you go into battle?'

The lieutenant reflected for a moment. 'In a manner of speaking, yes. Why? Is there anything nobler?'

White's passionate convictions excited Jenny. They were his

standout quality. If she were being honest with herself it was his youthfulness that attracted her most. The convictions were the clothes on an already attractive model. In Ancient Greece, White would have been an excellent soul; a tragic hero like Oedipus, who murdered his father and slept with his mother.

'What about the people you're fighting against? Those people who end up poor and homeless. War is a frightful waste.'

'The people who criticize war are usually those who have never experienced it.'

'Luckily for them.'

'And as abominable as it may be,' he went on, drawing her body to his, 'where would our nations be without war?'

'Alive?'

'Dead! In the dust!' White gazed intensely into his lover's eyes. 'Why, where would Europe be had its governments tried to appease Napoleon?'[43]

It was a telling example. Jenny had grown up under Napoleon's Civil Code and throughout her childhood had been taught to respect its founding principles. Without Napoleon, life would have been far less just, or simply unjust. Defeating a dictator such as Napoleon was the universal principle that Napoleon himself should have endorsed.

'I suppose you must be right,' said Jenny, if only to appease him.

She and the lieutenant prolonged their horizontal adventures whilst the children played in the corridor. She thought it better they played out there, where she could hear them, rather than in their room. When the lieutenant mentioned his exchange with the silver-haired bigot, she had insisted on it, instructing her daughters not to take any notice of the nasty old man and his wife, and to make as much noise as they pleased, the more the merrier.

'What about the Great Fear, girls?' said Jenny, to cries of approval.

She should have felt sorry for his wife, but on reflection had no sympathy for her. Women bore a duty to remain married in spite of their own feelings, which was deplorable. But that hardly entitled them to other people's sympathy. Jenny certainly didn't want any. She demanded respect, naturally, which included decent clothes. But to make a woman the object of sympathy was to assist in her public humiliation. Perhaps her husband's manifesto had it right, after all. Marriage in this world is nothing but a system of organized prostitution, both public and private. Mind you, Engels had written that part.

The lieutenant was an athletic lover. She expected as much. How could this swashbuckling Ares be anything less than magnificent? He tantalized her. The Baron used to tell her a story about a rich heiress, who married a younger man only to discover toward the end of her life that she had imagined it all: the man had never existed. Heaven forbid that White should turn out to have been a fantasy.

'But how could *she* exist then, Father?' Jenny had demanded.

'Well, of course, physically there was nothing wrong with her.'

'But she must have been mad!'

'Not exactly. As far as she was concerned, the husband was there.'

Jenny's interpretation of the story probably departed from whatever moral lesson her father had wished to convey. The Baron was like that. Perhaps it was meant as an apology for the rights of the criminally insane. Or perhaps it was a lesson in moral relativism. Far be it from any woman—or man, for that matter—to criticize the moral fibre of any other. All women should be grown up enough to live with themselves and the choices they make: for better or for worse, for richer, for poorer...

'Is there anything more I can do for you, Baroness?' said the lieutenant, in a state of mild exertion.

Jenny tried to give the question the attention it deserved, but couldn't think above the din. Her children were the cause of the disturbance. The sound from the corridor suggested that their class war games had enlisted several new recruits. The Great Fear involved a good deal of fuss and in Jenny's mind always spoke more about the activists than it did about *what* they were actually fighting for.

But the lieutenant could stop calling her "Baroness", for a start. She had already voiced her irritation, but clearly the moniker appealed to whatever fantasies he harboured. She had probed, gently at first, seeking a mature explanation for it, but he had put up a barrier guarded by a mother, who Jenny certainly wasn't going to try to compete with or impersonate. Some barriers were put up for good reason rather than simply to appeal to one's fantasies about oneself.

Chapter 27

There came a knock at the door and this time Marx rose in a new frame of mind. His sense of shame lingered. But Helene's handiwork had channelled those negative feelings in such a way as to bring about a novel set of forces and relations. The pain hadn't so much been destroyed as repurposed.

Even though it was pitch-black outside, Marx could see colour everywhere and detect phenomenal minute contrasts as if everything around him were being viewed under a microscope. But it wasn't to do with the infinitely small, where *every portion of matter can be thought of as a garden full of plants, or as a pond full of fish*, and *every branch of the plant, every part of the animal, and every drop of its vital fluids, is another such garden, or another such pool*. There lay the road to madness. He grasped the substantial forms, the modes striving to attain perfection only through themselves. As Helene's hand had crossed the dentate line and ventured up toward the Columns of Morgagni, the arrangement had surpassed pleasure and pain, good and evil. He and she. Once the new society had been attained free association would collapse such philosophical distinctions, would render all such "properties" redundant, since that was all they were, in essence: properties. Which, in essence, was not what they were.

'Dr Marx?' said the man at the door.

'Who are you?' he replied, adjusting his trousers.

The man removed his hat. 'My name is Dr Weiner and I'm in London on an urgent family matter. Please forgive the intrusion, Doctor. I'm trying to locate my brother, Heinrich. Our father fell gravely ill two weeks ago. He must be alerted to the news right away and brought back to Berlin.'

Marx blinked at the man, who was dressed matter-of-factly in a dark suit. He wore a thick moustache and wire spectacles, behind which were very narrow eyes. There was a badge on his lapel with writing on it too small to decipher.

'How did you find me here?' enquired Marx.

'Your landlady mentioned that a "Dr Mark" had just moved in to number 64. Previously I was told by several German artisans that you were a most helpful man to know. Trustworthy and considerate; a respectable gentleman. The men are all refugees and claim to have received financial assistance from the German Workers Society, of which the good doctor, I was informed, is one of the principal organizers. My brother knows of the Society's activities and wrote to my mother about it in one of his letters. He says he attended some of its meetings.' The man held out his card.

'Helene! Bring my loupe, will you?'

'In the course of my enquiries it was also brought to my notice that the *Manifesto of the Communist Party*, that landmark of socialist literature which, if you'll forgive the comparison, stands alongside the works of Saint-Simon, Weitling, Cabet, Owen, Fourier, to cite—'

'Yes, yes,' said Marx, 'don't overdo it.'

'—only the principal names,' the man went on, producing a copy of the green pamphlet from inside his jacket, 'was authored by the very same Karl Marx. Indeed, you can imagine the sense of pride I felt in knowing that my own brother must have made his acquaintance... Please forgive the intrusion, Doctor,' the man added, pausing to take a breath, 'I'm not long arrived in the country.'

Helene brought Marx his loupe and he examined the man's card, first up close, then at arm's length, like a botanist inspecting a flea-ridden specimen.

'My "influence",' said Marx, in a stately voice, 'does not extend to every workingman in whose circles I pass. Moreover, the Society has scores upon scores of members and I'm no longer involved in its day-to-day operations. In any case, I've never heard of your brother.'

'But maybe—'

'So I'm afraid I can't help you, Dr Weiner.' Marx handed back the card. 'Perhaps you could enquire at some of the local hostelries.'

'Might I—'

'Dr Weiner,' Marx interrupted, making his way to the table, 'it's getting late and I had intended to work. The night is when I work best. Less distraction.'

'Oh. Why, of course. Only...' Weiner peered out the window. 'What?'

'It's such dreadful weather and I was wondering... might I wait here? Just until the rain dies down. If it's not too inconvenient for you, that is.'

Marx heaved a sigh. 'This is London. I fear you may be in for a long wait.'

Helene took the man's coat and handed him the three-legged chair.

'You said you were from Berlin...' prompted Marx.

'Indeed.'

Marx picked at his quill with a kitchen implement. 'And what did you do there?'

'I was the editor of a medical newspaper.'

Marx broke off his vague activity. 'A *medical* newspaper? Which one?'

'The *Berlin Journal of Revolutionary and Social Democratic Medical Ethics*,' said Weiner.

Marx nodded. 'Never heard of it.'

'It was very underground,' said Weiner.

'Really?'

'Indeed. And revolutionary.'

'I see.'

'When the Prussian authorities learned of my involvement in it I was dismissed from the university.'

'Is that so?'

'It is.'

'I know several people at the university,' said Marx, approaching Weiner, who was most determined on staying upright on the three-legged chair. 'I dare say we share several acquaintances.' He leaned over him. 'Tell me, Weiner...'

'Yes... Doctor.'

'What would you recommend for the treatment of haemorrhoids?'

Thunder rattled the windows. The eye of the storm was still some way off, but it might have been heading straight for the house. The tempo of the water dripping into the bucket increased from allegro to vivace.

Weiner eyed Marx awkwardly. 'I'm afraid I'm not specialized in—'

'Arses? Come now, Weiner,' he cut in, unable to contain himself, 'we both know Berlin's full of them,' and let out a volley of laughter.

The man balancing on the chair remained impassive. 'Is there no one in London who can help you, Doctor? A professional gentleman like yourself must have numerous acquaintances.'

Marx looked down his beard at the man. 'Medicine is an expensive business, I need hardly remind you. I could paper these four walls with the bills I've racked up. House doctors always see me coming. I swear they look at me and mistake me for a pound note. In the meantime, my complaint festers on account of their "business".'

'"The bourgeoisie has stripped of its halo every occupation hitherto honoured and looked up to with reverent awe. It has converted the physician, the lawyer, the priest, the poet, the man of science, into its paid wage labourers",'[44] said Weiner, quoting the author's own words back at him.

Marx smiled. 'I see we're on the same page, Doctor.'

'Indeed we are,' Weiner affirmed.

'So! Perhaps we could assist each other after all. Dr Weiner, this is a rather... *delicate* matter. I suffer from aggravated skin lesions, mostly in the anal passage; though they have been known to grace my body in other areas about the torso, armpit, lower back and occasionally the face. All surgical interventions have failed to contain their stubborn persecution, whilst doctors and apothecaries have all proved themselves resoundingly incapable of offering me anything in the way of systematic pain relief. You may also be aware from your inquiries, Doctor, that I am currently completing a major theoretical treatise of crucial importance to the German Society and its members. The progress of the treatise is inversely correlated, so to speak, to that of the lesions. Ha! You'll forgive the comparison,' said Marx, picking up an orange, 'but the workingmen have been called worse in the European press.'

'Indeed you have,' retorted Weiner.

Marx frowned. 'What I am *saying* to you, sir,' he went on, peeling the orange, 'is that I have reached a decisive juncture in the development of my ideas. Or rather,' Marx corrected himself, chewing on a segment of the fruit, 'in the development of the *manuscript*!' Marx pinched his nose hard. 'It's a question of *stamina*. Wrestling with such unruly animals... Well! I wouldn't wish it upon my archenemies. Maybe some of them. There are greater tortures, mind. I can't presently say what they are.'

'Dinner's in five minutes,' said Helene.

Weiner forced a smile, unsure of how else to respond, or which response would result in the least chastisement, since the abstract ravings of his maniacal interlocutor seemed possessed of a logic all their own, while the man making them was a pure enigma.

'I see,' he managed.

'Really, Weiner? I fear not. I fear you do not see the *gravity* at stake. I'm not talking about the odd flash of inspiration; I could write another *Manifesto* in my sleep. No. I am talking about a systematic work that penetrates to the very core of the bourgeois society, that grasps the real movement, the development of the social forces and relations of production as a finite mode in the universal scheme of things. To put it bluntly, Doctor, the world in *transition*: from capitalism to communism. Change! Notwithstanding that "thing" in between.'

'Dr Marx?'

'Dr Weiner,' he replied, unbuttoning his trousers, 'I cannot journey there alone. I cannot penetrate to that "thing" in my present condition. There are hills and valleys and great mountains obscuring the view. And yet—and yet...!'

'Dr Marx, please—'

'They are the very mountains I need to climb in order to see it all. And at which point, if my dialectical intuitions are proved right, we will arrive finally at our common destination, in the very midst of that place where the thing is the thing. Let us stop beating about the bush, Doctor, as the English say. I wish that you conduct a thorough exploration of my anal passage and afterwards prepare me a medicine best adapted to the treatment based on your prognosis. My constitution won't tolerate a further surgical intervention at this time—time being, quite naturally, my overriding concern in all of this. I simply cannot spare a single day in my schedule. If you do this then I guarantee I shall have your brother found within 24 hours. Now, if you please,' announced Marx, dropping his trousers and bending over the table, 'to work.'

'Dinner's ready.'

Weiner froze. 'Dr Marx, forgive me,' he stammered, his eyes widening to reveal unusually grey orbits, 'much as it would be my... great *honour* to enter there...'

Marx turned to his physician in mild alarm.

'To, I mean, climb your mountain—' he checked himself. 'As one doctor to another, sir,' he began again, 'you do me the honour of trusting in my expertise.'

This struck the patient as an odd remark.

'Nonetheless, I cannot possibly commit to an examination on the spot without first garnering some more background information on your condition.'

'Very well,' Marx agreed, 'what do you need to know?'

'Past treatments. Doctors, apothecaries. You say not one of them was able to offer you effective pain relief.'

'Well. One of them,' Marx mused, '*supposedly* an apothecary... Ha! There lies a tale. Dietz!' He shook his head.

'Dietz?'

'Yes. From Berlin. I trust your medical training is better than his.'

'Dietz,' the other doctor repeated. 'I'm sure I must have met him. Where did he study medicine?'

'No idea. Look,' said Marx, shaking a bottle of the soothing balm, 'he prepares me these potions, but they scarcely do the job. It's little wonder given his party obligations.'

'Party?' said Weiner, very nearly toppling from his perch.

'Not exactly: the Communist League.' Marx thrust the bottle under the physician's nose. 'The problem with this stuff is it lacks the kind of viscosity—'

'Dr Marx, it's late and I fear I'm interrupting your dinner.' Weiner rose and his chair collapsed into a neat pile of firewood. 'I propose to conduct a thorough examination tomorrow. In any case my medical bag is back at my lodgings and I never practise without it.'

'Very well,' said Marx, pulling up his trousers. 'Helene, would you bring Dr Weiner's coat?'

'Before I leave, however, and since I have it to hand, perhaps you would do me the honour of signing your great *Manifesto*.'

Marx duly autographed the work, a novel experience given the obscurity into which it had fallen of late. Saint-Simon, Weitling, Cabet... The young cove was being facetious; although if he were really that desperate to find his brother then one could only hope that the latter had fallen into a very deep well, so that his return to Berlin might be stayed.

'Are you not eating?' asked Marx as he sat down alone.

'That's all there is,' replied Helene. 'You'll have to give me some money so I can go to market in the morning.'

Marx tucked into the food, a delicious beef stew with dumplings and vegetables, savouring every mouthful. In the centre of the table Helene had placed a snowdrop in a glass of water. A single flower. A peace offering. A settlement. Or perhaps something more.

'I'm off to the station to fetch Jenny,' said Helene in a burst of agitation. 'I'm late. Quick, come in here.' She led Marx into the bedroom. 'Guido's got a nasty cough, so keep your eye on him. He'll probably sleep, but if he starts coughing again you'll need to help him bring up the mucus. Do it like this,' she said, propping the child upright, 'and keep him there until it's all come out. He's already brought some up, but if there's any more you'll know what to do. And mind when you touch his tummy. Hold him under the arms like this.' She demonstrated. 'Have you got it?'

Guido looked at Marx quizzically. Although not knowing what to make of all the excitement, he was alert to the spontaneous transfer of powers.

'Argh!' said the child, pointing a worried finger at his father.

'It's all right, my darling. Papa's going to look after you.' She kissed the child on the forehead and handed him to Marx.

'Argh!'

Then she was gone, leaving him holding the baby. He watched her from the window as she bounded over the gleaming puddles and disappeared into the night. He thought he saw her turn and wave from the corner, but decided he must have imagined it.

She was a stunning specimen. Not beautiful like Jenny. But a formidable woman in her own right, whose capacity for bounding over puddles, making beef stew and being taken from behind by Marx she managed with the utmost proletarian dexterity.

The thought made him cringe. He had created a monster. The question now was: could it be caged? It was almost enough to revive some adolescent faith in the mystical power of the unknown. Mind you, wasn't that precisely what he was trying to determine with this magnum opus of his? The unknown?

Marx returned Guido to his cot and spread out his paperwork on the operating table. It was all here, everything. Everything and nothing. What a pile of nonsense! It was the first time he had taken a step back from the thing and really drawn a sense of the task ahead; apart from the other night, when he had gone into the operation with a different set of objectives. The other night had been a mere survey, a kind of quarantining exercise. But looking at *this* now, this... *train wreck* was enough to rob him of the will to live.

There were annotations upon annotations; notes in the "margin" so dense as to suffocate the main argument, which in any case had been rewritten over and over to the point of being indecipherable; references to articles that Marx either no longer had or couldn't remember having read; frequent random smudges and stains and cracks in the parchment itself, which in certain cases appeared to have been made deliberately; myriad caricatures (in Engels's hand) of Louis-Napoléon, including one of him being buggered by Heinzen; numerous banal "notes to self", stressing the importance of cooking as a model for writing. For example: "cooking well is not solely determined by a family's tastes", &c. As for the *content* of the work, aside from the List of Contents (which hadn't changed in months), it comprised a completely random collection of subjects (a wish list), which he had no firm grasp of and which, taken together, added up to a dog's dinner that no dog would dare touch. Namely, in order of appearance: the Great Fossil Lizard of the Thames Basin; the sexual dimorphism of crabs; the possibility of life existing on Mercury; the construction of piers; Kepler's two-body problem; Chinese versus Japanese syntax; mantra language texts in the

Yajur Veda; alienation; time travel; spiders in the Sahara Desert; fertility rites of the Pacific islanders; the mathematical concept of limit; the history of patenting in the United States; Balinese herbal remedies; the Jacobin legacy; the electromagnetic spectrum; the health benefits of tropane alkaloids; and pregnancy complications in cats. Cooking well was a question of taste. Why else would anyone want to eat the meal?

But then something else struck Marx as he recoiled in horror from the wreckage. The parchment was black, as black as the night. What was legible was only so at close quarters and only then with the aid of his loupe. In moving just a few inches from the page the text vanished. What had been written had at some point become more black than white as the space between the words and then the letters themselves dwindled. Only in this case there was virtually none of the white left and what little remained was at risk of being swallowed up by the ink, much of which was still damp and would only expand further still, thus sealing away his ideas forever. There was nothing for it but to copy out everything.

Lightning flashed and thunder rattled the windows. The storm was directly overhead. The tempo hit presto. Marx emptied the bucket and looked in on the children. They were both sound asleep. He refined his quill and contemplated the big oak table like a steamboat captain preparing to navigate the Congo River. He was in for a long night.

The tap-tap-tap of raindrops in the bucket did nothing for his concentration. The metronome might have been counting up or down. There were multiple suffering bodies within a mile's radius of the room. Marx had counted twenty shivering souls through the window of a downstairs flat earlier that evening. Multiplied by three for each house and 60 for the number of houses in the street equalled 3600. Multiplied by 10 equalled 36,000 for the quarter. Tap-tap-tap. There was a limit to how many raindrops the bucket could hold. But each one might have been a drop in the ocean. The sound combined in a delirious echo without rhyme or reason. It didn't help. The lightning flashed and the windows rattled, and this time the tap-tap-tap adjusted to the rhythm of clatters, rumbles and flanges on iron rails. It was the mechanical concert of a hidden code. Marx was back on the train.

The locomotive switched tracks hurling him into sacks of skin and bone. A welter of groans issued from the listless consignment of lost souls, the wretched of mind and body, ravaged by disease, war, poverty and hard labour. He righted himself and staggered on through the melee, passing through carriage after carriage of cramped cells, until he reached the ghostly compartments of bourgeois class, where space was at a premium but passengers were few.

He took a seat and contemplated the view. Something was happening out there that might have been monumental. But from in here all that registered was a remote turmoil. A mud-soaked plain revealed itself in a snippet of cannon fire. The panorama scattered and two life-size puppets tumbled down on wires: a rosy-cheeked Louis-Napoléon and a balding general in Prussian uniform.

The pair had been introduced into a clockwork diorama for some didactic purpose. There wasn't much subtlety to the display or complexity to its meaning. One battered the other with a wooden sword, then the other ran the one with a lance. A mousetrap dangled next to Louis-Napoléon, trapping then snapping off his arm.

The train rounded the bend and took on the treacherous terrain of the mountainside. The bridge with its middle span missing loomed. Marx exited his compartment and ran straight into the ticket inspector, knocking off his cap. Or rather, *her* cap.

'Tickets, please,' said Helene.

The uniform suited her and his first thought was one of relief that someone in the family was finally bringing home a wage.

'Quick!' he exhorted, 'the line's broken up.'

But Helene simply stuck out her chin and repeated the demand.

'Tickets, *please.*'

'Look! I haven't time for this—do you hear, woman?' and he pressed past her, only to be hauled back in her iron grip.

'I told you!' she screamed over the sound of the steam whistle.

The carriage lunged violently then hung in a state of sickening weightlessness. Marx came round hunched over the table in the front room. He must have been dead to the world, since he hadn't heard anyone arrive.

'Jenny?'

A figure appeared in the doorway. Something was gravely afoot. It must have been his wife. A candle on the floor threw a monstrous shadow against the wall and from its shuddering description Marx intuited the worst.

'I told you!' came Helene's voice again from the bedroom, only raised this time in a tortured howl, a heathen declamation directed at the gods.

Marx floated to the bedroom door. He regarded the scene, narrowly at first, in a concerted effort to filter out its bad part. But the image didn't yield to his will. He went to Guido's side and registered the lifeless corpse lying with its mouth open and head to one side. His wife's cherub-faced boy—the one destined to be a ballet dancer, whose every move his father would have idolized and cheered on from the balcony at Covent Garden whilst waving the red flag—was indeed dead. He touched the child's brow but felt nothing, not even the trace of his person. He must have been dead for hours. Marx felt a pain in his ribs and a noise in his ear, which presently served some narrative purpose.

'I told you to watch him!' sobbed Helene, lashing out again with her fists.

'I did,' protested Marx. 'I was checking every quarter of an hour, like you said,' but he couldn't be sure of it.

Mercifully the child hadn't suffered. The death had been sudden and couldn't have been prevented even if a team of physicians had been attending to him. Bauer had already been and confirmed as much.

Marx went to gather his son but Helene elbowed him aside. She thrust Guido's limp remains at Jenny, who clasped him to her breast and sunk to the floor. Then Helene began to repeat the same idiot mantra, 'I told you! Didn't I?' She circled the room in the fruitless panic of a caged animal. Fixing her eyes on Marx's paperwork she swooped on the debris, gathering up as many of the sheets as she could. Then, with a delirious cry of 'You're cursed!' she flung them out of the window.

Chapter 28

Guido was laid to rest the next day or the day after that. In the interim the house and surrounding neighbourhood fell into a state of limbo. People came in and out offering their condolences at odd times of the day and night. Marx should have known these people but didn't recognize a soul, apart from the landlady, which caused him no particular shame or embarrassment, managing his role as *paterfamilias* through instinct alone. Within hours he had borrowed two pounds from the Italian downstairs, despite having only asked for one, thus enabling him to retrieve his morning suit from the pawnbrokers and his wife's tailored jacket. How odd, he thought, that emotional turmoil brings with it clarity of purpose. Of course, he wasn't in total control of the situation. Far from it. Engels gave him the money for the coffin and the rest of the funeral expenses were made up in donations from the German workers, thus sparing Guido the indignity of a pauper's grave.

On the morning of the funeral the landlady was waiting at the foot of the stairs.

'I want you and Mrs Mark to know,' she whispered, taking Marx's hands in hers, 'that if there's anything you need — anything — then we will find a way.'

The cortege set off with Marx leading the wheelbarrow that carried his son's tiny coffin. The rest of the family filed behind, followed by Engels, Liebknecht and Schramm. Marx was heartened by the presence of several workingmen, including the wizened old chap from the Red Lion. They shook hands.

On reaching Whitefield's Tabernacle on Tottenham Court Road the party filed through a holly bush arch to a small patch of field circled by crows. Guido's grave had been prepared in the corner. It barely registered a graze on the muddy ground. However, on gaining the courage to peer inside, Marx instantly recoiled from the brow of a precipice. He was overcome by nausea and, retreating to the holly bush, brought up whatever remained in his stomach. On returning to the graveside he noticed bloodstains on his shirt.

The priest shook his hand, offered some consoling words and began his sermon after a brief incantation that the congregation repeated in halting English.

'This state and this society,' intoned the priest, 'produce religion, which is an *inverted consciousness of the world*, because they are an *inverted world*. Religion is the general theory of this world, its encyclopaedic compendium, its logic in popular form, its spiritual *point d'honneur*, its enthusiasm, its moral sanction, its solemn complement, and its universal basis of consolation and justification. It is the *fantastic realization* of the human essence, since the *human essence* has not acquired any true reality. The struggle against religion is, therefore, indirectly the struggle *against that world* whose spiritual *aroma* is religion. *Religious* suffering is, at one and the same time, the *expression* of real suffering and a *protest* against real suffering. Religion is the sigh of the oppressed creature, the heart of a heartless world and the soul of soulless conditions. It is the *opium* of the people.'[45]

'Amen,' affirmed the congregation.

Engels and Liebknecht lowered the casket on cords, and from that moment Marx began to experience the scene rather than witness anything real. He felt as if he were going down with the coffin. Then something unexpected happened: the world turned upside down. He reached out to steady himself, but it made no difference. He quickly adjusted to the sensation. Very soon the entire congregation was standing that way up, or down, or just suspended there. But in truth not really suspended at all, since nothing contradicted gravity.

The vault fell away and tapered sharply down a sheer cliff face to a point some distance underground. There, a great city populated by incongruous beings stretched across a vast plain.

Lower and lower the coffin descended into the bowels of the earth, passing through the circles of sin, exiting the state of Limbo, only to go through Lust, Gluttony, Greed then Wrath; Heresy, Violence then Fraud, finally coming to rest at the entrance to that ultimate well-pit guarded by giants, bound and chained, the Ninth Circle: Treachery.

He looked at Jenny. She was unflinching. Not a trace of sadness attached to her countenance as she held on to her sobbing daughters. It struck Marx then that his wife had a capacity for suffering that far exceeded his own. Her face wore an expression so noble, so replete with human dignity that he wondered at the cost. For everything, he knew, had its price.

As the sermon ended and the congregation drifted away, Marx stood by the graveside and asserted in the name of the providence that rules the universe that this was the end of it, and that henceforth every man shall be put to death for his own sin alone and no more: neither the fathers for the sins of the children, nor the children for the sins of the fathers.

PART II
FROM INFINITY TO ZERO

Chapter 1

London, April 1851

Within days the Marxes left number 64 for good. Jenny couldn't bring herself to sleep in the room where her son had died. Guido's death had made her ever more decisive. Marx understood the situation differently. It wasn't decisiveness that conditioned his wife's constitution. It was impulsiveness. She wasn't thinking clearly. She was in shock; in mourning. She needed rest.

But it was equally possible that everything Marx believed about Jenny was more a case of wishful thinking than reality and that when Jenny "suffered", it was because he believed she did or willed her to, for his own sake rather than hers. Perhaps it said something about the state of their marriage—or marriage in general—that the identity of the husband is defined through the wife or the mistress; and that the identity of the wife is defined through the husband or... who? Who was the other significant other in a woman's life?

'When a woman has a lover,' Jenny wondered out loud, 'what's the appropriate name for him?'

'Lieutenant White, of course.'

Jenny burst into a fit of laughter, which exposed her naked shuddering ribcage, the sight of which briefly compelled her partner to quit soldiering and join a monastery.

'No! I mean what's the male equivalent of a mistress called? Who would I be if you were a married woman and I were your lover?'

Had White been unaccustomed to Jenny's thought processes then he might have balked at the analogy.

'You're not my mistress. You're my baroness,' said the lieutenant, reaching across to kiss her somewhere about the ribcage.

A "gigolo", perhaps? Not unless mistress equated to "tramp" or "whore". But certainly not "master". In any case, some days after the Marxes moved into their new flat at number 28 Dean Street, Jenny ended her relationship with the lieutenant, deciding she no longer wished to be a mistress—or at least *his*—and congratulated herself for her decisiveness. Had Marx discovered the affair then no doubt Jenny's impulsiveness or decisiveness, whichever it was, would have been the least of their concerns; although the question itself was probably undecidable.

There were other changes afoot in the Marx household. On the fourth day after moving in Jennychen renounced the class war games, which came as a great relief to everyone, not least Marx, much of whose wardrobe had been expropriated by his daughter's Jacobin army in defending the Revolution. The mother was ecstatic.

'Karl, you'll never guess what our Emperor wants to do now,' said Jenny, clapping her hands in a flutter of excitement.

'Mmm,' he murmured from behind a mound of library books.

'She's going to be concert pianist! Can you believe it?'

'What?' was the father's curt reply, unsure he was hearing properly.

'You *know* how guilty it made you feel when the bailiffs took away her pianoforte in Brussels. Qui Qui was beside herself. Weren't you, darling?'

Jennychen shrugged.

'Karl,' continued the mother, 'I don't want you to be burdened by a feeling of failure any longer. We need to move on. But most of all, I don't want our daughter's dreams being frustrated any more. One only lives once. Now, I know there were issues last time to do with the piano tuner, the tutors and the fact that Qui Qui *never* practiced enough. Did you, sweetness?'

'Yes I did, *Maman*,' insisted Jennychen, who was playing chess with Laura.

'No you did not, my dearest.'

Jennychen stood up to make her point. 'Let me tell you really what happened,' she said, smoothing back her hair and adjusting her pinafore. 'Madame Veron was always giving me the Beethoven sonatas to practise on, which were *so* boring.' She counted out the sonatas on her fingers: 'Number 1 in F minor, number 2 in A major, number 3 in C major, number 5 in C minor, number 6 in F major—'

'You forgot number 4.'

'I did *not* forget,' replied the young musician. 'You know how I detest playing E-flat minor. *C'est comme ça.*'

'Oh,' said Jenny, slightly deflated. 'Well, never mind. I'm sure we can find you a more considerate tutor than Madame Veron. As for tuners, there must be dozens of them looking for work in your father's Society. Otherwise,' said Jenny, breaking into a smile, 'we can buy you a pony.'

'Yes! That would be splendid! I shall call him Robespierre.'

'And if it's a girl?'

'Robespierre. But only if I can keep him in the house.'

'Darling, you don't keep ponies in the house. They're animals.'

Marx listened to the conversation unfold in a state of utter incredulity.

'Jenny, at the risk of disappointing our pony-riding pianist, where do you suggest I find the money to hire a pianoforte?'

'Money?' The detail hadn't occurred to her. 'Why, I'll ask Uncle Lion, of course. Who else?'

'Uncle Lion is convinced that I was responsible for his shares taking a nosedive in the financial crash. He's no more likely to give us the money than he is to join the Communist League.'

'He might not give it to *us*. But he might if I tell him it's for our daughter. Cometh the hour, cometh the woman!' declared Jenny and with that, she packed her things to petition Uncle Lion in person.

She returned 10 days later from Holland with the tidy sum of 30 pounds in her purse, much to Marx's astonishment.

'But... how did you manage it? That uncle of mine's as mean as they come.'

'I have my ways,' said Jenny, enigmatic to a fault.

Marx was happy to leave it at that and no sooner was the money in his ink-stained hands than he was arranging for the hire of a Collard & Collard mahogany grand square pianoforte. It was rather old-fashioned, housed in a harpsichord case and lacking the new-fangled escapement action, which made it practically impossible to master the rapid playing of the modern works. Moreover, at six-feet four-inches long and two-feet nine-inches wide it took up considerable space in the front room, and infringed on Marx's meditation zone (an alcove by the window where he would pace and smoke his pipe).

Jenny managed to find a piano tuner herself. In fact, he was their old neighbour at number 64. At least he claimed to be a piano tuner. Marx was convinced he was smitten with Jenny and objected to him coming to the house, especially since he owed the man money.

'How am I ever going to manage our finances properly if you insist on reviving our debts?' Marx demanded.

'Karl, first of all, Francisco is not smitten—'

'Francisco? You mean you're on first-name terms with the Italian? Why, I should be... scandalized!'

'And,' Jenny continued, brushing aside the insinuation, 'if you wish to manage our finances properly and pay off the debt then I don't see why you don't do what everybody else does and simply *borrow* the money.'

Marx rolled his eyes. How little she understood. Credit was simply another commodity and perhaps the principal lever of primitive accumulation. Banknotes were merely the most widespread form of government IOUs. If he knew how to formalize the national debt then his book would be complete and their money worries a distant memory.

'I am not a bank. If I could print the money myself then I

would,' he replied, almost adding that a printing press would have been preferable to a pianoforte; though that would have been heartless (both together would have been better).

In any case the investment paid off. Jennychen's playing communicated great joy in the house. Even listening to the young impresario play scales was a delight, since Jennychen took "scales" to mean Bach. There was that moment in the Adagio in C major from BWV 564 where it moves from the Neapolitan sixths and quasi-pizzicato pedal into the Grave section, which Marx found simply devastating. Every time she played it he would put down his quill and swoon. It unblocked something in him; an aptitude for thinking the infinitesimals, together with the transcendental sublimity of the music, transporting him not on phantasmagorical train rides, but into the real-concrete and ad hoc historical grit of the *hic et nunc*. Butchers and bakers and bailiffs and fishmongers didn't enter the equation, and there was no longer any reason to worry about not being able to buy an infinite quantity of fish. But the renaissance didn't last and one morning in the second week of May, just when the manuscript seemed to be reaching some kind of completion, there came a knock at the door.

Chapter 2

'It's in the papers,' said Liebknecht, out of breath and handing Marx a copy of *The Times*.

"Communist Conspirators Arrested in Cologne", read the headline.

If Marx was out of the habit of attending Communist League meetings then it was for good reason. He had better things to do with his time, such as cleaning his fingernails and throwing scraps to pigeons in Trafalgar Square. But in light of the present emergency no amount of trivial pursuits appeared sufficient to prevent him from being dragged back to the Red Lion, which should have been renamed the Communist Knacker's Yard, for it had become the place where once noble beasts were laid to rest. *The Times'* article was only a column and the detail, not to mention most of the basic facts, needed corroboration. Someone had infiltrated the organization, resulting in a slew of arrests in Cologne.

On the short walk to the pub, Marx realized who that someone was. Nonetheless, attack being his preferred means of defence, he announced his arrival in the upstairs room at Great Windmill Street in the manner in which he meant to go on.

'I told you they were following me!' he declaimed in an opening salvo of recrimination. 'Why doesn't anyone ever listen to me?'

'Because you were being paranoid,' replied Engels.

Marx seized the only armchair and spread-eagled into it. 'But I was right, wasn't I?'

'I say,' said Liebknecht, 'I was thinking of getting a bacon sandwich. Can I tempt anyone else?'

'It's not a matter of being right,' replied Engels, who was dressed casually in a double-breasted frockcoat and light brown Manchester cloth suit. 'Paranoia is a delusional state and has little bearing on whether a man exists or not.'

Marx frowned. 'So what are you saying?'

'That's just me, then, is it?' Liebknecht observed.

'What?' said Marx.

'For the sandwich?'

Engels resumed. 'What I'm saying is that it might just as well have been anyone else following you.'

The point might have been flippant, ironic or profoundly spoken. Or all three.

'It was a spy!' insisted Marx, reaching out to strike the table, then deciding against it, 'not anyone else. You're making yourself sound ridiculous. Look, this Stieber[46] was on my back for months on end. First he was outside the hotel, then he was inside, then outside. He wouldn't leave me alone. He was following me all over the West End, everywhere I went. And you people just ignored it, pretended it wasn't happening. Bloody liberal-minded sceptics, the lot of you!'

'What do you mean "inside"?' said Engels.

'What?'

'You said he was "inside" the hotel…'

'The man was staying at the German Hotel! He was spying on me from his room, listening to everything I was saying. He must have been. Why, he was even taunting me, singing some dirge at all hours. I don't know what it was…'

'And how did he get hold of the party register?' said Engels.

Dietz[47] spoke up in his customary manner. 'As a point of order, gentlemen, might I suggest that we debate this matter under a separate heading pertaining to emergency resolutions? Otherwise I shall have to draw up a new agenda—'

'Fuck the agenda!' yelled Marx. 'I don't want to hear one more word about your lousy agenda! Am I clear?'

'Moor, can I suggest we adopt a more comradely approach?' Engels reached out his arms in an umpirely appeal for calm. 'Gentlemen, it's presumed from the few details we have that the party register provided this "Stieber" with the names and addresses of our comrades in Leipzig and Cologne. We need to establish how the register went missing from Dietz's lodgings. Dietz was burgled the week before. That's right, isn't it?'

'Indeed,' affirmed Dietz. 'The intruder broke in through the window and forced open my writing bureau.'

'And Marx believes,' Engels continued, 'that the spy discovered Dietz's whereabouts by spying on him or listening in.'

'Why, yes!' declared Marx, sounding vindicated. 'Or stole some paperwork from my hotel room. Or...'

'Or?'

'Or, well... You!' Marx blurted out, pointing the finger at Dietz. 'It's all *your* fault, this!'

Dietz didn't flinch. 'What Comrade Marx omits to say,' the acting chairman began, 'is that the impersonator turned up at my lodgings and presented me with this...'

He handed a sheet of paper to Engels, inscribed with the following words: *My arse is killing me. Send me the anal balm along with the party register at once. Karl Marx.*

'Oh, no!' Marx leapt to his feet. 'No, you don't! I won't stand for it! Do you hear?'

Engels offered Marx the sheet of paper for his inspection. 'That's your signature, is it not?'

Marx shook his head. 'Fred! Can't you see what he's trying to do? He's trying to dump me in the shit.'

'But the signature's yours? Just to be clear.'

Marx glanced at the note in Engels's outstretched hand. The signature appeared to be written on a sheet torn from a printed pamphlet.

'It might be. Who knows? It's possible, yes.'

Dietz interjected. 'Which is why, Comrade Engels, I handed over the party register, as instructed by Comrade Marx in his note, to the gentleman in question.'

'Give me that!' said Marx, snatching the note from Engels's hand. 'Look at this rubbish. Look!' He waved the thing furiously in front of Dietz. 'What about the rest of it? Does that look anything like my handwriting? Honestly? And how many times in the past did I ever send you a note like this by gopher mail?'

'Comrade Marx, I have dozens of them,' Dietz announced.

'Preposterous!' Marx retorted. 'I can't believe I'm listening to this. When did I ever employ an adult gopher?'

'By my reckoning not generally adult gophers, no. Children, in the main—'

'*Merci et voilà*. I rest my case,' Marx concluded, collapsing in the armchair and folding his arms.

'Children?' Engels sounded confused. 'You mean you're sending your children backwards and forwards to Dietz with the party register?'

'I don't know what you're insinuating, Fred. My son, I'll have you know, is growing in independence by the week. He... excels himself. He really does.'

'That being so, I'm not clear why you're in the habit of involving your son in party business. It's slightly... negligent.'

'I don't know!' Marx threw up his arms with the consternation of a worried parent. 'Perhaps the boy was intercepted. I can't follow him round the houses 24 hours a day, can I now? What I will say, however, is that the lad's streetwise. Christ! he knows these streets better than I do. Better than anyone! And he can spot a bailiff from 100 yards.' This admission was clearly a matter of some pride for the father.

'I rather fear we're straying off the point,' said Engels.

'Look,' said Marx, eager to refocus the inquiry, 'what do we know of this affair so far? What can be established? First: that Dietz *very naively* handed over the register to this Prussian meathead, which has resulted in the arrest of a certain number of our members.'

'Comrade Marx!' exclaimed Dietz, whose time-honoured

diplomacy was feeling the strain. 'I adamantly reject your insinuation.'

'Shut up! I haven't finished with you yet.' Marx went on in his forensic examination. 'Second: the breaking and entering of Dietz's lodgings *also* compromised the safety of a certain number of members. Now, since there are no witnesses to the break-in, we don't know if the robber was the same man as the spy or— correct me if I'm wrong—*how much* of what he made off with in each case led to all or some of the arrests.'

'What did he take from your desk?' enquired Engels.

'Letters in the main,' said Dietz. 'A notebook. A few scraps of paper. Nothing as comprehensive as a register, if that's what you mean.'

'Oh, "nothing as comprehensive, if that's what you mean",' imitated Marx. 'Comrade! Far be it from me to *insinuate* anything, but since there were no witnesses to your break-in, how do we know that *you* didn't just dispatch the information directly to Berlin?'

'Moor, please!' implored Engels.

Dietz hesitated as if struck by some fast-acting virus. 'I think... if anyone had wanted to give up the men to the Prussian authorities then he could have done so without going to the trouble of breaking in to my lodgings.'

'Or maybe you staged the break-in yourself,' said Marx, to a low murmur of disapproval. 'Eh?'

Engels cleared his throat and indicated to Schramm that he should strike the remark from the record.

'Comrade Marx,' Engels began, 'forgive me, but with all due respect, it seems that you may have acted a little carelessly in this affair. From what I can make out, Dietz has merely fulfilled a routine request from you—'

'Not me!'

Engels corrected himself, 'Or rather, the note received by Dietz and signed by you in your hand—'

'Oh, for fuck's sake,' Marx cut in, resignedly for a change. 'Look, it's all my fault. Is that what you all want to hear? *I* am responsible. Happy now? The Cologne lot are rotting in prison and it's all my fault. Why don't you minute that, son?' Marx goaded Schramm. 'Go on!'

'Don't minute that, actually,' said Engels. 'Moor, no one's seeking a confession. We just want to get to the bottom of it. That's surely reasonable.'

'Comrade Marx, if I may...' Dietz sounded a conciliatory note. 'Perhaps you could simply explain how this note came into being.'

Marx sighed. 'Fine. Very well. The Prussian came to my flat. I can't remember what he called himself then. Weiner: that's it.'

'The flat or the hotel?'

'Flat. We'd only moved in that afternoon. It was the day you were supposed to call round before leaving for Manchester. Anyway, the spy turns up claiming to be a general practitioner from Berlin looking for his brother. At first I said I couldn't help, but he persisted. He said he could make me some medicine but since he didn't have his medical kit with him, he'd come back the following day. He knew about me, who I was. He started waffling on about the *Communist Manifesto*, how it was a *chef-d'oeuvre* and blah-di-blah and would I sign his copy.'

'And that didn't raise your suspicions?'

'I was in pain. My mind was elsewhere. He caught me with my pants down. I'd just finished...'

'What?'

'Nothing. That's it. Anyway, he didn't come back. That was the last I ever saw of him.'

Engels leaned back in his chair and scanned the ceiling for clues. 'Well, I don't know. We'll have to organize their legal defence ourselves. No one in Germany's going to do it.'

Marx started. 'What do you mean "we"? You mean muggings here. How the *hell* do you expect me to finish my book with all this shit going on? Concentrate only on the book? The book and nothing else besides? Well? And now you want me to set up a legal department. That's what you're saying.'

An air of depression fell over proceedings. Marx got up and went to the stove. He poured himself a cup of coffee. It was stone cold and tasted horrible, but he drank it anyway.

'I've acquired some share capital in my father's business,' Engels said at last. 'Plus he's agreed to advance me some more cash to help renovate the house. I've decided I'm going to divert a fair proportion of it to Marx. It should be enough to cover all the extra legal work, and pay for postage and what have you; even employ a secretary to copy out documents. I can also do my fair share from Manchester. I don't have any outstanding career aspirations. The engine of our revolutionary enterprise is seated among us, gentlemen, in case anyone doubted it. We need to ensure that he stays on track. I think we can all agree, in light of this... unmitigated disaster, that we are reaching the end of the party's natural lifespan; and that the only logical thing left to do in the circumstances is to take a step back and let nature take its course. It's all up to you now, Marx. I can't guarantee you a regular salary. But I should be able to provide you with enough ready cash in order to keep your oil lamp burning and the hungry jackals from the door.'

'Might I raise a hypothetical point?' asked Liebknecht, at last returned in his quest for a bacon sandwich.

'Be as hypothetical as you like,' chimed Marx, 'seeing as we no longer exist.'

Liebknecht set down his plate on the table. 'I suppose it's more out of curiosity than anything else, and correct me if I'm wrong, but if Engels sends you money to help you write your book from his earnings in a capitalist enterprise, then wouldn't he be exploiting the surplus value created by his workers?'

There was a long pause, at the end of which Marx wrote something down in his notebook. It was a tiresome question, which required a painstaking reply and more energy than Marx could muster. The Communist League was dead. All that remained was the laying of its corpse to rest in the most dignified and efficacious manner possible.

Marx was no longer bound by the formalities governing a political organization. He no longer had to answer to Liebknecht or to any of the others. They could all mind their own business from now on. He was a free agent—albeit one still bound by another contract, the Contract of Contracts, the one he had entered into with Duncker. Not forgetting all the other contracts he had "freely" entered into over the years. Life was a pile of festering contracts.

Chapter 3

The next day Marx gathered the family together in the front room.

'It's going to be all change round here from now on,' he announced. 'I have some important news.'

Jenny's eyes glimmered. Marx never made announcements. Bad news tended to seep out like his wind. It had to be good.

'As you know,' he began, 'Engels has already moved to Manchester. Now, what that means is there's going to be a regular salary coming in from now on. It won't be enormous and it doesn't mean we can move house; not for the time being. But... all things considered, it's going to afford us a little more ready income.'

'What about Helene?' asked Jenny. 'I do hope this includes her. She needs money, too. She's been living in the same clothes for months.'

'Helene will have money for clothes,' Marx conceded, trusting that clothes were the only thing she needed money for. 'And the children can look forward to having a little more pocket money to spend.'

Jenny planted a kiss on the cheek of her eldest daughter. 'Did you hear that, darling? You'll be able to save up to buy your pony.'

'Can I have a pony too, *Maman*?' squealed Laura.

'Friends, if I could just hold your attention for a few seconds longer... There are certain conditions we all need to abide by in the changed financial circumstances. There are things I expect from all of you in return.'

Marx proceeded to explain that in between him pressing ahead and terminating the manuscript by the end of the month at the *very* latest, there was also the minor detail of organizing the legal representation for the Communist League comrades in

Cologne. It didn't demand any particular training or expertise, he said, merely legible handwriting, which Jenny and Helene definitely possessed, and Marx definitely did not. It occurred to him that so too did the children, especially Jennychen, and perhaps Edgar; although this last had concentration issues and would probably be better suited to his customary role as a courier, in this case ferrying letters and packages to the post office.

'I don't see why it falls to you to organize all this,' said Helene, folding her arms defiantly.

Marx erupted. 'Don't you see!' he cried, clutching his backside. 'The scoundrels have dumped this shit on me!'

His eyes bulged and his nostrils flared. A garbled diatribe ensued, most of which was unintelligible and punctuated by animalistic yelps.

After a time, he resumed in a monotone: 'There are certain obligations I must fulfil in order to be shot of the League's affairs and this is one of them. I'm not doing this because I care about these people. I'm doing it because it needs to be done. Some things in life just need doing. If someone doesn't do it then the thing doesn't get done.'

Jenny sighed. 'That someone is never just you. It's us.'

'We all have to earn our keep,' said Marx, which put paid to further discussion.

Jenny and Helene agreed to act as legal secretaries—a task that involved copying out affidavits, depositions and character references—on strict condition that Jennychen was left alone and allowed to concentrate on her piano-playing. That was fine by Marx. Edgar, however, was enlisted into making daily trips to the post office, which he did either by running as fast as he could to the depot on Long Acre or, when the situation was less urgent, riding there on his locomotive.

On setting out on one such mission he encountered the baker at the entrance to the house.

'Is that father of yours at home, son?' said the man, eager to settle one of Marx's innumerable overdue accounts.

'I ain't seen 'im, mister,' said Edgar, who then kicked the baker in the shins, snatched one of the loaves from his basket and scurried off down the street.

'My communist conspirator,' Marx dubbed his son after that.

Edgar was also his double agent. When he wasn't on a mission to the post office he would be out divining the word on the street and reconnoitring enemy positions. He also became a dab hand at ingratiating himself with the local shopkeepers and spreading false rumours among them regarding his father's health.

'My pap's proper sick,' he sobbed to the greengrocer one morning, to whom Marx owed 12 pounds and five shillings.

'Sick?' said the greengrocer, immediately roused to the state of his client's health. 'How sick?'

'Proper, like.' Edgar wailed a few times to get his point across. 'The doctor says if he don't eat plenty of greens he's going to d-d-d-die.' And with that the child burst into a flood of tears.

'Son, you take these cabbages home to your father at once,' said the greengrocer in a gust of benevolence.

'And loads of oranges,' added Edgar between the sobs.

By the time the artful dodger had repeated the routine with the butcher there was enough fresh meat, fruit and vegetables at the Marx house to last out the rest of the week and most of the next.

The house was a well-oiled machine: not exactly the printing press for banknotes that the master strategist would have preferred. Nonetheless, it was a fairly efficient one that first relied on Engels to appropriate the surplus labour of his cotton mill workers in the form of profit, pay himself a salary, extract a surplus from that sum and then send it on to Marx. Marx would then use it to pay the fixed and variable costs of his much smaller yet no less productive factory. The communist factory for the purpose of abolishing the factory.

The workers weren't as efficient as the atmospheric engines. There were times when Marx felt it would have been better if he and the women could have just kept going. That surge he felt at three in the morning when he put the snuff up his nose would only last so long and rarely took him over the edge. During daylight hours, Jennychen's piano-playing was an enriching tonic. She could buoy the mood with a Beethoven sonata. But none of them were machines and in any case, even if they were, there were limits to what could be done; albeit the very limits Marx needed to master if he was to complete his manuscript on time, since the capitalist society was nothing if it wasn't a question of limits.

'Your book, Karl,' said Jenny, replacing Helene in bed at seven o'clock in the morning after a night of copying out.

'What about it?'

'It's all a bit fruitless, isn't it? This capitalism,' she sneered. 'What does it actually amount to? It's all so vague. I know what a commodity is because I can see it. I can go and buy a scarf or a shawl—or could if you had enough money,' she giggled.

'And your point is?'

'My point is: where is it?'

'Where is what?' Marx snapped.

'Capitalism! Where is this *thing* of yours? Is it all around us? Is it in here or out there... or, where? Perhaps it's disappeared up your backside. Or is it just one of your fancy concepts?' Jenny remarked at her ingenuity. 'I often think you prefer invisible things to real things.'

'What you fail to consider is that they might both be the same thing.'

'But that's what I mean! You're obsessed with these ghost hunts of yours; always chasing after "things" that aren't there. If you can't see it and no one else can see it then why convince yourself it's there?'

Jenny's point was naïve but still rather persuasive, since she squeezed Marx's penis as she spoke in order to emphasize the *thing* itself.

'The point is to prove it's there,' explained Marx, who felt himself warming to his wife's position. 'And it is.'

'You only say that because you want to believe it's there,' insisted Jenny.

'No, it's because it's provable.'

'So prove it, then.'

'What do you think I'm trying to do?'

'Well, you should try *harder*,' she returned, squeezing him again for good measure.

His wife didn't usually touch him there. It was an understanding they had. She pinched him so tightly that he drew away for fear of what it might mean. But then, grasping her intent, he gave in to the demand. As she knelt over him and shook off her nightgown the dawn shadows scattered in a blaze of luminosity. She began speaking in tongues, her entire figure— menacing, furious—invested in some far-off incantation. Her cheeks flushed and skin shone, and her hair stood on end in a shock of electricity. It wasn't someone he recognized. Perhaps it was his chronic insomnia that reified the image before his eyes: an image of woman become flesh. There was no mistaking Jenny for another. But at no time before had he ever felt as distant from his wife. As much as it should have inspired him to see her like that it would demand more than a slight readjustment in his outlook before he could properly convince himself that any of this described his marriage.

Chapter 4

Despite the struggle of the Dean Street factory, seven out of twelve of the Cologne accused were found guilty of high treason. On 12 November 1852, they were sentenced to between three and seven years in prison. The defeat was compounded by a sharp downturn in Marx's fortunes when a few days later he received a letter from Duncker requesting that he repay the 100 talers that the publisher had put down on the manuscript, which was now three years overdue.

A flurry of letter writing ensued. Marx wrote back stating that the advance was 1500 talers, not 100, to be paid on receipt of the first draft. Moreover, he had never even received the 100 talers and requested that the publisher produce a receipt. The correspondence came back simply restating the firm's position: Marx was in breach of contract and was legally obliged to pay back the advance within 30 days. He responded by threatening the publisher with legal action. The situation was lamentable, but then what else could one do? It confirmed everything he had always said about the scurrilous and disreputable nature of the publishing profession. Never mind the money. What about some solidarity for a change! His entire family—including his children, one of whom was grappling with Beethoven on a substandard keyboard—was mortifying body and soul for the sake of communism, and all the publisher saw fit to do was start a war. The paradox was appalling; although since Duncker was only in the business of selling books the fact might never have occurred to the man.

It was also around this time that the true nature of the disaster hit home. The spy. It was all his doing. His intervention had orchestrated the dual collapse. The fiendish activity dating from the time of Guido's birth and culminating in the subterfuge at 64 Dean Street had been planned not merely to bring down the Communist League; that particular subterfuge was incidental. Instead, it had taken the form of an elaborate long-term persecution, one deliberately teased out over three years, for maximum psychological impact, and whose poisonous tentacles had reached inside Marx's house—his own house, no less!—which had precipitated the circumstances leading up to his son's death.

The spy was the most loathsome of criminals, beneath contempt even, and one could only wish for him an unseemly end courtesy of a backstreet cudgelling. Not content simply to steal the register of names and slither back to Berlin with the other snakes, the spy had set out to eliminate the communist movement in body and mind, slowly but surely disabling the intelligence of its chief theoretician the better to strike at the heart of its political organization. The revolution was frozen, only worse: it was dead and buried in the deep freeze of treachery.

Stieber. Who was he working for? The scheming cabbage Junkers in the Prussian Ministry of the Interior? Or did he have a direct line to the king[48] (who was probably being played by the Junkers)? Perhaps the king was playing them all (or thought he was). It was an unprecedented chess game that Marx was barely even aware of having played. If this were the model for future games then he would need a bigger board or a lunatic strategy, one that incorporated the world of contradictory things and relations. Kings that both were and were not kings. *Omnis determinatio est negatio.*

By and large the manuscript was all Marx cared about now. He would need to dig down to the wellspring of his reserves in order to put it to bed; although *merely* completing it was no longer an option. Satan's navel described his predicament perfectly: a centre without gravity. The book needed to chart the way back from that underworld, not by way of compensation for the League's destruction, but by way of imagining a completely new world. His book would not only need to advance a radical criticism of all that hitherto *had* existed; in other words, a critique of the bourgeois political economy. It would also need to pave the way for a new kind of economy, the proletarian economy, and for the new kind of human being capable of managing it.

Marx caught his reflection in the front room window. An affrighted specimen stared back at him. A wiry sponge sprouted from the patch of skin where his beard should have been; his eyes were red, his cheeks hollow and the wart had returned to his forehead. That imperceptible toppling over that lands the body in middle age from the prime of life had befallen him in an instant, depriving him of any sense of progress. Where had the time gone? But, more crucially still: what did he have to show for it?

The mere thought was enough to catapult him in the direction of the British Museum in a resurgent bout of panic. But barely had he made it to the end of the street when it dawned on him that he no longer had a publisher. The conflict with Duncker might also have done for his prospects with other publishers, in which case no amount of conceptual novelty would save his magnum opus, since no publisher would go near the work of an author in litigation. A serialization couldn't be ruled out. He was already receiving two pounds for each of his *New York Daily Tribune* articles. But a daily newspaper was hardly an appropriate outlet for a theoretical treatise on capital. The overhaul of the presentation was bound to compromise the argument to the point of superfluity.

'Afternoon, Mr Mark,' said the prostitute on the corner of Compton Street.

Who was this "Mark" fellow, anyway? No doubt a younger, more handsome and well-heeled fellow than he. A banker or stockbroker, perhaps. Or at least the woman's comely smile said as much. She sauntered up to him, hand on hip, a walking commercial transaction founded on the reproduction of her labour power. Supply and demand didn't enter into it. This was

Soho after all, and despite there being room for negotiation, fluctuations in price would average out over the course of her career.

''Ere my lovely,' said the sex worker, adjusting her cleavage, 'a thrupenny bit is all I'll charge yah, seeing as you're local.'

She was more attractive at close quarters. Her hair was naturally blond and glossy, stylishly fixed in a pomade. She had high cheekbones with a mole on one of them and wore a silk fichu over a pink bodice. Her debauchery was infectious, so to speak, somewhat in the fashion of Madame de Pompadour.[49] In fact, this woman of ill repute was almost radiant and could hardly be deemed desperate. For a fleeting second, the offer almost appealed to Mr Mark, whose sexual proclivities Marx might have been tempted to entertain, had it not been for the following unwelcome intervention.

'I say! Monsieur Ramboz!' The man had been running and it was only blurred vision that prevented Marx from responding in kind. 'Your boy ran off with one of my loaves last week,' said the baker.

'Oh,' was all Marx could manage. That was his boy all right.

'Indeed,' said he. 'Now, count me as the charitable type, which means I won't be adding it to your bill, providing you settle the account today.'

Marx weighed up his options. There was an alleyway across the street that he knew like the inside of his empty pockets. It was pitch-dark and uneven but, judging by the condition of the barrel-chested ape wheezing like a squeezebox, he could easily outpace him.

'Pardon me, sir, but that means right away. I know you're a respectable gentleman,' he added, clearly not knowing who he was talking to, 'much as it seems you've been doing your best to avoid me—'

'Do you mind?' interrupted Madame de Pompadour. 'We was getting down to a bargain before you stuck your oar in.' This shrill tirade did dispel further allusion to the court of Louis XV.

'Why, pardon me, duchess,' said the baker with an ironic bow.

'Go on and pardon yourself, mister!'

'Oh, fie-fie, madam!' retorted the baker, warding off the lady with an outstretched hand.

'You rotter!' she exclaimed and with that toppled from her elevated heels into the gutter. 'You meater! Go it!'

Marx, in no mind to expedite the lunacy, darted into the alleyway, successfully ducking the washing line that might have been set as a trap, slipped on the greasy entrails of an ex-animal, bounded over a barrel of tar, then clambered over the wooden fence at the end with the untamed enthusiasm of a military cadet completing an assault course.

'Oi! What the *fack* do you think *you're* doing!' demanded a fishwife floating her breasts in a sheep trough.

A rabid dog greeted Marx in the next courtyard, whose instinct to land its teeth in the intruder's backside met with the latter's determination to have done with the canine world. It was astounding what the body could do given the proper instruments. He clouted the mutt hard on the head with a metal dustpan. The animal showed remarkable resilience, a statement that might have held equally for Marx or the mutt.

'*Nec corpus mentem ad cogitandum!*' declaimed Marx, as if casting a spell; '*nec mens corpus ad motum!*' and he landed another blow to his rival's cranium, which sounded remarkably like the ceremonial gong at Wang's (he was working up quite an appetite with this); '*neque ad quietem, nec ad aliquid (si quid est) aliud determinare potest!*'[50]

Marx hit the bullseye again before hurdling another fence and landing unexpectedly in a walled flower garden. Potted geraniums and rhododendrons diffused giddy perfume and a row of boxwood shrubs were spaced out for planting. Marx hauled himself up from his landing pad and dusted himself down.

'Coffee?' said a septuagenarian.

It wasn't the word Marx would have chosen. But it would do. His host wore a thick pair of gardening gloves and stood brandishing a trowel. Her expression was strained and teeth clenched tightly as if in defiance of a creeping dementia. It might have been his presence to blame which, times being normal, should have counted as an intrusion. But then times were far from normal and in the grand scheme of things, when the history of the revolution came to be written, this mere footnote would count altogether differently, as the proof of some key proposition in his treatise (he wasn't planning a chapter on gardens; although he could probably add something to the appendix about them).

'Milk? Sugar?' enquired the gardener.

'Indeed.'

'Take a seat,' she said, showing Marx to the patio.

From here the street commotion receded to a distant hum. Marx reclined beneath the fan of a palm tree. Robins and blue tits bathed in an oval pond, and the scent of freshly dug earth and native herbs filled his lungs.

'What do you think of our hidden paradise?' smiled his host as she served Marx's coffee.

It was the ideal setting for drafting his communist treatise. But like any utopian idyll, it lacked a theory of transition. Eureka.

'More geraniums!' he enthused, gulping back his coffee in one, 'and a vegetable patch!' And with that he bolted through a doorway and on to pastures new.

Chapter 5

Back at the flat Jennychen was reciting Haydn.

'They're after us!' breathlessly Marx exclaimed, slamming the door behind him.

'Shhh!' said the child's mother. 'Once more, sweetness. *E nota bene un poco adagio*[51] for the second movement.'

'Quick! Do we have any more of that anal balm left?'

Marx bolted the door and as he spun round a tray of wine glasses went flying. He wasn't aware they kept wine glasses. They didn't any more.

'*Si, si, ovviamente,*' replied the daughter, '*e la cadenza durante tutto il pezzo.*'[52]

'Jenny!' Marx struggled in vain to intercede.

'Yes, darling, but not the third movement—'

'*Si, si—Rondò all'Ungarese,*' said the daughter. '*Non sono così stupido.*'[53]

'I say! Is anyone listening to me? Helene—'

'No! Absolutely not,' she replied from a rug in the alcove where the armchair had been until only this morning.

'You don't know what I'm going to say yet,' said Marx, even though it wasn't true.

'Yes I do and no I won't. I've just had a bath. That standpipe on the corner is on the blink again. I had to walk halfway along Wardour Street *four times*, if you don't mind. It took me an hour. And then! I had to go back later because we needed another bucket for the dinner—it's leek broth and *yes* it's gone cold again, just so you know. I'm tired and want to be left be. I've no intention of putting my hand up your backside tonight, so think on it. The last time I ventured up there I wound up with more than I bargained for—'

Marx relented. 'Fine, fine, you can spare me the sordid details. Jenny, bring the children over. I've an important announcement to make.'

'*Un momento!*'

'*Now*, please. And no, I have *not* bought Jennychen a pony. Is everyone here?'

'I think so, Karl. Unless you were *expecting*' —Jenny pretended to clear her throat—'someone else.'

Marx chose to ignore the innuendo. 'Gardens,' he began. 'What does that say to you?'

'Plants?' offered Helene eventually.

'Karl, our daughter is trying to complete Haydn before bedtime, so if you'd just make your point, *please*. I'm sure we've all got better things to do than play charades,' said the mother.

'Oh! if only for a little imagination. Look, it's not Hegel again if that's what you're thinking.'

'Thank the lord!' quipped Helene.

'No—look, forget it,' said Marx, becoming agitated. 'Forget gardens. Well! Don't forget them; we'll come back to them. It's far more straightforward, really. In fine.'

'Mummy, what's the Italian for "boring"?' chimed Laura.

'Hush,' said the mother, willing her husband to finish or run out of steam trying. 'What's all this about, Karl?'

Marx hesitated and for what felt like an eternity forgot who he was, let alone what he was on about.

'Is it about your *book*, perchance?' coaxed his wife.

'Of course it is! It is, yes!' and it all came back to him and he was off again. 'Forget gardens and think... fossil lizards. That's it! Creatures of the bog. Those giant, lumbering carcasses of yore: time. Or trains. Capital! Trains are better. Imagine you're travelling on one. And yet imagine you want to know *what time* you're due at your destination. Ha! How do you do it? How?'

'You—'

Marx interrupted. 'Oh, no! You can't.'

'You didn't let me—'

'Not on *this* train you can't, since what *I'm* talking about is your time of arrival down to the nearest fraction of a second, of a millisecond; of one millionth of a second; of one millionth of a billionth of a second. Needless to say the problem of approximation is where it lies: the problem. Hegel?[54] Why, the old bloodhound was snuffing out truffles in the dark—well, of course his dialectical reasoning was sound. But he was "limited", so to speak, in his time. In fine.' Marx coughed up a gob of phlegm and hawked it out of the window. 'But the limit—Kant calls it the *Grenzbegriff*—is *not* the restriction *in relation to which* the finite being thinks. Now. Granted, Hegel goes further. But how much? Well...'

'Karl, is this going to take long?'

'But *that's* what I'm talking about. Right *there!*' Marx screamed and very nearly punched the ceiling. 'Yes, I mean—precisely— that *is* the question.'

'*What* is?' Helene urged.

'How long's a piece of string? Why, it might be too long to measure should it turn out to be very, very long. Or—'

''Ow long is that, Dad?'

Edgar's question heartened his old man. The boy didn't ordinarily take much interest in his father's work; although Marx, too, was a late developer, in the sense that he didn't know how to answer the question either.

'Good question, son. Good question. Well...' Marx picked up a piece of charcoal and began writing on the wall. 'Think of it as bridging a gap. A bridge, if you will. A bridge we need to construct but can't until its span is determined with perfect precision.'

'Er... I doubt very much the landlady wants your pretty pictures on her walls,' observed Jenny.

'Too bad. We're out of parchment.' Marx resumed the lecture. 'The problem is not *length* as such. It's to do with the precision with which we approach the other side. It's the problem of reaching zero. What we call "infinitesimal" is the quantity posited by Leibniz as being smaller than any finite quantity without equalling zero. *Natura non facit saltus*? Ha! Madness, son. Contradiction! Leibniz gives us dy/dx for calculating the curve. But he treats quantities differing by a "mere" infinitesimal as being equal. Which leads to absurdities of the kind $dy \approx 0$; neither $dx = 0$ nor $dx \neq 0$; $dx^2 = 0$; $dx \rightarrow 0$; and...'

'Karl, this is all very interesting, but the children are tired, I'm tired, Helene's—'

'And! $dy/dx = 0/0$. The "quantitative" ratio wherein quantity can no longer be determined.'

Marx turned to Edgar half expecting to see the stirrings of a budding intellectual curiosity. But it was Saint Vitus, not Bishop Berkeley,[55] who moved this one's spirit and the cockney tearaway, in being allergic to grace, was bashing into the walls on his locomotive. The boy didn't know it yet, but history was on his side.

'You'll learn, son,' said the father, 'you'll learn,' and with that Marx was out the door and down the stairs shortly before bursting in again, then out again, then in again, then out and heading back to the British Museum; which, given the all-too-real possibility of bumping in again to his so-called creditors, he decided to approach by a circuitous route *qua* curve given by an algebraic equation, of which the hypotenuse of the differential triangle generated by an infinitesimal abscissal increment *e* is equal to the segment of the curve between x *and* x + *e*. Which was all so much *bunkum and balderdash* anyway, since for the curve $y = x^2$ it could mean, e.g., the infinitesimal hypotenuse between the abscissae 0 and dx coinciding with the tangent to the curve at the axis of abscissae between the two points *and* (dx, dx^2) lying on the axis of abscissae, meaning $dy/dx = 0/0$. *Contradiction.* Did he look like a walking indeterminate? So much for ideal magnitudes! It was all *madness* and as he bowled along Long Acre and passed the lunatic on the corner of James Street who thought he was Louis-Napoléon, and cut through Covent

Garden and the white veil of cloud on Bow Street rising from the depths of the Inferno, Marx felt sure he was on the verge of a great scientific breakthrough, not to mention a fundamental break with all existing philosophies, and that the days of this poor excuse for an earthly paradise were finally numbered.

Chapter 6

During the Enlightenment Jennychen played her pianoforte, Edgar rode his locomotive and the rest of the family played its respective parts in delivering Marx from the earthly paradise that wasn't, which they came to accept as the condition of disentangling each of their particular wills from their combined destiny. It went beyond enthusiasm, since the struggle for the book, which was a struggle beyond the book and for a normal life, increasingly passed off in the shadow of judgment, and in the fear of distraint and eviction. It had always been there. But if it happened again—as it had when their furniture was seized not long after moving in to number 28— then Marx feared for the integrity of his family and its general will, and without whom... well, without whom full stop.

The *chef-d'oeuvre* concentrated the mind. How was one to concentrate on anything else with *that* going on? Especially when it took the form of *everything* and when anything it had nothing to do with was also integrally related to it. Such was the contradictory reality the Marx family inhabited.

'Who are those men down there?' Helene would say first thing in the morning, a euphemism for "are they bailiffs"?

'It's no one,' Marx would respond, not even bothering to look up from his manuscript.

'Are you sure?' Jenny would ask, peering down at the handful of German workers, vagrants, autograph hunters, unemployed or just plain desperate who had washed up at their door that morning, pilgrims of an anti-Christ who evangelical lunatics would insist was about to save the world, of whom the man himself wanted nothing to do with.

'Who do they think I am?' Marx would mutter to himself, 'Emperor Nero? Mikhail Bakunin? I say!' he would call down to them, 'I don't do speeches from balconies. Please go away. I'm working.'

That would usually be the end of it.

When compared to other mundane challenges, such distractions didn't even rank as minor inconveniences. One particular morning, which serves as a model for the contradictory reality in question, Marx had woken up from the state of *not* being asleep, to be met by the experience of *not* having anything to eat or smoke, not to mention anything clean to wear, *no* money in his pocket and even *not* having anything to sit on. Helene was out; although *not* for the purpose of buying anything, since Marx hadn't given her any money. Meanwhile, Jenny was leafing through their ledger: a fine example of negative existence writ large.

'How much do we owe the butcher again?' she wondered out loud.

'Why?'

'It says five pounds three shillings and thruppence here, but I'm sure that can't be right.'

'Why not?'

'Well, because it can't be.'

Marx stood back from the wall the better to take in the differential equation he was applying to it, much like Caravaggio standing back from his canvass.

'That's a tautology,' he said, struck by the sublime beauty of his description of the continuity of functions.

There was something "poetic" about his reasoning; though no less savagely rigorous in his handling of Cauchy's notion of the infinitesimal. It was too early to say where it was going, however. After all, a brief appraisal of the rooms confirmed that he would very soon run out of wall space.

Jenny began to explain. 'Five pounds three shillings and thruppence for the butcher; 13 pounds three and two for the greengrocer; seven pounds seven and two for the baker; 17 and five for the ironmonger; seven five and 11 for the fishmonger; two 17 and 11 for the grocer... Now,' she said, slipping the buttons of her cardigan between jaundiced fingers, 'where was I? 31 for the rent; 67 and five in loans, 19 of which—note *19!*—you told me not to count, but I have anyway—and not forgetting the seven we owe Francisco; the 23! you owe Wolff—don't forget you said you could squeeze more out of him—the three! from Liebknecht—I'm counting it all regardless—the 23 three and seven and I can't even read whose name that is; the seven and 13 from the pompous arse who tried to seduce me in Hyde Park and the three from his wife—as did she!—and—last but not least...' Jenny played a crescendo on the piano, 'the 11 *and a penny* we owe the piano tutor.'

Marx could scarcely fathom what had triggered such obsessive bookkeeping, but was more concerned by the incident in Hyde Park.

'Well?' Jenny urged, wringing her palms. 'Don't you see? They're all prime numbers! Darling—it's—beautiful! Apart from the penny at the end. Why *is* it that 1 isn't deemed a prime number?'

It was rather a good question.

'Ha! You're a genius!' Marx declared, and with that he was out the door and down the stairs shortly before bursting in again, then out again, then in again, then out and heading back to the British Museum which, given the all-too-real possibility of bumping in *again* to his creditors, he decided to approach by a circuitous route. This time, however, it was far more circuitous than on previous occasions, given that no amount of precaution was too much in order to avoid disaster, despite his impatience to see this thing written up and completed by the end of the month, week, day, perhaps, since once outdoors in the community almost anything were possible. It was novel to be out among the people, his people, who were waiting for this book (without knowing it) and whose logic he was the mere servant of, a mind along for the ride—a finite mode or *res singulares*—which gave "him" no say in the matter.

He criss-crossed the planks, which had been a feature of the Piccadilly slime pools for so long that they must have been propping up the entire West End. Isolated columns vying with cranes for aerial advantage, in addition to the abandoned shacks of some Wild West outpost, it could have been a Christian mission in the Aztec jungle.

He descended Haymarket and for some reason—call it pure decision—he decided to double back along Panton Street, instead of rounding the arc of Cockspur and heading up the Strand. Outside Lyle's the greengrocers he almost had the shock of his life and darted into the alleyway adjacent to the shop.

Something echoed in the darkness. It might have been the contents of his mind. The stench of stale vegetables and ammonia took him back to his encounter with the homeless child all those years before. What had become of that poor soul? he wondered. He must have been grown by now, albeit in the imaginary incarnation of one lucky enough to live, slipped through the net of history or sucked through its black hole.

He heard voices in the cockney accent he had never managed to grasp—the ehs and ees and ahs and ois of its bovine syntax. He conjured up images of the tradesmen from Jenny's ledger, but all he could make out were the numbers and none of the faces of the corresponding Counts. It was the £2 7s. 11d. who had startled him; he recognized the figure's gait. Or possibly the £17 5s.

He tried to interpret the chalk drawing that had been scrawled on the wall. It was partly obscured by wooden crates and a film of grease. On closer inspection it was a 57 Lion, or the Stephenson perhaps, the locomotive with the big wheels on the front two axles. Had the artist ever travelled on one? In any case it was a fine etching. Perhaps the homeless child had made it. Then again, perhaps not, given the passage of time.

Marx stood taking the thing in for a while and then hit upon a novel idea. '*Res singulares*.' He knew what had to be done.

He flew back to the flat and grabbed the first thing he could lay his hands on—a mahogany box containing keepsakes and jewellery, half of which were broken anyway—then darted off to the pawnshop on Drury Lane, that proud showcase for proletarian merchandise, where he was bound to be able to strike a bargain with the proprietor. They had most of the family's possessions already: his suits, cravats and shoes without holes in; most of the children's clothes; their dinner service and silver cutlery; Jenny's dresses; Helene's, too; their best linen and family heirlooms, &c.

'These earrings are not solid silver, I'm afraid,' said the broker, who went further down in Marx's estimation every time.

'But the jewels are topaz,' said he, naming the first gemstone that came into his head.

The man peered over his half-moon spectacles and sighed. 'But the setting is not *solid* silver, sir. If they were—'

'Fine, fine—and the pearls?'

'The pearls are not pearls and I don't deal in... costume jewellery.'

'Costume jewellery?' demanded the client, almost foaming at the mouth. 'Costume! Why, that's really quite nonsensical.'

The broker looked fixedly at Marx, who swiftly changed tack.

'Look. My good man. You're a pawnbroker, am I right? And this is a commodity, is it not? And the money-form of any commodity is governed by the law of the general equivalent. Why, one is no longer trading under feudalism. Or...?'

The broker sat back from his rotund self. 'I can only repeat myself—'

'Fine, fine, just pay me the money, then,' and in no time Marx was out the door with the 10 pounds 10 shillings and ninepence required to make the purchase of the Birmingham Dribbler Kit.

Despite being a commodity like any other, on his way home from the Regent Street toyshop, Marx was convinced that he finally had in his possession the key to completing his work. His mind raced at the thought. It was almost as if the entire history of the Industrial Revolution had been squeezed into that commodity, which like a jack-in-the-box was poised to spill out its hidden secrets—if not exactly settle its unresolved problems, given that once his experiment was underway, it was sure to generate new ones—albeit none so unruly as to transcend the scientific framework he had already established. It mattered little.

Back at the flat he completed the assembly in no time and poured a mugful of his own urine into the boiler (the standpipe on Wardour Street was on the blink again), and with a lump of coal he had found on a scrapheap, he began to fire the burner. The frightful odour it gave off suggested it wasn't coal, at all—more likely desiccated dog turd—but it burned well enough.

As he waited for the boiler to heat up, he arranged the twelve sections of track in the front room, each roughly a foot in length—which wasn't difficult, since the only obstacle to negotiate was the pianoforte—and wrote out a working hypothesis. By the time Jenny and the others arrived he already had what he felt sure would end up as his preface. In any case it sounded both erudite and elegant.

'Listen to this!' he exclaimed, reading from a length of wallpaper resembling a Roman scroll. '"In studying social and economic transformations it is always necessary to distinguish between the material transformation of the economic conditions of production—"'

'Corrr!' cried Edgar, his eyes almost bulging from their sockets. 'Dad's only gone and bought the locomo-iff!'

'"—which can be *determined*,"' Marx raised his voice, '"with the precision of natural science, and the legal, political, religious, artistic or philosophic—in short, ideological forms in which men become conscious of this conflict and fight it out."[56] Well? What do you think?'

'Karl... What—have—you—done?' mouthed Jenny, doubting the veracity of the apparition, as Marx put the Dribbler through its paces.

'Mmm? Oh, that. It's my proof. More of a corollary, actually. A practical application of my theory—Edgar, don't touch the Dribbler, son, there's a good lad. You'll burn your fingers.'

'I'm not talking about *that*. I'm talking about... *this*.' Jenny stretched out a mortified finger.

'What?' Marx shrugged bemusedly.

'This, Karl. *This.*'

What Jenny was referring to was the image of death warmed up and which smelt twice as bad. It was as if Gluttony (the Third Circle) had regurgitated its entrails.

'Oh, I know,' shrugged the entrails. 'Over 10 pounds I paid and they didn't even include a rag.' He shook off the vestiges of a tar-stained shirt torn to shreds.

'But it was… the only shirt you had,' said Jenny meekly, almost in tears.

'It's nothing,' he replied, 'really,' in a consoling effort.

In the grand scheme of things it was all going to plan. The book was taking shape from the ground up, or ground down, its geometry being somewhat confused. Or not so much *confused* as inverted, since a man standing on his head was still the same man walking on his feet. Any gaps in the argument thus far were incidental to Marx's theoretical approach and could be ironed out along the way, put together in the process of writing, so to speak—drafting and redrafting and re-redrafting—the order of presentation being crucial, insurmountable. And yet the more he professed to know what he was doing the more he had the impression that *none of it made sense*—especially if it did—and that everything coming out of his mouth by way of explanation bore some *other* significance, a significance of which he was entirely ignorant. In sum, he would never understand what this damned book was supposed to be about. It was as if this confounded laboratory experiment of his, this Frankensteinian synthesis of everything under the sun and more, from the logic of differential calculus to soil erosion, bore implications far beyond the ken of mortal beings—albeit implications operating at another level, in an Other Universe, which could only be grasped on condition of some utter catastrophe.

'Is it house-trained?' asked Jenny of the thing scuttling round the room like a juvenile pet.

'The Dribbler is part of my experiment. Don't be afraid of it; but, equally, don't be confused. It's not an animal. It's a model for the transition to a new world.'

'It smells animal enough to me,' said Jenny. 'It smells like the gents bog.'

'What do you know about the gents bog?' Marx cringed. The Dribbler sprayed a jet of urine in a neat arc, much as a male pooch might have done. 'Look, you're missing the point,' he said. 'You need to take a wider view, see it in the round.' He marched Jenny into the centre of the room. 'It was your disquisition on prime numbers that set me thinking. A prime number has no divisors apart from itself and 1. Goldbach conjectures that every even number greater than 2 is the sum of two primes.'

'Gold back!' quipped Helene. 'Promises, promises.'

'Helene, would you open a window, please?' said Jenny. 'This thing's making me gag.'

Marx continued undaunted. 'But what about other numbers? What about the transcendentals? Why, π is positively sublime! 3.14159265357—'

'58...' Jenny corrected him. 'What's your *point*, Karl?'

He looked at her perplexedly. 'Precision,' he said, before hawking a gob of phlegm out of the window. '*That's* my point— bullseye. What if one were able to describe capitalism, plot the path of its movement, as a locomotive? What if it were possible to track its motion, its "real movement", so to speak, with such precision that one could measure its entire circuit in a formula?'

Jenny pondered the idea. 'You mean your little train is like capitalism.'

'My dear,' he declared imperiously, 'capitalism is "like" everything in the world! The train is a machine, not an analogy. It's a proof, by Zeus. It's a model *of* capitalism, if you like. But it's not "like" capitalism.'

His wife shook her head. 'No, you've lost me again.'

'Watch out!' Marx yelled, pulling Edgar from the track as the Dribbler sped past, accelerating. 'It's not a game, son. Go and ride your locomotive over there. This one's too small for you... Now, as I was saying, the aim is to "plot" capitalism with the perfect precision of a transcendental number. But note: precision.'

'And that's what your differential calculus is for.' Jenny was beginning to understand.

'Yes. But it lacks rigour. It might do the job when capitalism's going round in circles, repeating itself, moving at constant speed. In which case the ratio dy/dx matters naught.'

'No, you've lost me again.'

'But—stay with me, please—in order to ensure the necessary rigour we need to get beyond this nothing.'

'How? Nothing will come of nothing,' intoned Jenny in an operatic flourish.

'Ha! Speak again,' said Marx, striding forward masterfully.

Jenny fell on her knee and clutched at her breast: 'Unhappy that I am, I cannot heave, My heart into my mouth. I love your majesty, According to my bond, no more nor less.'

'How, how, Cordelia?' recited Marx. 'Mend your speech a little, Lest you may mar your fortunes.'[57]

Jenny rose, brushing the dirt and cobwebs from her dress. 'What fortunes? You're broke.'

'Listen,' Marx resumed, 'capitalism doesn't turn idly in circles and neither does it travel in straight lines. In the name of rigour and precision, we need to plot its peaks and troughs. Only it mustn't end there! *Verily we know nothing. Truth is buried deep.* We need to go further down, deep down to its core. But then where is "down" in matters infinite, since there's no geography there?'

'He's off again,' exclaimed Helene, sweeping up the cobwebs.

'We need to grasp capitalism through its deviations and detours. But more still do we need to chart its progress into the *future* through its random fluctuations and swerves. And to achieve *that*, comrades, there's only one thing for it: more track.'

Marx's face took on the fiendish aspect of a devil driving lost souls through the Gates of Hell: *Lasciate ogni speranza, voi ch'entrate.* 'Now,' he mused, eyeing the flat's contents, 'what's left?'

Instantly he expropriated Jenny's St Christopher, the silver necklace her mother had bequeathed her, then Helene's lever watch, the one they never had the money to fix, before sizing up the piano. It was tempting, and he knew a man who knew a man, but offloading that thing was theft pure and simple, and was sure to land him in Newgate Prison. Which left only one other item.

'Oh! no you don't,' said Helene, holding up the broom like a lance. 'Just you think on it!'

Instinctively she planted herself between Edgar and this Mephistophelian ogre, this revenant reject from the bowels of the earth, of a circle so "deep" it was numberless. But this pathetic gesture was no match for the Idea whose time had come and by shielding Marx's son from the creature, she merely fanned the flames of its diabolical plans. Marx wrestled the toy locomotive away from Edgar, almost carrying him off with it.

'Naaaaah!' the boy screamed, which would have broken glass had there been any left in the flat to break and which certainly lacked nothing in precision. 'Don't take my toy, Dad! Please, don't! Muuu-uuum!'

Jenny burst into tears and sunk to the floor. Helene jumped on Marx's back and was still on it halfway down the stairs.

'I'll throw you, woman!' he warned, buckling under her weight. 'Will you go off? Go off now or I'll launch you! Go off!'

'Stop! You... you... *violator!*'

The wall clattered into them and they bypassed the next flight of stairs entirely before hitting the landing with a thud. Marx groaned but stayed quite still. Helene, who had borne the brunt of the fall, pulled herself up by the banister rail and started to scream.

'Why do you want to abandon your son? Answer me!'

A foot landed between his legs. He should have felt that but didn't.

'Why do you want to abandon us? Answer me!'

Then another. He must have misheard. Another foot. Screaming, ranting, it was all garbled. She collapsed grief-stricken and presently began to sob. Marx remained motionless, rooted to the scene of a crime as perfectly lucid as it was unspeakable.

'Answer me!' Helene shuddered and the whole house with her, from the cellar all the way up to the attic, where Jenny listened and by the infernal noise must have known what it meant.

But she didn't act, didn't see fit to stand up to the ogre or put on a united front, since she knew in her heart of hearts that there was no alternative, and that despite all the pain and heartbreak she had to keep on going, if only by prolonging the agony.

Marx got up and left, already decided that there was nothing else for it but to pawn the stuff and buy up as much track as he could. What he must have looked like, this bear-chested apeman, smothered in blood and grease, didn't bear thinking about. He didn't think. Besides, the revolutionary war paint served to ward off the creditors.

Outside people fell over themselves to get out of his way. The streets emptied around him. He took one of his circuitous detours to Drury Lane, bypassing a demonstration of 3000 protestors or thereabouts, according to the police constabulary, and 30,000 according to the workingmen. Crucially 3 and 30 were the first and fourth numbers of the arithmetic progression modulo $q = 9$. That was a good sign.

Having completed the first stage of the mission, he began placing the different sections of track—51 in all! Some straight, some curved—without prejudice as to how they should all fit together, since randomness was not so much the aim of the investigation as the principle for unlocking a future world of revolutionary practice. Perhaps freedom would extend to being in two places at once in the future society.

Marx twiddled the regulator valve and a jet of steam shot out of the boiler, almost singeing his eyebrows off. The model was ready to go and in a split second he was back on the already moving train.

Things were difficult to make out at first. But closing his eyes sharpened his senses. The scenery came to him, gathering perspective, adding a third dimension to the reified landmarks: a castle, a lake, a tin mine, a church, green pastureland, rolling hills. There was hidden meaning in their random combinations. The locomotive tearing through space tore at its very fabric. Were they reaching some kind of threshold? *Prestissimo.*

The carriage went over a point, which he felt along the length of his spine, clenching the notes of an infinite keyboard. A melody began to unfold, one he should have recognized. Then a polyphonic steam whistle played the same tune: this anthem, the clarion call.

'Daaa-aaad!' said Edgar. 'Where are we going?'

'To a happy place, son. You'll see.'

'To the seaside? Are we going to the seaside?' Edgar sprang from his seat and pressed his face to the window.

'It's a place I've never been to but always dreamt of going. Your mother, too. Haven't you, my love?'

Jenny smiled, closed her eyes and inclined toward the light. She looked radiant. They were happy. Then she and Edgar were gone.

The dioramas receded into the past of an old-fangled clockwork theatre. As the locomotive rounded the minutest of curves a bridge spanning a deep ravine appeared. The image pulsed, then faded. The whistle sounded a monotone siren. Marx braced himself for the pain. His stomach fell away and the carriage rose high on its axles before landing in a sickening crunch, throwing up sparks and clouds of smoke. There was a screeching of brakes, a teeth-wrenching prelude to an almighty thud. *Scheisse.*

The sound of metal bending and buckling went on for some time. He waited. Meanwhile, a rebellion might have broken out in working class. Pity the lack of public information. When the clamour eventually died, all he could detect was the faint hiss of steam and the sound of the engine pounding like waves on a distant shore. He stepped down from the carriage and walked the length of the train. The engine was a monster of unprecedented proportions: a 4-12-4. Two front axles followed by six for the engine alone. Twenty wheels in all. The biggest wheels must have weighed a tonne apiece and towered over his tiny frame. Had *men* made this machine? And what was this *thing*?

The engine might have been carved from a block of granite blown from the Feldberg. There wasn't a seam, join or rivet anywhere to be seen. It was as if Momentum had been captured and customized in a unique substance. A slim aperture was its only facial characteristic, from which a mysterious red glow issued.

Marx scanned the featureless landscape for some idea of how long this unscheduled stop was likely to last.

'Hallo! I say! Workingmen! Anyone? Yooo-hooo!'

There was nothing, just a non-perspectival whiteness that extended to where the horizon should have been. It was hardly something. A small grey building stood out, the waiting room or ticket office. "Revolution Central" read the sign. The building was deserted.

He scanned the walls for a timetable. It wasn't easy to find, since bizarrely it covered the entire surface of the building. In fact, the timetable was all that there was. He touched its patterned fabric, which must have been some kind of ingrained code. How to follow this strange syntax wasn't obvious and was somewhat like trying to locate the end of a roll of cotton. He found the time of the next train. In fact, there was only one departure per day. Or, well… ever.

'Revolution Central,' he pondered, drumming his fingers on the wall. 'Now. Let's see. Departure.' And then written underneath the time:

00.00.0000000000000000000000000000000000000000000000000000
0000000000000000000000000000000000000000000000000000000000
0000000000000000000000000000000000000000000000000000000000
0000000000000000000000000000000000000000000000000000000000
0000000000000000000000000000000000000000000000000000000000
0000000000000000000000000000000000000000000000000000000000
0000000000000000000000000000000000000000000000000000000000
0000000000000000000000000000000000000000000000000000000000
0000000000000000000000000000000000000000000000000000000000
0000000000000000000000000000000000000000000000000000000000
0000000000000000000000000000000000000000000000000000000000
0000000000000000000000000000000000000000000000000000000000
0000000000000000000000000000000000000000000000000000000000
0000000000000000000000000000000000000000000000000000000000
0000000000000000000000000000000000000000000000000000000000
0000000000000000000000000000000000000000000000000000000000
0000000000000000000000000000000000000000000000000000000000
0000000000000000000000000000000000000000000000000000000000
0000000000000000000000000000000000000000000000000000000000
0000000000000000000000000000000000000000000000000000000000
0000000000000000000000000000000000000000000000000000000000
0000000000000000000000000000000000000000000000000000000000
0000000000000000000000000000000000000000000000000000000000
0000000000000000000000000000000000000000000000000000000000
0000000000000000000000000000000000000000000000000000000000
0000000000000000000000000000000000000000000000000000000000
0000000000000000000000000000000000000000000000000000000000
0000000000000000000000000000000000000000000000000000000000
0000000000000000000000000000000000000000000000000000000000
0000000000000000000000000000000000000000000000000000000000
0000000000000000000000000000000000000000000000000000000000
0000000000000000000000000000000000000000000000000000000000
0000000000000000000000000000000000000000000000000000000000
0000000000000000000000000000000000000000000000000000000000
0000000000000000000000000000000000000000000000000000000000
0000000000000000000000000000000000000000000000000000000000
0000000000000000000000000000000000000000000000000000000000

0000000000000000000000000000000000000000000000000000000000
0000000000000000000000000000000000000000000000000000000000
0000000000000000000000000000000000000000000000000000000000
0000000000000000000000000000000000000000000000000000000000
0000000000000000000000000000000000000000000000000000000000
0000000000000000000000000000000000000000000000000000000000
0000000000000000000000000000000000000000000000000000000000
0000000000000000000000000000000000000000000000000000000000
0000000000000000000000000000000000000000000000000000000000
0000000000000000000000000000000000000000000000000000000000
0000000000000000000000000000000000000000000000000000000000
0000000000000000000000000000000000000000000000000000000000
0000000000000000000000000000000000000000000000000000000000
0000000000000000000000000000000000000000000000000000000000
0000000000000000000000000000000000000000000000000000000000
0000000000000000000000000000000000000000000000000000000000
0000000000000000000000000000000000000000000000000000000000
0000000000000000000000000000000000000000000000000000000000
0000000000000000000000000000000000000000000000000000000000
0000000000000000000000000000000000000000000000000000000000
0000000000000000000000000000000000000000000000000000000000
0000000000000000000000000000000000000000000000000000000000
0000000000000000000000000000000000000000000000000000000000
0000000000000000000000000000000000000000000000000000000000
0000000000000000000000000000000000000000000000000000000000
0000000000000000000000000000000000000000000000000000000000
0000000000000000000000000000000000000000000000000000000000
0000000000000000000000000000000000000000000000000000000000
0000000000000000000000000000000000000000000000000000000000
0000000000000000000000000000000000000000000000000000000000
0000000000000000000000000000000000000000000000000000000000
0000000000000000000000000000000000000000000000000000000000
0000000000000000000000000000000000000000000000000000000000
0000000000000000000000000000000000000000000000000000000000
0000000000000000000000000000000000000000000000000000000000

At this point he stopped registering the digits, since they went on and on seemingly without end or interruption. It was certainly precise. Or was it? What type of train was being described here? None on the English networks, anyway. But as he circled the building and followed the negative chain into the waiting room, he wasn't worrying about the abstract nature of the problem any more. It was more a case of where it was leading. A sense of horror hit home as the door swung open on his past. The smell of rotten flesh escaped from inside. It brought to mind the Bingen cell he and Engels had been thrown into back in '49. There were no bars on the windows. Light poured in. Something was shifting on the floor, but the glare pushed him back.

He came to his senses. Was there a hope in hell he might be mistaken? He recognized those stripped concrete walls now. But what had been scrawled over them he had no recollection of, for it was nothing he could have done.

The maniacal graffiti screamed out the ravings of the committed, one of the godforsaken souls condemned to rot on Belle-Île.[58] Every inch of wall space confirmed the record of a monstrous tale. In some places the handwriting was minute. There seemed to be layer upon layer of it: competing formulas for branches of calculus and derived functions worked out for all of them; mathematical paradigms connected by arrows; the history of geometry since Thales; Pythagoras and the scandal of irrational numbers; arithmetic and prime number theorems... And then scrawled on top of it all, either in some act of pure desperation or delirium, the zeros had been lined up in rows. Thousands upon thousands, maybe millions of them. The search for an end. Or perhaps the final agonizing admission that there wasn't one.

The sun went behind a cloud to reveal human shapes. It must have been Jenny and the children. He looked away, mustering the courage to look back and willing it otherwise.

'Jenny. Can you hear me?'

It wasn't clear which of the two women should have answered. One was boiling some water on a stove, who must have been Helene, while the children clung to this other.

He reached out a mechanical hand then retrieved it—a stranger would have done the same—that this family might remain in limbo, concluding that it was better to do nothing than encroach on a disaster he himself had created.

His beautiful wife had aged horribly. The pain and suffering she had always managed to contain with her intelligence and grace no longer had beauty as its ultimate refuge. Her once porcelain skin was yellow and withered, and bore the unmistakable scars of the pox. He would love her still, but he wanted those scars to go away or at least to see past them. He had scars aplenty and was still alive, or at least must have been, since the pain he felt was more than a mere bodily state. It was part of his history and the record of a life. Theirs together.

'We will get through this, Jenny. You and I. You know it. I promise.'

He choked on the words and took her hand, trying to inject feeling into this murmured resolution. She squeezed him back with that iron grip of hers that always roused him in the small hours and a smile broke out on her face, a brief reflex, as if amused by the thought and the power she had to read his mind.

Edgar was collapsed in his mother's lap. His face was white as a sheet.

'Come on, Musch. Drink.' Helene gently inclined the boy's head.

He gulped down a mouthful of the mixture then collapsed.

'Hold him,' said Helene and Marx repeated what she had done, coaxing him to take a few more sips and then sitting him upright.

It was freezing. Edgar had the only blanket. Marx took off his jacket and wrapped him in it.

'He threw up some blood this morning,' said Helene. 'I couldn't find the doctor. Engels managed to raise him last week. He told me to heat this stuff up. He came over yesterday and said to keep him warm...'

'Edgar,' whispered his father. 'Musch. It's Dad.'

The child stirred.

'Would you like your locomotive?'

The eyes beamed. 'Locomo-iff.' The boy strained and nodded.

Marx wondered at the power of the word. A false hope rendered to sweeten the pill. But how could he possibly retrieve the toy? The flat was a shell. If he had had a knife he would have cut off his own hand for a half-crown; or donated his battered kidneys to science.

He got up and went to the bedroom. Nothing. But wait. It wasn't true. In the corner there was something. It shone like lost treasure, an amulet from a fairy tale. It was the silver picture frame with his father's startled face staring out of it. How that could have escaped his wife's obsessive bookkeeping was anyone's guess.

A snowstorm had put paid to all movement of creatures and infernal machines. A storm front had swept in and out, robbing the city of a dimension. The revolution was frozen and up to its neck. There wasn't a soul on the streets. Not a glimmer. Even the furnaces of the South Bank, whose doors always stayed open on holy days, were idle. The air was breathable again, as it must have been once upon a time, during one of the other periods supporting human life, or of history per se. No particles of any kind deviated Marx from the path he took to Drury Lane. It was all perfectly straight in his mind.

An omnibus had been abandoned on Whitehall next to the equestrian statue of Charles I. Icicles on the face of the tragic monarch made him look like Santa Claus.

'Deep and crisp and even,' hummed Marx.

There were several more abandoned omnibuses on the Strand. Marx counted a fifth. Henry the bus. A Bow and Stratford green had been submerged by a snowdrift, the colour inferred from its number, a placeholder on the top rail. Number 3. It resembled the cab of the revolutionary train, an igloo with a letterbox for the driver to peer through.

'Every even number greater than 2 can be expressed as the sum of two primes.' Marx recited Goldbach's conjecture to keep warm. 'But that can't hold for 4, because 1 isn't p-p-prime. Jenny's right. You're right, m-m-my love—1 isn't p-p-prime.'

A new-fangled pillar box mid-breast issued from the snow. Only when Marx surmised what the devil it was did the artificial slope give way and he fall through its frozen crust. He would be soaked through—assuming he ever made it back to dry land.

The pawnbroker's was closed. The workingman's boots had vanished from the vitrine, but Marx couldn't see much else through the condensation on the inside. Someone was in there. He banged and rattled the window so hard that no one alive in the West End could have possibly ignored it.

'Hallo! I say! Yooo-hooo!'

The broker appeared. 'We're closed,' he mimed.

Marx held up the silver picture frame. 'Solid silver, my good man!'

'Colonel,' said Marx, bursting back in like the Abominable Snowman. 'I got your locomotive. Your locomo-iff. Look.' Marx held out the toy in his frostbitten hands. The child was barely conscious. 'Later you can ride it. Would you like to? Why, I think it would be splendid. We can play together when the snow clears.'

Marx glanced out of the window. The sun was going down behind the rooftops, having given up for the day and failed to make an impression on the snow. Helene took Marx to one side. She didn't say anything, didn't need to. Just stared blankly. The doctor had called. She was boiling another of his mixtures. But...

'Dad,' said Edgar wistfully. He was feverish and still white as a sheet.

Marx held the child, but since he was wet through soon put him down again. Jenny and the girls were asleep. He sat with them, his back against the wall, shivering, breathing hard, exhaling puffs of steam. It was too cold to feel anything—fear, pain, emotion—which suited him fine. In fine.

Chapter 7

28, Dean Street, Soho
6 April 1855[59]

Dear Engels,

Poor Musch is no more. He went to sleep in my arms (in the literal sense) between 5 and 6 o'clock. I will never forget how your friendship has made this terrible time easier for us. My grief for the child goes without saying. My wife sends you her warmest greetings. When I come to Manchester I might bring her with me for eight days, in which case we should, of course, stay at a guest house (or perhaps take private lodgings). At any rate, I must try to help her get through the first days.

Your

K. Marx

Chapter 8

Things started to break down. Not that they could go any lower. Things had already hit rock-bottom and had it been possible to go any lower then surely they would have passed through the centre of the earth and come back out the other side. A man standing on his head was still the same man walking on his feet. Hell's geography wasn't adapted to the needs of its residents. Instead, in adherence to the breakdown, gravity failed. Which meant that with Edgar's death the relations dropped out of things. It was part and parcel of the aftershock. Impossible things would happen, seemingly all the time, albeit in a time unhinged, rendering futile any notion of "before" and "after".

Life without a past was a nightmare. Ghosts no longer haunted the present. Instead, they upped sticks and came to reside among the living. In addition to the past's migration, the future stopped. No longer was the future up ahead and just over the horizon. It was everywhere, stifling all forward-thinking, like a train already arrived even before having left the station. Or a constantly moving train that never arrived.

As for the workers, the train's future conductors, Marx began to suspect he was guilty of a monumental miscalculation. What if the risings of the workers in '48 were the very opposite of what he had thought? Instead of heralding the communist future, what if those revolutionary events were merely the death knell of the feudal past? Who was to say it wasn't still sounding? Perhaps the European revolutions signalled the extinction event of the communist movement, given that nothing seemed to be moving any more.

Much as he abjured Metternich[60] the latter was probably right in having described democracy as a matter of dissolution and decay. The only difference being that the German buffoon had forgotten to include the divine right of kings in his narrative. Why should the monarchs be immune to the collapse of democracy? There was only tyranny to come. Then again, since the law of gravity had collapsed, perhaps time would soon be running in reverse.

The Red Lion was deserted. It might have been a one-off. Marx had stopped frequenting the place years ago; 10 years at least, at the fag end of the Communist League. Much of the neighbourhood had been redeveloped. The ragtag cottages on Archer Street were gone and the workshops had been converted to private dwellings, which reflected the ups and downs of commercial lettings. The knackery had also been laid to rest. Back in the early 50s, he and Engels had pronounced the revolution frozen and entering a period of hibernation. In their naïve and exuberant enthusiasm they had invested in Marx's theoretical work. The Book would rescue them all and put the revolution back on track. Or at least it would provide a compass to navigate through it.

'How long before things get moving again?' would be Engels's opening gambit whenever they would meet, either in London or Manchester, in a clamorous bar or restaurant.

'Seems like things already have for you, friend,' Marx always felt like saying, 'by the look of your fine get-up.'

Engels always looked dapper in tweed and never would a hair of his immaculate coiffure contradict its wearer's crown. Since leaving London and becoming a cotton lord Engels's fortunes had blossomed. Despite having only agreed to join his father's firm in order to settle his gambling debts, he was now set up to be a partner. On each occasion he would never fail to mention how, despite it being a "damned squalid affair", in X number of years and counting, he would be drawing a pretty pension and setting up home in a leafy London suburb. In how many more years? 10? Some period of revolutionary hibernation. That would be 20 all told. A life, in fine. More than twice that of Edgar's and 20 times Guido's.

As for Marx himself, he didn't care to count. Years ago, he imagined earning enough to make a new start for the family, to put bread and snowdrops on the table, ship out of Soho and move "up" in the world. He and his wife had talked about Mayfair, where birds inhabited trees and the prostitutes were discreet.

Marx took a sip from his tankard. The grog was passable, better than he remembered. Perhaps if he drank one more it would taste awful. The barmaid, who was young and mildly attractive, asked if he wanted another. Miracles never ceased.

'It's much quieter these days,' Marx offered, scavenging his pockets for change.

'It's much quieter today,' she nodded, by which she meant since yesterday.

She contrived to smile, as if her grandpa had just announced that he had soiled his trousers and that without explicitly saying so, he expected her to wipe the shit from his arse. She could have done that readily and just as he was about to ask how much for, a figure appeared in the doorway. Marx would have recognized it anywhere. It was the floating graffiti on his retina. The wandering star of the revolution. Mikhail Bakunin.

At first the giant turned in circles, mightily perplexed by his missing public. 1849 was the last time he and Marx had locked horns, not long after his arrival from Paris. Their meeting had taken place in this very spot; albeit under different circumstances.

In an instant Marx could have snuck out of the back door. But it was too late now, as the giant stepped up to the bar.

'Well, well, well,' said Bakunin, taking off his hat and unwinding his scarf. 'If it isn't our Dear Leader.' He turned again in circles. 'It looks as if all the pretty birds have flown south for the winter. Landlord,' whom he saluted with a V-sign. 'I shall join you for one and then be on my way. You'll have one on me,' the host informed his guest, 'for old time's sake.'

Marx stared blankly into space as the Russian lowered himself onto his perch. His caution betrayed arthritis or an injury picked up on an Eastern front. Barely had he changed—he was still as big as a bronze statue—and when he peered down his beard at Marx, he took on the fearsome aspect of a Titan sizing up a mortal.

'Rebuses,' declared Bakunin, producing a copy of *L'Illustration* and dabbing it with sausage-sized fingers. He pressed a monocle to his left eyeball, which swelled monstrously in the lens. 'Tell me, is there something I'm *missing* there? I can see straight through these word games, Marx. Solving their riddles is a doddle.' The Russian was a walking caricature: a monocle-wearing walrus or beer-swilling woolly mammoth. 'There's a French countess I'm screwing who's fascinated by rebuses. She teases me and I play along. She studied at the Collège Royal back in prehistoric times. Architecture, of all things. "Comtesse," I tell her, "impress me not with your cultivation and learning, for I shall love you just the same." That riles her no end. Come to think of it, she must be—what—fifty? *"Tout trou est un but,"*[61] as they say on the Left Bank. I write her romantic poetry but she knows I rip it off. Always take the aristocrats from behind.' He stood up to demonstrate. 'That way you can size up their baubles. This stuff, though, there's more to it than meets the eye.' He let go a volley of wind. *'Je vous en prie.*[62] I mean this one's easy. Look.'

Bakunin pointed at the rebus on the back page which depicted, from left to right, a length of linen; the cheeks of a countess; a cartwheel; and a cogitating Enlightenment man. *'Drap. Peau. Roue. Je.* Obvious: *drapeau rouge.'*[63] He chuckled and the floor trembled. 'And yet! What if the meaning were hidden… elsewhere?' Bakunin leaned in to Marx, as if suspecting him of being part of the conspiracy. 'It's not *there!*' he boomed, in a voice that could have scared off a pack of wolves. He preached and prodded as if lecturing a cadet. 'Don't take me for an idiot, Marx. It's everywhere else! It's everywhere *but* there.'

The barmaid brought over two tankards and Bakunin

polished off his post-haste.

'But!' he resumed, spraying a mist of ale in Marx's face, 'don't by Jupiter tell me that it's not *there* all the same.'

Over the next hour or so, which for Marx might have been minutes or days, Bakunin expounded his conspiracy theory during the course of which more ale was consumed, an addendum to the initial "one"; which, needless to say, in matters of inebriation, is only ever the penultimate one, the one before last. The real rebuses weren't on the back pages of *L'Illustration*, the Russian asserted, they were scattered throughout the entire newssheet, in the form of secret codes introduced into notifications of novel treatments for rheumatism and shingles; cold-blooded mammals and pedigree cats; book signings and public lectures; the new labour-saving contraptions from America; the preparatory courses available to students sitting the baccalauréat and much else besides. There was nothing in the paper bearing on politics as such, hence nothing to raise the suspicions of Louis-Napoléon's censors. But the hidden messages were there, of that there could be no doubt, and they were political through and through. A keen eye was all it took to decipher them; although Bakunin's examples were completely ridiculous. In 48 pages of newsprint carrying three columns per page, almost any interpretation could be had, of anything from religious zealotry to consumerist propaganda. Moreover, if such "conspiracies" were being practiced in a bourgeois paper, then it only made sense to ask on whose behalf and to what end.

It was the typesetters, Bakunin maintained: those "workingmen" were part of a Europe-wide Tsarist reaction that led all the way to Alexander II. Ever since the Crimean War that bastard had been stretching out his tentacles and installing his agents in preparation for the coming world war. He was Frederick the Great and Napoleon Bonaparte all rolled into one. The people needed to wake up and open their eyes. It was staring everyone in the face.

'*Alors,*' he concluded, screwing the newspaper into a ball.

In truth the elaborate conspiracy theory had been so much flimflam, a mere preamble to the real business at hand. In the meantime Marx's mind had wandered, so that when Bakunin resumed his speech what the German doctor actually heard was far more lucid than it would have been had he absorbed everything that preceded it.

'You know, Marx,' Bakunin began again, 'I always knew it would turn out like this. Us together, I mean. We two here, in this place. That we were destined to end up together at this precise moment in time... Well! Would you credit it? Hmm. It's really quite remarkable. It's beyond science, if you ask me.'

The barmaid fetched over fresh tankards.

'Ну разве не чудесно вы выглядите сегодня?' said Bakunin, and 'спасибо.'[64]

Unlike her prehistoric forebears the girl wasn't Slav and a vacant smile was all she could manage. Bakunin quaffed a good measure of grog, slammed his tankard on the table and belched like a drain.

'Ask me where I've been!' he demanded. His speech was faster and more dedicated now.

'Where have you been?' Marx obliged.

'I'm glad you asked: Siberia. On a mission in the Urals, I was. I don't do things by halves, you know it. The Cossacks got wind of it and carted me off to Moscow. They locked me up. Tortured me.' Bakunin prized open his jaws and pointed at his missing teeth. 'They wanted a confession, but fuck them. I've never betrayed a comrade in my life. I told the tsar, told him straight to his face, wrote it down in my own blood. They had to let me go. He knows I know he knows what I know. *And* he knows it. But then it got me to thinking. That's where we should make our revolution.'

'Our revolution?'

'Damn right it is.'

Bakunin placed an envelope on the table and reclined. 'In this envelope,' he whispered out of the corner of his mouth, 'are secret plans for a Pan-Slavic uprising. I am placing you in charge of procuring field artillery. I count on you absolutely in this affair.'

Marx opened the envelope half expecting to be blown to smithereens. Bakunin had a reputation for being unpredictably predictable.

'It's a blank sheet of paper,' he noted.

'What!' retorted the Russian, 'you'd rather I inform the Russian ambassador? It's written in invisible ink.'

'Of course it is. I was forgetting.'

Bakunin heaved himself to his feet. 'We shall start in Poland,' he declared, 'working our way south-east and ending up in Kiev. The Russians and Upper Prussians have transformed the entire region into one gigantic police state. But we'll show them. Your contribution will be crucial in helping to win over the Ukrainians. They're backward, parochial types in the main: petty-minded bureaucrats. But they're coming round, slowly. *You* are going to help speed things up a bit. You're gaining quite a reputation for yourself, thanks to yours truly. Do you credit it? I circulated your *Manifesto*—only a few hundred copies, mind. Slipped them inside bibles and got them through customs disguised as a Franciscan monk. Worked a treat. Why, the parishioners lapped it up! The translation could have been more... muscular; I'll make a proper one once I'm back in Geneva. It's for the peasants, mind! They're the lynchpin in all of this. By rallying the peasants, we shall start the revolution in the countryside before swarming the towns. We're due to start 80 miles east of Lodz. You'll arrive from Gdansk. Take a barge to Weselno, then a mule to Rokitnica and await my instructions. Once we reach the secret location, we'll load provisions and begin the march to the Ukrainian border. With each new town we'll multiply our forces tenfold. Poland is like a powder keg. It's all waiting to go off. Once we've amassed 50,000 men we shall march on Moscow. *Et! Voilà.'* Bakunin concluded his presentation with outstretched arms.

Not knowing quite how to respond, Marx staved off mutual embarrassment by asking, 'Who else is involved?'

'It's top secret. I can't divulge any names or addresses at this time.'

'*Genau.* But numbers, roughly?'

'In all: no less than 20 peasants. They're holed up in a Ukrainian farmhouse awaiting my instructions.'

'20 peasants?'

It was an improvement on Bakunin's previous plan for the taking of the English parliament. This time he was up into double figures.

'No less than 20. Indeed,' affirmed the Russian. 'But think Spartacus and you'll get a sense of the overall scale and ambition.'

'So, to be clear: you plan to start a Pan-Slavic revolution with 20 Ukrainian farmers?'

'The brilliance of it, no?' Bakunin leaned forward. 'It's History in the making.'

Men made their own history, but not as they pleased. And certainly not in Poland.

'Mikhail?' said Marx, staring profoundly.

Bakunin mirrored the gesture. 'Yes, Marx?'

'You are out of your mind,' and with that he motioned to the door.

Bakunin looked mightily put out. 'Brother Marx,' said he, as a detachment of his Pan-Slavic army ebbed away. 'I say! I'm talking to you, comrade. I'm offering you a way out here. Don't throw it back in my face. Look at yourself. Can't you see? You're wasting away, Marx. Everybody knows it. You're finished—'

The German doctor swung round in a fit of delirious energy, which took both men by surprise, and landed his fist on the table.

'Have you any *idea* what I've been through? What I've been

struggling for? The merest *inkling* of what I've had to sacrifice just to *be* here? What I've *lost*? I'm a political refugee. *T'as compris ça?*[65] I don't have the luxury, more's the pity, of gallivanting round the globe from Paris to Timbuktu, leeching off rich countesses. And to what end? In order to cajole a barn load of Ukrainians without so much as a brain cell between them into following you straight back to prison? Your arrogance should astound and offend me, truly. But in point of fact, it simply bores me—as do you... *mon frère*. The day I take lectures from you on revolution is the day I join the circus. *Au revoir et bon vent.'*[66] Marx rasped and wheezed. Steadying himself, he resumed his progress to the door.

'I understand you, comrade,' called the conspirator after him. 'You need time to think it over. It's normal. Think it over as much as you like. Take your time; take all the time in the world... I say, Marx!' On reaching the threshold he turned and Bakunin resumed: 'I understand you, Marx, and far better than you think. Who knows? Perhaps better than you do yourself. But I'll tell you one thing that confuses me: someone's been messing with your head. It's written all over your face. Only *you* can't see it.' Bakunin traced a door on his own forehead, then opened it. 'Far be it from me to try to invade your headspace, brother. But when you find the bastard who's in there, make sure you kill him.'

The sky was the colour of an oil slick. With a bit of luck the orange debris would set the firmament on fire, sending him and the whole godforsaken shithole to kingdom come. A just and fitting transition.

He wandered aimlessly until darkness fell, putting off the inevitable, willing Jenny and Helene to be out by the time he arrived home. It wasn't through conscious volition that gravity had fallen out of his marriage. It was all down to the universal theory that he knew existed but had given up trying to understand. Nowhere were the postulates and proofs more confused than in his own marital realm. Why else could a statement such as "I'm going to Holland for a few days" or "I'm off to the coast with the girls" turn out not to be false, but meaningless?

Jenny and her mercurial behaviour would have surely baffled the modern physicists. It was enough to revise everything one took for granted about the nature of cause and effect. In the new world of things without relations, one had to assume that just because one's wife arrived home at seven in the morning, having left at six the previous evening, it didn't *necessarily* mean that she had been out the whole night. Or, indeed, that she had ever been out at all. Quite feasibly, the contradiction of her whereabouts might have been explained by anything, from a psychological amnesia on her husband's part to a tear in the fabric of time (which might also explain why she would often return home looking dishevelled—but even a look could deceive). In any case, it might have been a new and exciting age of time travel, if time hadn't been so fiendishly difficult to grasp.

His arrival at the house was greeted by the routine pandemonium. Jenny and Helene were drunkenly entertaining two soldiers who Marx hadn't seen before. When he came in, the men were quite startled, the women no doubt having neglected to mention anyone else lived there. Helene staggered toward him swinging a bottle of wine.

'Here he is!' she cried. 'All hail the saviour of the working class!' She dangled an arm round his neck, misjudging her own strength and causing him to stumble into her. 'Ladies and gentlemen!' she quipped. 'Welcome to the communist utopia! A world in which all your needs will be satisfied—' She raised her petticoats and threw them over the soldier's face to raucous cheers. 'Where everyone is equal and no man shall go without.' She lifted a bare leg and put her foot in the lap of the other one, who was balancing Jenny on his knee.

Marx's wife was paralytic; her face was green. At least his presence wouldn't cause her any embarrassment.

'Don't mind him, boys,' Helene added, 'he only works here!' to more raucous cheers and laughter.

Marx looked on blankly as if observing them all, himself included, from the nth dimension. It felt like the kind of near-death experience that patients recall of having migrated from their bodies to the ceiling, from where they observe themselves going under the surgeon's knife.

Helene steered him toward his desk. 'Off you go, my boy. And I want to see 100 pages before daybreak. Otherwise, I'll dock your wages!'

The room erupted again, and Helene led the chorus of some lewd and boisterous number. Marx watched impassively for a while before staring at the sheet of white parchment on his desk, unblemished as a fresh carpet of snow. Carte blanche. The white parchment stared back. It seemed a fair reflection of his work. What had he ever written? Aside from the *Manifesto*, which had been jointly authored by Engels in any case, and the *Contribution to the Critique of Political Economy*,[67] there was nothing to show for more than 15 years of non-stop graft. Even his *Contribution* was barely a contribution, more like a pathetic excuse for an introduction to the magnum opus he had planned but never managed to complete.

Aside from these two "books", what else was there? Notes! Nothing but notes![68] Rooms full of them. Walls covered in them. It had all been a colossal misjudgement, one that it pained him to accept. Instead of being a theorist of the here and now, he was destined to end up as a "posthumous" author, dug up like the Great Fossil Lizard by future generations and taken for a quaint observer of futures long since passed.

Chapter 9

The cherry blossom went up in funnels and came tumbling back down in flurries, landing on the heads of the young disciples.

'Thunder-ten-Tronckh,' said the fourth.

'Thunder-eleven-Tronckh,' said the third.

'Thunder-twelve-Tronckh, said the second.

'Oh, leave it be now!' said the first and the boys burst out laughing, all except him, their intrepid captain, discoverer of new worlds. Candide of the Kingdom of Westphalia.

'I heard she rides Andalusians!' said the fourth.

'Cunégonde?' said the third.

'Does she live in a castle, too?' said the second.

'Oh, leave it be now!' said the first and the boys burst out laughing again, all except him.

But so infectious was the laughter that soon he too was joining in, reinventing the names of the metaphysicians, sailing the fair winds for Paraguay and dreaming of his future bride.

They crossed the heaving fields to the shoulder of the hill and the cherry orchard overlooking the town, the source of this strange weather. She was there, the girl on the bench, alone. He blushed as she turned and smiled at him, for despite having done so countless times in the presence of her tutor, this was their first real encounter. In any case, it was her prerogative to make him blush, since what else was a young woman of 15 years to do with a boy of 11, if not seduce him?

Grasping the meaning of the regard, the boys pushed him forward, like would-be leaders of men whose job it is to select volunteers for the deeds they dare not perform themselves. He sat down next to her, knowing and expecting nothing, smiling petrified, finally resigned to whatever she had in store for him. She took his dimpled chin in one hand as if holding an apple, then placed her lips on his, then let him go; and as he floated away with the pink confetti she must have been impressed, because after that she never smiled at him in quite the same way.

Chapter 10

He woke up with a start. At first it felt as if he were back at the German Hotel. But there was none of the usual bustle, which meant it must have been a Sunday morning. Then he registered the culprit. It was another of the furuncles. As he stood up the pain held him in that brief state of beatitude before sacking the rest of his constitution. It felt as if an army of ants were marching through his arteries. It was so excruciating that he stood at the table in the living room for half an hour lamenting the fact that he would never be able to sit, stand or lie down again.

Then began the ringing in his ears, a polyphonic symphony that might have been bearable had it not been transposed roughly five octaves above the treble clef. How a human being could detect sound at that frequency was baffling. Perhaps his worst nightmare of being metamorphosed into a dog had finally come true.

The ringing stopped but the sound remained. Was it Jennychen playing the piano? No, not piano. Nor Eleanor's violin; although he recognized the melody straightaway. It revived his nocturnes at the German Hotel, when he would work by the light of the moon or the street lamp. He managed to tune back in to the outside world. It wasn't him; it really was there. The singing. Impossible but true. It was the singing of his tormenter, that portentous dirge sung in the same baritone.

He rushed to the window and there he was, the man in black, the wide-brimmed hat pulled down over his face as always, standing as bold as brass in front of the house. The nerve! Had he come back to challenge Marx to a duel? It wouldn't come to that.

He scrambled for his dressing gown and thought about what might conceivably serve as a weapon as he hurtled down the stairs—was there a pistol on the premises?—before simply clenching his fists and bursting out of the front door instead, ready, willing—if not entirely able—for an altercation. He hesitated between left and right before deciding the warbler must have cut down the small lane opposite the house, since Grafton Terrace was deserted.

After a minute in hot pursuit the muddy terrain yielded no clues. He was chasing shadows. There were no cobblestones to give away the intruder's whereabouts. It was a breezy spring morning. Birds and trees made the only music in this leafy neighbourhood. There was no other option than to run him down. He pushed on, trying to overcome a spastic reflex to give in and throw up. After 300 feet he felt the carbuncle burst, followed by a euphoric release that put a spring in his stride; 300 more and the blood or whatever it was discharging from his backside was making the exertion awkward; 300 more and it was agonizing. His lungs burned, he needed his pipe and he was ready to pull up when he recalled one of Engels's old sayings from their fencing classes at the German Workers Educational Society. Marx was a thruster, never a proper swordsman, and Engels had stressed to him the crucial importance of defence.

'Even when your opponent offers you an easy point, hold back. Let him err, then make your attack. Mark your gait, hold your form and wait.'

Marx repeated the mantra to the pattern of his stride, rasping and wheezing like a hyena, reaching Haverstock Hill on a second wind. But he was chasing shadows again. There wasn't a soul around and he might just as well have been running in the opposite direction. Whatever next! It was a vendetta. Clearly, Marx was being persecuted in retribution for some imagined blow to the spy's career, some personal fault that cried out for a scapegoat. Marx was that scapegoat. The spy knew where he lived, had tracked him down to the rural fringes of the city and was committed to shadowing him for as long as it took to drive his nemesis to the asylum.

Marx rasped and raved. The pain was gathering again. He threw off his dressing gown and ripped it to shreds. His pyjamas went the same way. He tried to rip his own beard off, but that failed. If a dog had been to hand, he would gladly have wrung the life out of man's best friend. In the event, and with nothing else to take out his anger on, he exploded in a fit of incandescent rage.

'You!' he howled, very nearly breaking his vocal chords. 'Who are you? Who! Are! You! Why are you doing this? Why? Haven't you had enough? Speak! Show yourself! You lousy Prussian swine! There's nothing left! Hear me, fucker! No! Thing!'

The tormentor refused to show. To his astonishment, however, on a slow, dejected walk home, Engels did make an unexpected appearance.

'Moor,' said his old friend, stepping out from behind a tree, 'I wonder how your manuscript is coming on.'

'Fred?' a startled Marx replied. He was about to add, 'How happy I am to see you!', when he noticed the giant zero where his friend's face should have been. The figure was large enough to put one's arm through. Barely gathering his senses Marx took off to the house at full pelt, screaming and wailing like a banshee, 'Let me out of the book! Let me out of the book!'

PART III

BACK TO THE FUTURE

Homo
Economicus

Chapter 1

2 Dec. 1863[69]

Dear Frederick,

A telegram arrived two hours ago saying that my mother is dead. Fate had to cart one of us away. Personally I already had one foot in the grave. In the circumstances it seems that I am needed more than the old woman.

I must go to Trier to settle the legacy. I was in considerable doubt as to what Allen's response would be, since I only began taking my half hour recuperative walks three days ago.

However, Allen gave me 2 enormous bottles of medicine and actually thinks it would avail me to go. The wound has not yet finished discharging, but I shall find enough good Samaritan women en route to apply the plaster for me.

I must now ask you to send me sufficient money by return, so that I can leave for Trier forthwith.

Salut.

Your

K. M.

Chapter 2

He stood to pocket 1000 talers from his mother's will but on the ferry to Ostend all Marx could think about were the 10 pounds he owed the butcher. Engels would send Jenny the money to settle up—although that was precisely what he was afraid of. One had to be relatively philosophical. If his home life was stuck in a rut then all manner of unpredictable seismic activity was to be expected. On the other hand, being philosophical couldn't resolve how he felt. It didn't ease his anxiety. There was no future in his life and as he boarded the train in Ostend it was 1849 all over again. This time, however, it felt worse, since now it was a journey *back* in time through ancient scenery. The memorials to failed revolts and past lives returned, the images of a Europe at war—the cannon fire and cannon fodder, the royal standards and red flags—a reverse Odyssey where, instead of a nostalgic trip home, one is carted back to a house in turmoil and upheaval.

Marx sat facing the direction of travel, but it didn't work. The scenery still went backward, not forward, and on alighting in Bonn he was so relieved that he knelt down and kissed the still earth beneath his feet.

On the outskirts of the city he hitched a ride on a horse and cart bound for Kretz. He had had enough of trains to last him a lifetime. The slower pace suited him and he slept for most of the way. To his surprise, on reaching Kretz, the mine, founded by the Romans, lay idle. So much for mineral wealth being the jewel in the crown of the Prussian state. Jewels were no match for capital. Capitalist modernity moved at a different speed. Mineral deposits might take millions of years to reach maturity, but capital could do it in a mere blink of the eye.

He set out to Koblenz on foot, but after 20 minutes renounced the folly. Dr Allen had recommended a half-hour of recuperative walking per day, not a mountain trek. He took a room for the

night and in the morning boarded a coach to Koblenz, and from
there a train that bypassed the Moselle. By the time he arrived in
Trier it was already dark, and after a quick chat with his sister
Sophie he retired to bed and snored his raging head off.

Dealing with his mother's legacy was a monumental bore.
Things would have moved far quicker had his *mater* not, in her
infinite wisdom, prepared two wills instead of one. The first had
named his younger sister Emile as the estate's sole beneficiary
and his uncle Lion as the will's executor. But the second shared
out the house contents and liquid assets among the siblings
without mentioning the uncle. Consequently, everything apart
from day-to-day living space had been placed under seal and
would remain so until the notaries arrived, who were on their
way from Holland. That might take several more days.

His mother had always surpassed herself in frustrating her
son and taking any opportunity she could to interrupt his money
supply. She was still managing it in death. When he reflected on
it now, Marx couldn't decide who had been the stingier of the
two, her or his father. His old man would always take her side
in arguments. The bias was never obvious when he was young,
since she always placed herself in the background. But the more
time went by the clearer it became.

Whenever his father wrote Marx those sermonizing letters of
his it was always the mother's voice Marx detected. Why had his
father always been swayed by her in his decision-making? His
letters might have carried a grain of truth in them—although
Marx couldn't rightly say what that was—but his father's
chastisement was dictated by his wife's moral prejudices. His
son was "living it up" in Berlin, "spending far too much" and
"making a name for himself", while she couldn't afford to pay
her decorator or build an extension on the house. His mother was
a simple-minded woman lacking in cultivation. He could readily
forgive her misguided prejudices. But the father he could not, for
the latter was a thoroughly enlightened man who was gullible

by choice. He wasn't his wife's puppet; nothing so benign. His father disguised himself as her puppet but was really his own. Or the largest in an ascending order of Russian dolls pretending to be the smallest. His had been an exercise in bad faith.

Marx got up late the next day and after lunch locked himself away in his old room. It was just how he remembered it. His sketch of Goethe was still in its frame. In the top drawer of the dresser lay all his school books neatly filed in chronological order. He opened the first and read the following:

Let your speech be perfect,
Let your thoughts be good and pure,
Love and obey your parents,
Always do your best.
Karl Marx, aged six years and three months.

He leafed through the rest, immersing himself for half an hour in every year of his school life. He turned every page and tried to recall every lesson. He remembered his algebra class. Was there any evidence of a precocious interest in differential calculus? Not as far as he could tell; although some of his books his father had kept in the upstairs study.

The door to the study was padlocked and a seal placed over the hinge. He thought about breaking it off. It was sure to land him a fine. Or worse. Then again, to hell with it. Time was money and they were wasting his. They could whistle for the money or send him the bill. Same difference. In any case he would deny all knowledge of it or put it down to sleepwalking.

He broke off the padlock and a mnemonic smell escaped from the room. It was his father's smell. He paused for several moments on the threshold. He didn't dare go any further; then again, he could hardly turn back. He found the key to his father's writing bureau on the mantelpiece, behind the ceramic statue of Frederick the Great. None of his schoolbooks were inside, nothing of interest. His father's papers and personal effects had no doubt been distributed or destroyed shortly after his death, 25 years ago. Marx had missed the funeral, delayed in transit, and afterwards hadn't outstayed his welcome.

He closed the door on the time capsule and went downstairs. It was quiet as the grave. He decided to venture outside. He wanted to see the Westphalens's old place on Neustrasse before it got dark. It would probably be the only opportunity he had before the notaries arrived. It felt exciting to be seeing the old place again. During his teenage years he came to regard it as his own house and by the age of 16 was already spending most of his free time there, playing Jenny and her brother, Edgar, at chess, consuming novels, composing avant-garde symphonies, dressing up her pet dog, Voltaire, and generally annoying the hell out of everyone.

An old man approached him. 'Is it really you?'

Marx felt embarrassed. He couldn't put a name to the face.

'Well, I'll be darned. It is! How are you, young lad?' enquired the man, slowly shaking Marx by the hand. 'How's that fine sister of yours?'

'Jenny's very well,' Marx replied. 'But she's not my sister. She's my wife.'

The old man was getting him mixed up with Jenny's brother, Edgar.

The man was deaf as a post. He cupped his ear and nodded. 'Jenny! Yes. What a sight she was. The most beautiful girl in Trier.'

He called out to passers-by, long-standing residents of the town whom Marx couldn't for the life of him recall, fault of his own poor memory or some misunderstanding on the man's part.

'Mrs von Pannewitz,' he shouted, 'come hither and meet the Baron's boy. He's taking a trip down memory lane.'

The old lady hobbled over wide-eyed and confused, as if it were her own husband risen from the grave.

'Baron?' she mouthed.

'You know!' said the man to the petrified dame. 'The brother of Jenny von Westphalen. Jenny! The queen of the ball!'

On hearing the words she was scarcely able to contain herself. 'Jenny? Jenny!' She began to shake.

'Yes, yes. Indeed, Jenny!'

Marx smiled. He didn't care for the approbation of strangers. But when it came to his wife he was happy to make an exception. Especially since the young woman they were talking about was how he preferred to picture her: the sublime portrait of eternal beauty, and of horizons infinitely great and small, yet to be traversed.

The man continued his nostalgic rambling.

'Your boy was mad to let her go,' he informed the lady, in what was meant as a whisper. 'Breaking off their engagement like that. Whatever could have possessed him? But we must let bygones be bygones.'

The old lady nodded forlornly.

'Handsome man, your Karl,' the veteran went on. 'A lieutenant, wasn't he? A patriot besides. Well, now!'

The old lady wiped her eyes with a handkerchief.

'They could have lived the life of old Riley, they could. And then what happens? Why, she ends up taking off with that... *terrible* young troublemaker. The Jew's son. What's-his-name? Mordechai?'

'Marx!' she blurted, as if purging an evil spirit. 'Karl Marx!'

'Devil!' said the man, crossing himself. 'God have mercy on us all!'

Marx stumbled back to the house, his exhilaration now dissolved in a concoction of bitter sentiments. He was feeling the future now and it was bearing down on him at 120 miles per hour, like the revolutionary train one might mistake for a patch of light at the end of a long dark tunnel.

'Von Pannewitz, von Pannewitz,' he repeated, sweeping the

cobwebs of his mind for the merest of clues. 'But no—that? It couldn't have been.'

On that particular day back in the early thirties he had arrived at the von Westphalens not noticing anything out of the ordinary; except for the telltale sign of Voltaire's barking. Jenny always chastised him for it. She wasn't there and the others seemed content to let the dog go on like that. It was as if he were giving vent in his canine tongue to some family disaster that went beyond grown-up language. Mercifully, no one had died. But when Marx had mentioned Jenny's name her mother left the room and her father came in to greet him, which was unusual, given he should have been at work.

'We're glad you're here, friend,' said the Baron, placing his hands on the shoulders of his young prodigy.

'I came... to see Jenny, sir.'

'Of course you did, Karl. Of course. I know. And Jenny very much wants to see you. She's in her room at the moment, preparing herself. But she'll be along soon.'

Jenny didn't emerge for seven days.

'Is she eating at all? I brought her this,' said Marx the next morning, handing her mother a ginger cake Sophie had baked for her.

'That's so very thoughtful of you,' said the Baroness. 'Do thank your sister, Karl. Jenny will be delighted,' and with that closed the door in his face.

It was all very strange. The next evening Marx went to the Neustrasse and lingered awhile across the street, trying to get a sense of what was going on inside. It was 10 o'clock on a cold November evening and the place seemed deserted. The lamps were all out. But as he walked away he heard the sound of a dreadful wailing. Or perhaps it was Voltaire howling.

The day after that he managed to sneak in and play Edgar at chess. It was an opportunity to pump Jenny's brother for clues.

'Whatever's the matter with Jenny, Edgar?' he managed at last, trying not to sound too concerned.

'Nothing,' the brother replied, to the sound of an almighty thud and a smashing window, followed by a bout of female hysterics.

Half an hour later the ranting and raving stopped, and was replaced by an awful chant: 'Why! Karl! Why! Karl!' It droned on for hours.

Karl? What did *he* have to do with it? He didn't understand. But then four days later he was summoned to the house, where everyone had been gathered in the reception. The Baron was dressed in top hat and tails, and his wife resplendent in a green silk gown and hood. Jenny descended the stairs like a ghost. No one made a sound. When she reached the final stair she came hurtling across the room and threw herself into Marx's arms. Both of them were overwhelmed. They looked at each other and wept.

The Baron smiled and nodded, then he and the Baroness departed for the opera. Whatever the problem had been before — and no one dared allude to it after that — Karl was no longer it. He neither needed nor sought explanation of any kind. To win Jenny's heart was affirmation enough. From that day forth he was no longer her plaything. They were equals whose love blossomed and whose passion radiated out in a beacon that lit up the whole universe.

This night's revelation cast everything in a different light. Marx wondered whether his wife had married the right man. Who did she really want? Who was she? The world was upside down. And he was still floating in space.

He arrived back at the family home and made a beeline for his father's study. He knew what he was looking for. In the bottom drawer of the bureau he found his father's mahogany box, the one inscribed with the Trier coat of arms. Locked. He ransacked the room in search of the key. It didn't seem right to break it open. He could probably spring the lock with a pin, but couldn't find one and didn't dare ask Sophie.

The father must have known this day would come, planned it, knew perfectly well when he locked the box and threw away the key that his son would one day return in search of it. It must have been his express wish, perhaps one of his final acts before he died. The box contained the message his son was meant to find and as he smashed it open he was moved to tears, both by the brilliance of his father's thinking and the dread of what he was about to read.

Chapter 3

The box contained the letters the father had sent the son during the latter's university days in Berlin. He began to read one:

Trier, 2nd March 1837[70]

It is remarkable how, despite my being a naturally lazy writer, I become quite inexhaustible when I have to write to you. I shall not and cannot hide my weakness for you. Sometimes my heart indulges in thinking of you and your future. And yet on other occasions I cannot dispel ideas which arouse in me sad forebodings and fear when, suddenly, I'm struck like a bolt of lightning by the thought: is your heart in agreement with your head and your talents? Does it have room for the earthly and finer feelings that offer such crucial consolation to a sensitive man who inhabits this vale of tears? And since this heart is obviously animated and governed by a demon unfamiliar to most men, is that demon heavenly or Faustian? Will you ever be capable—and this is the least of my heartfelt concerns—of truly human, domestic happiness? And—this is not the least painful of the doubts tormenting my heart, since I have come to love a certain person like my own child—will you ever be capable of spreading happiness among those around you?

What brought this train of thought to me? you will ask. Crazed notions of this kind have often assailed me, but I always managed to dispel them without difficulty for the sake of surrounding you with all the love and care of which my heart is capable, and I'm always happy to forget myself everywhere. But I note a striking phenomenon in Jenny. Owing to her total devotion to you and with her childlike, pure disposition, she betrays at times, involuntarily, a kind of fear, fear laden with foreboding, which does not escape me and which I do not know how to explain, and all trace of which she tried to erase from my heart as soon as I spoke to her about it. What can it be? I cannot make sense of it, but unfortunately experience tells me that I am rarely deceived in such matters.

That you should rise high in the world, the flattering hope of seeing your name in lights one day, along with your earthly well-being, are more than heartfelt wishes. They are long-cherished illusions that have struck deep root in me. Basically, such feelings are largely characteristic of a weak man, and are not free of all vices, such as pride, vanity, egoism, etc., etc., etc. But I can assure you that the realization of these illusions could not make me happy. Only if your heart remains pure and beats in a purely human fashion, and no demonic spirit is capable of estranging it from the finer feelings — only then would the happiness that for many years I have dreamed of finding through you finally be reached. Otherwise I would see the finest aim of my life in ruins. But why should I become too sad and risk depressing you? I do not doubt your filial love for your good, dear mother and myself, and you know very well where we are the most vulnerable.

I move on to positive matters. Jenny came to see us a few days after receiving your letter, which Sophie brought her, to speak about your plan. She appears to approve of your reasons, but fears the step itself, which is understandable. Personally I regard it as good and commendable. As she implies, she is writing to dissuade you from sending the letter directly — an opinion I cannot agree with. In order to put her mind at rest you should inform us eight days in advance of posting the letter. The good girl deserves every consideration and, to repeat, only a life full of tender love can compensate her for what she has already suffered, and even for what she will suffer still, given the extraordinary saints she has to put up with.

Compensate her? Was that what he was? Compensation? It made him sound like the booby prize at the village raffle. And what did his father mean "suffered"? It must have been an allusion to the traumatic incident. He went on reading:

Above all it is my concern for her that makes me wish that you will soon take a decisive step forward in the world. It would give her peace of mind; at least that is what I believe. And I assure you, dear Karl, that were it not for this, I would seek to restrain you from coming forward publicly rather than spur you on. But the bewitching girl has affected my old head too, and I wish above all to see her calm and happy. The task is yours alone and deserves your undivided attention, and it is perhaps to be welcomed that, from the very moment you begin to make your own way in the world, you are compelled to show human consideration, indeed wisdom, foresight and mature reflection, foregoing all demons. I thank heaven for this, for it is the human being in you that I will eternally love. Despite being a practical man I haven't become so jaded as to be indifferent to what is high and good. Nevertheless, I do not readily allow myself to be completely uprooted from the earth, which is my solid basis, and wafted exclusively into airy spheres where I have no solid ground under my feet. All this naturally gives me more reason than I would otherwise have had to reflect on the means at your disposal. You have taken up dramatic composition, and of course it contains much that is true. But bound up with its great openness and importance is, naturally, the danger of coming to grief in the attempt. The inner worth is not always decisive in life, especially in the big cities. Intrigues, cabals, jealousy, perhaps among those who have had the most experience of these, often outweigh what is good, especially if what is good is not yet elevated and sustained by a well-known name.

At this point the letter trailed off into career advice.

Marx caught his breath. He tried pacing the room, his preferred practice for the relief of the pain. Come to think of it, he hadn't paced a room with aplomb since his student days. His lodgings had always been too cramped and his flats even more so. Perhaps it was in this very house that he had last paced well, so well in fact that he ended up pacing straight out of the door all the way to Berlin, never to return. It was the last time he and his father would ever see each other.

It was the autumn of 1837. A huge row had erupted, his father warning that his son's "dramatic composition" was in danger of ruining everything. His father had expressed grave misgivings as to whether or not Marx would be able to support his future bride, given how recklessly he was spending his father's money and how little inclination he had for earning any of his own.

'Where are you going to find the money to keep her?' the father had demanded. 'Karl, I must speak my mind. You are marrying a von Westphalen. Hers is a *highly* respected family. You are placing me in a *very* awkward predicament. You enter this union in a nonchalant state at your utter peril *and mine*. You must assume adult responsibilities.'

'What responsibilities? We're in love!'

'I have grasped the fact only too well. Which is why I repeat: exaltations of love in a poetic mind are a recipe for disaster.'

'Oh! Father. Why must you forever conflate love with mundane things?'

'Because without mundane things there can be no love.'

The argument had turned in circles. Marx had been forced to act. But he knew that by defying his father he was turning the page on an entire chapter of his life. He was becoming an adult. Instantly. He had gone upstairs to pack his things. His father was reading in his armchair by the fire when the son reappeared.

'I am going to Berlin to finish my degree and when I return I shall marry Jenny,' the son announced. 'I have made my decision and will not be swayed.'

The father remained seated and placed his book on the armrest. He inclined ever so slightly his head. There was a quiver of emotion in his voice as he began to speak. But nothing could prevent him from delivering the verdict that he must have rehearsed in his mind a thousand times.

'You must choose, Karl. Marry Jenny or pursue your literary ambitions. But you cannot have both. If you do you will only live to regret it.'

Chapter 4

Their filial love went beyond the bounds of devotion. But as he arrived at Trier Cemetery it struck Marx that there had been too much love by halves. Too much love and not nearly enough care. Love overindulged and spoiled; the love so blind that it ends in resentment and self-loathing. Not caring less. He passed the line of portentous tombs with their Roman columns and Norman archways leading to nowhere before standing in front of the simple gravestone which read:

HEINRICH MARX
15 April 1777 — 10 May 1838

Mercifully the family had refrained from erecting a tomb flanked by archangels blowing trumpets. But still. It was a pity he and his father had rendered the other in marble and placed him on a pedestal.

His father's ultimatum was wrong-headed. Never had he managed to grasp the meaning of his son's philosophy. It wasn't the "content" that escaped him. It was the motivation, the practical ends it was meant to serve. As a student Marx had launched himself into poetry and metaphysics. It had taken him a small age to work through the competing systems. The German philosopher Hegel was a must. Not that he enjoyed grappling with the old dog. How anyone could put up with his craggy melody was a mystery. And yet for all Marx's hatred of abstract philosophical speculation there was no choice but to confront it, as one must the highwayman who steps out from the bushes on an isolated track in the woods. Idealist philosophy was the enemy and it had to be dealt with. But it couldn't be overcome once and for all. Instead, it had to be brought round — by force if necessary — to one's own ends. What ends? Revolutionary ones, of course. Communism, ultimately: the future society based on the free association of workingmen, and free in the sense of truly self-governing individuals. If the social criticism to which Marx adhered had any reason to be then it had to be practical. One couldn't be an abstract writer. One was a writer either by profession or else by dint of one's social class.

Explaining his philosophical motivations to his father was a lost cause; although, admittedly, Marx shared some of the blame for having failed to express himself clearly. He was young and his ideas were still evolving. Moreover, his communication with his father had become strained, mired in the son's own fantasies. Then again, his father's idea of philosophy was Voltaire (the French philosopher, not Jenny's dog). Thought experiments, bourgeois sermons, conundrums whose sole aim was to champion and defend the so-called intellectual status quo. But the status quo wasn't intellectual any more and it certainly wasn't fixed. Voltaire had by no means stumbled on an eternal truth. Neither had Hegel, for that matter. The revolutions they supported were old hat and out of date by the standards of their own ideas. History was going in a different direction, in the direction of an unprecedented proletarian takeover. A world revolution. Which made his father's statement meaningless. Choose? Jenny or the book? He couldn't have both? Why ever not, Father? Because "dramatic composition" is produced in the comfort of one's study, whereas marriage is a "solemn vow", albeit one dependent on a regular salary?

His father had no idea. In the future society Marx was working to achieve one *could* have it all: the wife *and* the book. The children, the dog, the pony and the piano... the whole damned affair! The fact that Marx didn't *personally* have the book yet was, admittedly, a poor demonstration of his theory. But that didn't mean his theory had been disproven. Indeed, he was about to put things right by finishing the book once and for all. He wasn't going to let his father have the last word.

He wanted to spend some time with his sister before he left and the following evening they talked. Could she throw any light on "Karl"?

'That was so long ago,' she sighed as if preparing to break a vow of silence. 'I only know what you know, Karl.' She touched his hand. 'Despite what happened all those years ago… Jenny loves you and always will.'

'They made me out to be an ogre,' he murmured, distracted by the sound of children playing outside.

'Who?'

'Mmm? Oh, no one. I went to the Westphalens's on Neustrasse. Some old codger. He mistook me for Edgar. I overheard him tell von Pannewitz's mother that I'd carted off Jenny; that "the Jew" had seduced her, as if ever I had it in me. Jenny was four years older than me. How was I meant to seduce *her*? If anything it was the opposite!'

Sophie opened her mouth but the words failed to come out.

'What were you about to say?'

'I was…' She was hiding something.

'What?'

'No, no… Only what I've said already. We all change, Karl. Our perspectives change with the passing years.'

'But that's not change,' he objected. 'What's your point?'

Sophie changed tack. 'Would you and Jenny still marry knowing what you both know now? If you had to go back in time would you still go through with it?'

Marx thought it over before responding. The question was either too philosophical or not philosophical enough.

'I can hardly speculate fairly given she's my wife now, can I? But of course I would. Why? What do you know that might make me reconsider?'

'No, no… I was curious, that's all.'

He became irritated. But the irritation was his fault. He shouldn't have forced the conversation in this direction. He went to bed and the following morning set out early for the station. He had unfinished business to attend to.

.

Chapter 5

In Cologne Marx felt ill at ease and couldn't work out why. Perhaps it was the gothic cathedral looming up like a giant spider as he haggled over oranges in the marketplace. He didn't pay heed to monsters or ghosts. There had to be a more rational explanation. That morning he had shaved off his beard as a precaution. But on reflection it seemed a stupid thing to have done, since his documents were all in order. His expulsion from the Rhineland, which had paved the way for his exile to Paris back in '49, was ancient history. Moreover, Cologne was hardly Prussia. A middle-aged man passing through Cologne on his way back to England from his mother's funeral posed no threat to civic peace. But then the more he reasoned thus, the more ill at ease he became. Politics played on the infinite chessboard had a different set of rules. Not only did he not understand them, he didn't even know whose move it was.

Stieber. He knew it. His discomfort defined in a single word. At the far end of the platform Prussian soldiers were stopping and searching passengers. A plain-clothes inspector was running the show. Marx tried to make out the face of the organ-grinder in the wide-brimmed hat. His monkeys were like bulls in a china shop, but the man himself betrayed the dedication of someone used to skulking round in dark alleyways. He knew what he was doing. The Prussian eagle was taking flight in search of fresh prey. In the meantime, just over the horizon, the Russian bear crouched. Bonaparte had predicted that the whole of Europe would in 50 years either be republican or Cossack. On reflection another of his pithy remarks seemed more apposite in the circumstances: "A spy who keeps his eyes open is worth a corps of soldiers." It seemed to sum up the inspector perfectly, who was clearly on a mission that had nothing to do with the Prussian state. He was being driven—almost consumed—by discipline for its own sake, a discipline that relied on the interception of innocents in a no man's land of officialdom, and ultimately presided over by unelected, unaccountable and irrevocable bureaucrats. The Germans had become objects of knowledge and Marx was one such object. He was the fly in Stieber's ointment. No doubt somewhere in the Berlin Police Headquarters there was a dartboard with a sketch of Marx's face pinned to it. The inspectors would throw darts at it whenever they needed to unwind, and do whatever else took their fancy in homage to his image. He must have been quite the pin-up.

It was Stieber all right. The cigar-shaped moustache and grey slits for eyes gave him away. Marx's train was due to depart in less than five minutes. But the odds of him being on it were rapidly diminishing. He began to perspire and rummaged for his handkerchief. The bottle of anal balm spilled out of his suitcase and rolled along the platform with a mind of its own. At first he decided to ignore it and pretend it wasn't his, before remembering that his name was written on the label.

'Herr Doctor! Dr Marx? You've dropped your medicine!' An interfering spinster divulged his name to the world, along with the nature of his intimate complaint.

Heads craned along the length of the platform. He thanked the lady through his teeth and willed a natural disaster. He drifted away. All he had to do was compose himself. Boarding a train wasn't rocket science.

A workingman recognized him and waved from inside one of the compartments. It was probably a case of mistaken identity. It had been known and had its advantages. Marx ignored him but the man persisted. There was no harm to it. Youngsters. Then some others joined in and soon several of them were hammering on the window. One of them shouted raucously through the grill. Marx shuffled away. He could take the next train, albeit at the risk of missing his connection in Brussels.

In the meantime, however, a constable had been alerted by the commotion. The train was due to depart in a minute's time and Marx had to be aboard. It was the train back to the future. His train.

'Constable, I categorically refuse not to be on that train,' he rehearsed himself saying.

'Why, Dr Marx,' the constable in his head replied, 'if you think the train provides the key to the enigmatic dimension of social reality that you have been trying to set down on paper for 30 years then, by all means, be my guest: board your train. But do hurry, because the train is about to depart.'

A steam whistle sounded setting the wheels in motion.

'Pardon me! If you please!'

Marx froze; a small uniformed man with pink teeth placed a hand on his arm. 'I need to ask you some questions, sir,' the man announced.

'That's my train!' said Marx, vocalizing his private wish and shaking free his arm.

The constable, who was small, frail and might have blown away in a stiff breeze, reached for his whistle. It was now or never. Marx ran away from a muddle of interpellations.

'You there! Halt!'

He was becoming quite accustomed to the Emergency Express, despite being unsure of how to board a moving train in the real world. He heard the exhortations of the workingmen behind glass, but it wouldn't be straightforward, since nuns of all people were congregating in large numbers on the platform up ahead and blocked his path.

'Coming through!' yelled the fugitive before ploughing into them like a rugby player hitting a haystack.

His suitcase went flying and landed on the head of one of the unfortunate congregation, but for whose placement his bottle of anal balm would have surely smashed. The Lord moves in mysterious ways. Amen. He recovered the case and made a beeline toward the platform edge. The carriages began accelerating away in a recursive line. The relative gravitational potentials of the moving bodies—theirs and his—were repulsing one another now.

He tried to lift his leg up onto the footplate. The manoeuvre required two hands and reaching out his good one caused his legs to buckle. He overbalanced and very nearly tripped, but managed to stay upright; nonetheless, the loss of momentum made the task even more improbable.

Marx ran through a cloud of steam and on exiting it the end of the platform came hurtling toward him. Then, on the verge of giving in to Newton, the workingman from the window flung open the door of the carriage—the last—and wrestled Marx aboard just in time to ward off gravity's impact. The workers cheered, ruffled his hair and slapped him senseless like a long-lost brother.

The revolutionary train of thought gathered momentum. The scenery was a vast unfurling tapestry in magnificent perspective. He set off along the corridor performing the requisite gymnastics. The space heaved with workingmen and several carriages further on, at the threshold of middle class, the confluence became a one-way stream of traffic.

'Ladies and gentleman! Tickets, please!' the inspector pleaded, but the appeal was lost in the melee.

The workingmen had taken matters into their own hands by invading middle class and commandeering the compartments, ignoring the remonstrations of those above their station, so to speak, and ushering in a free-for-all. Minded to establish some direction, Marx forged a path through the scrum and on reaching the end of the penultimate carriage, undid the chain separating it from the engine.

He approached the final door beyond which only drivers and engineers dared venture. Bracing himself and without a sideways glance he jumped onto the rear of the engine. The iron was hot and brittle. He climbed halfway up the ladder. The view peering over the driver's cab left nothing to the imagination. The wind rattled through him, blowing away the cobwebs, re-energizing his intellectual faculties and liberating those attributes of his mind he never knew existed. He was behind the screen of the diorama that separated the audience from its theatre. Cannons exploded to the left then right then left again. Streaks of fire ripped through the battlefield mapped out in the n dimensions of an infinite chessboard, stretching far enough back for the horizon to stretch itself to the point that no longer was a point. This was the final battle.

Louis-Napoléon and Bismarck[71] faced off on opposite sides of the chessboard, grandmasters in name only. Their Imperial Dinosaurs could survey all they liked for all the good it would do. This was real life seen through a lens as big as the universe, inscribed in universal laws, not patriotic announcements in the illustrated press. As they and their equestrian retinues receded into the distance they became as small and as threatening as toy figurines. How just and fitting—how logical—that in the game for ultimate control of the European chessboard neither man was going to win. History had delivered them their marching orders. Fait accompli.

'My Emperor, my Emperor is a captive!' cried Marx in a madcap fit of laughter.

A new ensemble cast appeared on the scene in the guise of women and children running behind a moustachioed general on a black charger. The light trembled, the scene darkened and the train rounded a bend.

The carriages fell in line and the engine put on a spurt. Marx watched up ahead imagining that the miscalculation was his. But the suicidal apparition of the bridge was real. Suddenly he knew how the college-goers, drunks and lunatics must have felt as the murky waters of the Thames came hurtling toward them. There was nothing he could do. Either he was going over the bridge this time or going straight to hell. There was no middle ground—or ground at all—and no possible synthesis. *Hic Rhodus, hic salta*!

The bridge with its span missing resembled one of his most

recent formulas. But imagination wouldn't do when the solution went far beyond common sense. Think. The problem had always been how to overcome a "limit" that continued indefinitely. How to make the jump from ∞ to 0? It was like trying to land the front wheels of a train on a sixpence.

Throwing his notebook to the four winds he gulped down his final breath and prayed they would never find his body. The whistle played its polyphonic symphony in a delirious key and signalled to anyone who cared that this godforsaken crate wasn't making any more unscheduled stops. Less than 1000 yards of track left and the engine accelerated toward zero, the axles squealing a monstrous siren of protest and the furnace threatening to blow.

'You're free, Prometheus!' yelled Marx. 'Come! Throw off your chains! Throw them!'

500, 400, 300... It was all in the lap of the Titans or those mad scientists convinced that by throwing sufficient mud at the walls they were bound to hit upon a novel idea.

'I have you now, Prometheus, you damned imposter, you!'

And yet the solution was there. A body travelling sufficiently fast *could* span infinity, reasoned the mad scientist, insofar as mass is equivalent to energy and one is convertible into the other. He was heavier than usual when he felled the nuns by virtue of his momentum. Had he hit them at twice the speed he would have been heavier still, &c. Ditto the revolutionary train. Travelling at many thousands of miles per hour made it a different beast from the one stood idly on the platform. Why, it wasn't the same "thing", at all.

The same held in the sphere of money circulation. Variable magnitudes could be converted into variable quantities of capital. All that is solid melts into air; although what melts into air doesn't just disappear. Whereas a commodity was meant to be consumed, money never could be. Like physical matter, which could neither be created nor destroyed, capital could always adopt new forms, from the sale, purchase and loan of everything from labour power,

Prussian armies, natural resources, model train sets to capital itself. In fine, capital was limitless. It was the lord and god of the world of commodities.[72]

Had he retained his notebook he would have set the idea down on paper. Instead, he merely screamed his last word in defiant rebuke to the parochial reason of this planet: M-C-M.

Whether the train was defying gravity or tumbling into the void was impossible to say. It made little difference given that the Earth had already been falling into the sun for somewhere in the region of 4.543 billion years at the moment the train left the tracks. In that moment an infinite pattern appeared, comprising everyone he had ever known and loved, detested, disliked and felt damned indifferent toward.

Light migrated into a long tunnel, a transparent container of his visual field. At the very end was a small window. He was going through the window. Perspective froze momentarily and he lost his sense of direction. As the front wheels touched down his vision resumed, as did gravity, which brought up most of his dinner. A staccato of thuds rattled his bones and threatened to shake him off his perch. He clung on to the ladder for dear life as the remainder of the galloping leviathan caught up; or most of it. Petrified screams carried on the breeze, followed by a low rumble. Then a hideous explosion confirmed that the rear carriage hadn't made it across the gap.

'The theory needs some work,' Marx shrugged. 'What do you want me to say?'

The train continued its progress. So fast was it travelling that even its shadow appeared to be blurred, which didn't make sense; although, on reflection, his eyesight was shot to pieces. As the engine slowed the terrain flattened out and the scenery changed to reveal a gathering on a public square and people making speeches from a balcony. A cannonade sounded. It was the Hôtel de Ville in Paris.

The image dissolved and Marx came to, his nose pressed against the window of his compartment. He was back in the terrestrial hell; the pain from his nether regions confirmed it was real. The whirlwind trip had taken it out of him and he resolved to take a bath the moment he reached the house. Hot, cold, it didn't matter, providing the water was clean.

He wiped the steam from the glass. The train was pulling into Waterloo Bridge. Over the river the clock tower appended to the Tory talking shop was nearing completion; the Great Fossil Lizard was showing off its new member.

On account of some masochistic urge to experience comfort Marx decided to travel home by cab. On reaching Primrose Hill the driver veered off on a detour. They were probably repairing the roads again. One could barely keep up with the changing landscape. He peered out at the monoliths, each one more imperious than the last and wholly at odds with its surroundings. Volcanic islands of capital.

Eventually, the cab turned into a crescent and pulled up outside an almost palatial residence, a three-storey terrace house set back some way from the road. The cab driver opened the door and Marx alighted to the sound of nightingales warbling *prestissimo*. A wad of bills in his wallet took him by surprise. He handed over the fare and without thinking instructed the driver to keep the change. The panic subsided and as he walked the garden path and climbed the steps to the red door flanked by Roman columns he wondered whether the solution lay in the number: 1.

'Afternoon to you, sir,' said a man in an apron. 'Spring's arrived!'

Marx ducked instinctively, but the salutation was genuine, not the usual preamble to a summons. The tradesman smiled, tipped his hat, climbed onto his butcher's van and cantered off whistling a familiar tune.

On entering Marx almost swooned. He could hardly have been more at home. The hallway was fitted with red carpet, which extended all the way to the top of the stairs. There were potted plants, indoor palms and geraniums on stands, and fresh ivy decorated the foot of the banisters. Bright sunlight issuing from the back room filtered through stained glass and overall the ambiance was positively charming. He could smell coffee.

He heard voices being raised. Not an argument. More the vigorous discussion of a progressive ladies seminary.

'It's hardly immoral, Mother,' said a voice. 'This is 1867 and the story was published in 1856. Morality goes with the times.'

'I'm not denying it,' replied the other. 'What I'm saying is it's not a moral book according to taste. It goes against the grain of public decency.'

On the marble-topped dresser by the front door a parcel addressed to Herr Marx lay unopened. His heart sank. Judging by its size and heft it had to be paperwork relating to one of his legal wrangles. Duncker, he surmised, aware he would never manage to shake off the curse of Berlin. But the postmark said Hamburg, not Berlin.

He unwrapped it, daring not to open his eyes until the book had been in his hands for a full minute. It was a bulky tome and judging by the smell of the paper newly printed. A first edition. He opened his eyes and glanced at the cover:

Capital
A Critique of Political Economy
By
Karl Marx
First Volume
Book I: The Process of Production of Capital

'If a man doesn't truly know the woman he marries, Mother, then all morality might as well go out the window... Father!' Eleanor bounded over and kissed him on the cheek. 'Mother! Papa's back!'

She led him by the hand to the sitting room, where the women were taking their elevenses. He acknowledged his wife, as did she, tilting her head and appraising him through the lorgnette eyeglasses perched on the end of her nose.

'Well?' she said. 'Did everything turn out as expected?'

'I'm back,' was all he could say with certainty.

'I'm glad, Karl,' said she, nibbling her scone. 'We're always glad to get you back. Aren't we, Eleanor?'

'Father,' said the daughter, 'aren't you going to tell us what's in the parcel? Helene! Father's here!'

He was still clutching the book but declined to break the seal lest he should be horrified by some typographical error. He and Engels had pored over the proofs for months. The relief of seeing it in print came from knowing that now it was done he could really get to work on the second volume; that was the place for setting out the real argument.

Giving in to temptation, he flipped it open to the first page. How appropriate, he thought, to have dedicated his magnum opus to Wolff,[73] "bold and faithful champion of the proletarian cause". Well said. *Capital* was Marx's Silesian moment,[74] his intellectual rising. It was a work of the transition to a new way of thinking bourgeois political economy. But what was he saying? It *was* a new way of thinking all unto itself. He should have felt immeasurably proud—and did! He would brandish it everywhere he went, even have a new suitcase made, a leather one, for the express purpose of transporting his copy.

'So,' said Helene, setting down a china teapot on the dining table, 'what's all the fuss about?'

'Father has a special announcement,' said Eleanor, who clearly knew what it was.

'Well, go on, Karl,' said Jenny, 'don't keep us all in suspense.'

'My book,' he said, handing her the 600-page doorstop.

'Oh!' she replied, straining under the impediment to feminine decorum. She placed it on the table, as if divesting herself of a snake or lion cub, whose mere presence in the room gave cause for concern.

Meaning to open it but quickly changing her mind, she said, 'Congratulations, Karl,' and reached for her embroidery.

It was a valid response to a whole life's work and to a book she was already in. Whether or not she recognized his achievement — and naturally she did — she had still been instrumental in helping him bring it to fruition. They would no doubt discuss it when the time came. There was time at last. Now the book was published they had all the time in the world.

'Capital!' exclaimed Eleanor in a flutter of excitement, who in spite of her 12 years could reel off the book's main concepts and proceeded to do thus.

Of course, he recognized his own voice in hers, like the talking bird that parrots one's favourite expressions. But his daughter's enthusiasm made him satisfied beyond words, since hers was the generation for whom his work had really been intended. They would be its standard bearers. The thought rekindled his optimism — a new experience, given how long it had been blowing in the wind and languishing in mental torment. A fine feeling. As for Helene, she was unmoved; though, later on, Marx embarrassed her by sneaking back to the sitting room and walking in as she was nearing the end of the first chapter.

'It's all Greek to me!' she exclaimed, throwing up her arms, which was her way of paying him a compliment. She could hardly plead total ignorance when it came to economy, at least not in the domestic sphere.

Later that evening he retired to his study where finally he found the courage to go through the text. The few typographical errors he discovered he could live with and in any case would have to until the second edition came out. The content was the thing. On balance, the misgivings he had harboured about the book's presentation had probably been justified from the start. A mere impression, but delving into the tome as any non-specialist reader might, Part I stood out. On reflection, and along with Part V, he should have confined it to the appendix. It was a minor oversight. Serious readers would skip them. After all, his was a scientific enterprise and by definition a work in progress. The book wasn't a bible. It was raw material for experimentation. Proving his theory was a matter of coming to the table armed with the correct interpretive apparatus. After all, a man aiming to produce diamonds might possess an abundance of igneous rock and yet, for lack of proper equipment, would fail to cut a single gemstone.

Capital, Marx decided, should be "read" in the same spirit. Mere understanding wasn't the only issue. Every workingman could grasp what he was saying, since Marx had invested their struggle—which was *his* struggle, too—in every line. The book marked a beginning, planted a flag in a battlefield. Where it would end wasn't presently clear. The important thing to bear in mind, however, was that the revolution wasn't far off and that based on the seismic rumblings filtering back from various quarters, the workers, through their revolutionary deeds, were already putting his theory to the test.

Chapter 6

In the new decade Marx was determined to learn Russian. He had no desire to speak the language. But the beat of the tribal drums confirmed the crucial importance of all manner of goings-on east of the Danube. Bonaparte's famous dictum that all Europe would in 50 years either be republican or Cossack had of course already been realized by the nephew in the monstrous synthesis of the Cossack republic.[75] But there was nothing to fear from imperial demagogues. Their days were numbered. The east was the land of the rising sun. Things happened there first by necessity.

'Are you not going to drink your tea, Father?' said Eleanor. 'And it's "чай", in *case* you were wondering.'

And then there was Ireland. There were obvious parallels between the mad inhabitants of the Emerald Isle and the Slavs. Peasants could more easily be hoodwinked than the industrial working classes—

'It's getting cold: холодно,' chuckled Eleanor.

Not to mention Germany. That was where things were really heating up. Its recent war with France only went to prove that the working classes were the only people with a true foreign policy. The bourgeoisie got off on sycophantic patriotism, imagining there to be someone in Heaven watching over them, without recognizing that very someone as their own mirror image. There was no future in narcissism. The gates of Heaven would soon come crashing down on their heads.

'Father!' said Eleanor, becoming exasperated, 'if we don't leave now then we'll miss all the speeches.'

'Mmm?'

She handed him the mug. '*Drink* your чай.'

'Very well, very well,' said he, becoming exasperated, too.

'And don't even think about coming back early,' warned Helene with a raised finger. 'I've a pile of housework to get through. As for that study of yours—'

'You can do as you please up there,' Marx cut in as he rummaged through his coat pockets, 'but don't touch any paperwork. Rearrange the furniture—redecorate the place, if you like—but kindly do *not* touch the paperwork. It's arranged just how I like it.'

Helene stopped what she was doing and folded her arms. 'And what did your last servant die of?'

'I'm just saying,' said Marx, finally locating his wallet in the pantry, 'in case you get any ideas.'

'I was about to say,' said Helene, 'before you butted in, that I shan't be going anywhere *near* your study. So think on it. You can't teach an old dog new tricks. You've made your bed and as far as I'm concerned you can lie in it.'

'Oh, that's quite unfair! He's getting better, Lenchen. Aren't you, Father?' Eleanor brushed some crumbs from his lapel and straightened his cravat.

'More organized with every passing day,' said Marx, distractedly. 'Keys! I knew I was looking for something…'

'Out!' said Helene, herding them into the hallway, 'both of you.'

'But I need my keys!'

'And don't be back before six!' she said, slamming the front door.

'Wait a moment! I forgot my newspaper,' but Helene turned a blind eye to Marx's pleading and closed the curtains on the front window when he tried to persuade her to let him back in.

'You can buy a copy of *The Times* on the way,' said Eleanor, grabbing him by the arm and leading him down the garden path. 'I know you're a stingy old sort, but still—'

'Stingy! Stingy?' Marx dug his heels in. 'I'll have you know, young lady, that I paid for your violin in cash.'

Eleanor blushed.

'That's right. You're right to turn a certain shade. I haven't heard you playing *that* for a while. The other girls in the neighbourhood were green with envy when I bought it. Your mother thinks I spoil you. Stingy? Indeed.'

'Well, I didn't mean *that* type of stingy,' said the daughter sheepishly. 'I meant… economical. Anyway, can we *please* stop talking about money? It's too squalid.'

Marx nodded and offered her his arm. 'That's better.'

Eleanor counted the new-builds as they flew down Primrose Hill. On reaching Regent's Park, however, the omnibus hit traffic.

'56!'

'Mmm?' said Marx, squinting at the newspaper the gentleman opposite was holding.

'I've counted 56 new detached houses in the past half-hour. They weren't there a month ago.'

'You must have a memory like an elephant,' said the father, inspecting his inside jacket pocket. 'Did I not bring my monocle? You didn't pick it up by any chance, did you?'

'Now *why* would I pick up *your* monocle, Father?' the daughter huffed. 'You left it on the kitchen table, if you *must* know. It was there right in front of you.'

'Oh! And you didn't think to tell me?'

'Your memory is like is sieve,' said Eleanor, shaking her head and gesticulating wildly.

'It doesn't lose the important data—fortunately.' Marx politely tried to attract the gentleman's attention, but the sour-faced top hat, whose top hat occupied its own seat, hid behind his paper.

'So!' said Eleanor, contriving to change the subject. 'Who are you most looking forward to listening to today?'

'Me?' said Marx, showing their tickets to the conductor. 'Oh, I'm not bothered. When you've attended as many of these events as I have you know more or less who's going to say what.'

'Yes, but you must admit there's nothing like a rousing speech, is there? It's the Irish, after all. When an Irishman speaks it's like hearing a rebel orchestra.'

'I see you're wearing your green ribbon,' Marx noted. 'Very smart.'

'It was a present from Auntie B.' Eleanor began to sing "God save our flag of green" to the tune of the national anthem, which provoked disgruntled noises from the other passengers. Marx laughed heartily at the irreverent ditty and enjoyed it so much that by the end of the first verse he was outdoing his daughter by improvising a second:

> Fenians march again
> Blow up the houses of
> Parliament.
> Confound its politics
> And the Brits' dirty tricks
> And feed them arsenic
> Long live the Celts.

Eleanor invented a third that departed from the political theme and included a risqué reference to the queen's "purple-faced mutton chops". The rebel choir collapsed in a riot of laughter. The conductor refused to see the funny side, no doubt owing to the fact that by Oxford Circus most of his passengers had deserted the drunken boat.

'I say, conductor!' said Marx, aiming to get a rise out of the man, who by now was visibly fuming. 'Won't you come and join in our sing-song?'

The conductor broke into a temper. 'That's it! Off you get!'

'Do I detect an Irish accent there?' said Marx archly.

'Certainly not!' came the reply. 'Off!'

When the rebels reached Hyde Park the speeches were already in full swing. Eleanor was more informed than her father, who was rather put out by the presence of Odger[76] on the platform. She gave a running commentary, introducing each of the speakers with a brief biography and explaining *au fur et à mesure*, with the aid of dialectical reasoning, why revolutionary violence had to be adopted in the struggle for Irish independence. Marx understood his daughter's position, which in the true dialectical spirit of the times he vehemently opposed, albeit with the aim of overcoming their opposition in a higher synthesis.

'I can't agree with you, Father,' said Eleanor, affirming the impasse. 'One mustn't compromise with the baddies of Empire.'

Before long Marx's rear end began to rebel in its own inimitable style. There was nowhere to rest it. Not wishing to inflict the tragedy on the audience, he wandered downwind far enough for the smell to disperse in the outdoor container—although, since the crowd were tightly packed, he was soon exiting the park through the main gates and wandering off along Piccadilly.

He took a pint in the Queen's Head then went up Bond Street to the Burlington Arcade, where he thought about purchasing a new straw hat for the summer (Eleanor's dog, Whisky, had eaten his old one). The ones he preferred were exorbitantly expensive and despite having the money he decided to keep strolling instead, since the exercise did him good and there were very few people on the streets.

On reaching the east gate of St James's Park he wasn't remotely tired and kept going, eager to see what progress had been made on the Westminster clock tower and whether or not the time was ripe for a Fenian assault on Parliament. He stood at the base of the granite monolith somewhat in awe of the operation. One of the clock faces was being winched into place. It never occurred to him that there would be four clocks to tell the same time.

Since the Waterloo terminal wasn't far he decided he might as well kill two birds with one stone and book tickets for the family's spring jaunt to the coast. But on entering the station's main concourse he instantly regretted his decision.

'I'm afraid we're not able to sell you a ticket that far in advance,' said the man in the ticket office, whose being behind bars spoke volumes.

'But it's a month away,' said Marx, distracted by the general commotion and a creeping sense of déjà vu.

'It's no longer the company's policy, sir. The terms of refunding tickets have changed.'

'But I don't want a refund. I want to purchase tickets.'

'That doesn't alter the policy, sir,' said the man. Logically speaking, his argument was quite correct. The problem was that it was meaningless.

Marx headed for the exit in an irate mood. He waved away the hawker and pressed himself through the crowd before remembering his newspaper. Another hawker appeared screeching himself hoarse, then another, and on regaining the station entrance it occurred to him that the great commotion far exceeded the routine bustle of commuters, many of whom had interrupted their journeys to appraise themselves of the news.

He scanned the evening edition of *The Times*. Adverts, nothing but adverts. Then he realized he was looking at the back page. He turned over, almost anticipating the surprise. Almost. "The Workers Rule Paris", read the headline. He dropped the paper and punched the air so hard it almost ruptured his spleen.

'Worker power!' he shouted at the top of his voice.

A lady cradling her poodle very nearly had a heart attack.

'There, there,' cooed Marx at the animal that wanted to bite his finger off. 'Nice doggy.'

From this day forth he would love dogs, petition the revolutionary government in Paris to establish a national holiday in their honour. Open a Ministry for Dogs. Cats could hardly be left out. Although Marx drew the line at rats. Granted they were mammals, but one should heed Darwin. The mental capacities of human beings were different in degree from other mammals, not in kind. That being said, the human race was a distinct species.

The bodies separated and he drifted back toward the river, retracing his steps without so much as a thought for anything more than the simple act of placing one foot in front of the other. He could manage that in the new society. He could drift.

It was all so different without having changed that much. All on account of a tiny earthquake. But the shock would spread. It was building; one could feel it. Marx surveyed the map of the city whose scale was 1:1. How strange to think he was finally seeing the real thing. Was the world ready for change? It didn't matter. It was already there; only more so. The bone-crushing factories still stymied the senses; more boats were jostling for control of the narrow section at Westminster Bridge; more factories cannonading the orange soot — a sudden burst brought him to his senses — and more working up of raw materials into finished goods. More, basically.

And yet there was something *even more* remarkable about it than the spectacle he had first set eyes on back in '49. Capitalism was fast running out of places to hide. It could no longer move unseen like some mythic creature of the bog.

A concrete embankment had been built upstream as far as the distillery at Vauxhall Stairs, the upshot being that the Upper Lambeth Marsh was no longer prone to flooding and disease. On the North Bank, where once he had sunk in mud up to his knees, was another embankment. It was only a matter of time before the infernal factories would be reined in and their activity curtailed; no thanks to the top hats in that palatial talking shop yonder, but to the workers themselves and their unshakeable demands for a real life.

How ironic, Marx thought, that the Tories had constructed a giant clock for overseeing it all: a clock for counting down the time on their own destruction and to the arrival of the new society. Year Zero. How admirably progressive and revolutionary the bourgeois class were. Once fully arrived in the new society one would no doubt need a new type of clock.

His walk back to Hyde Park took much longer than expected. He had to sit down and rest several times on account of his bunions. On reaching Hyde Park Corner most of the crowds had gone. A band of Irish folk players were treating a young lady to their merrymaking. She kept trying to shoo them off but her objections only gave impetus to their routine. They yelped and hooted and made more noise with their tongues than music with their instruments. The ringleader, who played the penny whistle, for every few bars of delirious music would remove his hat and hold it directly under her nose. Drawing closer, Marx recognized the lady as his daughter. She had tears in her eyes.

'Father!' she said with a huge sigh of relief. 'You had me worried silly! But where *were* you?'

The musicians promptly scattered. Eleanor clung to him and planted a kiss on his cheek. She started to sob profoundly. Marx took her in his arms. He could barely contain himself and presently they were both in tears. He gently stroked her hair.

'Tussy, Tussy,'[77] he whispered over and over until the emotions settled.

She dried her eyes and made light of the panic. He handed her *The Times* and she duly read the news. By now her face was quite composed. When she had finished reading she handed the paper back to him.

'Now,' she said, adjusting the ribbon in her hair, then ever so slowly observed, 'you know what this means, don't you?'

'No,' said the father.

'It means… we need those darned musicians back!'

And with that they cried and hugged again before dancing the Irish jig all the way up Park Lane.

Chapter 7

At the beginning of July 1870, Prince Leopold of Hohenzollern, the nephew of King Wilhelm I of Prussia, withdrew his candidacy for the Spanish throne. The French Emperor Napoléon III had staunchly opposed the marriage between Prussia and Spain. However, not content with the royal climb-down, he instructed his ambassador in Berlin to gain assurances from the Prussian king that no Hohenzollern prince would ever petition for the Spanish throne again.

The king refused and broke off contact with the ambassador. He instructed the Prussian chancellor, Otto von Bismarck, to publicize the incident and state for the record the crown's position. When Bismarck's edited version of the Prussian king's "snub" hit the French newsstands on 14 July, Bastille Day, the public mood hit fever pitch. On 19 July, Bonaparte declared war on Prussia.

In the days that followed, England's Queen Victoria wrote to her eldest daughter, the Princess Royal and future Queen of Prussia, lamenting the "unjustifiable conduct of the French".[78] In the satirical magazine *Punch* a cartoon appeared of Marianne attempting to restrain Bonaparte from entering into "a duel to the death".[79] France's declaration of war had been "cynical", according to Robert Browning.[80] On 2 September, 6 weeks later, Napoléon III surrendered at the Battle of Sedan, precipitating the fall of the French Empire. The French might have been excused for their unjustifiable conduct.

Petrified by the prospect of another worker uprising on the scale of the June revolution of 1848, republican deputies scrambled to the Hôtel de Ville, where they set up a National Defence government. It soon became clear, however, that this government had no intention of defending the nation. A Janus-faced strategy ensued. On the one hand, the foreign ministry began negotiating with Bismarck while the Prussians marched on Paris, surrounded the city and occupied large parts of the French provinces. On the other hand, the Minister of War and of the Interior Léon Gambetta led a campaign of national resistance. In Paris itself the National Guard, comprising some 240,000 men, stood armed. However, they did not enter into the government's "defensive" strategy.

The French army generals had no intention of resisting. The government's priority, according to its monarchist president General Trochu, was the defence of "religion, property and the family". But its other priority, a corollary or condition of the first, was to pay the Prussians a war indemnity courtesy of a loan from the Bank of France, for which the government's leading negotiators, Jules Favre and Adolphe Thiers, had their eyes set on a hefty commission. The price of the indemnity: five billion francs in gold. Bismarck had demanded eight billion, but when Thiers broke down in tears it was agreed that France would cede part of its eastern territories in Alsace and Lorraine instead.

On 31 October, in a climate of mounting frustration and hostility, a crowd invaded the Hôtel de Ville and held its cabinet hostage. Following further defeats and capitulation on the battlefield, the suspicion among leftist republicans was that the government was conspiring to bring about the total defeat of the French armies the better to pacify and submit the nation to the demands of its Prussian invaders.

Gustave Flourens[81] climbed onto the cabinet table and called for a revolutionary dictatorship. Following a period of confusion and indecision that extended into the small hours, forces loyal to the government arrived and the crowd was dispersed. The attempted coup leaders were either arrested or went into hiding and the government held a snap plebiscite, in which 84 per cent of Parisians expressed support for its leadership.

The status quo continued. In the provinces the resistance for the most part paid lip service to the principle of national defence. Meanwhile, behind the scenes, the government made secret plans to negotiate a truce with Bismarck at a time when 1000 Parisians per week were dying of starvation owing to the Prussian army's blockade of the city. Such was the skulduggery involved that on 26 January 1871, the French Foreign Minister Jules Favre agreed an armistice behind the back of War Minister Gambetta, who was only informed two days later. With the election of a staunchly monarchist French government on 8 February, led by Adolphe Thiers, all that remained to be done was for France to pay its indemnity.

On 1 March the Prussian invaders conducted a victory parade along the Champs-Elysées. The only onlookers were statues draped in black flags. The staunchly monarchist government thought better of entering the city and kept its distance in the relative safety of Versailles, 12 miles from the capital.

A week later Thiers ordered the disarmament of the National Guard and the cancellation of its salary. Paying off the Prussians demanded austerity. The defenders of Paris were going to have to foot the bill for the nation's defeat. During the June revolution of 1848 National Guard militia had joined in the army's massacre of Parisian workers. But in the intervening years its social composition had changed. Now predominantly working class, its revolutionary energies were coordinated by a central organization, the Central Committee of the National Guard.

On 18 March regular army units began executing Thiers's orders for the confiscation of National Guard weaponry. Everything had been going to plan until soldiers of the 88th regiment of the line, under the command of General Lecomte, reached the slopes of Montmartre. A militiaman was set upon, shots rang out, and crowds flooded along cobblestone streets and alleyways to Le Champ polonais, where 171 cannons stood in defiance of their would-be captors. (The cannons had been manufactured during the Prussian siege and funded by public subscription). A nurse by the name of Louise Michel[82] arrived to treat the wounded man, as did Dr Clemenceau, the mayor of Montmartre. The militiaman, Germain Turpin, a bricklayer, was pronounced dead at the scene.

Militia swarmed and civilians thronged and both faced off the soldiers and their commander, who by now were marooned in a sea of bodies. A stand-off ensued. The two sides fraternized and one by one the soldiers dropped their weapons, exited the ranks and were swallowed up by the crowd. A drum roll sounded, the line took two paces back and the shrieks of the women were answered by a rattling of bayonets. The soldiers raised their rifles. A falling hand signal. Nothing.

'Rabble!' howled Lecomte. The general sprung forward, enraged. 'Fire!'

Besieged at Bitche, beaten back at Beaumont, clouted at Chilleurs, licked at Ladon, the 88th regiment, having already been humiliated in the eastern provinces of France, had no desire to add insult to injury in the northern districts of Paris. The crowd erupted in a dithyrambic orgy. Lecomte was set upon and whisked away to the sound of drums, bugles and indecent wisecracks. Later that day he and General Clément-Thomas, one of the architects of the repression of June 1848, would be executed in a garden at Château Rouge.

An avalanche of militia, army mutineers and plebeians descended on Place Pigalle, where the remains of the 88th regiment were lingering. Seeing the riotous assemblage hurtling toward them the army officers froze, unsure of whose side to take. A sabre-rattling cavalry officer was upended and his animal butchered in several dozen choice cuts. Barricades were thrown up here, there and everywhere. Regiments retreated and soldiers vacillated in the anomie of rebellion.

From Belleville to Montmarte, Bastille to Château d'Eau; from the 13th and 14th arrondissements to the Latin Quarter and all along the Rive Gauche and over Place de la Concorde, the workingmen and its proletarian militia mounted the barricades and stormed heaven. The historical tragedy of 1848 had given way to the historical epic of 1871. On 27 March the Commune of Paris was declared. A crowd of several hundred thousand converged on the Hôtel de Ville to salute the new municipal government, the government of and by the people, who finally commanded their own destiny.

Chapter 8

London was in the grip of dinosaur fever and on the journey from Hampstead to the British Museum—where the "Exhibition of Preserved Specimens, Extinct Species, Antiquities and Pre-historic Remains, &c. ", was being held—Jenny and her daughter speculated on how the city must have looked in pre-historic times.

'This was probably all the same,' decided Eleanor as the omnibus reached Primrose Hill.

She remarked at how the chimney stacks on the horizon looked rather like the giant conifers of the Mesozoic Era, albeit ablaze.

'It would have been much warmer,' surmised Jenny. 'All the reptiles wouldn't have liked it that much had the weather been cold.'

'Imagine London with reptiles!' Eleanor enthused. 'Well, not London. But the place as it was. I think,' she reasoned, 'I would like to have seen the dinosaurs in their natural habitat. I mean, I know they were hardly pets, but... I'd like to think I could have befriended them.'

'I'm sure they would have loved you too,' said Marx. 'They would have gobbled you up in an instant!'

'Father!' she protested. 'No, they wouldn't have. Anyway, I'm not talking about living there. I'm talking about going back to their time as a visitor in a special travelling vessel, then coming back just in time for supper.'

Helene approved, 'As long as you're home in time for supper I can't see any harm in it.'

'As long as you don't bring any of the dinosaurs back with you,' Marx added. 'Jennychen once wanted to keep a pony in the house.'

Eleanor giggled.

'Oh, it might sound funny now,' said Marx, 'but in those days we were living in a two-room flat in Soho. Your sister was quite determined.'

'She is still,' added Jenny.

'If she could have adopted a dinosaur when she was little then she would have,' said Marx.

'Probably a flying one,' reflected Jenny.

'I'm still waiting for someone to answer my question about why all the lizards became extinct,' said Helene.

'Dinosaurs,' said Eleanor. 'No one calls them lizards any more, Lenchen.'

Marx folded his copy of *The Times* and began to explain. 'First of all, one should bear in mind that they were creatures that roamed the Earth millions of years ago. The fossil evidence is scattered all over the world, since the African and South American continents are thought to have once fitted together. Gathering their remains is a bit like doing a jigsaw puzzle. But natural selection seems the most likely explanation. And although not lizards in the modern sense, Helene's right. A great many *were* antecedents of today's lizards.'

'Ha! Imagine being buried on two separate continents,' said Eleanor. 'Your top half is in Guinea and your bottom half in Brazil.'

Presently, Helene said, 'That's just careless if you ask me.'

'Lenchen!' Eleanor laughed. 'It's not *careless*. It's natural history. The continents became separated.'

'Well, some history it is that splits you in half and leaves you in two different places. Just you mind that doesn't happen to me.'

'I can't very well promise to look after your remains for a million years, now can I?' said Eleanor.

'In a million years I very much doubt that mankind will still be around,' said Marx, unfolding his newspaper. 'A million years on this lonely planet would seem quite enough for any civilization.'

At Oxford Circus a gang of public schoolboys boarded the bus accompanied by their schoolmaster, who Marx said resembled Gladstone. In being impossibly tall the man had to crouch down some way in order to avoid banging his head on the roof of the bus. He wore a high starched collar, talked in a gratingly high-pitched tone and wielded his cane like a shepherd herding sheep.

'What sort of dinosaur is *that?*' whispered Eleanor from behind her hand.

'He looks more like a giant cricket,' Helene whispered back and the two of them cracked up.

'Featherstonhaugh! That's not the appropriate place for your cane, lad,' said he, sounding like a geography teacher. 'Remove it from Soames's ear at once. And St John! Give Fiennes back his hat, boy.'

'I'd say it was almost an extinct species,' Marx surmised.

The Marx party waited on the steps of the British Museum for Engels to arrive. He was late. The spring weather was bright and sunny with patches of clear blue sky. There was a chill north wind. It didn't do for Marx's furuncles, which were back on the scene, nor for Jenny's long list of ailments, especially her rheumatism.

'What time did Engels say he'd arrive, Karl?' asked his wife.

'Midday.'

'It's already a quarter past.'

'Oh, Father, *please* can we start without him?' said Eleanor, jumping up and down to keep warm. 'We've been waiting so long I'm beginning to feel as if *I* am a dinosaur.'

'Very well, very well,' he replied, eager to see the exhibition himself.

First they visited the Paleozoic room, which housed the trilobite fossils and the giant clams. A scale model diorama had been set up depicting primitive fish emerging from a swamp. A Dicynodon the size of a Labrador but more serene and with lizard legs posed on a rock in the centre.

'He looks like Whisky,' said Eleanor, who Marx swore blind was a wolf and called Wilhelm.

'Far prettier, anyway,' he said. 'And less noisy, I'd imagine.'

Next came the Mesozoic room where the Plesiosaurus skeleton was on display, along with several colour illustrations of the animal swimming in a blue ocean.

'How odd he appears,' said Eleanor.

Helene agreed. 'Why, he's neither one thing nor the other. They've given him the head of a crocodile and the body of a whale, and his arms—'

'Fins, Lenchen,' interrupted Eleanor. 'They're fins.'

The land creatures were fascinating. Marx circled the scale model of the megalosaurus. It towered over him bearing its teeth in a fiendish grin. How the evolutionary theory could account for the extinction of that merciless great predator was a question and a half. Extinction didn't seem the correct description for dinosaurs. Species evolved as one geological era transitioned to the next. One couldn't simply jump between them. Matter, after all, could no more be destroyed than created. All that was solid melted into liquid before evaporating into steam. It didn't melt into *thin* air. Granted, the phase transition of sublimation, where a solid converts directly to a gas—

'You're under arrest!' barked a voice in his ear.

Marx gasped, 'Why... you... you... horrid lizard man hybrid, you!'

Engels doubled up in laughter.

'I should set that thing on *you*,' said Marx, adjusting the seat of his trousers before seeing the funny side.

'Just checking to see you're still with us,' said Engels. 'You looked as if you were lost in time.'

'I was: in the Jurassic Period. Come! Let's jump forward 200 million years.'

Marx escorted Engels to the Cenozoic room, where he shared

the fruits of his most recent reading on geology and palaeontology. The skeletons here were less monstrous and almost exclusively mammalian. The Megaloceros, the Anoplotherium and the Megatherium wouldn't have looked out of place in the London Zoological Gardens—had they been alive and covered in fur.

'Well, Moor,' said Engels, poking his head into the ribcage of a giant sloth, 'you did it.'

'*We* did it, you mean,' said Marx.

'We? Oh, yes... I suppose.'

'I was never out for glory, Fred.'

'Me neither,' Engels confessed, standing back from the skeleton. 'Four tonnes? It must have been the size of an elephant.'

'It was,' said Marx. 'I think that's a juvenile specimen you're looking at.'

'Oh, right... It's some achievement, mind.'

'What? The Megatherium?'

'No,' scoffed Engels. 'Not the bloody dinosaur. Your book! *Capital*, you old fool.'

'Why... yes!' Marx recoiled from the giant bat hanging over his head. 'It's a beginning, Fred; a beginning. I still have my doubts regarding the presentation.'

Engels looked almost aggrieved. 'Oh?'

'Part I: I should have dumped that in the appendix. Talk about wire-drawn. It lacks theoretical rigour...'

'Really? I don't find it wire-drawn. On the contrary. It... grows on one.'

'Oh, but it is,' Marx insisted. 'It's taken me a couple of years to digest all my errors and misjudgements. I'm still satisfied with my approach, mind. What pleases me most is the way in which the book sets out a truly *scientific* approach.'

'Indeed.'

'Finally, I'm doing for social and economic history what Darwin has been doing in natural history for donkey's years.'

'Oh, I think you've gone beyond Darwin,' said Engels. 'After all, Darwin's work is retrospective. He studies evolution to the present day. Yours is all that and more. Why, it's prospective! You've produced a theory of history that is progressive in every sense of the word.' The thought stopped Engels in his tracks. 'You've invented a science capable of seeing into the future.'

'Steady on,' said Marx, more in embarrassment than disagreement. 'It's true I've uncovered an approach to history broadly compatible with the natural philosophy. But,' he cautioned, 'I've still got Volumes II and III to get through. It's not over until the fat tenor sings.'

'Well! be careful what you wish for,' said Engels, peering into a display case containing a coprolite. 'And remember,' he added, 'you really must be more careful about what you write, Moor. It seems your book's inspired a revolution in Paris.'

'Ha!' laughed the Red Doctor, 'don't you start! I'm already being slandered in *The Times*. Look! Hark at the rubbish they write. Blah, blah, blah: "and the Paris Police Commissioner", who they don't even name—'

'Currently tending his allotment in Versailles—'

'—"has let it be known that the *notorious* Karl Marx, the German exile presently *residing* in London—'

'And has been for over 20 years—'

'—"has been *orchestrating* much of the current lawlessness in the city through his International Society for Workingmen." Well, now! What a genius I am to be "orchestrating" a revolution from my study.'

Engels produced a notepad from his coat pocket and began to sketch. 'Have you written to them?'

'Written to them? I hardly have time to do anything else! Every time I turn my back they invent another fairy story.'

'It'll calm down. Once the press gets over the shock of a revolutionary dictatorship.'

'Never, in other words.'

'Mind you,' recalled Engels, 'Bakunin must be feeling

remarkably stupid.'

'Dear oh dear.' Marx shook his head. 'He grows more self-absorbed with age.'

'For all his talk of Pan-Slavic revolution, I don't see many peasants storming the Winter Palace.'

'Quite,' Marx affirmed. 'He tried to get me involved in one of his hare-brained schemes.'

'Oh?' said Engels, gazing up from his sketch. 'I don't recall you telling me.'

'Years ago. On his way to or from Geneva, I forget which.'

Engels turned the page and began afresh. 'On second thoughts, I think you did. Following his escape from a Siberian dungeon.'

'Yes, that's right.'

'He turned up in Lyon last autumn.'

'I heard.'

'Paraded into the town hall, climbed onto the balcony and declared a workers' republic. Just like that.'

'Problem was no one had bothered to tell the workers!'

The men laughed into their long beards. Marx hugged a column to prevent himself from falling over. Regaining his composure, he began intoning like Hamlet.

'Times have certainly moved on, Fred. We're entering the dawn of a new age. Science is in command now. Not bourgeois science. Proletarian science. A science adapted to the betterment of the workers; one finally equipped to serve their true interests.'

Engels held up his sketch of the Megatherium for Marx's approval. Jenny, Helene and Eleanor arrived, and immediately burst into fits of laughter. Then Engels joined in. Marx had performed his soliloquy standing next to a sign pointing straight at him which read: "Neanderthal Man".

'What?' said the unwitting exhibit. 'Did I say something funny?'

Chapter 9

That evening Eleanor performed Lady Macbeth's soliloquy. It moved Jenny and Helene to tears, and even Engels needed a handkerchief. Marx too was moved by it; although he did feel awkward when his daughter delivered the line, "unsex me here".

'She wants to be an actress, Mr Engels,' said the mother, drying her eyes.

'Your daughter has talent,' he observed, before swiftly changing the subject, no doubt eager to avoid encouraging a career that he might ultimately have to pay for. 'I'll be heading off now, Moor,' he said.

'It's too late; stay in the guest room. We can talk.'

'I would, but I've a pile of correspondence waiting for me at home. Let's meet later in the week.'

Marx walked his friend to the door, who handed him an envelope containing 20 pounds. It was more than enough to cover the rent and pay for the spring excursion. It would do the family good to breathe some sea air for a change.

'I trust you're ready for a drubbing tonight,' said Marx, pouring himself a scotch and lighting a cigar.

'I trust *you* are, you mean,' Helene replied, cracking her knuckles and rolling up her sleeves.

Marx fought mercilessly from the off. Helene, playing White, opened with d4. Marx responded with a Benoni Defence. After that nothing much happened until White h3. Then Black gifted a horse to the king on f2. White might have checked the knight's advance on its right flank—as indeed a more republican Marshal Bazaine might have checked the advance of the Prussian VIII corps at Gravelotte.[83] An engagement taken in isolation comes to define the battle only in retrospect. The fact that a player may miss a key move can hardly be put down to poor judgment, since who's to say the mistake wasn't induced by the opponent's strategy?

'How long is your game going to last this time?' quipped Jenny. 'A week? A month? A year?'

'It shall last as long as it takes,' said Marx. 'By Zeus!'

Bc4.

'That's it,' said Helene, sinking back in her chair. 'I'm done.'

'Really?' said Jenny. 'That was awfully quick, Helene. I felt sure you were going to triumph tonight.'

'Were you, indeed?' said Marx. 'Well, now. Perhaps you can rally to her aid. Come! Your opponent awaits.' He offered up his seat.

Jenny regarded her husband narrowly.

'He's off again,' said Helene, shaking her head. 'I told you he was losing his marbles.'

'Really, Lenchen? You think you can beat her this evening, do you? So! Let's make a bet.'

Helene laughed. 'Money, eh? Well, there's a first.'

Marx exited and returned moments later brandishing a gold sovereign. Placing the coin on the table, he said, 'Come, Jenny. She's yours for the taking. *Allez!*'

Jenny sighed. 'Karl, I'm really not in the mood for any of your silly games. I feel quite weary tonight.'

'Games?' Marx frowned. 'What games, pray? Chess is no game. Why, it's a struggle to the death. It's part of life.'

Jenny looked askance. 'Chess. You want *me* to play chess. Really, now?'

'Really, yes,' he insisted, patting the armchair.

'I see. And why should I want to do a thing like that?'

'Well, because you... *play*, for one thing,' said Marx, holding firm to the conviction.

'Well, if it makes *you* happy, Karl, then yes, I'll *play* Helene at chess. Although, seeing as I barely know the rules, I strongly suggest you take back your sovereign.'

'Oh, trust you to spoil it, now,' said Helene. 'Of course she knows how to play. But you can make yourself useful and serve us a nightcap. Something with plenty of alcohol in.'

'Yes, do, Karl! It shall improve my concentration.'

Helene joined in the jest. 'What about champagne?'

'Yes, champagne!' mimicked the wife. 'To celebrate my win,' and the two women fell about laughing.

Marx froze. Unsure quite what it all meant, he floated from the room feeling mildly embarrassed, like a man become the butt of his own joke.

On entering his study he shivered. He went to shut the window and looked outside. Finally the council had erected a street light opposite the house. That would save him falling down any more potholes. It was rumoured they would tar the road soon, too. Progress. The bourgeoisie might have laid the foundations of democracy, but they were mere foundations. A new class was taking over. One only had to consider what was happening in Paris to get a sense of what the future would bring. One marvelled at how the workers had taken control of Europe's illustrious capital. The new government was making major strides in almost every field: in providing education for all; in advancing women's rights; in novel artistic experiments (the collapsing of the Vendôme Column was a particularly moving work); in reining in the bakers; disbanding the mercenary army; and, most importantly of all, making the municipal government directly accountable to the people. At last a government that represented the majority for a change. It was all unprecedented. There was no doubt about it: mankind was entering a new phase of world-historic proportions—

Marx's hand froze. A bead of ink dropped from his quill. He recognized the tune immediately. There was no chance of him not, it being the rallying cry of the persecution, the signal of all the misery and strife he had suffered down the years; and that, by the law of probability, if not by universal providence, he had long ago finally laid to rest. Or so he thought.

'Greetings, my son,' said a voice and a figure appeared by the fire, seated in Marx's armchair.

Immediately he recognized the scene as the same one he had walked out on all those years ago in Trier. Only he couldn't walk out on it this time.

'Good evening, Father,' he said, lowering his quill.

'Well, Karl. What can I say? You did it. It took you more than 30 years, mind. But! You did it.' The father read the title of the book that hovered impossibly in the air in front of him. '*Capital: A Critique of Political Economy* by Karl Marx. Your masterpiece, indeed. My heartfelt congratulations.'

Heinrich Marx found his feet. Or rather he levitated to them.

Eventually, Marx forced out the immortal line, 'What are you doing here?' and fumbled to his.

'Is that any way to greet the ghost of your dead father?' Heinrich replied. 'Come!' and with that he glided across the room. The apparition reached out to embrace the son, but instead simply passed straight through him like the London mist. 'Ah, yes,' he said, remembering. 'After 33 years of haunting I still can't get used to that bit. It's a pain, I'll admit it.'

'I... I...' Marx stumbled on the verge of a coherent thought, a reaction even, 'I don't understand,' being all he could muster.

The father removed his wide-brimmed hat, which flew across the room of its own accord and landed neatly on the armchair. He was smart and clean-shaven, the image of the daguerreotype in the silver frame, at least looking as "healthy" in death as Marx remembered him in life. Perhaps it was his shimmering figure, the halo which, in spite of being stripped from the bourgeois professions in this world, clearly returned in the next. Not that he was in the next. Yet.

'You summoned me, Karl.'

'What?'

'You *summoned* me,' pronounced the ghost.

'No!' the son insisted, denying both the fact and the apparition.

'What was it now?' Heinrich recalled the words from memory: '"Just as they seem to be occupied with remaking themselves and things in revolutionary ways they anxiously conjure up the spirits of the past..."'[84] It was a quotation from one of Marx's old essays written 20 years ago. 'It seems you've been writing me pen letters all these years without even knowing it.' Heinrich raised an eyebrow before breaking into a smile. 'I'm dead, Karl,' he said. 'Permit me some *humour* at least. But come now, did you seriously think you could go on writing such things without raising my interest?'

'But... you're *dead*,' said Marx, unable, or unwilling, to reconcile the idea with the thing itself.

'Yes. If only,' muttered the ghost. 'Not wholly, I'm afraid. In limbo. You know Dante. Of course you do. Anyway, that's where I ended up. On the shores of Acheron. I said to the ferryman, "Look here! There must be some mistake," as he was rowing off. He told me to take it up with Minos—not the easiest man to see, I'll grant you. Eventually he looked at my case and told me I was a "virtuous non-Christian adult". I told him I'd converted from Judaism. "Doesn't count," he said. Anyway, the long and short of it is I have to wait. I'm hoping for a reprieve. God knows I've been patient enough. But I digress. What was I getting at?'

Marx thought about pouring himself a drink, but dared not take his eyes off the apparition. Even if his mind were playing tricks on him—and it had been known—he needed to be sure how far it had led him astray.

'The book! Of course. Indeed. How wrong I was. It took me all these years to understand what you were trying to achieve. What can I say? You got there in the end. You know, Karl,' said the ghost, wistfully staring through the wall, 'when you were young and headstrong, I couldn't see where your life was headed. More importantly, neither could you. You rebelled against me. I can't say I blame you. I dare say I would have done the same had I been in your shoes. The future seemed like a foreign land back then. Well! You don't know the half of it, son. Try looking into the future when you're dead. One might as well be walking backward. Have you ever hurtled into a long dark tunnel without there being any light at the end? Without even being sure there's a way out? Well, that's what it's like. How little we mortals know. That's one of life's great tragedies. What was it Hegel said? "Only when the dusk starts to fall does the owl of Minerva spread its wings and fly." We only discover the truth when it's too late. That's why I had to follow you.'

Marx partially came round. 'It was... *you* outside the hotel.'

'God, yes,' the apparition affirmed, wincing. 'How you lived in that hovel is beyond me... Yes. It was I, Karl. I who followed you. I did warn you about big cities. My, how you moved around—'

Suddenly Marx exploded. 'I was destitute! I didn't have a pot to piss in! Or were you too busy to notice?'

'I know, I know,' said the ghost, anticipating his son's anger. 'I hope my behaviour didn't strike you as insensitive. Self-respect is one of death's first casualties. I'm sorry, Karl. I hope you can find it in your heart to forgive me.'

'Insensitive? I almost died. My *sons died.*'

Marx's objections seemed not to register, as if the ghost's entire speech were rehearsed and these words the only ones he possessed; as if the apparition were a beacon, instead of a thinking being, flashing on a distant rock, whose enigma is dashed the moment one sets foot ashore.

The ghost resumed its rhetorical dialogue.

'You remember my letter, the one I sent not long before you walked away from home, never to return. It broke my heart, Karl. You broke my heart. You stopped responding to my letters. I don't blame you for my death. Then again, I'm only human: "Hath not a Jew eyes? Hath not a Jew hands, organs, dimentions, sences, affections, passions, fed with the same foode, hurt with the same weapons, subject to the same diseases, healed by the same meanes, warmed and cooled by the same Winter and Sommer as a Christian is? If you pricke us doe we not bleede?"[85] I remember the words I wrote to you, for in setting them down on paper they were engraved on my heart and I feel them still, even though my heart no longer beats and is just a memory now; as am I.'

The father cited the letter: '"*That you should rise high in the world, the flattering hope of seeing your name in lights one day, along with your earthly well-being, are more than heartfelt wishes. They are long-cherished illusions that have struck deep root in me.*" Vain? Yes, it was vain of me to write those words. And egotistical. I admit it now—I did then. But I couldn't help myself. How could I when you refused to write, ignored my letters, refused to come home to see your mother and me. You gave me no choice, Karl. I became the father you wanted: a ghost. And such remains my dying regret.'

The light in the hearth dimmed and the ghost's face shone forth differently, at first a flicker, then a giant Olympian beam rising from the bowels of the earth. Marx peered over the brow of the precipice half expecting to be met by Helene's disgruntled expression through the hole in the floor. But the light emerged from another dimension. Staring into its source he could make out the tapestry of the firmament. Not the heavens as such, but their ornate description in formulae. Suddenly a gale-force wind rattled through the room, whose unexpected ferocity threw Marx's beard backward, along with its wearer.

'And yet!' declaimed the ghost, raising his voice above the gale, his compassion departed and newly possessed of a diabolical power. 'How your talents matured! How your heart beat like a man's in achieving your masterpiece! How you kept your demons at bay! How you pursued your research to its dying embers! Truly, your name will be remembered down the ages, such heights have your ideas scaled. And Jenny...' The gale relented and the apparition dimmed.

'Dear, sweet Jenny. She was the source of my greatest anguish, as I admitted in my letter, betraying a kind of fear laden with foreboding. I could never understand it...' The ghost paused, then looked away, clasping his hands tightly behind his back. 'I was quite taken by her, Karl, I should tell you frankly. She could work magic, your Jenny, with her bewitching smile. I think... I was...' The ghost checked himself. 'It matters not, for truly in your marriage she spurred you on. You spurred each other, in the progressive spirit of the age, which, despite being a liberal man, I don't pretend to grasp fully, or indeed endorse. It matters not, Karl. Jenny became the molten rock of your revolution, flowing in all directions, and in so doing helped you overcome all obstacles. She was your great love and your great strength, and without whom nothing truly would have been possible. What more can I say? You proved me wrong. Forgive me for ever having doubted you.'

Marx surveyed the room, which seemed miraculously unscathed. For a moment he wondered if anyone else might make an appearance; his mother, perhaps. She had only been in the ground for eight years, whereas the father 33, and on reflection probably needed more time to put her speech together.

The son was still in shock. But the emotion, if that's what it was, was waning. In any case, he felt little emotion as he readied himself to speak, since he lacked none. His father's words had moved and instilled in him a novel self-consciousness. For if the speech had one thing confirmed, Marx thought, then surely it was how desperately alike they were. If the father and the son had loved each other so intensely then the former's message brought it home, and in such a manner as Marx would be given to set out.

'Father,' he began, 'dear Father. You always were a vain and egotistical man. You admit it and I know it. Let me speak frankly, for since you're no longer alive it seems I'm no more

318</br>

capable of damaging your ego. In any case, our passions are so similar that in talking to you now I suppose you may not be here, after all; at least not completely. There's plenty of room for doing harm to the other when the other is part of oneself. It's a feeling I've had about Jenny too down the years. Anyway, Father: yes, I admit. When we last met it went badly. I stormed out with but one thing on my mind. Or two: Jenny and my writing. You dared me to choose between them and I refused. Compromise was never my strong suit; nor yours. What did you expect from your own son? I asked nothing more of you, so what else was there to say? I loved you as a son should always love his father, only more. The same was true of you, which makes us equals in a manner of saying. Anyway, perhaps your "no" spurred me on; perhaps I carried it with me through the years in some secret compartment of my soul, not even recognizing it was there until now. And Jenny... Until just now I was mystified as to why I put up with her all these years. No doubt she has harboured similar thoughts. Well, you and I both knew. It was because we were in love. We pushed each other to the outer limits, then beyond, which is what lovers are bound to do. We didn't renege on our marital bond, in the sense that it kept us together. It withstood the pressures that assailed us from all sides. It didn't break. It hasn't yet, anyway. It held firm. Perhaps I was never at the height of her passions. But then, as you say, "Hath not a Jew hands, organs, dimentions, sences, affections, passions..."?

'You make a fair assumption and I suppose it may be the case that you vouchsafed our love affair, watching over us like a guardian angel. After all, you were the one who helped our union in the beginning and sheltered us from Jenny's family. I remember what you wrote in your letter about that *bewitching girl*. Then again, I must say, as tempted as I am to admit that your intervention was decisive, I shall resist doing so, since when two people fall in love, the father, it seems to me, is more hindrance than help. You'll forgive me, Father, but I am not so "liberal" as ever to contemplate a *ménage à trois* with my own parent. This "Jew" you see before you has his *own* hands to feel—I was never much persuaded of the influence of an invisible one—and I have used my passions to perfectly good effect, even if the fruits of my loins... well, I won't go into the sadness. There is precious little time for it, at least between *us*. You're dead and our meeting is just a bodily state, albeit one whose truth I won't deny. As for the book, well! I admit to being shocked at first, and beside myself with worry and shame, when heeding what you said just now. When you first started to speak your words conjured an image that quite horrified me, making me question my motivation and whether or not my only aim all along had been to have the last word; as if my aim in writing the book had merely been to have something, rather than nothing, to will. You're right, of course. I rebelled against you. But ask yourself this, Father: to what end? I firmly reject your insinuation that this was somehow "your" book or the one I wrote to win your approval. Despite my faults, I also had a wife and family who needed me, who I struggled for and would have died for too, had it been necessary. We live by necessity and all the necessary accidents too, for which I readily accept my share of the blame. We can't change the past and I, no more than you, can change who I am.'

Marx moved away from his desk to where the ghost was in the centre of the room. The apparition was taking it all in, and nodded from time to time, for even if he agreed with some parts of the son's speech and not with others, it was still his son who was speaking and he was bound to listen.

'But, Father,' the son went on, 'let me tell you the real reason why your ego deceives you and why your interpretation of my life is wrong. For there is one illustrious actor you failed to mention, despite you and me; one party to the drama that escapes your attention, despite being a far bigger elephant in the room than you, and even more so for not being here.' Marx reached out his hands and was about to lean them on the father's shoulders, before realizing they couldn't touch.

'Communism!' he exclaimed, staring into his father's eyes and seeing right through them, all the way to the bust of Zeus that stood in the corner. 'Communism is the only spirit in this house. Why, it makes your apparition look, well... *frightful* by comparison. "A spectre is haunting Europe—the spectre of communism." No doubt you remember those lines from my "love letter". If you had even bothered to read the newspapers,' said the son, shaking out a copy of *The Times*, 'then surely you'd know that communism is no longer just a figment of my imagination. It's already here! Do you *seriously* believe I wrote this book for you? Ha! Well, who knows, Father. Maybe I did. Just *maybe* I did. But the fact that Paris is presently governed by a proletarian dictatorship suggests, does it not, that my 600-page missive may have wider significance beyond the four walls of this room?'

The son's eyes welled with tears, for in spite of himself and everything he was saying, he realized now that this was the speech he had rehearsed in his mind a thousand times before. 'Don't you see?' he yelled, 'I didn't write this book for *you*! I wrote it for the *workers*! I wrote it for the *Revolution*!'

The words seemed to hang in the air. The ghost had surely heard them, but what he was about to say told a different story, since he was frozen in time. Being the trigger for another imperative, as the clock on the mantelpiece began to strike midnight, the final countdown to zero, the voice said this: 'My time here is at an end, Karl. You made your father very proud. Never forget that I love you, my dear, dear son,' and with that he disappeared.

A strange finale to an unhappy consciousness, Marx thought, as he signed off his letter to Kugelmann, no more distracted by the wandering spirit who would truly be at peace now, having exited the halfway house of being and appearance. He arranged his paperwork in a neat pile and put out the lamp—the one in the street remained undimmed—and since his loupe was downstairs he put off reading the evening editions until morning.

Chapter 10

TO THE PEOPLE OF PARIS,
TO THE NATIONAL GUARD,[86]

Citizens!

Down with militarism and the general staff in their gold braided uniforms!

Make way for the people, for the combatants, for the vanguard! The hour of revolutionary war has sounded.

The people may not be versed in cunning manoeuvres, but with rifles in their hands and cobblestones under their feet they have nothing to fear from all the strategists of the royal military school.

To arms, citizens! To arms! You know what's at stake: defeat the reactionaries and the clerics of Versailles or fall into the merciless hands of those miserable wretches who, by their deeds, have handed over France to the Prussians, and who are making us pay the ransom for their treason!

If you want the blood that has flowed like water for six weeks not to be fruitless; if you want to live freely in a free and egalitarian France; if you want to spare your children your sorrow and sufferings, you will rise up as a single man and, faced with your fearsome resistance, the enemy, who thinks he can enslave you once more, will be shamed by the pointless crimes with which he has besmirched himself for the past two months.

Citizens, your representatives will fight and die alongside you if need be. But in the name of this glorious France, mother of all revolutions of the people, permanent home of the ideas of justice and solidarity that must and will be the laws of humankind, march on the enemy, and let your revolutionary energy show

him that although he betrayed Paris, Paris can never surrender
or be defeated.

The Commune counts on you; count on the Commune![87]

Civilian Delegate of War
Ch. DELESCLUZE

Committee of Public Safety
ANT. ARNAUD, BILLIORAY, E. EUDES,
F. GAMBON, G. RANVIER

Notes

1. 'Nachrichten aus Paris,' in Marx, K. and Engels, F. *Marx Engels Werke, Band 5* (Berlin: Dietz Verlag, 1959) p. 116. [Translated by G. M. Goshgarian].
2. College-goer — Victorian-era slang term for factory worker.
3. *Raus mit euch, Ihr Tierquäler!* / Off with you, animal abusers!
4. *The whole difficulty in understanding the differential operation…* Marx, K. 'On the Concept of the Derived Function,' in Yanovskaya, S. A. (ed.) *Mathematical Manuscripts of Karl Marx* (London: New Park, 1983) pp. 3–4. The following mathematical expressions also appear in the same location.
5. *Come with your gods…* Marx, K. 'Difference between the Democritean and Epicurean Philosophy of Nature,' in *Marx and Engels Collected Works*, Vol. 1. (London: Lawrence and Wishart, 2010) p. 104.
6. *Every portion of matter…* Leibniz, G. *Monadology and Other Philosophical Essays*, Schrecker, P. and Schrecker, A. M. (eds.) (New York: Bobbs-Merrill Co., 1965) section 67.
7. Louis-Napoléon Bonaparte (1808–1873). President of the French Second Republic (1848–1852) and Emperor of the French (1852–1870). Became Emperor in a *coup d'état* on 2 December 1851. Thereafter officially known as Emperor Napoléon III. Not to be confused with his uncle, Napoleon Bonaparte (1769–1821), who also took power in a *coup d'état*, on 9 November 1799 (the so-called 'coup of 18 Brumaire'), becoming First Consul of the Republic, then Emperor of the French (1804–1814).
8. Mikhail Bakunin (1814–1876). Revolutionary anarchist and author of influential anarchist works *Statism and Anarchy* (1873) and *God and the State* (1882). In the first week of May 1849, he and the composer Richard Wagner took part together in the Dresden uprising, where for five days the

town was ruled by a revolutionary government. As E. H. Carr writes, 'On May 6th the insurgents had set fire to the Opera House, where Bakunin a few weeks before had heard the 9th Symphony conducted by Wagner.' *Mikhail Bakunin* (New York: Vintage, 1937) p. 193. Bakunin was subsequently arrested and spent eight years in prison. In July 1848, Marx's Cologne newspaper the *Neue Rheinische Zeitung* printed allegations that Bakunin was a spy of Nicholas I of Russia. The allegations were corrected in a subsequent edition and, according to Marx, in August 1848 the pair met on good terms in Berlin. Marx describes the affair in *Marx and Engels Collected Works*, Vol. 7, p. 630 note 210.

9. *Nihil movetur nisi corpus, ut probatur* ('Nothing is moved except a body, as the Philosopher says'). Saint Thomas Aquinas, 'The substance of the angels absolutely considered,' in *Summa Theologiae*, Question 50, Objection 2 (Grand Rapids, MI: Christian Classics Ethereal Library, no date) p. 574.

10. Gottfried Wilhelm Leibniz (1646–1716). German philosopher and mathematician. Sir Isaac Newton (1642–1727). British mathematician, physicist and astronomer. Their respective works stand as landmarks of Enlightenment thinking. In the field of mathematics, both men contributed to calculus and to the problem of how infinitely small quantities (or 'infinitesimals') can be precisely measured in the real world. There are two varieties of calculus: differential and integral. The first is concerned with calculating the rate at which quantities change. The second is concerned with calculating the volume of that change. In the final years of his life this abstract mathematical problem began to preoccupy Marx. He criticized what he saw as the inherent deficiencies of Leibniz's and Newton's differential formulas and notations, and the idealist philosophical tendencies of calculus in general. Apart from his own notes on the subject,

Marx's *Mathematical Manuscripts* includes an accessible explanation of what he was trying to achieve with calculus and how it relates more widely to the history of philosophy. See C. Smith's 'Hegel, Marx and the Calculus,' in Marx's *Mathematical Manuscripts*.

11. Спасибо, дорога́я — Пожалуйста / Thank you, ducky — You're welcome.

12. Joseph Arnold Weydemeyer (1818–1866). Former lieutenant in the Prussian army, editor of the *Neue Rheinische Zeitung* and member of the Communist League. In spring 1849 he settled briefly in Frankfurt where he would edit the *Neue Deutsche Zeitung* until the paper was suppressed in December 1850. In 1851 he went to live in New York and set up there *Die Revolution*, a radical German language newspaper that would publish several of Marx's essays, including 'The Eighteenth Brumaire of Louis Bonaparte.'

13. Louis Althusser describes capitalism's emergence in the Po Valley as follows: 'In untold passages, Marx — this is certainly no accident — explains that the capitalist mode of production arose from the "*encounter*" between "the owners of money" and the proletarian stripped of everything but his labour-power [...] We can go even further, and suppose *that this encounter occurred several times in history before taking hold in the West*, but, for lack of an element or a suitable arrangement of the elements, failed to "take". Witness the thirteenth-century and fourteenth-century Italian states of the Po valley, where there were certainly men who owned money, technology and energy (machines driven by the hydraulic power of the river) as well as manpower (unemployed artisans), but where the phenomenon nevertheless failed to "take hold".' *Philosophy of the Encounter, Later Writings, 1978–87*, trans. G. M. Goshgarian (London: Verso, 2006) pp. 197–8.

14. George Julian Harney (1817–1897). British Chartist leader

and radical journalist who from 1845 edited the *Northern Star*. Contributors to the paper included Marx and Engels.

15. 'Jenny Marx an Joseph Weydemeyer in Frankfurt a. M., 20. Mai 1850,' in Marx, K. and Engels, F. *Marx Engels Werke*, *Band 27* (Berlin: Dietz Verlag, 1963) pp. 607–610 [Translated by G. M. Goshgarian].

16. Georg Weerth (1822–1856). German writer, poet and journalist, and member of the Communist League. Worked as a clerk in Bradford from 1843 to 1846.

17. Arnold Ruge (1802–1880). Republican activist. Collaborated with Marx in Paris in February 1844 on the short-lived radical German language newspaper, the *Deutsch-Französische Jahrbücher*. Their correspondence of 1842-43 was printed in the paper's first and only issue. Like Marx, Ruge fled to London following the 1848–49 revolutions. Marx and Engels paint a disparaging portrait of him in their essay, written in 1852 (and unpublished in their lifetimes) 'Great Men of the Exile,' in *Marx and Engels Collected Works*, Vol. 11.

18. Oswald Dietz (1823–1898). Republican activist and Communist League member who took part in the Baden uprising of 1849 before eventually fleeing to London in 1850. Emigrated to America in 1852, where he worked as an engineer and a labour union organizer.

19. Wilhelm Liebknecht (1826–1900). Republican activist and Communist League member who fled to London in 1850. Returned to Germany in 1862 and became a founding member of the General German Workers' Association, a forerunner of the Social Democratic Party of Germany.

20. Konrad Schramm (1822–1858). Revolutionary activist and Communist League member who fled to London in 1849. Fought a duel against August Willich in 1850 in order to defend Marx's honour. He was believed dead at first, but returned to England from Belgium, where the duel had been

fought, having survived a glancing shot to the head. Wilhelm Liebknecht relates the incident in *Karl Marx: Biographical Memoirs*, trans. E. Untermann. (London: Journeyman Press, [1896] 1975). Available at: <www.marxists.org/archive/liebknecht-w/1896/karl-marx.htm> [accessed 27.06.17].

21. Johann Gottfried Kinkel (1815–1882). Poet and member of the Communist League who fought alongside Engels in the Baden-Palatinate revolutionary campaign of 1849. During the retreat of the Baden-Palatinate Revolutionary Corps from Rastatt in late June 1849, he was wounded and taken prisoner by Prussian troops. He later escaped from Spandau Prison in Berlin and eventually fled to London. Like Ruge, Kinkel was the subject of a disparaging portrait by Marx and Engels in their essay, 'Great Men of the Exile.'

22. Karl Heinzen (1809–1880). German revolutionary agitator who contributed articles to the *Rheinische Zeitung*, the radical newspaper Marx edited in Cologne from 1842 to 1843. Spent time in London in the aftermath of the 1848–49 revolutions, then sailed for America in the autumn of 1850. The subject of a disparaging portrait by Marx and Engels in their essay 'Great Men of the Exile.'

23. Marx's *Theses on Feuerbach*, from which this quotation is taken, was written in 1845, but first published in 1888, five years after Marx's death. The exact wording of the German original is: '*Die Philosophen haben die Welt nur verschieden interpretiert, es kömmt drauf an, sie zu verändern*' ('The philosophers have only interpreted the world in various ways; the point is to change it'). 'Thesen über Feuerbach,' in Marx, K. and Engels, F. *Marx Engels Werke, Band 3* (Berlin: Dietz Verlag, 1978) p. 7.

24. Mary Burns (1821–1863). Irish partner of Engels.

25. *Monsieur! Veuillez accepter mes plus sincères excuses pour le désagrément — Je me mettrais volontiers à plat ventre devant vous, mais je crains que, ce faisant, je resterais par terre indéfiniment —*

Dans le mille! / Sir! Please accept my most sincere apologies for the disturbance—Readily I would prostrate myself before you, but I fear that, in so doing, I would be unable to get up again—Bullseye!

26. Heinrich Cornelius Agrippa (1486–1535). German occultist and theologian. Cited in Mary Shelley's *Frankenstein* as an influence on Victor Frankenstein's scientific experiments.

27. Long Millgate and Ducie Bridge appear in Engels's famous account of working-class Manchester life. The book was originally published in 1845 (in German) and in 1887 (in English) as *The Condition of the Working-Class in England.*

28. *Pas d'histoires et gentil. C'est vu?* / No messing about and be nice. Got it?

29. *Ich kann nur ein bisschen Deutsch—Ja, aber nicht viel—Es ist immer schön, beim Reisen Leute kennenzulernen, die deine Sprache sprechen* / I speak just a bit of German—Yes, but not well—It's always nice when travelling abroad to meet people who speak the same language.

30. Marx, K. *Capital. A Critique of Political Economy*, Vol. 1, Engels, F. (ed.), trans. S. Moore and E. Aveling (Moscow: Progress Publishers, [1867] 1887) p. 27.

31. Marx, K. *Capital. A Critique of Political Economy*, Vol. 1, p. 27.

32. Marx, K. and Engels, F. *Manifesto of the Communist Party*, trans. S. Moore and F. Engels (Moscow: Progress Publishers, [1848] 1969) no page number. Available at: <www.marxists.org/archive/marx/works/1848/communist-manifesto/ch02.htm> [accessed 27.06.17]

33. Marx, K. and Engels, F. *Manifesto of the Communist Party*, no page number. Available at: <www.marxists.org/archive/marx/works/1848/communist-manifesto/ch02.htm> [accessed 27.06.17]

34. Marx, K. and Engels, F. *Manifesto of the Communist Party*, no page number. Available at: <www.marxists.org/archive/marx/works/1848/communist-manifesto/ch01.htm#007>

[accessed 27.06.17]

35. Marx, K and Engels, F. *Manifesto of the Communist Party*, no page number. Available at: <www.marxists.org/archive/marx/works/1848/communist-manifesto/ch01.htm#007> [accessed 27.06.17]

36. Marx, K. and Engels, F. *Manifesto of the Communist Party*, no page number. Available at: <www.marxists.org/archive/marx/works/1848/communist-manifesto/ch04.htm> [accessed 27.06.17]

37. Dr Marx! How nice to see you!—Good day, Mr Wang—Why don't you come to see me any more?—Work. I have no free time—You work far too hard, Dr Marx. Like me. But what can we do? London is the city of workers.

38. William Shakespeare, *Hamlet*, Act 1, scene 5.

39. Marx's poem 'To Jenny' was written in November 1836 and included in a 'Book of Songs.' Containing 53 poems in all, Marx dedicated the album to his father. See Marx, K. and Engels, F. *Marx and Engels Collected Works*, Vol. 1, p. 522.

40. *Was soll das denn heißen!* / What is the meaning of this!

41. John Russell, 1st Earl Russell (1792–1878). Whig and later liberal politician and British Prime Minister (1846–1852 and 1865–1866). From July to August 1855, in six instalments of the *Neue Oder-Zeitung*, Marx published a damning portrait of the man to whom Charles Dickens would dedicate *A Tale of Two Cities* in 1866. See 'Lord John Russell,' in *Marx and Engels Collected Works*, Vol. 14, pp. 371–93.

42. *nudo come mamma ti ha fatto* / in my birthday suit.

43. Napoleon Bonaparte. See footnote 7.

44. Marx, K. and Engels, F. *Manifesto of the Communist Party*, no page number. Available at: <www.marxists.org/archive/marx/works/1848/communist-manifesto/ch01.htm#007> [accessed 27.06.17]

45. Marx, K. 'A Contribution to the Critique of Hegel's Philosophy of Law,' in *Marx and Engels Collected Works*, Vol.

3, [1844], p. 175. Translation modified.

46. Wilhelm Stieber (1818–1882). Law student who joined the criminal division of the Berlin Police and rose swiftly through the ranks to become its chief in the aftermath of the March Revolution of 1848. His memoirs recount a series of (at best) semi-plausible adventures that read like a 1930s spy novel. In Marx's 'Revelations Concerning the Communist Trial in Cologne,' published anonymously in 1853, Stieber's involvement in the circumstances leading up to the trial is explained at length and in some detail. See *Marx and Engels Collected Works*, Vol. 11.

47. In Marx's 'Revelations Concerning the Communist Trial in Cologne,' published anonymously in 1853, Dietz's involvement in the circumstances leading up to the trial is explained. Note that the present fictional account differs significantly from Marx's. See *Marx and Engels Collected Works*, Vol. 11, pp. 403–7.

48. Frederick William IV (1795–1861). King of Prussia (1840–1861).

49. Jeanne Antoinette Poisson, Marquise de Pompadour (1721–1764). Chief mistress of Louis XV of France.

50. Benedictus de Spinoza, 'Ethica,' in *Opera quae supersunt omnia*, Vol. 1. Bruder, C. H. (ed.). Leipzig, Bernh. Tauchnitz Jun., [1677] 1843. Pars III, Propos II, p. 274: 'The body cannot determine the mind to think, nor can the mind determine the body to movement, or rest, or to any other state (if such state exists).'

51. *E nota bene un poco adagio* / And note a little adagio.

52. *Si, si, ovviamente, e la cadenza durante tutto il pezzo* / Yes, obviously, and cadenza throughout the entire piece.

53. *Si, si—Rondò all'Ungarese. Non sono così stupido* / Yes, yes—Rondò all'Ungarese. I'm not that stupid.

54. Georg Wilhelm Friedrich Hegel (1770–1831). German philosopher and intellectual figurehead. Arguably the

most significant name in Western philosophy and the key influence on Marx and his generation. Occupied the chair of philosophy at the University of Berlin (1818–1831), where Marx would study from 1836 to 1840.

55. George Berkeley (1685–1753). Christian and idealist philosopher who in 1734 published *The Analyst,* a book criticizing the faulty reasoning of Newton's and Leibniz's calculus.

56. Marx, K. 'Preface,' in *A Contribution to the Critique of Political Economy* (Moscow: Progress Publishers, [1859] 1977) no page number. Available at: <www.marxists.org/archive/marx/works/1859/critique-pol-economy/> [accessed 27.06.17].

57. William Shakespeare, *King Lear,* Act 1, scene 1.

58. Under the French Second Empire the Belle-Île-en-Mer penitentiary was used to detain political prisoners who included, from 1850 to 1857, France's most celebrated/notorious revolutionary, Auguste Blanqui.

59. 'Marx an Engels in Manchester, 6. April 1855,' in Marx, K. and Engels, F. *Marx Engels Werke, Band 28* (Berlin: Dietz Verlag, 1963) p. 443.

60. Klemens von Metternich (1773–1859). German Austrian statesman and diplomat whose conservative politics helped to conserve the hegemony of Austria, Prussia, Russia and the United Kingdom in the aftermath of the Napoleonic wars.

61. *Tout trou est un but* / Every hole is a goal.

62. *Je vous en prie* / You're welcome.

63. *Drap. Peau. Roue. Je* / Sheet. Skin. Wheel. I. This rebus makes no sense in English, but when the pictures are correctly interpreted in French they spell out the word *drapeau rouge,* or 'red flag.'

64. Ну разве не чудесно вы выглядите сегодня? Спаси́бо / Don't you look beautiful today? Thank you.

65. *T'as compris ça?* / Have you got that?

66. *Au revoir et bon vent* / Goodbye and good riddance.

67. The book was published in 1859 by Franz Duncker of Berlin.

68. Note that many of the 'books' that now bear Marx's name appeared in the years following his and Engels's deaths. In many cases the works represent abandoned or unfinished projects not intended by their authors for publication. For example, the *Grundrisse. Foundations of the Critique of Political Economy*, was published in German in 1939–41 and comprises rough notes that Marx wrote in the late 1850s. A substantial work Marx *did* complete in his lifetime was published in German in 1860. Entitled *Herr Vogt*, it was similar in tone to Marx and Engels's 'Great Men of the Exile,' and took apart a little-known German democrat called Karl Vogt, who in 1870 was revealed to have been a spy of Napoléon III.

69. 'Marx an Engels in Manchester, 2. Dec. 1863,' in Marx, K. and Engels, F. *Marx Engels Werke, Band 30* (Berlin: Dietz Verlag, 1974) p. 376.

70. 'Heinrich Marx an Karl Marx in Berlin, den 2ten März 1837,' in Marx, K. and Engels, F. *Marx Engels Werke, Band 40* (Berlin: Dietz Verlag, 1968) pp. 626–29. [Translated by Jason Barker and G. M. Goshgarian].

71. Otto von Bismarck (1815–1898). Prussian statesman and Chancellor of Germany (1871–1890).

72. See Marx, K. *Capital. A Critique of Political Economy*, Vol. 1, pp. 105–6. Marx argues that whereas the circulation of commodities satisfies 'use-value,' as, for example, when someone buys a commodity and consumes it, the circulation of money 'satisfies' so-called 'exchange-value.' However, unlike a commodity, money cannot be consumed, since what money is as such is secondary to the value it represents. Money, in other words, can never fall out of circulation: whenever it seems as if capital has disappeared, it has merely adopted a different form. .

73. Wilhelm Wolff (1809–1864). Radical journalist, member of the Communist League and editor of the *Neue Rheinische Zeitung*. The author of numerous articles describing the plight of Silesian weavers and their famous rising of June 1844. Politically active during the revolutionary period 1848–49 and, like Marx and Engels, and many of their German comrades, fled to London in its aftermath. Settled in Manchester where he worked as a schoolteacher.

74. See note 73.

75. From Marx's 'The Eighteenth Brumaire of Louis Bonaparte,' published in *Die Revolution* in 1852: 'The French bourgeoisie had long ago found the solution to Napoleon's dilemma: "In fifty years Europe will be republican or Cossack". It solved it in the "Cossack republic".' Available at: <www.marxists. org/archive/marx/works/1852/18th-brumaire/ch07.htm> [accessed 27.06.17].

76. George Odger (1813–1877). Trade unionist who, along with Marx and Engels, was a prominent member of the International Workingmen's Association from 1864 to 1872. Promoted to the Association's General Council without being elected by the Council. Marx accused Odger of being a careerist who contributed nothing to the organization. See *Marx and Engels Collected Works*, Vol. 42, pp. 314 and 519. Crucially, when it came to Marx's address to the General Council supporting the Paris Commune, written in July 1870–May 1871 and published as 'The Civil War in France,' Odger renounced the document.

77. Eleanor was known to intimates as 'Tussy' from a young age.

78. '20 July 1870,' in *Letters of Queen Victoria, Vol. 5 (1870–1878)*, Buckle, G. E. (ed.) (Cambridge University Press 2014) p. 44.

79. *Punch*, London, 23 July 1870.

80. '19 July 1870,' in *Letters of Robert Browning*, Hood, T. L. (ed.) (New Haven: Yale University Press, 1933) p. 138.

81. Gustave Flourens (1838–1871). French Jacobin revolutionary, chemist, radical pamphleteer and Marx family friend. Active in the Cretan uprising of 1866. Participated in the worker uprising of 18 March and elected to the Paris Commune by the 19th arrondissement in the municipal elections of 26 March 1871. Summarily executed by gendarmes on 3 April following a skirmish on the western outskirts of Paris.

82. Louise Michel (1830–1905). French revolutionary activist, schoolteacher, medical orderly and National Guard member. Deported to New Caledonia in 1873 for her active participation in the Paris Commune. Returned to France in 1880 following the amnesty for the Communards and continued to agitate for revolutionary causes right up until her death.

83. François Achille Bazaine (1811–1888). Commander-in-Chief of French Forces during the Franco-Prussian War of 1870–71, who caused a public outcry by refusing to defend the nation once Napoléon III had surrendered on 2 September and the Empire had fallen, despite the Prussian army's continued occupation of France.

84. Marx, K. 'The Eighteenth Brumaire of Louis Bonaparte.' Available at: <www.marxists.org/archive/marx/works/1852/18th-brumaire/ch01.htm> [accessed 27.06.17]. Translation modified.

85. William Shakespeare, *The Merchant of Venice*, Act 3, Scene 1.

86. *Journal officiel de la Commune de Paris du 20 mars au 24 mai 1871. Fac-similé intégral en un volume.* Ovtcharenko, C. (ed.) en collaboration avec la Bibliothèque Paul-Emile-Boulet de l'Université du Québec à Chicoutimi, no date, pp. 2089–90.

87. The Paris Commune was the revolutionary workers' government that ruled Paris from 28 March to 28 May 1871. This proclamation was made during the so-called Bloody Week (21–28 May), when troops loyal to the Versailles government entered and conquered the city by force, massacring 30,000 people in the process.

About the Author

Jason Barker is Professor of English at Kyung Hee University in the School of Global Communication. He has published widely on Marx and Marxism, and is the writer, director and co-producer of the documentary *Marx Reloaded* (2011).

Zero Books

CULTURE, SOCIETY & POLITICS

Contemporary culture has eliminated the concept and public figure of the intellectual. A cretinous anti-intellectualism presides, cheer-led by hacks in the pay of multinational corporations who reassure their bored readers that there is no need to rouse themselves from their stupor. Zer0 Books knows that another kind of discourse - intellectual without being academic, popular without being populist - is not only possible: it is already flourishing. Zer0 is convinced that in the unthinking, blandly consensual culture in which we live, critical and engaged theoretical reflection is more important than ever before.

If you have enjoyed this book, why not tell other readers by posting a review on your preferred book site.

Recent bestsellers from Zero Books are

In the Dust of This Planet
Horror of Philosophy vol. 1
Eugene Thacker
In the first of a series of three books on the Horror of
Philosophy, *In the Dust of This Planet* offers the genre of horror
as a way of thinking about the unthinkable.
Paperback: 978-1-84694-676-9 ebook: 978-1-78099-010-1

Capitalist Realism
Is there no alternative?
Mark Fisher
An analysis of the ways in which capitalism has presented itself
as the only realistic political-economic system.
Paperback: 978-1-84694-317-1 ebook: 978-1-78099-734-6

Rebel Rebel
Chris O'Leary
David Bowie: every single song. Everything you want to know,
everything you didn't know.
Paperback: 978-1-78099-244-0 ebook: 978-1-78099-713-1

Cartographies of the Absolute
Alberto Toscano, Jeff Kinkle
An aesthetics of the economy for the twenty-first century.
Paperback: 978-1-78099-275-4 ebook: 978-1-78279-973-3

Poor but Sexy
Culture Clashes in Europe East and West
Agata Pyzik
How the East stayed East and the West stayed West.
Paperback: 978-1-78099-394-2 ebook: 978-1-78099-395-9

Malign Velocities
Accelerationism and Capitalism
Benjamin Noys
Long listed for the Bread and Roses Prize 2015, *Malign Velocities* argues against the need for speed, tracking acceleration as the symptom of the on-going crises of capitalism.
Paperback: 978-1-78279-300-7 ebook: 978-1-78279-299-4

Meat Market
Female Flesh under Capitalism
Laurie Penny
A feminist dissection of women's bodies as the fleshy fulcrum of capitalist cannibalism, whereby women are both consumers and consumed.
Paperback: 978-1-84694-521-2 ebook: 978-1-84694-782-7

Romeo and Juliet in Palestine
Teaching Under Occupation
Tom Sperlinger
Life in the West Bank, the nature of pedagogy and the role of a university under occupation.
Paperback: 978-1-78279-637-4 ebook: 978-1-78279-636-7

Sweetening the Pill
or How we Got Hooked on Hormonal Birth Control
Holly Grigg-Spall
Has contraception liberated or oppressed women? *Sweetening the Pill* breaks the silence on the dark side of hormonal contraception.
Paperback: 978-1-78099-607-3 ebook: 978-1-78099-608-0

Why Are We The Good Guys?
Reclaiming your Mind from the Delusions of Propaganda
David Cromwell
A provocative challenge to the standard ideology that Western
power is a benevolent force in the world.
Paperback: 978-1-78099-365-2 ebook: 978-1-78099-366-9

Readers of ebooks can buy or view any of these bestsellers by
clicking on the live link in the title. Most titles are published
in paperback and as an ebook. Paperbacks are available in
traditional bookshops. Both print and ebook formats are
available online.

Find more titles and sign up to our readers' newsletter at
http://www.johnhuntpublishing.com/culture-and-politics
Follow us on Facebook at
https://www.facebook.com/ZeroBooks
and Twitter at https://twitter.com/Zer0Books